A
Matter Of
Loyalty

ALSO BY ELIZABETH EDMONDSON

VERY ENGLISH MYSTERIES

A Man of Some Repute

A Question of Inheritance

OTHER WORKS

The Frozen Lake

Voyage of Innocence

The Villa in Italy

The Villa on the Riviera

Devil's Sonata

Night & Day

Fencing with Death

Finding Philippe

Anselm Audley & Elizabeth Edmondson

A Matter Of Loyalty

Text copyright © 2017 by Anselm Audley & Elizabeth Edmondson
All rights reserved.

Published by Thomas & Mercer, Seattle

www.apub.com

Amazon, the Amazon logo, and Thomas & Mercer are trademarks of Amazon.com, Inc., or its affiliates.

ISBN-13: 9781542046589
ISBN-10: 1542046580

Cover design by Lisa Horton

Printed in the United States of America

To my co-authors:

P.C.A.
1942–2011

E.A.E.
1948–2016

Chorus angelorum te suscipiat
et cum Lazaro, quondam paupere
aeternam habeas requiem.

Saturday

Scene 1

The defection of Bruno Rothesay was headline news. Hugo Hawksworth had run through the news items, from the screaming tabloid headline, *ATOM SCIENTIST MISSING*, to the more sober report in *The Times* that a physicist from the Foxley Atomic Energy Research Establishment had disappeared. As Foxley was barely five miles from Hugo's desk in Thorn Hall, the Service's archive facility in the hills above Selchester, it was of more than academic interest. Sir Bernard, head of Thorn Hall, had been forced to cancel a weekend's shooting and summon his key staff in on a Saturday.

Hugo put the last of the newspapers down – nothing there to indicate a leak – and looked out of his window. It was a cold January day, fog blanketing the valley. The spire of Selchester Cathedral was quite invisible, the room around him chilly. Thorn Hall's magnificent summer views of the valley came with a price: high on a north-east-facing hillside, its failing Victorian plumbing not among the Service's priorities, it was never warm. The aged cast-iron radiator under the window was cranking itself up with an alarming series of gurgles and thumps.

The telephone on his desk rang. It was Mrs Tempest, secretary to Sir Bernard. 'Sir Bernard asked me to let you know that Inspector Jarrett is on his way over.'

'Inspector Jarrett?'

'Inspector Jarrett is from Special Branch, he's come down from London with regard to the investigation of Dr Rothesay's disappearance. He wants to know more about Dr Rothesay's background, so Sir Bernard said he had better talk to you.'

Hugo replaced the receiver. *Thank you, Sir Bernard.* That was all he needed, one of those disagreeable Special Branch men who thought the intelligence services had no business with a place like Foxley. He could press the button to summon Mrs Clutton, his Archivist, but instead he got up from his desk and limped the few yards down the corridor to put his head around Mrs Clutton's office door. Best to be prepared.

In the usual way, she had anticipated his request. Bruno Rothesay's file was already on her desk.

It was quite a recent thing, this investigation into the pre-war backgrounds of the scientists at the Atomic, as the locals called Foxley. They knew perfectly well what went on there, just as they knew Thorn Hall was no Government statistics office, whatever the sign on the gateposts might say.

Any scientist employed at Foxley was security-vetted by London before they were allowed to set foot on the premises, but it had become all too clear that some information was leaking from the establishment. Hugo, office-bound ever since a bullet wound in a Berlin street had confined him to the sort of intelligence work he could do behind a desk, was duly tasked with combing through the records. Allegiances, tidbits, dust-dry interviews, with more than a sprinkling of spiteful gossip.

He was no more than halfway down the first page when Jarrett barged in without knocking. He was tall and dark, with cold eyes and an aura of hard if disagreeable competence about him. 'Good morning.

You're Hawksworth? I'm Jarrett. Sir Bernard told me to come and see you. I want to find out what you've got on Rothesay's past.'

He sat down in the chair opposite Hugo, rather as if he owned the place. Hugo, disliking him on sight, flicked open the file. He said crisply, 'I'm not finding anything suspicious in his record up to 1939. That's the period that Sir Bernard asked me to investigate. I know during the war he was involved with the Manhattan Project at Los Alamos, but the records on that will be elsewhere.'

Jarrett said, 'I'm well aware of that. I want to know about the time when he was a student and doing his first research jobs. He wasn't at Cambridge, that's one thing.'

Hugo suppressed a smile. Since Burgess and Maclean's defection, the equation in too many corners of the intelligence community had been laughably simple. Cambridge had been a hotbed of Communist sympathies in the 1930s, the Service's two most embarrassing defectors were Cambridge men, *ergo* if there were any suspicion of treachery, Cambridge was probably at the bottom of it.

'No, he was an Oxford man. Pembroke College. First in physics, 1921. Then on to the Roberts Laboratory, to work on electron physics.'

Jarrett said, 'Of course, while we know that Cambridge bred spies, no reason to suppose that there weren't just as many at Oxford.'

'Perhaps the Oxford spies are clever enough to avoid detection,' Hugo said. He disliked the way Jarrett's eyes lit up at the possibility of finding more traitors, as if that were something to be relished.

'Treason is no laughing matter. If you haven't found Rothesay's Communist links, you just haven't looked hard enough. Given that someone is clearly passing information from Foxley, I'd expect you to have left no stone unturned to discover the sympathies of the people working there.'

Hugo said, 'I've been working my way through all the records, and I must say I'm surprised about Bruno Rothesay. From his record, his history, and his known political views, he wasn't high on anyone's list of suspects.'

'That just shows how wrong you can be. Letting opinions get in the way of the facts. Man's defected, that's quite clear. He'll have skipped the country now with that wife of his.'

Hugo said, 'I'm surprised the whole thing was allowed to reach the papers. I'd have expected it would have been kept under wraps until it was known for certain that he had defected.'

Jarrett frowned. 'That's what I'd have done. My lord and master, Chief Superintendent Pritchard, decided that the publicity might help catch him before he left the country. But it's nonsense.'

His tone suggested that this Pritchard was overdue for retirement. Possibly involuntary.

Hugo said, 'You think his wife is with him?'

'Certainly. She's obviously in this with him. We've been investigating her background. She seemed blameless enough, but she must be involved. No living relatives, nothing she couldn't leave in a hurry. She telephoned the laboratory three days ago to say that he was ill and wouldn't be in, that's why it took a while for the alarm to be raised.'

Hugo knew this already from Superintendent MacLeod, the local police officer who was involved in the inquiry. On the second day, in accordance with Foxley regulations, two colleagues from the Atomic had gone to Rothesay's cottage on the outskirts of Selchester, to check what was wrong with him and see that he was getting proper medical attention.

There had been no reply to their knocks. The house had a deserted air, with curtains drawn and lights out. In the end, they had broken in. 'Nobody there,' MacLeod had said. 'Everything neat and tidy. He must have left early, the breakfast things were washed up on the draining board. Post from that day and the day before lying on the mat. Wherever he is, he hasn't been at home ill.'

'Damn sloppy to leave it two days,' Jarrett said sourly. 'Bunch of amateurs. You've gone slack down here in the sticks.'

'Perhaps,' said Hugo, fixing a cold eye back on him, 'you can advise the Select Committee as to which operations should be closed down to free up some extra funds.'

Jarrett ignored him. 'But then, you've had quite your share of security breaches here, too. A double agent right under your nose, and weren't you suspended from the Service yourself in the autumn? Meeting a known MGB officer without permission.'

Hugo had indeed met Colonel Orlov without permission, and found him considerably better company than Jarrett. He had a concern for what was right and what was not. God only knew how he'd held on to such a sense in the MGB, it was hard enough in the Service.

'If you know about that, you know the inquiry has been resolved,' Hugo said.

Jarrett's expression made it clear that he held no higher a view of the authorities involved than he did of Pritchard. Hugo wondered whether he'd ever actually met a Soviet intelligence officer, principled or otherwise.

'You lodge at the Castle, don't you?' said Jarrett. Hugo thought it unlikely that he was changing the subject. 'Imposing place. I suppose it's rather empty without the late Earl's presence.'

'I never knew it before,' Hugo observed. He thought it was probably a much more comfortable place now than it had been. The late Earl had not been a pleasant man. His unexpected successor, Gus, had until recently been an American classics professor, and possessed a great deal more basic decency.

Hugo turned over a page, without much hope that Jarrett would take the hint.

'His niece still lives there, too, doesn't she? Freya Wryton.'

'Yes,' said Hugo, without looking up.

'Buried in some tedious family chronicle, so I hear.'

'I believe she's writing a history of the Fitzwarins.' Which would have been far from tedious, had that actually been the subject of her labours. Her ancestors had been a turbulent lot, he gathered. Troublesome barons in the Middle Ages, uppity earls from the time of Richard III, bitter recusants and recalcitrant Royalists thereafter. More than a whiff of the Machiavel about them, with the odd note of brimstone here and there. Fine subject for a historian, but Hugo very much doubted Freya was up to anything quite so worthy.

'How is she finding life as a maiden aunt?'

This time Hugo did look up. That was a thoroughly personal question. He wondered who this Jarrett was, and how he knew her.

He was saved a reply by the shrill peal of the telephone.

'Hawksworth here. Oh, it's you, Superintendent.'

Jarrett leaned forward, a raptor's gleam in his eyes. Not a man Hugo would want to have on his trail.

Hugo listened to Macleod. Well aware that Jarrett could only hear one side of the conversation, he was careful not to say anything too specific. 'Has she? Where? How did that . . . Oh, I see. You've had it checked, I take it? All above board. And the call? No idea. Nothing from the exchange? You're looking into it. Says it's all stuff and nonsense. I see. Thank you. I imagine our guest from London will want a word. Yes, he's here. In my office. I'll send him over.'

Hugo put the phone down before Jarrett could demand to speak to MacLeod himself.

'That was Superintendent MacLeod, of the county constabulary.'

'I know MacLeod,' said Jarrett. 'Don't waste my time.'

'Dr Rothesay's wife has turned up,' said Hugo, with quiet satisfaction. 'She's been staying with her sister-in-law in Wales this last fortnight. Hill farm in Radnorshire, no telephone, snowed in until yesterday. Plenty of witnesses, including some neighbouring farmers and a Methodist minister. She didn't make the call, and she has no idea where Dr Rothesay might have gone. Says this defection story is stuff and nonsense, and he hasn't a treasonous bone in his body.'

Exactly the conclusion Hugo had come to, as it so happened.

If Jarrett was taken aback, he didn't let it show. He was on his feet in an instant. 'Curious thing for a wife to do, in the depths of winter,' he said thoughtfully. 'There's more to this than meets the eye. Where is she?'

'At the police station.'

'I'll be over again this afternoon,' Jarrett said, looking down at the files as if he could spot a lie even through a manila envelope. 'You can show me everything you've got on the wife.'

In a moment, he was off. He didn't bother closing the door behind him, and an icy draught swirled around Hugo's desk. The dull ache in his leg sharpened to a twinge.

'Peace and quiet,' said Hugo, getting up to close the door. 'For now.'

The phone rang ten minutes later. It was Mrs Clutton.

'Sir Bernard wants to see you,' she said.

Scene 2

Sir Bernard was standing at his big eastern window with his hands behind his back, looking out over the fog. It was his great-man-of-affairs pose, and the room suited it, even if Sir Bernard didn't. He was stocky, ruddy-faced, very much the image of an English civil servant.

'Ah, Hawksworth,' he said as Hugo limped in. Sir Bernard's enormous office was wood-panelled to within an inch of its life, even the ceiling, but that did make it rather warmer. That, and the maintenance crew's natural tendency to pay attention to their chief's office first.

'Sir Bernard,' said Hugo. He was waved to a seat. Sir Bernard took his.

'Bad business at Foxley,' Sir Bernard said, steepling his fingers. His hands weren't long or elegant enough to pull the gesture off.

'I take it all the usual things are being done?' said Hugo.

'Oh, yes,' said Sir Bernard. 'But I'm afraid this is all rather too late. A man doesn't just defect on a whim between one day and the next. He'll have planned it all. Meticulous types, these scientists.'

'He knew we were investigating him,' Hugo pointed out.

'You've been doing that for weeks, on and off. He could tell we weren't taking it too seriously, or you'd have been on it full-time. Plenty of time to let his controllers know, plan the getaway.'

'There's still nothing in the files to point at him,' Hugo said. It might not be the politic line to take, but as far as he was concerned, Bruno wasn't the leak.

'Nonsense,' said Sir Bernard, cutting him off. 'You just haven't found it. London wants results. I want the missing thread. You know it's Rothesay now. Go back through the files with a fine-tooth comb. His background is your only task until further notice.'

Hugo knew enough of the Service, and of Sir Bernard, not to say any more. Keep your mouth shut, and there was room for manoeuvre.

'Oh, one more thing,' Sir Bernard said, with a distinctly apologetic note in his voice. 'I'm afraid your assignment includes assisting this Jarrett with his inquiries. Some bureaucratic hoo-ha going on in London. Give him any help he needs.'

Hugo gave a reluctant nod and stood up. As he turned to go, Sir Bernard spoke again. 'I know you're not wild about this, Hawksworth. Nor am I, and nor is the Chief. He doesn't want Special Branch to have the slightest excuse for poking its nose into our affairs down here. Find Jarrett his proof, convince him we're quite on top of security, and get him back to London as soon as you can.'

Scene 3

'It should be working now, Miss Freya,' said Ben, ducking through the passage from Lady Matilda's wing. 'I'll go back in every couple of hours to see how it's doing.'

Freya Wryton looked up from her detective novel with a guilty start. She was sitting in the warm Castle kitchen, far from her typewriter, with tea by her side. A purring Magnus was draped across her lap, flexing his claws back and forth in her oldest, most disreputable tweed skirt.

Ben was half the Castle staff in these straitened times – handyman, gardener, groom and caretaker all rolled into one. At the moment, most of his time was spent knocking Lady Matilda's wing back into shape for the new Earl and his family. Already displaced by his sudden elevation from widowed New England classics professor to Earl of Selchester, Gus had drawn the line at installing himself and his two daughters in the old part of the Castle. Neither Polly nor Babs had been happy at the prospect of beams, bare stone, and walls six feet thick.

Lady Matilda's wing, built with every mod con the 1890s could boast and still in good shape, had been ideal for them, with the added benefit that Freya, Hugo, and Hugo's sister Georgia had been spared the hunt for new lodgings.

The same, however, could not be said of the ballroom. Sometime over the New Year, more of the makeshift Army plumbing had given up the ghost.

'No bodies?' Freya said, remembering what had happened the last time the Castle plumbing broke.

'No bodies, Miss Freya,' Ben said.

'I suppose we're clean out of missing earls,' said Freya. She might not actually be writing a worthy tome on the Selchesters, but she knew enough of the history that she wouldn't have been so very surprised to find a few minor scions of the family buried under the floorboards here and there.

'Tisn't good to speak lightly of the dead, Miss Freya,' said Mrs Partridge from the scullery. Mrs Partridge was the other half of the staff, cook and housekeeper and witch of all work.

'What dead?' said Georgia, Hugo's sister, coming down the passage from the front door with a blast of cold air, all shapeless uniform and long legs. She dumped a bag full of used games kit on Mrs Partridge's meticulously scrubbed floor and looked around. 'You're procrastinating,' said Georgia, taking in cat, book, and kitchen all at once.

'I'm not procrastinating,' said Freya. 'I'm taking a break.'

'You hadn't even started that Margery Allingham this morning,' Georgia said. 'You were at the end of an Edmund Crispin. I noticed, because you said I could have it when you were done, and you weren't. Now you're nearly at the end of the next one. You haven't done a jot of writing today. Or yesterday. You got through two then, and now you've moved on to Allinghams.'

Georgia was, as usual, absolutely right. Freya gave her a quelling look, which had no effect whatsoever.

Mrs Partridge, whose keenly honed sense for disturbance had brought her back into the kitchen, had better luck. 'Take that bag off the floor, young lady. You can sort it out in the laundry room. Whites and colours separated, please, not in a messy pile like the last time.'

'Why are you so late?' Freya asked, looking at the big old kitchen clock.

Georgia's expression turned quite murderous. 'Miss Harrison was lurking in the library passage. Said I ought to be at games, what was I doing sloping off like that. Horrible woman. I bet Judy Woodley put her on me, too. She never does games, but she's forever lecturing the rest of us about it. Always some certificate to get her out of it, and she's as strong as a horse. Looks like one, too.'

'Off with you!' said Mrs Partridge sternly.

Georgia slung the bag back on to her shoulder with bad grace. 'Have they caught that boffin yet? It's the talk of the school. They say he's gone off to Russia with his mistress. I thought all these Atom men were married to their work.'

'Out!' Freya said.

This time Georgia went, giving a fair impression of Magnus's I-meant-to-do-that look.

'The laundry is to the right, young lady!' Mrs Partridge called after her as Georgia headed off towards the stairs and her waiting French horn.

'Fair handful, she is,' said Ben, who had wisely refrained from taking any part in the conversation.

'She's a right hoyden, sometimes,' said Mrs Partridge, 'but it's not right for a girl, being moved around all the time, and with different people. Maybe she's settled now, but it was only a couple of months ago you were all expecting to be on your way, new Earl and all that.'

Freya's opinion was that Georgia would have been a handful no matter what happened to her, but there was a good deal of truth to Mrs Partridge's words. Georgia had lost her first home and her mother in the Blitz, her father at sea. Her guardian, an aunt, had remarried and moved to Canada, which left only Hugo.

Who might be fully in his element dealing with Russian colonels and suspicious policemen, but who found a gangly, devastatingly blunt thirteen-year-old a complete mystery.

'Did that Atom scientist really have a mistress?' Freya asked. If there was Selchester gossip Mrs Partridge didn't know, it probably wasn't worth knowing.

'They're not monks up at the Atomic, I shall say that,' said Mrs Partridge.

'Do tell,' said Freya.

'I think you'll want to be about your writing before Miss Georgia comes down asking more awkward questions,' said Mrs Partridge, with a witchy look. Freya was quite sure Mrs Partridge knew exactly what she was really up to, but her lips were – on this one subject – sealed.

Freya tucked her Margery Allingham away on the little shelf behind her and slid off the bench, depositing Magnus on the warm patch she'd left behind. He gave her a distinctly baleful look. 'I shall go for a ride,' she announced.

'Go for a ride indeed,' said Mrs Partridge to Ben as the door closed behind her. 'Miss Georgia is spot on. She's not writing a word. She's already late with this one, and then where will she be?'

'I'm sure they're used to writers' ways up in London,' said Ben, who knew as well as Mrs Partridge that Freya's worthy and endlessly spun-out family history was nothing more than the convenient cover for a series of exceedingly successful Civil War bodice-rippers.

'Don't be so sure,' said Mrs Partridge darkly.

Scene 4

Saul looked around at his future abode and place of business.

'It's rather a wreck, I'm afraid,' said Vivian.

Wreck was an understatement. The old Selchester Gallery looked as though the Army had abandoned it during a retreat. The floors were bare, the walls tattered, and every imaginable variety of junk was piled in the corners. It hadn't seemed this bad when he'd looked around it, but that had been on one of December's rare fine days, with sun flooding through the grimy windows facing School Lane. Vivian, in her tailored two-piece and exquisitely draped fur, could hardly have looked more incongruous. Rather like a film star in a barracks, not that any of his units had ever received such a visit.

Saul had signed the lease almost at once. Space in Selchester was hard to come by, and it was pure luck he'd been in town on the day when the protracted legal battle over the Gallery's ownership had finally been resolved. The Gallery and the flat above were both free to let, and he had snapped both up. A place to live, a life to rebuild.

'I've seen worse,' said Saul, who had been in the Army and the Foreign Legion.

'Of course you'd say that. It quite deadens the spirit. Now let me show you the important bits, hand you the keys, and then we can be out of here. Jamie is keeping my table at the Daffs.'

It took longer than they'd expected. In the end, Vivian simply pressed the remaining keys into Saul's hand. 'You know what to do and where to find me,' she said. 'I'd never have agreed to look after the keys if I'd known there were this many.'

By the time they reached the Daffodil Tearooms, Jamie was besieged. The café was packed, the windows steamed, the noise deafening.

'Oh, thank God you're here,' he said, installing them by the window with indecent haste. 'Half of Selchester has come to gossip, and when they see an empty table they'll hardly take no for an answer. Your usual, Miss Witt, and for you, Mr Ingham?'

'Why, whatever's up now?' said Vivian, scanning the room for a newspaper she could read the headlines from.

'Such a to-do at the Atomic,' said Jamie over the din. 'One of their boffins missing for two days, and now it seems he must have taken himself off to Russia. Quite frightful. You wouldn't catch me doing that, no matter how much I believed in the brotherhood of all men.'

Vivian made a face. 'So the whole place will be swarming with beastly reporters again.'

'I had to evict two of them from your table,' said Jamie, shaking his head. 'They were quite rude. Richard had a word with them, though. Such a palaver.'

Jamie was small, round, and a conscientious objector who had served as a medical orderly in the war. Richard, the other Daff, was tall, with a chef's authority, and had been a naval gunner. Saul could imagine him making short work of two reporters.

'Don't they know you're here?' he asked, as Jamie bustled off with their order. Vivian was a film star, and Selchester her bolthole.

'They do, but it's a slog to get here, and everyone would give them the cold shoulder if they came just for me. If they're here for something else, they'll all be writing colour pieces on Selchester to fill the time. We've rehearsals to be going on with, too.'

Vivian's attention was much taken up with the *Murder in the Cathedral* rehearsals. It would be the climax of Selchester Cathedral's thousandth anniversary celebrations, half the town involved and the rest wanting to be. She was directing it, not without a certain opposition from the stodgier local worthies.

'Talk of the devil,' she said. 'There's our newest committee member and honorary patron. Stanley twisted his arm last week.' As chief of the Feoffees, Selchester's arcane version of a City Council, Stanley Dillon was adept at twisting arms. Even when they belonged to earls.

The tall figure of the new Lord Selchester was standing in the doorway, looking around for a space. Vivian waved him over, and Jamie pushed through the throng with an extra chair.

Saul gave Gus a guarded but courteous greeting. It had only been a few weeks since he'd come up to the Castle in a whisky-sodden haze, with the intent of doing something to the Earl he'd almost certainly have regretted. Only later had he learned that the Earl he sought, a man who liked to have others in his power and wasn't above blackmailing them to ensure it, had met his much-deserved end seven years before. The new Earl seemed to be animated by quite a different spirit, but it was still unsettling to be sitting at a table with him.

'Good morning to you both,' said Gus in his soft New England accent. 'I see the town's in quite a frenzy. Already had two of those reporters ask me for an opinion.'

'Did they know who you were?'

'I think so,' Gus said. He couldn't be comfortable with that yet, Vivian thought. He had enjoyed a certain distinction in his old life, but the fame which came from making a first-rate translation of the *Iliad* and *Odyssey* wasn't much preparation for this.

'What did you tell them?'

'I told them it was a matter for the authorities. They kept wanting more, but I didn't see what else there was to say.'

'Oh, my,' said Vivian, with a wicked laugh. 'They'll have loved that.'

'I was hoping I'd find you,' said Lord Selchester. 'Dinah tells me your next rehearsal is tomorrow. Stanley said I ought to make an appearance, see what I've got myself into.'

Vivian's eyes betrayed a flicker of amusement. Dinah, chatelaine of the Selchester Bookshop, would be involved in the production, probably backstage, but she didn't think that was the reason Gus was popping into the bookshop every day.

'Three until six. There was some muttering about rehearsing on Sunday, but it can't be helped. Next weekend I've all the professionals down except Sir Desmond himself: we'll be at it Sunday afternoon again and half of Saturday, too.'

Sir Desmond Winthrop was a friend of Vivian's, a theatrical knight with a Selchester connection who'd agreed to play Becket.

Selchester nodded gravely, and turned his attention to Saul for a moment. 'Are you involved?'

Saul shook his head. 'Too much to do at the Gallery. It'll be a month's work just to make it ready, never mind filling it.'

'I'm sure he'll end up being dragged in,' said Vivian, with a ruthlessness which spoke of using every asset at her disposal, willing or otherwise. She'd have made a formidable partisan. 'Now, closer to the time, I was wondering whether you might come to one or two things in London . . .'

The door banged again, and one of Mrs Partridge's witchy cronies – was it Martha Radley? – sat herself down at the table behind Saul. Her voice was quite penetrating.

'Such a thing I saw in the tea leaves,' she said. 'This Dr Rothesay, terrible business. I see a watery death for him.'

There were low shrieks of horror.

'You think he's drowned on the way to Russia?' said another witch.

'I don't think he ever left these shores,' said Martha. 'There's water aplenty in the Sel, isn't there?'

Unnoticed by the others, Saul went quite still for an instant.

'Would you excuse me for a moment?' he said. 'I'm not sure I turned the gas tap all the way off. Don't want to blow the place up on my first day, not unless I can take some of the reporters, too. I shall be back before you're done with the schedule.'

Vivian and Gus were deep in plans, and waved him away. It was a while later, after the third time she'd fended off an excuse to seize his empty chair, that Vivian wondered what was keeping him.

'It's too bad of him,' said Vivian. 'I keep trying to involve him, but he will be a cat who walks by himself.'

'I can't say I know him well enough,' said Gus. 'He does put me in mind of Ajax, though.'

'Is that the big Ajax or the little one?' said Vivian, who'd been in her share of classical tragedies.

'Ajax, son of Telamon, who went mad after he lost the fight with Odysseus.'

'Killed all the Greeks' sheep then fell on his sword, didn't he? An odd character. Capable on the surface, but angry underneath. Wouldn't you be, in his shoes?'

'I can't imagine the things Saul went through,' said Gus, thinking of Saul's wife and daughter on the far side of the world, resolutely refusing to have anything to do with him. The trial and condemnation, seven years in the Foreign Legion, and all for a crime he hadn't even committed. 'All because my father needed a scapegoat. God forbid I should ever end up like that.'

Vivian shuddered at some buried memory. 'You couldn't. That kind of evil takes a lifetime of practice.'

Scene 5

It was a weary Hugo who limped into the kitchen that evening, an hour late and thoroughly out of sorts.

Mrs Partridge bustled over to the stove, where Hugo's dinner had been keeping warm. Hugo eased himself on to a bench and winced as Magnus took the opportunity for a spot of kneading.

'No luck?' said Freya. They'd heard nothing new on the six o'clock news.

Hugo shook his head. By no stretch of the imagination could two hours closeted with Jarrett constitute *luck*. The Special Branch man had turned the file upside down and inside out looking for Communist sympathies, but there wasn't a thing there which didn't apply to every physicist old enough to have been working in the thirties.

'They aren't making you go in again tomorrow, are they?'

'Small mercies,' said Hugo. 'The Foxley administrator won't hear of calling his staff back on a Sunday.'

'I wouldn't have thought they set much store by the Sabbath.'

'He doesn't. He's just looking out for his people. If Dr Rothesay has defected, he'll be on the far side of the Iron Curtain by now, and there's not a thing we can do. No point hauling everyone in so Jarrett can rake them over the coals.'

Freya started. 'Jarrett, you said? Jarrett of Special Branch?'

'Yes. London have sent him down to put the fear of God into everyone. He asked about you.'

'I suppose he would,' said Freya. 'He was Roddy's best man.'

Freya had ditched Roddy Halstrop quite literally at the altar, running down the aisle and jumping into a taxi. Her parents had been

17

horrified, her uncle, Lord Selchester, coldly furious. It was the one time she'd tasted the edge of his temper, aside from the argument they'd had on the last evening of his life.

She'd never regretted the decision. Roddy was safely married to someone else now, thank God, but she had his measure. Jarrett was quite another matter. She'd never known how to deal with him. If Hugo was a Renaissance courtier, smooth and silent, Jarrett was one of Cromwell's major-generals, a starched zealot in a three-barred helmet. An involuntary shudder ran down her back at the idea of him loose in Selchester.

Hugo didn't see the shudder, but he caught the sudden tightness in her face. This is someone who scares her, he thought. She had been at ease when he came in, pleased and solicitous. Now she was wary, her eyes distant.

'Did he cause you trouble?' said Hugo sharply.

She pulled herself together. He would be here for a couple of days, tearing Foxley apart, then back to London and a different world.

'No,' she said. 'Nothing like that.'

'Is there anything I should know about him?' Hugo asked, as Mrs Partridge carried his plate over.

'If you've met him, you know him.' Another comparison came to her, from a world full of black doublets and ruffs, silken words and ready treachery. 'Think of those men who tore country houses apart looking for priests in priest holes.'

Hugo rather doubted this Jarrett would be gone as quickly as Sir Bernard hoped.

Sunday

The rehearsals were held at the Feoffees' Hall, being Selchester's equivalent of a town hall. When he first arrived, Gus had admired its fine classical frontage, tall windows looking out over the market square, but he hadn't been inside. There was a rather splendid Jacobean staircase, but the main hall at the top was less impressive.

'It's like Spode china inside,' Freya had said, on the steps. She was curious to see some of the rehearsals, and suspected Gus would appreciate a familiar face. 'All blue and white.'

'It doesn't sound as if you like it much.'

'I can't say I do. It's rather sentimental.'

Looking around, Gus was forced to agree. Not the neoclassical at its finest, and rather too pale and cold for a room in this climate. The sky outside was a dark, louring grey.

Mrs Partridge had been positively aglow with doom and gloom before he left. 'Storm coming up-Channel, so they say. Gale-force winds on the Cornish coast, and a ship in trouble off the Lizard. We're in for a right bucketing here, and no mistake. There'll be chimneys down, and the river right up. It was into the town this time last year.'

Bucketing was the word in older parts of the Castle, apparently. There was a store of buckets in a downstairs cupboard, and more in the attics, to catch leaks at their source. Six years of war and seven of legal limbo had taken their toll on the Castle. Ben had his work cut out just making temporary repairs.

Dinah waved as they came in. The hall was full of a cheerful medley of cast members, plus a few who didn't really seem to have any business aside from curiosity.

'I didn't know you'd be needed so early,' said Freya.

'I like to see how they're getting on,' said Dinah.

Or else she'd heard Gus was coming, and decided to put in an appearance.

'Gosh,' said Freya, spotting a couple among the milling throng. 'Are they involved?'

'Yes, they're with the production team. She's helping with the costumes, and he apparently knows something about the nuts and bolts of lighting rigs. Besides, they have a van – it'll be very helpful come show time.'

'I'm surprised they've started taking an interest in local affairs,' said Freya.

'Who are we talking about?' Gus asked.

Freya pointed them out. 'The couple from Nightingale Cottage. Not their actual name, that's Pierce or Pearson or something. They're freethinkers, and folklorists. Always wandering around asking farmers for old stories and the like. There's something of a competition among the locals to see who can make them believe the most outrageous thing.'

Gus, scholar to his fingertips, frowned. Some of his colleagues had done excellent work teasing out ancient stories in Greece and the Balkans. 'That's not sporting of them.'

'I suppose not. Only they do seem to swallow anything they're told.'

Watching the couple come towards them, Gus found that quite hard to credit. They had the look of a pair accustomed to watching carefully and fitting in. He could see them coping with life among South Sea Islanders, for example. But where did anyone in England get the money to spend their life collecting old country stories? Everything seemed to be rationed here, except gossip.

'You must be Lord Selchester,' said the woman, extending a hand. 'Miranda Pearson. This is Jeremy, he doesn't talk much.'

'Glad to meet you,' said Gus, rather bemused by this un-English introduction. Jeremy was a big man, bearded and inscrutable, his greeting more conventional. Not a happy soul, Freya thought. He had a weary look in his eyes.

'I don't approve of the peerage at all,' Miranda declared. 'It's a thoroughly outdated institution, but if we're to be stuck with it, I'm glad to see new blood. I hear you're a classical scholar.'

'I am indeed. Although I doubt I shall have as much time for it as before.'

'Jeremy and I are students of folklore,' Miranda went on. 'Old stories are full of radical notions, much more so than people give them credit for. We're giving a talk on Friday – I hope you'll come to hear it.'

'I shall,' said Gus, intrigued.

The noise died down. In the silence, Vivian clicked her fingers. 'We'll start at the entrance of the knights. Toby, you'll read in for Sir Desmond again. This table will be the high altar . . .'

As the actors took their places, the first raindrops fell outside.

Monday

Scene 1

The last of the rain was still drumming on the windows when Georgia's alarm clock went for school.

'Beastly weather,' she said to Polly over the breakfast table, thinking of the long, wet drive and the climb to school on the other side.

'At home we had ice storms,' Polly said. 'When we lived in the boondocks, the power went out for days and we had to sleep around the fire. I've never been so cold.' Gus had spent the freezing winter of 1947 teaching at a small Catholic college out in the wilds of New Hampshire, far from the city lights of Boston. His daughters had never quite forgiven him.

'Bet they'd cancel school for that. We just get everything more sodden and grey than usual.'

'We couldn't even go to school once.'

'If only,' said Georgia wistfully.

'School would have been warmer. Besides, I rather like it.'

'More fool you. Do you want the dusty bits at the bottom of the cereal packet, or can I have them?'

The rain had stopped by the time they climbed on their bikes.

'Take care on the drive, young ladies,' said Ben, tramping past in dripping overalls. 'There's a nasty slip by that bend, where you can't so much as see the road ahead.'

The sky was full of angry grey clouds still, and the drive covered with puddles. They'd been bundled out of the door on schedule, but they were nonetheless running late by the time they turned out of the drive on to the main road. The vegetable van, on its way up to the Castle, flashed its lights at them. Georgia gave a cheery wave and nearly fell into a puddle.

They stopped at the bridge to let a lorry full of sheep through.

'Isn't the river high?' Polly said, peering over the stone parapet. The water was twice as high as it had been on Saturday, swirling around the ancient arches.

'Branches everywhere,' said Georgia with satisfaction, watching half a tree come through the centre span. 'Maybe it'll flood and we won't be able to go in.'

'Georgia,' said Polly in quite a different voice, just as the van crested the hump, 'what's that?'

She pointed at something dark, snagged on the end of the branch. Something long and log-like, but which didn't look like wood, and had pale bits.

Polly hadn't lived through the Blitz and the doodlebugs. Georgia had, and she was just old enough to remember it.

'Oh,' she said, feeling very queer indeed. She jumped off her bike and waved the driver down.

Scene 2

'It's Dr Rothesay all right,' said MacLeod, coming back into the office where Hugo and Jarrett were waiting. The Selchester police station was like every other in England – square and imposing on the outside, shabby and institutional on the inside. 'Right down to the scar on his left cheek. He was at Heidelberg for a while. I'm told it's a scar from one of the duelling clubs they have there.'

'I want a second identification,' said Jarrett at once. 'There must be no doubt.'

As if there were likely to be multiple bodies in the Sel with German fencing scars on their cheeks.

'My men are bringing one of his colleagues down from the Atomic,' said MacLeod.

Jarrett frowned. 'Its name is the Atomic Energy Research Establishment, Foxley, Superintendent, and I shall trouble you and your constables to refer to it as Foxley. We have professional standards to maintain.'

MacLeod and Hugo exchanged a weary glance as Jarrett paced over to the window.

'Do you have a confirmed cause of death?' Hugo asked, leaning back in the uncomfortable police chair. His mind kept flickering back to Georgia. She and Polly had been packed straight off to school after giving brief statements; there was nothing they'd seen that two farmers and four other witnesses hadn't spotted seconds later. What bothered him was that she should be involved at all. She'd seen too much death for a girl of her age.

MacLeod opened his folder, as put out by the interloper from Special Branch as Hugo was. Jarrett had all but taken charge of the recovery operation, directing constables this way and that as they struggled to recover the body safely from the swollen Sel. He'd been ready to leap in and do the job himself, although every local knew they'd not have seen him again if he'd been so foolish. The Sel had a vicious way with it.

'One gunshot wound to the back of the neck. Our surgeon is retrieving the bullet for analysis. Condition of the body consistent with several days in the water. Marks on the neck and legs suggest it may have been weighted down. Some mud and grass stains on the collar and trouser legs. We'll get what we can from those, but we're lucky to have a body at all. The valley looks pretty on railway postcards, but it's a quagmire. Sand and clay – bad mixture. Doesn't let go easily.'

'So if yesterday's storm hadn't pulled him loose, we'd never have found him,' said Jarrett.

'Indeed.'

In which case, Hugo thought, Dr Rothesay would have been tarred for life as a traitor to his country, instead of being seen as the victim of a cold-blooded murder. The real sleeper agent at Foxley would have been free to continue his work.

'This is a priority for Special Branch,' said Jarrett. 'I'll bring some more people down from London. MacLeod, I'll need your men to do the legwork in Selchester. Questioning his neighbours, movements in his last days, that sort of thing. Hawksworth, you'll go through all the background material on Rothesay's colleagues and connections, see what you can turn up. You can come up to Foxley with me now, put some faces to the names.'

In other words, MacLeod and his men would do everything Jarrett thought beneath his personal notice. MacLeod said only, 'I'll see to it.'

'Come along, Hawksworth,' said Jarrett. 'No time to lose.'

He was out of the door before Hugo had stood up, barking at his men in the corridor.

'Sooner you than me,' said MacLeod. He and Hugo hadn't seen eye to eye much, but on this they were united. Until Jarrett found a convenient scapegoat, at which point MacLeod might well endorse his suspicions simply to get rid of him.

'Will your men need to speak to my sister again?' Hugo asked. 'I don't like her being involved.'

'I shouldn't think so. If she'd been walking along the river path and found it, we'd have had a good many more questions, but she did the right thing, and we've plenty of witnesses who saw it floating along. None from further upriver, mind you, where we need them.'

'Thank you,' said Hugo.

'I should warn you,' MacLeod said, 'a couple of those journalists were poking around. They'll have seen my men taking statements.'

Hugo grimaced.

'Nasty characters, some of them,' MacLeod went on. 'Real gutter press, here to dig up whatever dirt they can throw at the Government for the sake of a headline. They can say what they please now, not like in the war. You might want to tell her not to speak to them.'

Scene 3

Foxley lay in a valley of the Selchester Downs, east of the city. It was seven miles away, miles spent with gritted teeth in the front seat of Jarrett's powerful car, Hugo trying his best not to hang on to the dashboard while his leg protested at the bitter cold. The car was already freezing, and Jarrett wound the windows down. He didn't like condensation, apparently.

It had, at least, been a quick journey and a silent one. Jarrett drove the way he talked: with intent, single-minded concentration, and a total disregard for the comfort and well-being of others. At the first corner on the London Road, he nearly pushed a small van into a ditch. Hugo caught a glimpse of the driver as he shuddered white-faced to a halt on the verge. Jamie, proprietor of the Daffodil Tearooms. He'd be all a-fluster about that for a week.

Jarrett's only response was to shift up a gear, roaring away on the long, straight road up to Hammick Down. The fields either side were huge, stony, and empty. Over to the right sat the big lonely bump of Pagan Hill, its crown of trees hiding an old stone circle. Selchester superstition held that the place was haunted. With that odd folklorist couple in Nightingale Cottage busy asking daft questions about it, all the old stories were having a fresh run.

Foxley was on the wrong side of Hammick Down, an old and rather ugly Victorian stately home surrounded by an array of prefabs, Nissen huts and one or two small hangars. Thrown together during the war, of course, for weapons research. Repurposed afterwards, as the Government frantically tried to make up ground on the Americans' Bomb.

A barbed-wire fence ringed the perimeter. The guard at the barrier made a show of checking their papers, only to be barked at when he didn't do it quickly enough. Another guard, more attentive, directed them to the office of the Administrator, Brigadier Caundle, in a dark-green prefab.

Caundle was a small, fussy man with ginger hair and a permanently screwed-up face. He'd been a senior quartermaster in the war, and had kept the Eighth Army in provisions right through from Sicily to Naples before the powers that be had decided to park him in an obscure research institute to shuffle scientists around. He'd been here ever since. Easy to underestimate, Hugo thought, but he'd faced Jarrett down over the weekend interviews and won.

Caundle greeted his two guests without pleasure. He knew Hugo from previous visits, gave a brief nod.

'Yes, yes, I've heard,' he said, before Jarrett could launch into his spiel. 'Terrible thing to happen. Saw him myself last Tuesday, day before he disappeared. Leaves you cold to think of it. Lying at the bottom of the river all that time. I was expecting MacLeod, with news like this. I thought bodies weren't your thing.'

'One of your researchers is dead, Brigadier, shot in the back of the head and dumped where he'd normally never be found. This is still a national security matter.'

'You think one of my people might have done it?'

'We don't have a defector,' Hugo put in, 'but we still have a leak.'

Caundle frowned. 'I suppose you'll still be wanting to haul every-one over the coals, then, as if any of them could be involved in a thing like this.'

'I'll speak to his immediate colleagues and superiors first,' said Jarrett. 'Then anyone who had dealings with him in the last two weeks. My sergeant will be here shortly to go over your security procedures. Can't have any repeats of this. I trust I'll have your full cooperation.'

'Of course,' said Caundle briskly. 'I'll take you to Dr Oldcastle first. He's the head of reactor physics – that's Dr Rothesay's division.'

As Caundle led them along a maze of concrete paths, Jarrett inter-rogated him as to this Dr Oldcastle's character. Hugo listened atten-tively, his eyes roaming the camp. An uninspiring place to spend your days, but then he'd thought that about Selchester, before he came. He'd always lived in London, amid the bright lights and the bustling goings-on. Valerie, whom he'd barely seen since coming down to Selchester, was still quite appalled that he'd lingered there so long.

'Darling, Thorn Hall is death even in the Service,' she'd said on the phone, a note of more than usual impatience in her voice. 'Graveyard of ambition.'

'How would you know that?'

'I keep my ears open,' she said. 'I had lunch with Philip and Una Frome – you must remember them. Philip sends his regards, he's doing very well. Says there'd be a place for you at Mowbray & Cavendish any time you liked. They like men who can keep their mouths shut, although I honestly don't know why they bother, it's all so very arcane.'

Hugo remembered Philip Frome, had served beside him in Italy and the Balkans. A handy man in a tight spot, good company, the out-fit's practical joker. He'd resigned his commission in 1946, as soon as the Nuremberg tribunals were over, and gone into one of those immensely discreet firms which looked after old money. They'd met up for lunch at Philip's club last spring, and Philip had spent two hours straight boring for England. When Valerie had asked about it afterwards, Hugo hadn't been able to remember a single thing he'd said.

Was that what awaited Hugo if he left the Service? A lifetime of solid respectability, shuffling figures around and watching former comrades vegetate in wood-panelled rooms?

'I can hear what you're thinking,' Valerie had said. 'I can tell you don't like what you're doing down there. You can't go back into the field, so why keep at it? Digging up old bones, finding skeletons in everyone's closets, living in a draughty castle in a provincial nowhere. Why in God's name are you still doing it?'

Hugo had asked himself that question more than once.

She had sighed. 'Got to go. *Swan Lake* at Covent Garden. Simply divine, I hear. You're missing it all. Talk soon!' Hugo hadn't rung her since.

Another row of prefabs, then around the side of a hangar to Oldcastle's office, a temporary building bolted on to the hangar's side. Foxley had been an airfield for a while, during the Battle of Britain, but a marginal one at best, closed and converted to other purposes as soon as the immediate danger of invasion was over.

Oldcastle's secretary, Miss Fitzgibbon, ushered them into his office at once. Oldcastle was tall, spare, a little stooped. His office, large and well furnished, would have been more at home in Whitehall than in this maze of temporary buildings. The door had a glazed opening, the secretary's desk positioned so Oldcastle could catch her eye without stirring from his seat. A man who valued creature comforts. Or perhaps he simply found the whole place as dismal as Hugo did.

'You'll be here about Dr Rothesay,' Oldcastle said, shaking hands with them one by one.

Jarrett had spent much of the walk insisting that he and Hugo would conduct the interviews alone, without Caundle present. Caundle had stood his ground, but Jarrett had police procedure on his side.

'I'll leave you gentlemen to your work,' Caundle said, with somewhat ill grace. 'Miss Fitzgibbon can call me when you're done here.'

He stumped out. Oldcastle offered them chairs, had his secretary bring them tea. Fortnum & Mason, Hugo noticed, in a proper tea set.

'An indulgence,' Oldcastle said, noticing his attention. 'Proper tea was very hard to come by at Los Alamos. I try not to repeat the experience.'

It wasn't his only indulgence, Hugo noticed. There was a little wooden rack with four fountain pens. Good ones, too, with Osmiroid nibs and several bottles of ink.

Jarrett didn't waste time complimenting Oldcastle on his taste. He fixed the scientist with a cold eye and ran through the opening questions: what was Oldcastle researching, how many people did he have under him, how long had he been there? All things both Jarrett and Hugo knew. Dr Oldcastle was courteous, apparently quite unfazed by Jarrett.

'Who did Dr Rothesay usually work with?' Jarrett demanded.

Oldcastle folded his hands in front of him. 'He was the division's best theoretician, a first-class mind, so he worked with almost everyone over the years.'

'Your division is fairly new, isn't it?' Hugo asked.

'Yes, it was only established last winter, when my staff and I moved here from Ulfsgill in Westmorland. Given the problems we've had with our plutonium, and the key role of reactor design, it was felt appropriate to hive off the relevant experts into their own department, for better cross-fertilisation.'

Jarrett spoke before Hugo could say anything more. 'Who was Dr Rothesay working with at the time of his death?'

'His immediate superior was Dr Edward Vane. He's my right-hand man, as it were, and responsible for keeping an eye on Dr Rothesay day by day. Rothesay was a rather temperamental character, you understand.

A Scots-Italian from Edinburgh, went to Oxford on a scholarship. There was a certain touchiness to his brilliance, so he needed careful handling.'

'Did he have any office-mates, immediate colleagues?'

'Only Dr Wood, he's a New Zealander from Auckland. Rather younger than Dr Rothesay. Served in the New Zealand Navy during the war – fought at the River Plate, in fact. Took his doctorate at Manchester when it was all over, came straight here. Very practical turn of mind, he and Rothesay were due to be working together for the next couple of months, but that's been delayed. He went home before Christmas. Father on his deathbed. I pulled some official strings to put him on a military flight, he wouldn't have got there in time otherwise.'

That took Wood right out of the picture, at least for Rothesay's murder. Hugo knew Jarrett would want to confirm Wood's presence in New Zealand, though.

Oldcastle ran through a list of other staff, none of whom seemed to have worked particularly closely with Rothesay of late. There was a smattering of Danes, Germans, Canadians, Eastern Europeans. 'We're a very international outfit here,' said Oldcastle proudly.

Jarrett looked as if he'd swallowed a wasp. *Very international* was Special Branch's idea of a nightmare. As for Los Alamos, those who'd been there were in a category all their own, like Cambridge men.

'How long had you known Dr Rothesay?' Hugo asked.

'We go back a long way, before Los Alamos.'

'Were you friends?'

'I wouldn't say we were friends. Dr Rothesay didn't have close friendships with his colleagues, particularly not in the last few years. I believe he had one or two colleagues at Oxford with whom he was close. He was, as I said, prickly, rather prone to taking offence.'

'But he'd worked with you the whole time?'

'More or less. When he was assigned to work in my team at Los Alamos, I found his ideas very fruitful indeed. I tried as best I could to give him opportunities to show his capabilities. He was my first pick when I was appointed to head a team at Ulfsgill, and I made sure he was transferred here with me, to a position perhaps better suited to his talents. He was rather out of his depth in the more applied environment of Ulfsgill, got himself involved in a serious accident.'

Hugo had noticed that in Rothesay's file. There had been what the scientists referred to as a serious 'criticality incident' at the Ulfsgill facility while Rothesay was working there. A scientist had died from radiation exposure – a sobering reminder of the forces these men were working with.

'How much information did he have access to?'

'I should say anything the division did, and a fair bit of the work the other divisions were doing, if need be.'

'Don't you have security procedures for that sort of thing? Barriers between divisions, as recommended by Ministry instructions?'

'If we did, Inspector, we'd be trailing the Swedes in the atomic stakes, let alone the Russians. Of course, I tried to ensure that no one had access to too much, but as one of our top theoreticians, Dr Rothesay's work naturally affected all of us. He was often given access to experimental reports where his theories had been put to the test, to refine his calculations for the next stage of experiments.'

'I see,' said Jarrett. 'Let's go through this in order, then. When did you last see Dr Rothesay?'

Scene 4

Freya was in her tower, deep in another Edmund Crispin. She had turned her chair to face one of the windows, partly to catch the wan sunlight and partly so as not to have to look at her typewriter. A blank sheet of paper sat accusingly in the feed, gathering dust.

She looked up at the sound of a car crunching on the gravel. It came to a halt by the doorway. A door banged, then someone rapped on the heavy Castle knocker.

Curious, she put the book down and went over to the window, peering down through the thick leaded glass. It was Sir Bernard's Rover. Ben's voice came up.

'Sir Bernard. What can I do for you?'

'Is the Earl at home?'

'Why yes, but he's in Lady Matilda's wing now. Let me show you the way.'

'Much obliged,' said Sir Bernard.

Their voices died away. Puzzled, Freya returned to her book.

Scene 5

Gus was wrestling with a line of Virgil when he heard footsteps outside, a gentle rap on the door.

'Come in.'

It was Ben, with Hugo's chief Sir Bernard in tow.

'Beg your pardon for interrupting, sir, but Sir Bernard is here to see you.'

Gus pushed his chair back. 'Of course, come in. Take a seat. Can I get you something?'

'No, thank you. On duty.'

Ben shut the door, his footsteps receding.

Sir Bernard looked around the big, panelled room Gus had chosen as his study. It tended a little to sombre Victorian Gothic, like the rest of Lady Matilda's wing, but had a big, sunny bay window and a view out across the gardens. The one thing it lacked was books. Gus's library was still in New England, being packed up to join him in his new life.

'What can I do for you, Sir Bernard?'

Sir Bernard shifted in his chair, a little uneasily. 'Come to ask you a favour. Rather a big one, at short notice.'

Six months ago, the idea that senior members of the British intelligence service would have been asking him for favours – and feeling awkward about it – would have seemed quite absurd.

'I'll help if I can,' said Gus.

Sir Bernard crossed his legs and folded his hands, like a man sitting for a portrait. 'We have a defector. Hungarian scientist chap. Came over about six months ago, just before things started to thaw there, although God knows if that'll last. Been debriefing him at one of our other sites, but headquarters wants him to spend time with one of our people here. We need somewhere to put him up that's quiet and out of the way, and I thought you might be able to help. He's had rather a rough time of it, and a few days somewhere like this would do him a lot of good.'

'Is there any danger to my family?'

'Heavens, no. Even if the Soviets found him, they wouldn't bother coming after him this late in the day. They'll assume he's told us everything he's going to.'

Gus considered this. 'But he hasn't, if you'd like him to spend time with another of your officers.'

Sir Bernard looked almost embarrassed. 'A great deal of the initial debriefing was done by people who were, perhaps, not sufficiently acquainted with the intricacies of his field. We have someone here who's done a lot of work on it recently, for another case.'

In other words, thought Gus, they were trying to get themselves out of a muddle.

'I'd be happy to help, Sir Bernard, but it seems to me that Selchester isn't the easiest place to keep a secret. There doesn't seem to be a man, woman or child in the town who doesn't know what your establishment is really up to, and right now the place is swarming with newshounds after a trace of this scientist.'

Sir Bernard gave a small but definite sigh. 'I did suggest to my superiors that it might be wise to wait a few days. But no, London proposes, and we must dispose. The decision has been made, the personnel assigned, and we must make the best we can of it.'

'I'm surprised you're willing to lodge your defector with an American.'

'Well, you're not an American any more,' said Sir Bernard. 'Peer of the realm, although I suppose the formalities are still under way there?'

'They are indeed. Quite a process.' He'd been up to the House of Lords to see one of the heralds only last week. It had been like stepping back into the nineteenth century. Or the twelfth.

'So I imagine. No, ah, problem with changing your nationality? I'd be happy to put in a good word for you.'

'It was easier than I thought it would be. Given the circumstances.' He'd been expecting it to drag on for years, but so far it was all going smoothly. Political pressure on the relevant departments, he reckoned. A murdered earl was embarrassment enough for the Government.

'As I expected. Doesn't do to have an earl caught in that kind of limbo, could lead to all sorts of complications. Your solicitors are a sound lot, though, they'll be on top of it all. Excellent chaps. Know a couple of the partners from my club.'

Sir Bernard seemed to have run out of Establishment small talk, so Gus returned to the original subject. 'When would this be?'

'When? Ah, of course. Well. We'd like to drive him down this evening, arrive after dark, if that's acceptable to you. He'd be here for a week, perhaps two. He's indicated he'd like to go to America in the end, and they seem willing to have him. Colleagues there, you see. I thought he might find you interesting company.'

'I see. And what do we tell Mrs Partridge and the Selchester rumour mill, when a Hungarian scientist turns up in the middle of the night? I can hardly pretend he's my long-lost cousin, we've had quite enough of that sort of thing already.'

Sir Bernard fingered his moustache.

'One of my London colleagues had a suggestion. Seems our fellow is well read, knows his Latin and Greek. Not like some of our chaps, can't tell a hexameter from a handsaw.' He seemed rather pleased with his alliteration. 'We'd like to pass him off as a classicist. Émigré, fleeing Uncle Joe's thought police, standing up for Western civilisation and so on. Where better for him to take refuge than with a fellow Greats man? Although I suppose you don't call it Greats on your side of the pond.'

'Thorn Hall is officially a Government statistics office,' Gus pointed out. 'An odd place for a classicist to spend his working days.'

This point did not please Sir Bernard, perhaps because his superiors hadn't considered it. Gus didn't have much experience with Sir Bernard's American counterparts, but he could spot a career administrator when he saw one. 'They all know what we're up to at Thorn Hall, however much we'd wish it were otherwise. Perfectly natural for us to be interested in him.'

This was an unexpectedly candid admission from Sir Bernard. Gus paused for a moment, tapping his fingers on the arm of his chair. For his own part, he was more than happy to offer temporary refuge for a man without country or home, fugitive from a monstrous tyranny. As father of two daughters recently caught up in a murder investigation, he was a little more cautious. True, Babs was away at art school, returning to the Castle only during the holidays, but that left Polly even more exposed. He trusted Freya and Mrs Partridge implicitly, and there was Georgia, but it was still all very new and unfamiliar.

'If you can give your word there's no threat to my daughter,' he said at last, 'you have my permission.'

'You have it,' said Sir Bernard. 'I'm a father myself. Sons, in my case, but a man has his duties.'

'Very well,' said Gus.

Sir Bernard uncrossed his legs. 'Thank you, Lord Selchester. Much appreciated. I'll let London know. I imagine you can expect him this evening, around nine. Best not to entrust anything to the telephone, I think.'

Gus walked Sir Bernard back to his car in the pale sunshine. Ben had turned it around, but was nowhere to be seen. Sir Bernard gazed appreciatively over the lawn and the ruined walls towards Thorn Hall, across the valley.

'I take it I can tell Mr Hawksworth and Miss Wryton about this,' Gus said.

'Of course. I'll have Hawksworth fill you in on his background.'

'Can you tell me his name?'

'Yes, of course. You'd better know it now you've agreed. Dr Árpád Bárándy. Well, Lord Selchester, you have the thanks of the Service, and the gratitude of your adopted country. Sorry to have sprung this on you so suddenly. I'd like to have done it properly, but as I said, London was adamant. If there's anything I can do to return the favour, do let me know.'

They shook hands, as one English gentleman to another, and Sir Bernard drove off. Gus let out a long, deep breath, and tried to imagine the FBI or CIA allowing a defector to lodge with a visiting Brit who'd just inherited an oil fortune or some such. Quite unthinkable.

He headed for the door. Time to find Mrs Partridge.

Scene 6

Dr Edward Vane was a thin, correct man with a severe expression, like an old-fashioned schoolmaster. He had his own office next to Oldcastle, a neat desk with everything in lines, rows of periodicals on shelves in the corner.

His view of his colleagues was rather dim. Or perhaps it was fairer to say he was more alert to their faults than their virtues, particularly if those faults were in some way disorderly. Dr Wood, the New Zealander, was far too casual, prone to call people by their first names, as apparently was the way at home. Thorogood, the materials man, liked to work late and sleep late.

'And Dr Rothesay?' Jarrett asked. His eyes were alight, no sign of boredom. 'What did you think of him?'

Not *When did you last see Dr Rothesay?* Hugo noted.

'There was very little order to his thoughts, for a man in his profession. Perhaps if he had been better able to discipline his mind, he might have achieved a rather greater scientific eminence than he did. As for his personal conduct outside work, it was nothing short of scandalous.'

'What do you mean?'

'I mean he had affairs, Inspector. With married women.'

'Do you know who?'

'I did not enquire, and he did not tell me. They came and they went. Sometimes they came back. I can't imagine why.'

'Did any of them ever come to Foxley?'

'I should think not. Brigadier Caundle is most punctilious about security, and I can't imagine his men would ever have allowed Dr Rothesay to bring his various mistresses to a secure installation. Nor can I believe he would have wanted to do so.'

Hugo wondered idly whether Dr Vane were the sort of man who would secretly have liked to have mistresses of his own (plural, of course) and couldn't forgive Dr Rothesay for being a man who did. Then again, mistresses were apparently considered disorderly, so perhaps not.

'Do you think he discussed his work with them?'

'I very much doubt it. It was difficult enough to get him to discuss his work when he was meant to be doing it. He considered himself a man of high culture and wide interests. He liked to talk about them during his breaks. Dr Oldcastle has always tried to encourage a culture of scientific discussion among his staff, as he believes great things can come of apparently casual conversations. Dr Rothesay's attitude was not conducive to such discussion.'

Here was a man who had no trouble speaking ill of the dead.

'How was the quality of his work?' Hugo asked.

'He had a first-rate mind,' said Vane grudgingly, 'which he employed at a fraction of its capacity. I was pleased to see, since we moved here, that he was paying more attention to his work, coming in earlier and leaving later.'

Jarrett was on that like a shot. 'You mean he was here at times when few others would have been?'

'I like the staff to keep regular hours where possible, between nine and six. There are, as I said, certain members of staff who prefer a more irregular pattern, despite attempts to discourage them' – Thorogood the materials man, no doubt – 'but Dr Rothesay's habit had become to arrive early and leave late. I must admit, the quality of his output had improved.'

Hugo could all too easily imagine Dr Vane behind a desk on the other side of the Iron Curtain, forever hassling his staff over the minutiae of factory production targets and steel quotas.

'Would he be here alone?' Jarrett asked, scribbling furiously in his notebook.

'Sometimes. At the end of the day, though, every member of staff is required to lock all their materials away and take the key to Reception, where it is in turn locked away for the night. The night-duty guards are unable to access the keys.'

Jarrett clearly approved of this. 'Good procedure.'

Hugo asked, 'Could you put a more exact date on when his behaviour changed?'

Vane began to tap his fingers against one another. 'I would say that it changed around the time we arrived at Foxley.'

Hugo flipped through his own shorthand notes, rather less copious than Jarrett's. A field agent had to have a good memory; it was dangerous to commit things to writing.

'This was about a year ago, then.'

'We moved here at the beginning of December 1952.'

'And do you know of any reasons why Dr Rothesay might have become more dedicated to his work?' Hugo asked.

'I was not in Dr Rothesay's confidence.'

'Indulge me with some speculation.'

Dr Vane said nothing for a long time. Jarrett's thumb began to twitch.

'I should say that he had begun to see the error of his ways, perhaps after he had such a close call at Ulfsgill. To be a first-class scientist, it's not enough to rely on intuition and hunches. It takes careful, sustained work. Dr Rothesay had rarely exerted himself to the limit of his abilities, and time was beginning to catch up with him. Perhaps if he had bestirred himself earlier, he might have left a more fitting scientific legacy. It's a tragedy that he didn't.'

Scene 7

Knowing full well that Jarrett would be away at the Atomic all day, Freya had taken herself into town while the coast was clear. She'd go to the bookshop, she decided, seek out some worthy tome on Restoration England or the Sun King's France and see what gems it yielded. That at least would be research.

The Selchester Bookshop was dimly lit, its smell familiar and comfortable. Dinah, in her favourite crimson sweater and much-darned trousers, was in a chatty mood.

'Busy this morning,' she said. 'All the ladies who lunch are at the Daffodils. Body in the river and all. How's Georgia?'

Freya had heard about the body. Inevitably, it had been Mrs Partridge who had brought the news.

'They've found that scientist,' she'd said as Freya passed through the kitchen. 'In the river. I heard as it was Miss Polly and Miss Georgia as spotted the body on their way in to school.'

Freya stopped. 'Dead? Georgia saw it?'

'That's what I heard,' said Mrs Partridge. 'There was a right crowd on the bank when I went in, police vans and all. No sign of Miss Georgia or Miss Polly, mind you, but Farmer Loveless, lives up Nethercoombe way, said it was those two girls tipped him off to it, just as he was on his way home.'

'Is she all right?' said Freya.

'He said she looked a bit chalky, but a good day's school is just what she needs. You be here when she gets home, mind. Mr Hawksworth might be out till all hours, now there's a body on their hands, and she'll want familiar faces around her.'

Of course Freya would be back. Such an awful thing for anyone to see, let alone a thirteen-year-old.

'She'll be fine,' said Dinah firmly now. 'Shaken, for a while. It's not an easy thing, coming face-to-face with mortal remains. She didn't see her mother's body, did she?'

Georgia and Hugo's mother had been killed by the doodlebug which left Georgia trapped under the rubble for several hours.

'I don't think so,' said Freya. Hugo had mentioned it once, something about small mercies. His mother had been in another room of the house when the V1 hit. 'I just wish things would settle down for her.'

'Get Leo down,' said Dinah. 'If she'll talk to anyone, it'll be him. He's the closest she has to a father, never mind his Roman collar. Gus was very impressed by him. Says he's known good men and good priests, but Leo is the best of both.'

Leo was Hugo and Georgia's uncle, a Catholic priest who lectured in physics at Oxford. Roman collar aside, Freya wouldn't be surprised if in twenty or thirty years' time Hugo looked just like his uncle. Leo had been in intelligence, too, during the first war.

'Hugo can ring him this evening,' said Freya, glad of the suggestion. 'How is Gus's latest translation going?'

'You live in the same Castle,' said Dinah, going around to the far side of the counter.

'Mmm,' said Freya, recognising a delaying tactic when she saw one. 'He's buying a lot of books.'

'He needs a lot of books,' said Dinah, with a glint in her eye. She liked her secrets, too, which Freya could well understand. 'Were you looking for something, or did you just come for a break from your chronicle?'

'I was looking for things on the Stuarts,' Freya said.

'Are you still on the Stuarts? You were in here, what, a year ago, asking for things on Charles II.'

'The Selchesters were up to all sorts of things at the Restoration,' Freya said, and then, improvising wildly, 'I've found an interesting offshoot of the family. Early eighteenth century. Descended from the ninth Earl's illegitimate son, who had all sorts of adventures during the Interregnum.'

'He was the one married to Countess Maude, wasn't he? The one you like? I wouldn't have thought he had the spirit for illegitimate children.'

Freya did indeed have a thing for Countess Maude, who had valiantly and skilfully defended the Castle against a Parliamentary army during the Civil War. She'd quietly abstracted the Countess's portrait from the Gallery, to hang on her wall.

'Oh, he had plenty of spirit for dashing about in Cavalier finery and sweet-talking the Southwark wenches. Less so for the privations of a siege.'

'Was the mother a Southwark wench?'

'No,' said Freya, inventing herself even further into trouble. 'A gentleman's daughter. Quite scandalous. All hushed up, but of course everybody knew.'

'Just like Selchester,' said Dinah gnomically. 'What did he get up to? This is like a Rosina Wyndham, and to think I imagined your research was dull.'

'I'm not sure yet. Spying for the Royalists, maybe. I'm looking for some background,' Freya said, back-pedalling furiously. There were Rosina Wyndhams to Dinah's left, a whole row of them staring accusingly out at her. She'd had no problems coming up with plots for any of them before. Why was it so difficult now?

'The Interregnum . . .' said Dinah thoughtfully, walking over to the history section. The Interregnum wasn't at all what Freya was after, but she'd dug herself into a hole now, so it would have to do. She could always pick out some other books for good measure. Or come back, following her imaginary trail forward into the Restoration. 'You're in luck. This came in a few months ago, hasn't had any takers.'

She pulled a heavy tome off the shelf and dropped it into Freya's hands.

'*John Thurloe, Cromwell's Secretary of State,*' Freya read. '*The author is a Fellow and Tutor in early modern history at Trinity College, Cambridge* . . . It looks awfully worthy.'

'Isn't history always worthy?' Dinah said. She patted the book. 'Never mind the dull title, he was in charge of all Cromwell's spies. It'll be just what you need. You'll see. Now get along, or I shall think you're only using me as an excuse not to work. Shall I wrap it for you?'

Five minutes later Freya was standing in the chilly street, poorer by a considerable sum and richer – if one could call it that – by one distinctly dull book she didn't need. Still, she could take it to the Daffodils and pretend to read it over a cup of coffee.

She made for the tearooms.

Scene 8

Jarrett's campaign to turn the Atomic inside out, one scientist at a time, came to a swift halt with a phone call from MacLeod. Bruno Rothesay's wife was back in Selchester. Hugo had to endure another white-knuckle drive back to the police station to interview her.

Alice Rothesay, brittle, and expensively dressed in a well-cut, light tweed suit and a hat that was far too smart for the country, had a similar silver-gilt beauty to Freya's cousin Lady Sonia. In Mrs Rothesay's case, the beauty was on the wane – more through temperament, Hugo thought, than time. Her mouth was set in a frown, and she was ill at ease in the interview room without a cigarette. Jarrett didn't allow his subjects to smoke, said he didn't want them at their ease.

It was the first time Hugo had met her, his previous acquaintance being only through her husband's security file. Eight years younger than her husband. Daughter of a High Court judge, old family of no great distinction, no political involvement. Degree from Oxford, which meant she was clever. The competition for places at the women's colleges was intense. Married Bruno a couple of years after graduating, while she was working as an assistant in the chemistry department of University College London. No children, one brother killed in the war, no living family aside from this Welsh sister-in-law.

All in all, a thoroughly uninformative file.

'Anything more on this sister-in-law?' Jarrett had asked MacLeod, pausing in the corridor outside the interview room.

'Nothing yet. The Radnorshire police are taking their time.'

'Sloppy,' said Jarrett. 'Probably out combing the hills for some Taffy's lost sheep. If you haven't heard tomorrow, I'll give their Chief Constable a rocket. Can't have them dragging their heels in a case as important as this.'

The Radnorshire police, Hugo rather thought, might not hold the same view of their priorities. Particularly when forced to contend with snowdrifts deep enough to cut whole villages off for weeks at a time.

Now the three of them sat opposite her in a bare green room, a deliberate intimidation. Jarrett snapped a file open, launched straight into his questions before MacLeod could say a word.

'Mrs Rothesay. You left Selchester for Radnorshire on the thirtieth of December, correct?'

Alice Rothesay lifted her head. 'I believe it customary in civilised countries for gentlemen to introduce themselves. My father used to say that an absence of manners was the surest sign of a Bolshevik.'

Jarrett clamped his jaw shut and allowed MacLeod to make his interrupted introductions.

'We've already met, Mrs Rothesay. May I introduce Inspector Jarrett, of Special Branch, and Mr Hawksworth.'

'Of the Statistics Office, so I hear. Is my visit to Radnorshire of economic interest? I'm flattered.'

Hugo was beginning to like her.

'If you would repeat the account of your movements that you gave to me,' MacLeod said, 'that would be greatly appreciated.'

'Of course, Inspector. I didn't go straight from Selchester, as a matter of fact. I went to London, to see the New Year in with some friends and go to the theatre. Not much opportunity to do that in Selchester. I left for Staffordshire on the seventh to visit an old friend of my parents on her sickbed, and arrived at Anne's on the evening of the eighth.'

'Anne is your brother's widow?' Jarrett asked.

'Yes.'

She was determined not to give Jarrett an inch and, Hugo suspected, taking a certain bitter pleasure in it.

'How does a senior judge's daughter-in-law come to live on a Welsh hill farm?'

'She married again.'

'And you went to stay with them for two weeks, in January.'

'I went to stay with them for four or five days, but it snowed. I was stuck.'

'When did you last speak to your husband?'

'In London. We spoke on the telephone before I left for Staffordshire.'

She was keeping her hands very still, tightly clasped around one knee.

'What did you talk about?'

She shrugged. 'I don't really remember. I know I ought to, since it was the last time I spoke to him, but it didn't register at the time. I think I told him about the plays I'd seen, and he pretended to be interested.'

'Did he speak about his work?'

'His work was classified, Inspector. I dare say he made a few remarks about his colleagues. I pretended interest in turn. I told him I'd be back around the thirteenth, and we left it there.'

'Mrs Rothesay,' said Hugo, intervening before Jarrett lost his temper, 'I take it your marriage was not a happy one.'

She paused, her fingers tightening in their clasp. 'No, it wasn't. My husband was a disappointed man, Mr Hawksworth. He wanted to be one of the greats, you see, like Rutherford or Bohr. But he also wanted to be more dashing than they were, a Renaissance man. While they were at conferences talking about physics, he was living the high life with the locals. Wine, women and song, it was all very diverting for him. Then he found himself up in a godforsaken valley in Westmorland, working yet again for Laurence Oldcastle, who's half the scientist he was. He realised he'd flunked it.'

Jarrett scribbled a few words on his notepaper.

'I suppose you think that makes him ideal spy material, Inspector, but you'd be quite wrong. Whatever his other faults, my husband was no traitor.'

'Did he change after that?' Hugo said.

'He became a bore, obsessed with making his mark on science. It was bad enough in Westmorland, never mind the appalling weather. After he was transferred here, I hardly saw him. I was a widow of the Atomic long before I became a widow in fact.'

'Did he talk about an accident at Ulfsgill, a brush with death which might have changed his outlook?'

She rolled her eyes. 'Yes, I know he was involved in an accident – he wouldn't shut up about it. As to whether it gave him a greater appreciation of his life and career, perhaps. Mostly he grumbled about it, said he was being blamed. I was simply glad we were moving somewhere a little more civilised.'

'He thought he was being blamed?'

'My husband never thought anything was his fault. I gathered that someone else at Ulfsgill had blamed him, a theoretician, for getting too involved in some experiment. He, on the other hand, considered that his colleagues were doing mere engineering, and that his talents were being wasted.'

Jarrett took over again: had she noticed any change in his behaviour recently, had she any reason to suspect he was hiding something, had she noticed him with any new people? Her answers were short, to the point, and as uninformative as her section in Bruno's file. No, no, and no. He left early and came home late, she lived a quite separate life with frequent trips to London.

Finally Jarrett could stand it no longer. 'I must warn you, Mrs Rothesay, that failure to divulge evidence in a case of this importance could have very serious consequences.'

'I don't respond well to threats, Inspector,' she said coolly. 'I've given you the answers you deserve.'

'Don't you want your husband's murderer brought to justice, Mrs Rothesay?' MacLeod asked. Hugo had never found him the most tactful or observant of men, but beside Jarrett he was a model of sympathy and understanding.

'I do. I loved him once. Even if I hadn't, he was murdered in cold blood, and I should like to see his murderer hang for it, whoever he or she might be. But you mistake our relationship if you believe I was privy to any but the most superficial acquaintance with his affairs.' There was ever such a slight emphasis on the last word, one Jarrett picked up immediately.

'Are you suggesting your husband was having an affair?'

'My husband was always having an affair, Inspector. The war didn't put an end to that. If you're going to ask me who was the current object of his attentions, I'm afraid I can't tell you. He had two or three last year, they seemed to overlap with one another. There were a couple of local women, some ambitious young graduate student from London. Now I've had enough of your questions and your manners. If you want to talk to me again, I shall insist on having a solicitor here. My father lodged a generous sum of money with Hare & Warren in London to ensure that my legal affairs would always be taken care of. As I've barely touched it, there should be more than sufficient to deal with any nuisance you may cause.'

It was left to MacLeod to show her out. Jarrett began writing, his pen heavy on the notepaper.

'She's hiding something. You know as well as I do.'

'We all hide things. The question is whether it has any bearing on the case.'

'It's our job to hide things. It certainly isn't hers. I suppose her father taught her how to lie with a straight face. Still, the truth will out. I'll have her followed.'

'Won't work,' said Hugo, who was as tired of Jarrett as Alice Rothesay had been. 'Selchester is too small. She'll find out in half an hour, and you'll be the laughing stock of the town.'

'I'll thank you to keep to your files and let me do my job, Mr Hawksworth.'

Hugo knew an opening when he saw one. 'Then perhaps we should divide our efforts. It's hardly efficient to have us both in each interview, when you're taping everything up at the Atomic.'

Jarrett's eyes lit up at the word 'efficient', although not without a certain suspicion. 'What did you have in mind?'

'The circumstances of Dr Rothesay's death suggest someone with capabilities rather out of the ordinary. When I went through the files before, my instructions were to concentrate on political connections.

Now it seems we're looking for a man with war service, perhaps not even directly connected with the Atomic. It might serve us well for you to concentrate on the circumstances of his death while I look into the background. That is, after all, why I'm here.'

He was taking a risk. There were always things to be learned from an interrogation, even one conducted by Jarrett. Nuances of body language, a flicker of the eyes, could open up whole new lines of investigation. But instinct told him a more flexible approach was needed.

Jarrett gave a curt nod and took up his pen. 'Keep me updated every day. Let MacLeod know on your way out.'

Hugo shut the door behind him with a silent sigh of relief and set out down the corridor. He heard a snatch of conversation from another room, something about stolen farm equipment. A constable was taking a statement about a local ne'er-do-well, a name Hugo recognised. It was all pleasantly mundane, a world away both from Jarrett's disagreeable questions and from Hugo's own previous life.

When had all this become so reassuring? He'd been a city-lights man, yet all of a sudden Selchester seemed normal, and this world of files and spies distinctly alien.

He turned a corner to see MacLeod handing some papers to a secretary.

'Dispensed with your services, too, has he?' MacLeod said.

Hugo sketched the agreement they'd come to, and the Superintendent allowed himself an appreciative smile. 'Wish I could do that.'

'Haven't you duties to attend to here?'

'Only until Special Branch need something.'

Hugo judged MacLeod in an amicable mood. They hadn't the easiest of relationships, MacLeod far too willing to toe London's line when it had been decided to pin the late Lord Selchester's murder on an innocent man, but on Jarrett they could agree.

'What's his background?'

MacLeod knew exactly what Hugo was asking, and was willing to be drawn. 'I hear he was in counter-intelligence in the war, debriefing German spies. Went over to Germany in '45, to hunt for traitors like Haw-Haw. These days it's Russians, I suppose. He has a reputation for efficiency. Everything in tip-top condition.'

'And his superior, Superintendent Pritchard?'

MacLeod's expression was almost reverent. 'Now, there's a real policeman. Not much to look at, mind you, but no one better on a tricky case.'

Hugo heard a door slam, purposeful footsteps in the corridor. Time for a quick getaway.

Scene 9

The pale-eyed man was waiting just out of sight of the school gates. Georgia was deep in conversation with Daisy about their planned expedition through the woods to Pagan Hill. She didn't see him until it was too late.

He appeared, as if from nowhere, with a notebook poised in his hand. His manner was friendly, but his eyes were a washed-out blue, and very cold. He ignored Daisy, focusing his attention on Georgia. Polly was somewhere behind them; she'd left her exercise book in Miss Ormskirk's classroom.

'Might I have a moment of your time to ask about your discovery this morning?'

Georgia wasn't having any of that. She didn't want to be reminded of the body in the river, stiff and pallid. They'd heard at lunchtime who it had been – the headmistress had called her and Polly in to tell them. Miss Winscomb wasn't grand like her sniffy old headmistress at Yorkshire Ladies', but there was a quiet authority to her which inspired more respect. Even in Georgia, who wasn't prone to take much notice of headmistresses.

'This is, regrettably, an affair of some importance,' Miss Winscomb said, looking at the two of them over her desk. 'All of the reputable papers and some of the less reputable ones, too, have sent journalists down to root around. If any of them are so devoid of manners as to approach you, say nothing to them. Don't linger on your way home this evening.'

Polly nodded, looking across at Georgia with a warning in her eyes. For once, Georgia wasn't inclined to be stubborn.

'Good,' said Miss Winscomb. 'If there's any trouble, I should like to know about it. Any reporter who bothers you will find himself in very deep water. Figuratively speaking, that is.'

Now Georgia tried to walk on, but she found him blocking their way across the road. She couldn't tell how he'd moved so quickly. She didn't like him one bit.

'Can you give me a few words on what it was like to find the body?' the reporter asked. Only she wasn't at all sure this was a reporter. She'd seen them loitering that morning. They all had much the same look and manner. Newshounds, they were called, and there was a certain bright-eyed curiosity to them all.

This man was quite different. His eyes didn't wander, and his tone wasn't right. She rather thought she recognised him.

'Would you please move out of the way?' she said, with more firmness than she felt.

He didn't. They couldn't turn, because he'd positioned himself in the way of their bikes.

'Who are you?' Georgia demanded. 'I've seen you before; you're always poking around. I shall report you to the police.'

The threat didn't move him, but something else did.

'You there! What's your name?' came a sharp voice from behind them. Georgia nearly died of relief. It was Daisy Dillon's father, Stanley Dillon, chief Feoffee of Selchester and a man not at all to be trifled with.

The man's eyes tightened with frustration. He turned and strode away, ignoring Stanley Dillon, slipping into the alley behind the row of Victorian houses down the road from the school.

Stanley Dillon's face was hard and resolute, but it was the face of a man very definitely on their side.

'Are you all right?' Stanley asked, his eyes following the man's passage. He'd been worried about something like this, and had taken the rare step of coming to pick Daisy up and check on the other two. Only a van had dropped its load on Garver Street, and he'd been late.

The two girls nodded. Mr Dillon tightened his lips in sudden anger. That this should have happened to any girl, almost within sight of the school gates . . .

'Did he say anything about where he was from?'

'I've seen him before,' Georgia said. 'He was here last year. But he wasn't a reporter then.'

Stanley Dillon would have laid odds the man wasn't a reporter now. 'Come on,' he said. 'We'll leave your bikes at Mrs Gumble's. You can pick them up tomorrow.'

Scene 10

Despite Hugo's best efforts, Jarrett gave him a lift home to the Castle, roaring up the drive and through the gate arch with fractions of an inch to spare. He screeched to a halt outside the door.

'Looks the worse for wear,' he said, jumping out to have a look at the gaunt dark bulk of the Castle. 'Still, I suppose this Yank has grand plans for it, they always do. Do the place good to be brought up to date. It's like one of those Hammer Horror flicks.'

Hugo levered himself out of the car, rather more slowly. There was a great cawing of rooks in the trees, aggrieved by the violence of the new arrival.

The door opened. It was Freya, bundled up in an ancient Arran sweater. She stopped abruptly at the sight of Jarrett, a shuttered look on her face.

'Oh, it's you,' said Jarrett. 'Still stuck in the sticks, I see.'

With some effort, Freya ignored him.

'Hugo, Georgia needs you.'

That was an odd thing to say.

'Of course.'

'Oh, that sister of yours,' said Jarrett. 'Don't know what you're thinking of, sending her to school in a place like this. She should be in a proper boarding school. Otherwise she'll end up like Freya here, a lifelong spinster.'

'I believe Freya went to Yorkshire Ladies' College,' said Hugo neutrally. 'Goodnight, Inspector. Thank you for the lift.'

He turned for the door without a further word.

The door slammed, the tyres squealed, the engine gunned. The rooks rose in another chorus of protest.

'Thank God,' Hugo said. 'What's this about Georgia?'

Scene 11

Georgia was in the cheerful chaos of the kitchen, arguing with Polly over their history homework. Daisy Dillon was doodling on a scrap of paper, rather more interested in the treacle tart Mrs Partridge was making. Gus and Stanley Dillon had retreated to the calm of the South Drawing Room.

'What rubbish this is. There were hardly any real Protestants in England,' Polly declared. 'Just the ones Henry got to come up with reasons he could have his wicked way with Anne Boleyn.'

'Anne was a Protestant,' Georgia pointed out.

'See? Lust. One of the seven deadly sins. Nothing more.'

Mrs Partridge, already scandalised at this rank Popery being bruited about in her kitchen, shot her a stern look. 'None of that, Miss Polly.'

'Then why did we all become C of E even after Henry died?' Georgia demanded.

'Because Elizabeth hung and drew and squashed anyone who disagreed with her. They had to hide in priest holes.'

'It's hanged, not hung, don't you know anything? And what do you mean, squashed? She chopped people's heads off, like the Earl of Essex.'

'Essex was a nobleman, and anyway he was guilty. If you didn't plead, they squashed you under a stone until you died.'

'Did they teach you that in your American school?' Georgia asked, rather envious of a curriculum with such details. 'I thought you didn't learn any history before the *Mayflower*.'

'I read it in a book,' said Polly, who had been to a convent school in Boston. 'School had all the lives of the saints with those lugubrious illustrations, just as dull as Miss Ormskirk. But less wrong.'

'She's not wrong,' said Georgia stoutly.

'That wasn't what you said when we did Richard III,' said Daisy. 'Can you put more treacle in, Mrs Partridge?'

'Now, Miss Dillon, it may not be rationed any more, but that doesn't mean there's plenty to go around.'

'You should ask my father – he can get you more.'

Hugo and Freya came through from the corridor, Hugo looking distinctly weary.

'You were talking about me,' Georgia said. 'You don't need to. I'm fine.'

'But wrong,' said Polly.

Georgia elbowed her in the ribs. 'I should think you need attention more than I do,' she told Hugo. 'You look like someone picked you up and shook you. Who was in that noisy car?'

'I was given a lift back by Inspector Jarrett.'

'Poor you,' she said, remembering him from this morning. He hadn't actually questioned her, that had been stodgy old MacLeod, but she'd heard him berating a pair of policemen for not jumping to it quickly enough. 'I bet he drives like the clappers. Probably always getting stopped by the police and then flashing his card at them, like some Soviet commissar, so they have to salute and watch him zoom off. Have a stiff whisky, you need it.'

'Are you all right?' Hugo asked.

'Of course,' she said scornfully. 'I'm going to get better marks than Polly in history this week. She'll write all sorts of Papist propaganda and Miss Ormskirk will give her an E.'

'I shall have my reward in heaven,' said Polly with a sidelong glance, 'while you roast with all the other heretics.'

'Heretics are much more interesting,' Georgia declared. 'They say what they think. I bet Miss Ormskirk would have been in the Inquisition.'

Hugo decided this would be a good time to ring Leo, as Freya had suggested. The clamour of an argument renewed, following him down the stone passages into Grace Hall, where the Castle's telephone resided.

Hugo's call to his uncle was brief. He well knew Irene from the exchange would be hanging on his every word, and his recounting of the news was brisk, contained. Leo had seen the headlines, and would know to read between the lines.

'I have tutorials tomorrow and a Mass in the evening: I'm deputising at the Chaplaincy. It'll have to be Wednesday. I can leave first thing.'

Not as soon as Hugo had hoped, but it couldn't be helped.

'There's something else,' Hugo said. 'Bruno Rothesay was an Oxford man. Pembroke, early twenties. Tallish, black hair, later picked up a Heidelberg scar.'

'Say no more,' said Leo. 'Then I shall be on the three-fifteen.'

A crisp click of the receiver. Such a nuisance, having to watch every word you said on the phone. Then again, Grace Hall in January was nearly as cold as his office, and he had no desire to linger.

'Wednesday,' said Hugo, spotting Freya in the doorway. 'Will she . . .'

'She'll be fine,' said Freya. 'As Gus would say, she's a tough cookie.'

Hugo tapped the phone with a finger, lost in thought. 'That man, though. Time and time again he's turned up, and we're none the wiser as to why.'

They'd all encountered the pale-eyed man before. Jenkins was his name, or at least the name he went by. Freya had endured some unpleasant questions from him on the way back from Selchester's funeral, and he'd followed the newly minted Lord Selchester across the Atlantic, only to turn up again in Selchester at Christmas.

'Stanley will ask a few questions. Daisy was caught up in it, too. He's not happy about that, and he doesn't like this sort of thing happening on his turf.'

'Nothing helpful from the police, I suppose.'

'They'll have a sharp word with Jenkins if he does anything of the kind again, but there's nothing more they can do. We already know he's a private investigator. MacLeod thought he might have had some police experience at one point. He has a very good idea of just what he can get away with.'

Footsteps in the passage.

'Ah, there you are,' Gus said, coming out into Grace Hall with Stanley Dillon behind him. 'We were wondering whether that car was our Hungarian friend arriving early.'

Hugo looked blank. 'Hungarian friend?'

'I was just about to tell him about our visitor,' Freya said, cursing Gus and Stanley for their curiosity. She couldn't tell Hugo the whole thing now, as Stanley Dillon didn't have security clearance. Gus had told her when she returned from town, leaving her with a sense of unease and a desire to get the low-down from Hugo.

Hugo, however, was quite in the dark.

'Hasn't Sir Bernard briefed you?' Gus asked.

'I haven't seen hide nor hair of Sir Bernard today,' said Hugo. 'I've been up at the Atomic with Jarrett.'

There was a perplexed silence.

'I think,' said Stanley after a moment, 'that the three of you need to talk. I'll take Daisy off. It's time she had her dinner.'

'She was rather hoping to have dinner here, I think,' said Freya. 'Something to do with a treacle tart.'

'There's more afoot than Mrs Partridge's cooking, by the sound of it. Sir Bernard can be a crafty one when he wants to be, for all that dignified exterior. I'll take my leave here, Lord Selchester, if you don't mind, and let you know if I get anywhere with this Jenkins fellow.'

Scene 12

They repaired to the South Drawing Room, where Gus filled Hugo in on the afternoon's visit.

'He's arriving tonight?' Hugo asked.

'Nine or thereabouts.'

Hugo smelled a rat. Chaotic the Service could be, occasionally bureaucratic, prone to keep secrets even from itself, but this had all the feeling of a clever manoeuvre on someone's part.

'Spit it out,' Gus said. 'You look as if you've sucked on a lemon, and I'd rather hear it plainly than wrapped up in weasel words. Sir Bernard didn't sound too happy about it either. Apologised twice for doing everything in such a hurry.'

'As well he should,' said Freya, who had no time for Sir Bernard, and didn't like the sound of this one bit. 'He's acting as if he were still a trustee, and the Castle a place he can park inconvenient guests. Present company excepted, of course.'

'As I recall,' Hugo said, 'you weren't too happy to have me and Georgia pressed on you either.'

She lifted her chin. 'I'm glad you came here, if not with the manner of it.'

'Spoken like a true Selchester,' Gus observed.

Hugo said, 'I think someone was relying on your ignorance of British ways, and particularly the Service's ways.'

'In other words, I've been had.'

His father would never have been had. The late Lord Selchester might never have risen as high as he had clearly wished, but Freya had never seen anyone successfully cross him. One didn't. Perhaps it was a point in Gus's favour that he could make such a mistake, that he lacked her uncle's ruthlessness.

'They pulled a fast one,' Hugo conceded.

'Literally.'

Freya glanced at the clock. Half past six. Too late for Hugo to go back to the Hall and have his secretary pull Dr Bárándy's file before he arrived.

'Do you think this Dr Bárándy might be a danger to Polly and Georgia?' Gus said. 'If he is, I'm not having him in my house, gentleman's agreement or not.'

'They wouldn't put a peer's daughter at risk,' said Hugo. 'Too much danger of the whole story getting out, more scandal and bad press. We've had enough of that with Burgess and Maclean. More likely they're just playing on your sense of hospitality to get themselves out of a tight corner.'

'Why keep you out of the way, though?' Freya asked. 'Pick a day you were out of the Hall, make very sure you didn't know about it in time.'

'I'd have queried it with the Chief,' said Hugo. It didn't normally do to go around the chain of command like that, but the Chief had sent him to Selchester because something was amiss here. Now it seemed something was amiss in London as well.

Gus nodded. 'I shan't do your Service another favour in a hurry, that's for sure. I suppose we'll have to make the best we can of it. Whatever the Service may be up to, Dr Bárándy deserves our hospitality. Mrs Partridge thought we might put him in my father's room, to give him some privacy. It has its own private sitting room next door.'

'From Communist Hungary to an earl's bedroom,' said Freya. 'Quite the change for this Dr Bárándy.'

Scene 13

'Some brandy, that's what you need,' said Mrs Partridge from the doorway.

Freya looked up from Cromwell's England with a start. She'd been curled up on the sofa since supper, deep in the tangled webs of John Thurloe. Why would she need brandy?

She didn't. Hugo did, limping across to a chair by the fire. The library was the warmest of the Castle's grand rooms, particularly on a January night with a wind howling outside. Polished wood, faded leather, a deep carpet, the crackle of seasoned logs, there was nowhere better to read.

'You look almost cheerful,' she said.

With an hour or two to recover from the various unpleasant surprises, Hugo was feeling rather more himself. One learned to be adaptable in his line of work. He sank down in the chair, glad of the warmth.

'Chalk it down to the prospect of working on my own again,' he said.

Freya folded the book shut, keeping her finger on the page. 'Do tell.'

He caught a glimpse of the cover. 'Thurloe. Research?'

'Unexpectedly fascinating. Dinah pushed it on me. I always thought, what a dull decade, no theatres and no Christmas, but such goings-on. A seethe of intrigue.'

'Better at a distance?'

'Perhaps. I'd rather have lived in the Restoration – such mischief – but you have to look at the years before to see why. All those plots and counterplots, informants everywhere, Cromwell making up the rules as he went along. No wonder everyone wanted strong drink and loose women once Charles was back on the throne. They were lucky to be in one piece.'

'I suppose your ancestors were in the thick of it.'

'Not in the most edifying way. The ninth Earl tried to buy his way back from exile by betraying a Royalist plot, but his wife found his letters and threatened to send them to the King unless he behaved. Thurloe called her some quite colourful names in his correspondence.'

'Here you are,' said Mrs Partridge, coming back in with a glass of brandy.

'What's this about working on your own again?' Freya said, her attention diverted back to the present.

'I convinced Jarrett we should work from different angles.'

'Heard as Mrs Rothesay gave him a piece of her mind,' said Mrs Partridge with satisfaction. 'Good job, too, coming in like one of Uncle Joe's commissars and hauling law-abiding citizens over the coals.'

Hugo had long since given up wondering how Mrs Partridge got her information so quickly, but he wouldn't have guessed Alice Rothesay would be so ready to tell.

'I didn't know she spent that much time here,' said Hugo.

'You'd be surprised,' said Mrs Partridge. 'Her husband may have spent all his time at the Atomic, but not all his colleagues had work on their minds.'

On which oracular note, she swept out.

Hugo took a sip of his brandy. An affair with one of her husband's colleagues made a certain sense. None of Jarrett's business, necessarily, but enough to put Mrs Rothesay on the defensive with a policeman prone to see the worst in everything.

'How well connected is Jarrett?' Hugo asked Freya, then added, 'If you don't mind talking about him.'

'He was well connected when I knew him,' she said. 'All his own work, though. He's the sort of man who Gets Things Done with great vim and vigour, turns places inside out. Someone the Government calls on when they need to be seen to be doing something.'

She paused, with a frown.

'Roddy told me once that he'd interrogated and hanged more German agents during the war than anyone else. As if it were important that he'd dealt with them properly.'

Hugo well knew that most of the agents the Germans had landed had never stood a chance, put ashore on alien soil with no backup and no real idea of where they were going. It was war, and a vicious war at that, you couldn't be sad that they'd failed, but to count them up like trophies was wrong nonetheless.

'I shall be glad to be spared more interviews with him, at any rate,' said Hugo. 'It's back to Thorn Hall for me, combing through the files. While Jarrett is throwing his weight around at widows and boffins, there's someone loose in Selchester with the training and disposition to shoot a man in the back of the neck, and I'd very much like to know who it is.'

Scene 14

True to the slapdash nature of the whole operation, it was a quarter to eleven before an engine finally sounded on the drive. Polly and Georgia were long since in bed, Hugo looking weary, and Gus casting irritable glances at the clock.

'Poor Mrs Partridge,' said Freya, as they made their way down to the door. 'She gets up earlier than any of us.'

'Poor Mrs Partridge, my hat. She wouldn't miss this for anything,' said Hugo.

The low clouds had cleared, the sky was bright with stars and the air bitterly cold. Freya paused in the corridor to pull on a coat, came out to see Hugo talking to the driver and Gus greeting a dapper, dark-haired man with a lively face. Another man retrieved a valise from the boot.

'Welcome to Selchester, Dr Bárándy.'

'Thank you,' said their guest. 'They said they were taking me to a castle. I thought perhaps this was a euphemism – one of those English stately homes which is only called a castle – now I see they were quite correct.'

'I hope they didn't lead you to expect butlers and armies of servants. We're a small and select establishment.'

'Yes, I see, there is no butler with a disapproving expression, or footmen like statues, and perhaps also no long grim corridors full of armour and the heads of deer?'

'There's the Long Gallery,' Freya said cheerfully, 'but the girls use it for a bowling alley.'

'My cousin, Miss Wryton,' said Gus.

'Ah, the writer,' he said, with a twinkle in his eye. She extended a hand, which he kissed with great courtliness. 'Enchanted.'

'We should let these gentlemen get on their way,' said Hugo, who clearly wasn't having much luck getting information out of the driver.

They exchanged polite courtesies, ushered their guest through into the kitchen as the two men drove off. Mrs Partridge was waiting by the stove, kettle to hand if needed, while Magnus watched, sphinx-like, from the end of the bench. 'No point putting him out at night,' she was wont to say, 'when there's enough mice in the Castle to keep a legion of cats busy.'

Their guest wondered at the kitchen and charmed Mrs Partridge before turning his attention to Magnus, who deigned to have his chin scratched.

'He likes you,' said Freya. 'Just don't try to ruffle his stomach, or he'll sink his teeth in your hand soon as look at you.'

'He has pride, as a cat should. Or a horse.'

'You ride?' she asked, interested.

'I grew up on the Great Hungarian Plain, the steppe as you call it. Before I could walk, I could ride. But not for many years now. No more horses.'

In the light, she could see too many lines on his face, dark shadows under his eyes. He was an exile in a strange land, moved from pillar to post by a foreign intelligence service. No wonder he was exhausted.

'Would you like tea, or shall we show you to your room?' Gus asked.

'If you please, I should like to sleep, and you have all been up waiting, because the car was late. This Service of yours, Mr Hawksworth, it is not punctual, no? Always muddling things up. Locking the stable door after the horse has bolted, is that how you say it? I have been picking up these things from your colleagues.'

There was a twinkle of mischief in his eye.

He was less sanguine when they showed him his room, its thin veneer of Georgian panelling and Victorian wallpaper hardly sufficient to conceal the thickness of its walls. It was a comfortable room, no vast mausoleum, with a fire crackling in the grate and a hot-water bottle in the bed, but it was still very much of its place.

'There must be some mistake – these are your rooms, surely?' he said to Gus.

'These were my father's rooms, in his time. My daughters and I live in another wing. This part of the Castle is a little too archaic for American tastes.'

Dr Bárándy regarded the bell pull beside the bed with a wary expression. 'I have never stayed in a house with such a thing, but in Sherlock Holmes . . .'

'Quite safe, I assure you, not a snake in sight,' said Freya. 'Magnus would have caught them long ago.'

'Magnus? Ah, the cat.' He paused, his eyes on Gus. 'Your lordship, I thank you for your hospitality, for putting a stranger up in your house at such notice. It is a kindness, no matter how many such rooms you have to spare, and I am grateful.'

Tuesday

Scene 1

Georgia came down for breakfast to an appetising smell of bacon, and a strange man sitting at the table. She'd dragged herself out of bed early on purpose, to beat Polly down. Polly never had any problems waking up for school; it was unnatural.

'Hullo,' she said. 'You must be Dr Bárándy.'

'Good morning. You are one of the Earl's daughters, perhaps?'

'I'm Hugo's sister. Mr Hawksworth, that is. Georgia.'

He looked surprised. She stuck out a hand, which he shook gravely.

'That's Polly on her way now. She's the Earl's younger daughter. Babs is the elder – she's away at art school in London.'

Polly came running through from the other passage. Georgia gave her a triumphant look and quickly snaffled the next plate.

'Two rashers, Miss Georgia, no more,' came Mrs Partridge's voice from the pantry.

'Yes, Mrs Partridge,' said Georgia, making sure she took the two crispiest, and extra egg. Polly gave her a dirty look as she sat herself down at the table opposite the Hungarian.

'A healthy appetite, I see,' he said. He'd cleared his own plate.

'You're up very early. You didn't get here till late, either.'

'And how would you know that?' Mrs Partridge asked.

'Not likely I can sleep through a car driving up, and all that tramping along the corridors, now could I?'

'I did,' said Polly.

'You were in another wing. Miles away.'

'Sleeping the sleep of the just and righteous,' Polly said. 'I expect you were haunted by visions of hellfire, all that heretical nonsense you were saying yesterday.'

Dr Bárándy looked from one to the other of them in interested confusion.

'School history,' said Polly scornfully. 'Henry VIII.'

'Ah, the Reformation.'

'Did you have one in Hungary, Dr Bárándy?' Georgia asked.

'Only in Transylvania, in the mountains. And please, call me Árpád bácsi, as I once called my father's friends. We cannot be forever standing on formality.'

'Where Dracula comes from,' Georgia said, intrigued. 'I thought that was in Romania.'

'It was Hungarian land once, but it was taken from us. Like many other things.'

'Árpád bácsi,' Polly was repeating, 'Árpád bácsi. I like that. What does that mean?'

'Bácsi is what Hungarian children call friends of the family. Strictly it means uncle, but we do not use it only for real uncles. And Árpád is my name, after the first chief of the Hungarians, long before we had kings.'

Polly's eyes narrowed. 'A pagan?'

'Oh yes. The old gods lasted a long time in Hungary before we became Catholic. Now, of course, we have a different sort of heathen in charge.'

'Is that why you left your home?' Polly asked, with one of her thoughtful, inquisitive looks. Georgia knew perfectly well that, if they'd had more notice, she'd have been down to the town library looking for a serious book about Hungary, the better to know what she was dealing with.

'In part. Now is not a good time to be a Catholic in Hungary. Many priests, even our Cardinal, were arrested and tortured, many churches destroyed. It is hard to see such things happen – places you love destroyed by vandals, people dragged into black police cars by thugs – and then to hear those same thugs and vandals declare how they are making a better world.'

Mrs Partridge came back into the kitchen with a stern look on her face. 'Now, Miss Polly, Miss Georgia, I doubt our guest wants to talk of war and destruction. Can I get you anything more, Dr Bárándy? And just say if they're bothering you with their questions.'

'There is no bother,' said Árpád. 'They are terrible things I would not wish on any people, not even Russians. But they have happened, and so I must face them. Just as I must face that I will never see my country again. But now, tell me, for I am confused. You, Miss Polly, are the daughter of the Earl, who is called Gus?'

'Yes. And Babs is my sister, and we live through there.' She pointed in the direction of Grace Hall.

'Actually, it's that way,' said Georgia. 'You've forgotten there's a turn in the passageway.'

'And you, Miss Georgia,' Árpád said, 'are the sister of Mr Hawksworth.'

'He's much older,' Georgia said. 'Our parents died in the war, so he has to look after me. He's not too bad at it. I like being in Selchester.'

'It is an interesting place to live, I can see. Never did I imagine I would end up in the room of an English earl. But there is no, what would you say, earl-ess? This does not seem right.'

'Countess,' Polly and Georgia said, at the same moment. It was Polly who went on. 'An earl's wife is a countess, but my mother was never a countess. She died during the war, of tuberculosis.'

'I am sorry to hear this, it is a hard thing to lose a mother so young. And then there is Miss Wryton, who is engaged to Mr Hawksworth?'

Polly and Georgia gave one another a look. Mrs Partridge stirred the pot of scrambled eggs quite unnecessarily, and said nothing.

'No,' said Georgia. 'I think he ought to be, but he isn't. He has a girlfriend in London, she's called Valerie and she's useless. Wants Hugo to work in some dull bank with dull people in dull suits, and me to go off to some Proper Boarding School where all the mistresses are sadists.'

'You said Miss Harrison was a sadist,' Polly whispered.

'All games mistresses are sadists,' Georgia whispered back.

'And your father,' Árpád said to Polly, 'he is an American, but also an English earl. How can this be?'

They were still halfway through the story of Gus's unorthodox parentage when Freya came in, looked at the clock, and with an exclamation packed them off to get ready for school. 'Ben will run you down, since your bikes are still there, but you'd better hurry. Hugo needs the car to take Dr Bárándy to Thorn Hall.'

'To look at classical statistics, I suppose,' said Georgia as she vanished.

'I hope they didn't bother you, Dr Bárándy,' said Freya. 'They can be quite a force of nature.'

'As I said to Mrs Partridge here, no, not at all. They remind me of my own sister when she was that age. Now, perhaps you can finish for me this story of Gus's father and the French craftsman's daughter. Such wickedness, to marry in secret and then deny it. I was told English aristocrats only have time for dogs and horses. This is clearly not true.'

Scene 2

The call came in just as Jarrett was leaving for the Atomic, MacLeod counting down the minutes. Constable Tarrant answered from the dispatch desk, pen at the ready. A male voice, rough and indistinct.

'Selchester Police Station . . . Could you repeat that, sir?'

He made an urgent motion towards MacLeod's office. Phyllis, the quickest-witted of the secretaries, sprang up to fetch the Superintendent. Tarrant's pen raced across the paper. 'I see. The Selchester Gallery, you say. Could you hang on for a moment, sir, I'd like to put you through to someone more senior.'

Click. The line went dead.

'What is it?' MacLeod asked, appearing in the doorway. There was always the chance of another big case, something the Chief Constable would want him to take a personal look at.

'Anonymous tip-off, sir. Says we might want to take a look at the Selchester Gallery's new tenant in connection with Dr Rothesay's murder, particularly the cottage he's staying in.'

MacLeod looked puzzled. 'What new tenant?'

'Mr Ingham,' said Phyllis. 'The man who was staying in Nightingale Cottage when there was that to-do at the Castle. Just took the Gallery this week.'

'Ah,' said MacLeod.

'What's this?' said Jarrett from behind him. The man had the ears of a fox.

MacLeod explained.

Jarrett frowned. 'Saul Ingham. I know that name.'

'Convicted of fraud in '46, skipped the country. To join the Foreign Legion, as it turned out. Cleared in his absence. Turned up here at Christmas making death threats against Lord Selchester.'

'The American?'

'No, the previous one. Hadn't heard he'd died.'

'Foreign Legion,' said Jarrett thoughtfully. 'A man who knows how to kill. Get me a judge.'

Scene 3

Stanley Dillon had been at his desk bright and early, wrestling with the latest absurd directive from the Ministry of Supply. Rationing might be on the way out, but it seemed the Ministry would make itself a nuisance to the last.

His secretary, an ample and capable Welshwoman named Miss Rhys, popped her head around the door.

'Call from the Town Clerk, Mr Dillon. Problem at the Feoffees' Hall. They need you there at once.'

Stanley picked up the phone, listened, asked a few short questions. Two minutes later, he was in his car.

'I hope the Super doesn't catch him driving like that,' Miss Rhys said, hearing the roar of the engine as he drove off. She liked to call MacLeod the Super, the way people did in detective novels. Working for Mr Dillon was a good job, an interesting job, but there was a part of her which longed to be a senior policeman's secretary, a fly on the wall as they did all their detection.

'The Super has other things on his mind,' said her office-mate Martha Radley, Mrs Partridge's crony. 'What's up at the Hall? Do tell.'

'Such a to-do. He'll be in quite the temper when he gets back, let me tell you . . .'

As it happened, Constable Tarrant did spot Stanley's car going rather too fast down Station Road, but he wisely chose to turn a blind eye. With that Special Branch man making a pest of himself, now was most definitely not the time to muddy the waters by hauling the chief

Feoffee in for speeding. That was the sort of thing Fred Camford would do, and Constable Tarrant prided himself on being several notches above Fred Camford where intellect was concerned. Superintendent MacLeod shared this estimation of Tarrant's merit, which was why he'd been sent to keep an eye on the suspect's movements while Camford took his place at the dispatch desk.

Stanley pulled his car into one of the spaces outside the Feoffees' Hall and leapt out, taking the steps two at a time. Handsomely classical it might look on the outside, but it was a real hodgepodge under all those mouldings, with a Tudor council chamber and a mediaeval roof.

A roof which had decided, sometime during the storm, to abandon its centuries-long struggle against the elements.

Upstairs in the Hall, the Town Clerk, Mr Simmonds, looked like a particularly lugubrious sheepdog as he stared up at the ruined ceiling. John Brodrick, whose firm looked after the fabric, picked up a piece of fallen plaster and sucked in his breath.

'How bad is it?' Stanley demanded.

It looked bad enough. There was a great brown stain on the painted ceiling, centred around a small, dark, dripping hole. As he watched, a shower of fragments tumbled down on to the parquet.

'Disaster waiting to happen,' said Brodrick with relish. 'A wonder it lasted as long as it did, false ceiling like that. They should have taken the whole thing down, put in a proper roof. Knew what they were doing, those Georgian builders – look at the Royal, two hundred years old and good as new.'

The Royal was the Royal Selchester Hotel, up by the station.

'What happened?'

'Tiles worked loose in the wind, by the chimney. All that rain poured in, spent yesterday seeping down into the false ceiling. Plaster's sodden. Beams'll be all right, but you can kiss goodbye to they mouldings and curlicues.'

Good riddance, thought Stanley, who had always loathed the blue-and-white roof with its mouldings of Arcadian shepherdesses. If only it could have held off for another six months.

'How long to make it safe?'

'Can't. Water's spread right through. Could come down any moment.'

'What a thing to happen, with the anniversary celebrations coming up,' said Simmonds, quite unnecessarily. 'All those dinners and ceremonies, and what'll Miss Witt say?'

Scene 4

Miss Witt's first response, when Stanley rang her, did not bear repeating. They had known one another for years. Stanley was one of the very few people outside the theatrical world with whom she could be quite honest.

'Can't that builder of yours do anything?'

'He wants to knock the whole thing down, build something new. Less trouble.'

'Oh, how ghastly. Don't let him.'

Stanley had a certain sympathy for Brodrick's point of view – the whole place was one huge sink of money – but he knew Selchester too well to imagine there'd be any support for it. The whole city would be up in arms.

'No danger of that. I told him he'd be run out of town in a hail of rotten vegetables if he tried.'

'Quite right, too. Can he fix it?'

'He thinks he can do away with the whole Georgian ceiling, fix the tiles and take us back to the mediaeval beams, but it'll be most of the year before he's done. Grand opening in November or some such. Until he's done, we're short one town hall. I thought I'd ring you first, give you a chance to lock in another performance space before anyone else does.'

'How extremely tiresome. Thank you, Stanley.'

A series of muffled thumps came from the corridor outside his office, probably Brodrick making his way up into the roof space. They'd most likely have to move out lock, stock and barrel while the work was done.

'There's the Methodist Hall.'

She sighed. 'They're booked up until April, the Dramatic Society has a long-standing arrangement. Besides, no Sunday rehearsals.'

'You could try the Chapter House. The Dean has no hang-ups about the Sabbath, and he's as keen on this as anyone.'

'Darling, my cast would resign in a body. It's colder than Siberia in there, and too small besides. I shall ring that temporary headmaster at the Cathedral School, what's his name? Dr Pilchard or something. Looks like a throwback to the nineteenth century. Shouldn't like to be one of his boys.'

'Dr Pilton,' said Stanley, who as one of the board of governors was obliged to refrain from airing his thoughts on the subject, at least where anyone might overhear. 'Let me know if I can do anything else, word in someone's ear or the like. Good thing we've a meeting of the anniversary committee this evening, make sure we can get it all wrapped up as soon as possible.'

More steps in the passageway, another thump. This time the chandelier in Stanley's office shook.

'Darling, what on earth is that noise? Is the rest of the building falling down about your ears? If a moulding falls on your head I'll have to deal with that tiresome deputy of yours, and he's as deaf as a post. So please do get out in time, if it's all the same to you.'

Crash. A bellow in the corridor. 'How're they beams bearing, John?' It was one of Brodrick's men, the one built like the side of a barn. Surely Brodrick wasn't about to let him loose in the roof space? They'd have a hole in the floor, too, if he came through, never mind another body on their hands.

'Must go,' said Vivian. 'Good luck. I rather think you'll need it.'

Scene 5

'I'm afraid I can't sanction the use of our hall for any outside use. The school's charter is quite clear on the matter. Now, if you'll excuse me, I have a scholarship class to teach. Good day, Miss Witt.'

Vivian slammed the phone down, giving it – and, by proxy, Dr Pilton – a look of pure venom. He knew perfectly well the previous Head had allowed all sorts of people to use the school's hall. She wondered if the problem was more that she was a woman doing a man's job, in this case directing a play, or that he was intent on reversing every single one of his predecessor's policies.

After trying, and failing, to persuade the Methodists that hosting a rehearsal on Sunday would be an act of charity rather than a breach of the Fourth Commandment, she took herself off to the Daffs for coffee and inspiration. It was a quiet time of day, so she had no problem snagging herself a table. The windows were blessedly misted, no one could see in.

Jamie had nothing good to say about the Head.

'Such a frightful man. I do hope they don't make him permanent. To think of a school like Selchester being run by someone like him in this day and age, it makes me shiver.'

'Any dreadful stories? We could give all those reporters something to do.'

'I won't have them in here,' said Jamie. 'They take up all the tables, order one cup of tea and don't eat a thing, just sit there with their ears cocked. I hear one of them cornered Miss Georgia yesterday, asked her all sorts of nasty questions about how she found the body. Unpleasant type. I hear he's been sniffing around here before, back when there was that to-do over the late Earl.'

Vivian was only too familiar with that sort of reporter from her life in London, where the gutter press was always ready to jump on the slightest hint of scandal and blow it out of all proportion.

'Have they caught anyone yet?' she asked, although she could be fairly sure she'd have heard by now.

'No, although I hear that Special Branch fellow has been turning things inside out up at the Atomic. He was downright rude to Mrs Rothesay when he interviewed her. Taught him a good lesson, though, she did.'

'She always could look after herself.' Except perhaps in her marriage, which had been a disaster.

'I didn't realise you knew her.'

'Only distantly. We were at the same school for a year; they wouldn't have me any longer. I lowered the tone of the establishment, they said.'

Jamie's eyes glinted. 'Do they claim you as one of their alumnae now?'

'Oh no. Their girls go on to finishing schools in Switzerland, not to RADA and the stage. But tell me,' she said, returning to the immediate problem, 'where else in Selchester there might be a hall big enough to use for the rehearsals.'

'Well, I'd have said the Methodists, you know, they host the Selchester Players.'

'Tried them. Too much on, and they definitely won't do Sundays.'

'Such a shame about the Town Hall. Have you tried the Castle?'

'I hardly think the new Earl wants half the town trooping through his sitting room. He has enough to deal with already.'

'Of course not. It's his ballroom I was thinking of. I used to help out there, before the war, when the late Earl held his occasions. Such an experience they were! All the bigwigs down from London, everything immaculate for the evening, and his lordship quite splendid in tails.'

Vivian had never seen the ballroom, and had no particular desire to be reminded of the late Lord Selchester. The Castle was a place she'd rather avoid, thank you very much.

'Is it habitable still?' In the Castle's current state, she could very well imagine bats flitting around the ceiling. The more the better, as far as she was concerned.

'So Mrs Partridge tells me, and with Lady Matilda's wing being opened up, the pipes are in working order and everything. Oh, do ask him, it would be ever so good to see it used again.'

She scribbled it down in her notebook. 'Now, where else? We can't be out of church halls, surely. The one at St Aloysius's? I'd think that Irish padre would be up for it, he's a merry soul . . .'

Scene 6

At lunchtime, Hugo dropped in on Harriet Godwin. She was Thorn Hall's new interrogator, a youthful and breezy Yorkshirewoman who'd blotted her copybook in London and been sent here for her pains.

She was also, as he'd suspected, in charge of debriefing Dr Bárándy. She'd come to the Service from a physics degree at Manchester. Not a normal background, but she was far more useful in this day and age than the likes of Hugo. Most of the scientific defections had been the other way, naïve idealists passing the Manhattan Project's secrets to Russia, but there had been the occasional foreign defector, too.

Like Dr Bárándy.

Harriet was sitting at her desk in a refreshingly unladylike way, legs up on a chair, eating a sandwich and flicking through a stack of papers. 'Thought you'd be along,' she said.

'Splendid work in Washington.'

'And other places,' she said, with a sidelong look.

He inclined his head. She'd gone to interrogate a British scientist picked up by the FBI, landed herself in quite a tangle of traitors' secrets.

'How was it?' he asked. 'Washington, I mean?'

'Cold. Foggy. Paranoid.'

'Just like London, then.'

'Not as lively. Give me New York for city lights. Billboards, theatres, people know how to enjoy themselves. Everyone in Washington lives in a perpetual stew of intrigue.'

'That's why we have jobs,' he said, sitting down on the other empty chair. Her office was small, poky, and chilly, as opposed to his, which was large, gloomy, and chilly. Her regulation square of carpet was barely big enough to fit her desk. 'Rather that than the sticks?'

Further acquaintance with Selchester had done little to undermine Harriet's initial conviction that she didn't belong.

'Any day.'

'Where's Dr Bárándy?'

'Woolhope whisked him off for lunch. Hungarian is his latest language.'

Peter Woolhope was the Hall's most interesting resident, a lean and wild-haired figure in rumpled tweeds. Much the most imaginative man in the outfit, prone to odd hunches and flights of fancy. And practical jokes, which was what had landed him down here. 'How many will that be, eight?'

'Nine. He speaks Slovak as well as Czech.'

'I'd say Hungarian would be more of a challenge, but I doubt it'll slow him down for long.'

'So,' Harriet said, putting her sandwich down, 'you're here to ask what's afoot.'

Hugo tried to lean back a little in his chair, to spare his leg, but it was unyieldingly uncomfortable. At least Harriet didn't do her interviews in here. 'Yes.'

'I wondered that myself.'

'When did you find out?'

'Yesterday morning. No mention of them landing him on you, or I'd have slipped you a note. They hauled me back to quiz Dr Rothesay's colleagues when it looked as if he'd done a bunk. Now it turns out he's dead, they've put me on to this instead.'

'Interrogating someone who came over six months ago. Not exactly urgent.'

'Did you know it was Dr Bárándy who put us on to the leak at the Atomic?'

'Sir Bernard neglected to mention that.'

Harriet made a dismissive noise. 'For a man who loves the sound of his own voice that much, he's been remarkably close-mouthed about this. It was Bárándy all right. They stuck him with regular interrogators, peppered him with questions about Soviet bombs and missiles and so on. Wasn't until someone who knew their business took over that we discovered he'd known as long ago as February about the accident at Ulfsgill, not long after it happened. Once we started probing, it turned out that was simply the earliest detail the Russians knew about, and you know the rest.'

Hugo did – there had been a trickle of information from Foxley to the far side of the Iron Curtain. They'd had their suspicions back in October, confirmed it in December. 'Wind back a moment. No one has told me the first thing about Dr Bárándy.'

'Old Hungarian family, not that distinguished. His uncle once held a minor post in Admiral Horthy's government, and his sister had married a major in the Hungarian army, for which unspeakable crimes the whole family was shipped off to Siberia in '48. Once the Soviets found out he was a physicist, they offered him better conditions for his family if he'd work on one of their projects, so he spent four years in some closed city in Siberia, helping Uncle Joe build his Bomb. They let him go after Stalin died, upon which he found out that his parents and sister had died in their first two months in the gulag.'

'How did he get over?'

'There are ways across the Yugoslav border.'

'You're the expert.' She'd ended up in the field, so he heard, pursued by the Hungarian secret police. A nasty outfit, even by Eastern Bloc standards.

She grinned. 'He had rather an easier time crossing than I did. Walked into our embassy in Belgrade, asked for asylum. I suspect he might have preferred the Americans, but there were some dubious characters watching their place. We'll have to get used to being the second choice.'

'I can see why you're so popular in London,' he remarked. 'It'll be Ulan Bator for you next.'

'There's a queue. You might even be ahead of me. Roger Bailey is out for your blood, and you're none too popular in London after you spoked their wheel over the late Lord Selchester's murder.'

'That was mostly Freya Wryton's doing.' Credit where credit was due.

'Miss Wryton isn't in a position to be blamed. Though she's attractive. I can see why you're standing up for her.'

'I'm otherwise engaged, thank you very much,' said Hugo curtly.

'Yes, that Valerie Grisewood, whom you've left to languish in London.' Mischief glinted in Harriet's eyes.

This wasn't at all what Hugo had come to talk about. 'She does not languish, thank you very much, and if she did, it would be my business, not that of the Thorn Hall gossips.'

'Her business, too, I rather think. She cornered Roger Bailey at a party on Saturday, quizzed him on your life down here.'

Hugo winced. Their colleague Bailey disliked him intensely, for reasons he'd never quite fathomed. There wasn't a worse person Valerie could have seized on. No doubt Hugo would be hearing about it all too soon.

'I have no doubt you'll do the decent thing in the end, Hawksworth, but take it from me, sooner is better.'

He gave her a cold look. 'Can we return to Dr Bárándy?'

Harriet held up her hands. 'I've said my piece.'

'More than.'

She was quite unruffled. 'As I said, it turned out the Soviets knew what we were doing almost as soon as we did. Hence your work these past few weeks.'

'So Bárándy blew the whistle on a traitor at the Atomic.'

She tapped the desk. 'Once we knew what questions to ask him.'

'What was he working on?'

'Improving the yield of the A-bomb. We know they have an H-bomb project going, too, like the Americans, but he wasn't working on that. Worse luck.'

'So,' Hugo said carefully, 'we have a defector who blows the whistle on a leak at Foxley. We have a dead scientist at Foxley . . .'

'Not the leak?'

'Nothing in his background to suggest it.'

'Sir Bernard likes the idea that Rothesay was the leak, tried to get out, and was shot by his handler.'

'Not the most plausible.'

'But so convenient.'

'Finally,' Hugo went on, staring out of the window at a slope full of gloomy conifer trees, 'we have the defector foisted on Gus – Lord Selchester – the very day Dr Rothesay turns up with a bullet in the back of his neck. All of which is done very carefully behind my back.'

'They can't have known about the body when they sent him down here. I found out first thing yesterday, which is about when it turned up.'

'They could have changed their minds, sent him somewhere else.'

'Pigs might fly. I think you're reading too much into this. Far be it from me to read the minds of our illustrious superiors, but what we have here is on the one hand a good old-fashioned bureaucratic bodge-up, and on the other someone in London who wants to teach you a lesson. See, the queue for Ulan Bator.

'In fact,' Harriet continued, 'I'd hazard that someone, whoever they may be, reckons a couple such nudges might push you out of the Service altogether, into some line of work where you'll stop being such a nuisance. We all know a desk job isn't the same as fieldwork. What could be more natural than to throw the whole thing in, start something new?'

'You'd move up the queue,' Hugo murmured.

'They'd like to get rid of me, but they can't. Not as long as men like Bárándy are important.'

He turned his attention back to their guest. 'Is he important?'

'He's blown the lid on the mole here. If he does nothing else, he's made his contribution. He'll do well in America. He's a born survivor. The more important question right now is, are you?'

Scene 7

MacLeod led a team of four constables and a sergeant to search Ingham's place. Jarrett, of course, came too.

'It's in Long Combe,' MacLeod said. 'Fisher Walk. Woods on two sides, path to the river. Make sure you cover the exits, and search the outbuildings. I took the precaution of getting a warrant for the Gallery too. We'll move on there if necessary.'

'He wasn't in occupation there when Dr Rothesay disappeared,' said Constable Tarrant helpfully.

'Indeed he wasn't,' said Jarrett. 'But there's a great deal of junk in there. It's an ideal place to dispose of evidence.'

The constables eyed one another unenthusiastically. Fred Camford had looked in on the Gallery a few months back, when some of the junk stored in the flat had fallen over during the night, alerting a zealous neighbour.

'A right dog's breakfast, it was,' he'd said. 'Falling to bits, it were. Wonder it hadn't all toppled over before.'

They parked their van a little way along, and trooped down through the woods. Number 3, Fisher Walk was a small, neatly appointed cottage, with roses trained up the front and a wisp of smoke coming from the roof.

'Bit nice for the likes of him, isn't it?' whispered Constable Gibbert, a raw youth with big feet who'd joined the month before.

'Belongs to a gentleman as . . .' Constable Tarrant began.

Sergeant Barkwith wasn't having any of this. 'Quiet there! You're policemen, not gossiping fishwives. Gibbert, how about you don't trip over anything this time?'

After a long pause, Saul opened the door. He was covered in dust and grease, with the look of a man doing a hard day's work and enjoying himself. The satisfaction vanished at once, replaced by a suspicious wariness. 'Superintendent MacLeod,' he said, tight-lipped. 'What can I do for you?'

'We have a warrant to search the premises, Mr Ingham. Please stand aside and don't touch anything.'

'Search it for what?' Saul said bitterly. 'I thought we were done with this, and you were ready to bring charges against that—'

'This is a different matter, sir.'

'Let me see your warrant.'

Saul examined the warrant, then with a sigh stepped back to let them in. He could see one of his neighbours, the nosy one, peering through her window. This would be all over Selchester by the end of the day. 'That Saul Ingham in trouble again. Always knew he was no good . . .'

The constables fanned out, heavy-handed and industrious. Jarrett looked around, appraising the cottage at a glance. Plainly furnished, almost spartan. The bare minimum.

'So what's this about?' Saul demanded.

'The murder of Dr Bruno Rothesay, Mr Ingham,' said Jarrett, having troubled to introduce himself this time. 'Do you know him?'

'We were distant acquaintances,' said Saul, 'but in case you haven't noticed, I only moved to Selchester this week.'

'Let us be the judges of what's relevant, sir,' said MacLeod. 'What was the nature of your relationship with Dr Rothesay?'

'What is there to tell? I met him a few times when I lived in Oxford, and I moved here the day he turned up missing.'

'What did you think of him?'

'Not much,' said Saul shortly. 'We moved in different worlds. He was gown, I was town. I didn't have much to do with him.'

'Found something here, sir. Out in plain sight, by the bed.'

Constable Camford came downstairs with a pistol and holster in one meaty hand, a box of ammunition in the other.

'That's my service revolver,' said Saul.

'Let me have a look at that,' said Jarrett. He flipped the gun over once in his hand, looked at the ammunition, and shook his head. 'Wrong calibre. That's a Webley, one of ours. Keep going. Pay attention to loose floorboards, the backs of cupboards, drawers, places like that.'

'I'd like to know what makes you think I had anything to do with this,' Saul said.

'We'll be the judges of that, Mr Ingham. If there's nothing suspicious on the premises, you've nothing to worry about.'

'This isn't my house, Inspector, and I've better things to do than go burrowing in somebody else's drawers. It's a temporary base for me, nothing more.'

The search continued, heavy footsteps on the ceiling, Saul's belongings turned inside out with a clumsy show of efficiency.

'Don't like doing this with him watching,' said Gibbert to Tarrant, as they went into the bathroom. *Him* was Jarrett, the station's current bête noire.

'That's why you're up here and he's down there. Sarge knows his business. You just keep out of trouble now. There won't be a gun in his shaving things, neither.'

Gibbert picked up the container of shaving cream. 'They's all French.'

'Stands to reason. He was in the Foreign Legion, Sarge says. Been out in Indochina or whatnot, fighting the Commies.'

Gibbert's eyes went wide. 'The Foreign Legion? Well, I never. Did he murder someone?'

'Way I heard it, he was framed for something, fled the country. Hullo, what's this?' He rattled the panel on the side of the bath. 'Give me a hand here, will you? No, wait, comes off easy like. There's something in here, too.'

'Aren't we supposed to use gloves, so they don't get our fingerprints confused?'

'When it's time to pick anything up, I'll tell you. What have we here? That's one of they German pistols, that is, like they have in the movies. Now what would an honest man be wanting with something like that, I ask myself? Run and fetch the Super now, and don't trip on your way down.'

Fetching the Super inevitably brought their unwanted guest upstairs, his eyes alight. Saul stood waiting under Constable Camford's watchful eye, unable to make out a word of the conversation upstairs.

Jarrett thundered down the stairs, full of hard triumph. 'Would you care to explain this, Mr Ingham?'

His gloved hands held a German Luger and a stack of ammunition.

'That's a Luger,' said Saul, puzzled. 'Where did it come from?'

'Germany, Mr Ingham. By way of France, if the markings are anything to go by.'

'I've never seen that gun before.'

'It was in your bathroom, Mr Ingham, carefully hidden away.'

'Then perhaps you should ask the house's owner.'

'That won't do. I'm afraid you'll have to come with us to the police station, Mr Ingham. You have some questions to answer.'

Scene 8

It was Gus's first meeting of the anniversary committee. Stanley Dillon had roped him in soon after New Year, ignoring all his protests about not knowing the town well.

'Of course you must be on it,' he'd said briskly. 'Do you no end of good, and help people get to know you. Besides, it'll give the committee some heft to have an earl on it. Next meeting's two weeks on Tuesday. Get Freya to fill you in – she knows all about it.'

The meeting was in the Masonic Hall, which had earned him a glare from Polly, and some muttering about secret societies. 'What would the Pope say?'

'Where does she pick this up from?' he asked as he drove Freya and Hugo to the meeting. 'Back in the States, the Masons are just like the Rotary Club, they meet and they do good works. From the way she goes on, you'd think they were something out of a John Buchan novel.'

Gus had discovered a complete collection of Buchan novels in the library, and had been reading his way through them. Freya wasn't entirely sure where they had come from, since her uncle had never been a great reader.

'They're a little more influential than that here,' said Hugo. 'She must be thinking of the European Freemasons – they're a much more anti-clerical bunch.'

'She's got quite firm about things like that all of a sudden,' said Gus. 'I mean, I've brought her up as a good Catholic, with a proper sense of right and wrong, but since we've been here, she's taking it all more seriously. I don't want her to grow up one of these people who won't have anything to do with the world outside the Church. It's not good for a young woman to think like that.'

'She's just hanging on to the things she knows,' said Freya from the back seat. 'She's been uprooted from her home, her country, everything she's used to. The Church is the one thing which hasn't changed, so of course she'll hang on to that. Give her time and she'll reach her own balance. No need to worry about her taking holy orders or the like.'

'If you say so,' said Gus. 'Of course, if she wants to become a nun . . .'

Freya knew perfectly well Polly had no intention of becoming a nun. 'She likes baiting Georgia. It's part of the game they play.'

And, perhaps, her father, too, but Freya wasn't about to say that.

The anniversary meeting was open to the public, and rather fuller today than was usually the case. With the damage to the Feoffees' Hall and the sensational news about Saul Ingham, the meeting was a perfect excuse for gossip. Freya and Hugo took their seats with the hoi polloi in the hall, while Gus was ushered solicitously towards a chair on the dais.

Sir Bernard intercepted him, with – rather to Hugo's surprise – Dr Oldcastle at his side. Gus greeted Sir Bernard courteously, but perhaps a trifle stiffly.

'He'll have to learn a bit more sangfroid,' Freya whispered to Hugo.

Dinah had slipped in beside her. 'What was that?'

'You'll find out,' Freya replied, as Stanley called the meeting to order and introduced the new Earl.

'Before we get down to our scheduled business,' he said, 'there's the urgent matter of finding rehearsal space for our flagship event, the production of *Murder in the Cathedral*. As you've all doubtless heard, the Feoffees' Hall suffered severe ceiling damage as a result of Sunday's storm, and will be closed for several months. There are four days of rehearsals scheduled this weekend and next, with several of the professional actors in attendance, so it's very important that we find Miss Witt a venue. Ideally the same venue.'

'I can help you with a venue on the Saturdays,' said Father Maloney of St Aloysius's, 'but not on Sundays, I'm afraid.'

Nor, it seems, could the Presbyterians, who had sent their jolliest elder to the meeting, nor the Methodists, whose Miss Shaw seemed rather relieved to be let off the hook for Saturdays, too.

'She should never have scheduled rehearsals on Sundays,' Dinah whispered to Freya. 'It must be quite normal in London, but she's forgotten what a bunch of stick-in-the-muds we are down here.'

There followed a round of rather fruitless discussions – could the Masons help out? The schools? The YMCA? – before Gus intervened.

'Excuse me.'

The hall fell silent, perhaps rather more quickly than he'd expected. He did have rather the look of the previous Lord Selchester in a certain light, tall and commanding, and most people here were used to a man in the Castle you didn't want to cross.

'If I understand this rightly, Miss Witt, your immediate problem concerns the next two weekends, particularly the Sundays?'

'Yes, it does.'

'Then why don't you use the ballroom at the Castle on all four days? It seems you're in a bind, and I'd be more than happy to help you out.'

Vivian had been hoping that wouldn't happen, thought Freya, catching the tiniest flash of discomfort as she turned to look at the Earl. Freya couldn't blame her, after the treatment she'd had at the late Earl's hands. Of course, no one knew about that.

The suggestion made, it was received with general relief. Freya didn't think Stanley had set it up – how could he have known the ceiling would fall down? – but he was a man who liked getting things done, and here was something very definitely done.

'He'll end up hosting school fetes in the ballroom if he's too obliging,' Freya said to Dinah, in the general round of congratulations which followed.

'He won't,' she said firmly. 'He may be new to this, but he has far too much good sense to let himself be used. At least, more than once.'

So Dinah already knew something of the Árpád story. No surprise there. Gus wouldn't have let anything important slip, he was much too honourable, but Freya was ready to bet he'd consulted his friend on how to deal with the British Establishment in future.

'Where's your guest?' Dinah asked, confirming Freya's hunch.

'Back at the Castle, putting his feet up. Wouldn't be fair to drag him out where he can see us all gossiping about him.'

'Gus thought he might be interested in Miranda Pearson's talk on Friday. She's been all over the place, apparently, there might be some Hungarian folklore.'

'I shall be going, I'm dying to know what she makes of all those ridiculous stories the farmers tell her.'

'So will half the town.'

Stanley was speaking again. 'While Lord Selchester's kind offer has put a roof over the actors' heads, it sounds as if we'll still be short of chairs and refreshments. Can anyone who can help transport those please talk to Mr Frankland at the end of the meeting?'

Edgar Frankland was the producer, an old theatrical friend of Vivian's who'd retired to Selchester and had been itching to get his fingers into a really big show again.

'Now, on to item one . . .'

The rest of the meeting passed less eventfully and with relatively few interruptions, since most of those present were really here for the Dean's free refreshments and the gossip.

Hugo's attention wandered. His leg had been aching after half an hour, even on the comfortable chairs the Masons had outfitted themselves with. He needed to get up and move at regular intervals, the physiotherapist kept telling him. Time was, he'd have been able to stay stock-still for hours at a time.

It was almost a year since a fake message had lured him to a trap in an East Berlin backstreet, putting an end to his field career and very nearly to his life. It was intruding on his thoughts again, a puzzle he couldn't solve. Something had been out of kilter, but neither Hugo nor the officers who'd debriefed him had been able to pin it down. His instinct for trouble had surfaced at the last minute, so a bullet intended to kill had only lamed.

He'd seen it when they'd extracted it from his leg, to be filed in the Service archives.

'Wool-gathering?' said Freya. Hugo realised the meeting had broken up. He stood with a grimace, pushing his chair back too quickly and earning a basilisk stare from the biddy behind him.

'Very sorry, ma'am,' he said, receiving only a beady look over her shoulder as she headed along the row.

'Don't take any notice of her, she's got the sharpest elbows in Selchester,' said Freya. 'She's just cross because you blocked her exit, now Mrs Seathwaite will get to the cakes first.'

Another equally snowy-headed old lady had indeed contrived to be the first at the refreshment table, even though half the hall hadn't so much as got to their feet.

'She usually parks herself on the end of a row,' Dinah remarked. 'Sloppy of her not to be here early enough.'

It sounded as though men in flat caps ought to have been taking bets.

'Did you notice the couple from Nightingale Cottage are here?' Freya said.

Jeremy and Miranda Pearson were indeed present, making their way over to talk to Edgar Frankland.

'I didn't know they were involved in town things,' said Hugo. Nightingale Cottage had been mooted as a potential home for him and Georgia before Gus invited them to stay on at the Castle, so it was a small slice of Selchester gossip he knew something about. Opinion had tipped the couple for a speedy departure, but here they still were.

'Oh, they are now,' said Jamie, appearing from behind them. 'Forgive me, I'm a terrible eavesdropper, but I couldn't help overhearing. They're at that stage where they make a big effort to keep everything together, as if that'll save things. It won't last.'

'Is that why no one thinks they'll stay?' Hugo had never got to the bottom of those rumours.

'Oh, such terrible fights they have.'

'I wouldn't have reckoned he had the spirit for it,' Freya said, watching the two of them in conversation with Edgar.

'Wears him quite out, so they say. But they put a good front on in public. It's all these peculiar ideas of theirs. One needs a certain radicalism – there's an awful lot of stuffy old baggage in society – but one can't help feeling that sometimes people take it too far.'

'Saul did mention they had separate bedrooms.'

That, of course, brought the conversation around to Saul's arrest, news of which had only reached Hugo just before he left the Hall. Selchester, it seemed, was split between those who thought there could be no smoke without fire, and those who thought Saul had simply become the police's favourite suspect. Jamie was firmly in the latter camp.

'It's just too obvious,' he declared. 'That poor man, constantly being accused of things he hasn't done, as if we don't all have our guilty little secrets. What if he decides to take himself elsewhere after this? We need a gallery, some proper culture would do us no end of good.'

'Does that mean you'd be singing a different tune if he weren't opening a gallery?' Dinah asked.

'Dinah Linthrop, you're a wicked woman to suggest such things.'

'Don't call her a wicked woman where his lordship will hear you,' said Freya.

It was Jamie's turn to look sly. 'My lips are sealed.'

'Are they sealed on the subject of Foxley?' Freya asked. Dinah gave her a quick, grateful smile.

'What more would I know about that than our esteemed investigator from the hush-hush place? Although I did have Dr Oldcastle's secretary in just now, Miss Fitzgibbon. She's a great friend of Miss Rhys who works for Stanley Dillon, and by all accounts he's quite relieved there's a suspect. It'll get that nasty man from Special Branch out of his hair.'

'I thought he was quite pally with the Special Branch fellow,' said Dinah.

Freya shot a glance at Hugo, who was standing quietly, with an expression of polite interest and nothing more.

Jamie knew all about that. 'Oh, they're both so Establishment it almost hurts. Probably glad to find kindred spirits down here in the sticks. See Oldcastle with Sir Bernard over there, aren't they two peas from the same pod? Metaphorically speaking, of course. I'm sure this Jarrett is on his way to great things, hopefully a long way from here, and I hear Dr Oldcastle has already been tipped to become a panjandrum. There's a big position coming up in London, whoever gets it is almost guaranteed a knighthood. Miss Fitzgibbon is very excited. She says he'll get her an invitation to anything really important, and she loves some good pomp and circumstance. Don't we all?'

Hugo thought of Harriet Godwin, who had no time at all for pomp and circumstance, nor indeed the whole apparatus of monarchy and peerage, but held his tongue.

'He can't have liked one of his subordinates turning up dead, now can he?' said Dinah. 'Worst possible thing for him at a time like this.'

'Like a mad wife in the attic,' said Freya. Although of course that was a Romantic trope, appropriate for its own time. In Rosina Wyndham's era, there were more effective ways to get rid of inconvenient relatives than locking them in the attic. Unless a man like Thurloe found out, and then you were in the soup.

'No wife, mad or otherwise,' said Jamie, a little disappointingly. 'Though I do gather he has his lady friends from time to time. Discreetly, of course, if anything in Selchester can be discreet.'

Indeed they weren't monks up at the Atomic, as Mrs Partridge had remarked, but why should they be? They were as human as anyone else, for all the cult of the cool and disinterested scientist.

'I should catch Vivian,' said Dinah, spotting her through the crowd. 'I'm now officially assistant stage manager, and apparently she wants a meeting of the production team at the weekend.'

Freya nudged Hugo. 'That'll be you, too. I hope you've been in touch with that friend of Vivian's about the lighting.'

'Perhaps Gus will end up hosting that at the Castle, too. There'll be a lot of people on site.'

'Mrs Partridge will be delighted,' said Freya. 'She's dying to have more going on at the Castle.'

Sir Bernard was bearing down on Hugo, Oldcastle in tow. 'Ah, Hawksworth. Might I have a word?'

'Of course, Sir Bernard.'

Sir Bernard bore them over to the quiet corner where all the high-backed officers' chairs had been stacked. 'We shan't be bothered. One advantage of everyone knowing what's really going on up at Thorn Hall.'

'What can I do for you, Sir Bernard?' said Hugo.

'Oh, don't be so damn stiff about this business with Dr Bárándy, Hawksworth, just rather a messy business up at Headquarters. Can't think what they were doing, but there you are, they propose and we dispose.'

Sir Bernard was fond of that phrase, particularly when attempting to palm off responsibility for an unpopular decision on to his superiors in London. Everyone at the Hall knew he still cherished hopes of promotion to the Chief's job. Thorn Hall might be the graveyard of the Service, but in Sir Bernard's view, he'd demonstrated his credentials for running a considerable establishment.

'Curious thing Dr Oldcastle said to me earlier, in light of this business with Saul Ingham. Thought you should hear it.'

Oldcastle and Sir Bernard might be two peas in a pod in terms of character, but there was no denying that Oldcastle had rather more style. Away from the relentless presence of Jarrett, Hugo had no trouble imagining this man as guest of honour at a conference, or mingling with the great and the good. There was a certain patrician air to him which Sir Bernard, for all his efforts, had never managed to cultivate.

'Sir Bernard has brought me up to date on the progress of your investigation,' said Oldcastle, 'and it jogged my memory. I've heard Ingham's name before. Wasn't he here over Christmas?'

'He was,' said Hugo.

'That's the curious thing. Foxley doesn't do much over Christmas and the New Year, too many people want to take holidays at the same time. I can't say I blame them, it's a miserable place to be in the winter. Now when we came back, Bruno was in a good mood. As I said, he wasn't always the easiest man to work with.'

He rubbed the back of his neck with his hand.

'It's this stoop of mine, gets painful as you get older. Where was I?'

'Rothesay's good mood,' Sir Bernard prompted.

'Yes. He even had an amiable chat with my secretary Miss Fitzgibbon on the subject of Italian feuds and quarrels. It seems – and I'm afraid this won't exactly cast Dr Rothesay in the best light – that he had encountered an old enemy in Selchester, and was pleased to find him desperate and down at heel.'

Sir Bernard frowned. 'Sounds more like a mafioso than a respectable British scientist.'

Hugo had dealt with a number of mafiosi in Southern Italy during the war, and found most of them more congenial company than Sir Bernard. It was a fair comparison, although a bona fide mafioso would have made sure to riddle his enemy with bullets before going on his way. Just to make absolutely sure his fortunes didn't change for the better.

'And this was Saul Ingham?' Hugo asked.

'He mentioned the name to me later that day, when I suggested that this wasn't exactly the scientific spirit. I didn't pursue the matter, and there was no reason to remember the name.'

'What did he say?' Hugo asked out of curiosity. He wasn't the only curious one, either. People were casting interested glances at the three of them from across the room, quite certain that Important Government Business was being discussed right before their eyes. At least no one was trying to edge closer. Good manners prevailed that far.

'When?'

'When you took him to task about the scientific spirit.'

Oldcastle gave the faintest of smiles. 'He said it was the human spirit, never mind the scientific spirit.'

'And you never found out what had caused their enmity?'

'No. Although I shouldn't wonder if it were a woman. Quite the Lothario, Bruno was.'

'I shall have Jarrett informed of all this in the morning,' said Sir Bernard. 'Of course, he'll want to take statements, but it does look as if the two of you might be on to something with this Ingham fellow. Who knows, if he does turn out to be responsible, perhaps Jarrett was on the right track with Rothesay being a sleeper agent after all. We could have this settled by the end of the week.'

Sir Bernard was positively beaming at the prospect, and Hugo couldn't entirely blame him. Jarrett had been over at the Hall briefly, banging doors and leaving chaos in his wake.

'I should very much like to know who tipped the police off about Ingham,' said Hugo. 'A quarrel between him and Dr Rothesay is one thing, but we're left with a third party who doesn't wish to reveal themselves, hardly above board.'

Sir Bernard harrumphed. 'Plenty of reasons for a source to remain anonymous, you should be used to that. Well, I've done my bit, and with luck so has Dr Oldcastle. Got to be off. My wife will be waiting to hear the latest on the play. Laid up with a twisted ankle, or else she'd be here herself.'

Hugo watched them go, vaguely uneasy. Freya threaded her way through the gossiping throng to join him.

'What did Sir Bernard have to offer?'

'The easy answer,' said Hugo.

'My aunt says that's why they parked him here.'

'Which aunt? Lady Priscilla, I presume.'

Lady Priscilla was married to a well-connected MP who sat on the relevant committees in the House. She'd know the low-down on Sir Bernard if anyone did, although she wasn't above trying to sit on inconvenient secrets herself when it suited her. She'd done her utmost to block Freya's investigation into Gus's parentage.

'Indeed. Priscilla only really pays attention to the country round here and her Catholic goings-on, but in those circles, there's nothing she doesn't know about. Aunt Hermione – Lady Selchester as was – never wanted anything to do with that world while she lived here, although I dare say she knew a few of Selchester's secrets just the same. Self-preservation, you might call it, to have some cards up your sleeve when you're married to a man like that. No wonder she took herself off to Canada.'

The easy answer. Perhaps that was the malaise the Chief had sensed at Thorn Hall. A man who always took the path of least resistance, in charge of one of the Service's most important – if least well-regarded – departments. A lot could slip through the cracks with someone like Sir Bernard in charge.

Freya glanced across the room. 'Heavens, we'd better rescue Gus. He's been cornered by Mrs Baxter, wants to bend his ear about how an earl ought to behave. He'll be eternally grateful if we can whisk him off.'

Scene 9

At the Castle, Polly and Georgia had taken Árpád on their very own tour. It was based on a mixture of recollections, things Freya had told them, things which had happened – including two murders – and pieces of a nineteenth-century book on the Castle Polly had found in the library.

Georgia was little impressed. 'Terrifically dull when he talks about the state rooms and so on, not too bad when he gets to the people. You can see why Freya wanted to write a history, if that's what she's really writing.'

Polly, possessed of a more scientific mind, said, 'Why hasn't she got it with her in her tower?'

'I suppose there are lots of copies. Maybe your ancestors bought up the whole print run, so no one would know all their dark deeds.'

'If I were full of dark deeds, I'd want everybody to know, then they'd be afraid of me. Didn't someone classical say it was better to be feared than loved?'

Árpád had been more than game when they had suggested the tour, even though night had fallen long since, and some of the finer points would perhaps have been better appreciated in daylight. They had trekked all the way around the West Lawn, following the line of the old curtain walls above the valley.

'There's the Old Tower,' said Polly, pointing at a dim shape in the darkness, visible mostly for the outline it made against the moon. A chill wind was whipping at their heels, blowing leaves around the old inner bailey, and their coats flapped around them. Ben was keeping a discreet eye from a distance, at Mrs Partridge's request.

'Can't say as I'd want to go outside on a night like this, but they're bent on it, and who knows what foreigners like to do with their spare time. Just keep an eye on them, make sure they don't go anywhere they shouldn't.'

She had managed to catch Árpád away from the two girls for a moment, and given him his instructions. 'Now don't let them get carried away. They'll neither of them be the first to admit to being cold, so you make sure they come in when they ought. Heaven knows there are enough rooms to see inside without venturing out in such a chill.'

Árpád promised to guard them with his life, and once again complimented Mrs Partridge on her cooking, which she took in very good form. She would never have admitted it even to Freya, but she was rather pleased to have so interesting and charming a foreigner to stay. Even if he didn't have a ration book.

'The Old Tower is where Miss Freya works?'

'No, that's the New Tower, over there,' said Georgia, pointing at a closer and somewhat less tumbledown bulk. 'That was built in Richard III's time. The Old Tower is from sometime in the Middle Ages.'

'Henry III,' said Polly smugly.

'Who wants to remember anything about Henry III?' said Georgia airily. 'Even Miss Ormskirk didn't. She just went on about Simon de Montfort and Parliament until we were all glad to get to Edward Longshanks hammering the Scots. His own subjects probably forgot he existed, and that's why they were building towers all the time and throwing peasants into dungeons. Might is Right and Heft is Beft.'

'It's best not beft. They just couldn't draw 's's properly in the olden days.'

'It doesn't rhyme if it's an 's'. Hullo, what's that?'

They were far enough from the main Castle to be able to see over the rooftops, towards Pagan Hill.

'What's what?'

'Those lights on Pagan Hill.'

Polly peered through her thick glasses. 'I can't see anything.'

Árpád, blessed with perfect eyesight, was quick to see it. 'Yes, there is a flickering, behind trees perhaps? Not quite at the top.'

'There's a grove of trees at the top,' said Georgia. 'And a barrow.'

Árpád was puzzled. 'A barrow. Like a wheelbarrow?'

'No, a tomb. A mound, with a pagan king inside and all his gold. Probably human sacrifices underneath, to haunt it for all eternity.'

'There's no gold there,' said Polly. 'It's a Bronze Age chambered barrow. The book talks about it.'

'It's still haunted, there are all sorts of stories about it. Even Bobby Sackbut won't go there at night.' Bobby Sackbut was Selchester's chief tearaway.

They watched the lights flickering back and forth between the trees until Árpád noticed Georgia was beginning to shiver.

'I think we have seen enough of the outside in the dark,' he said. 'I should like to see it in the daylight.'

'You'll have to wait till the weekend,' said Polly practically. 'Or Freya can show you. But she won't tell you all the interesting bits.'

As they came back past the gatehouse, a white shape swooped overhead.

'See,' said Georgia. 'I told you there were owls in the Castle. Only you have to be outside when it's dark, or you won't see them.'

Polly stared curiously after the owl. 'Where do they live?'

'Somewhere up on the rooftops above the Long Gallery, Ben says. There're all sorts of closed attics and things up there, it's a real hodge-podge. Magnus probably goes up there to pass the time of day with them, have a good moan about the quality of mice these days.'

'Austerity mice,' said Polly, who hadn't quite forgiven her father for bringing her to a country still recovering from sugar rationing. She liked her creature comforts. 'Thin starved creatures.'

'They can't be too thin and starved. Look at the size of Magnus.'

They came back into the warmth and light of the Castle, where Mrs Partridge gave Árpád an approving look.

'Twenty minutes, girls, then it's bedtime. You can show Dr Bárándy the rest of the Castle another night, when you don't have school in the morning.'

'We always have school in the morning,' Georgia muttered. 'I bet they'd put school on Sunday if they could get away with it.'

'What was that?' Mrs Partridge asked.

'Nothing,' said Georgia. 'Come on, let's go up to the Long Gallery, that's the best bit of the Castle. He hasn't seen all the portraits yet.'

The Long Gallery ran the whole width of the Castle, a great echoing Jacobean room with acres of leaded glass, five huge fireplaces, and an array of formidable Selchester ancestors. At night, uncurtained, it was full of stern faces and dim immensity.

'For what did they use such a room?' Árpád asked as he wandered along the row of portraits. 'It was not surely for receiving the guests, up all those stairs?'

'They used it for exercise on rainy days,' said Polly knowledgeably. 'Much better than taking a turn about the room like the people in Jane Austen. Up and down, up and down, you could walk a mile in here. Terrific views, too. There's a priest hole somewhere, only we've never found it.'

Árpád frowned, not understanding the word.

'A tiny little cupboard,' said Polly, 'where priests hid when the Protestants were looking for them. With a secret entrance, all concealed in the panels or something. They had to spend days and days there, sometimes they couldn't even stand up.'

'We use the Long Gallery for skittles,' said Georgia, anxious not to hear any more talk of small enclosed spaces. 'Not much else it's good for now. Only the floor isn't level, so you have to practise. See what happens if you just let fly.' She took one of the skittle balls and rolled it along the wide oak floorboards. It veered around in a curve before banging into a vast iron grate. 'I bet Polly's ancestors used to torment their visitors like that,' she added with a sideways glance.

'Only when they were young,' said Polly smugly. 'After that they were too busy enduring terrible things for the Faith. Look, there are the Headless Earls. Fourth, fifth, and seventh, all beheaded by the Tudors. And there's the seventh Earl's brother, who was a Jesuit.'

'Full of casuistry,' said Georgia, 'and plots.'

'I don't believe you know what casuistry is,' said Polly belligerently.

'What about the sixth Earl?' Árpád asked, to head off an argument.

'He died in the Tower before they could top him,' said Georgia. 'Did away with himself, the inquiry said, but how can anyone suffocate themselves under their own pillow?'

'Men do not change,' said Árpád softly.

Polly caught a distant look in his eyes and thought it best to change the subject. 'Come on, let's show him the Methuselah Earl.'

They clattered along the floor, via the Stuart Earls and the missing ninth Countess – appropriated by Freya for her study – to a bewigged ancient who resembled nothing so much as a vulture, his eyes bright with avarice. Behind him was a glass cabinet full of skeletons, and below the portrait the legend *Theophilus Fitzwarin, Eleventh Earl, 1689–1788*.

'Supposedly they're there because he fancied himself an anatomist,' Georgia said. 'Actually, they're all the people he outlived. Sons, grandsons, wives, enemies. There's a chest full of gold, too, packed with his ill-gotten gains, but it's too faded to see in the dark. He was the one who restored the family fortunes after his pa frittered everything away on horses and mistresses in Charles II's time.'

'You know a great deal of this history,' said Árpád.

'That's because it's far more interesting than anything at school,' Georgia said. 'Freya knows all the stories. I suppose she needs to for that history she claims to be writing.'

Wednesday

Scene 1

Hugo was off to Thorn Hall as soon as it opened, but even then he found the insufferably efficient Jarrett had been a step ahead of him.

'A file on Mr Ingham?' said Mrs Clutton. 'We do have one, but Inspector Jarrett has already requested it.'

Damn the man. 'Has it been taken over to him yet?'

'No, Susie's fishing it out.'

'Could I perhaps have a few moments to look through it before it goes?'

She gave him a shrewd look. Mrs Clutton was no fool. In fact, she could probably have run the whole operation far more competently than Sir Bernard. She also had no more love for Jarrett than anyone else at Thorn Hall.

'I might be able to do that. But you'll owe Dick a little something.'

Dick was the Hall's long-suffering messenger, who had made his opinion of the incomer quite plain after being reproved for a short delay in bringing over some other materials.

'No gentleman, he is, for all his hoity-toity ways. Belongs in one of they Russki uniforms. They're welcome to him.'

'Look on the bright side,' said Amos, who ran the post room. 'Now he's got a suspect, he'll be out of here in the blink of an eye. His type doesn't hang around.'

'We'll owe Dick a week's convalescent leave, if this goes on much longer,' Hugo said. 'Do we have anything separate on Alice Rothesay, or is it all on her husband's file?'

'Nothing more, Mr Hawksworth. If we had separate files for everyone, we'd need the Castle to store it all, and you'd be out on your ear. Ah, here's Susie with your file. Be quick, mind you.'

Hugo retreated to his office with the precious folder.

There wasn't much in it. The Service only had a file on Saul because he'd been assigned to a special unit towards the end of the war, rounding up German scientists before the Russians could get their hands on them.

As to why he'd been chosen for that, it was obvious at once. He'd worked behind enemy lines in Greece and North Africa, then with the partisans in Yugoslavia. Several citations and as many reprimands. Not a man who thrived in a strict hierarchy. Here was a note from a commanding officer early in the war. Prone to minor disciplinary infractions, some quarrels, an argument with a colonel. A personal observation: *Lieutenant Ingham has decided opinions about the competence of some of his superiors, and has yet to learn to keep those opinions to himself.* Ouch. He'd seemed destined for a military prison until a more sympathetic CO had seen him in his element during the evacuation of Crete, passed his name to a friend looking for oddballs and misfits.

Saul certainly seemed to have a chip on his shoulder – well, Hugo knew that already. He flicked back to before the war. Rural Oxfordshire, son of a labourer, employed as a porter at the Ashmolean, moving pictures and sculptures. He'd flourished in the art world, picking up invaluable hands-on knowledge, gone straight back into it as soon as he was demobbed – no hanging around in the Army for him – and ended up in a tangled situation with the late Lord Selchester.

He had a chequered history, and clearly not an entirely honest one. There was a great deal of murky business in the art world. Saul, fighting for a niche in that world, had done whatever paid, and not scrupled too much about it.

No sign of Communist sympathies at all. He had a pithy lack of respect for his social superiors, which had given one interviewer pause, but it seemed to be rooted principally in the conviction that they were all idle layabouts. Communism, he'd said, was just a different way of living off the sweat of others' backs.

After the war . . . only a bare record, added sometime in these last few weeks. Nothing Hugo didn't know already. Conviction for fraud, later overturned, fled the country and vanished, seven years in the French Foreign Legion.

It all made sense. Saul had a prickly temperament, the right background, and an old feud with the dead man. Hugo himself had given Jarrett the angle he needed. He'd look for someone with the right training, he'd said. Lo and behold, that someone had turned up. Sir Bernard was pleased. Jarrett would be pleased.

Hugo jotted down a few salient points and the name of Saul's next of kin before handing the file back to Mrs Clutton. No point keeping Dick waiting any longer than was absolutely necessary.

'Find anything helpful, Mr Hawksworth?' she asked.

'Nothing I didn't expect to see there.'

'That'll make Inspector Jarrett happy.'

He gave an absent-minded nod, turned back to his office.

'I've seen that look on you before, Mr Hawksworth,' she said. 'Gets you into trouble every time.'

'Mrs Clutton,' he said over his shoulder, 'you know me too well.'

'There'll be trouble all right,' said Susie darkly.

Scene 2

In Oxford, Leo was on the case. He'd only met Bruno Rothesay once, at a conference in Göttingen in the early thirties. Not a face you forgot, with that great Heidelberg scar on it. A good conversationalist, full of *joie de vivre*, although perhaps a little too prone to move on when someone more exotic appeared.

Oxford being what it was, though, there were plenty willing to talk and give pointers, helpful or otherwise. An amiable chat in the Senior Common Room at St Giles led Leo to a former colleague of Rothesay's, now living in retirement out at Woodstock, and thence to Rothesay's closest Oxford friend, a chemist working at the Dyson Perrins Laboratory on South Parks Road.

A swift walk across the road under grey winter skies, through the Lamb and Flag Passage, past Keble into the untidy warren behind the Museum. Behind the grand façades on South Parks Road, the science area was a warren of Nissen huts, pipes, cylinders, and vents.

A pair of graduate students ambling past gave him cheery nods. He'd taught them both. Of considerable ability but indifferent keenness, not like the lot who'd come through in the years after the war. This pair were just too young to have fought.

He found his man in another Nissen hut bolted on to the back of the Dyson Perrins, badly ventilated and overly full of noisy equipment. Dr Thomas Marston. A dapper, sandy-haired man with a bright, cynical glint to his eye, looking on with a certain exasperation as a pair of technicians dived into the bowels of the only silent machine in the room.

'Can't hear a thing in here,' Marston said, brushing off an introduction. 'Let's go somewhere quieter.'

They stepped out into the alley. Marston pulled a cigarette case out of his pocket; Leo declined.

'Father Leo Hawksworth,' said Marston, 'of St Giles. Heard your talk at Leiden last year, in that strictly-for-the-curious session Lemaître organised at the end. "What can science learn from theology?" Dangerous business, asking that kind of question. Can't say it went down well with my colleagues – those who bothered to sit through it.'

'What did you think of it?' Leo asked. At a gesture from Marston, they began walking in the direction of the Parks.

'It's a brave man who asks.'

'Or a curious one,' Leo said.

'We,' Marston said, waving his cigarette to encompass the whole grimy, war-weary labyrinth of the Science Area, 'unleashed far greater horrors on the world than Torquemada ever contrived, and we're just as convinced we were in the right. A salutary lesson to see our arguments reflected back at us from all those centuries ago. Makes you wonder how far we've really come.'

'Wonder? Or do something about it?'

Marston shot Leo a knowing look. 'You know the answer to that as well as I do. That takes imagination, and there's not enough of that in this whole department to fill a thimble.'

They came out through the gate into the raw, leafless landscape of the Parks. Clouds scudded overhead, darker grey against lighter. The wind was cold, relentless. Over by the Cherwell, the geese were making a terrific racket.

'I think you do your colleagues a disservice,' said Leo.

'Probably,' said Marston carelessly. He had left his coat open, and seemed quite heedless of the cold. 'But you weren't sitting in the bar with them afterwards. Now, tell me. What curiosity brings you to my door? I can't say I'm sad to be given a break from Bouncing Betty's latest tantrum – she's the antique you caught us all crawling around in – but I admit to a certain curiosity of my own.'

There was no reason to beat about the bush with this man who watched too much and forgave too little. Leo could make a shrewd guess as to why, given the Establishment's shabby treatment of Professor Turing.

'Bruno Rothesay.'

'Ah,' Marston said. 'I was sorry to hear about that. If you're involved, I suppose it wasn't an outraged husband finally catching up with him.'

Of course, he knew more than he ought about Leo's past and his other work, just as everyone in Selchester knew more than they ought about Foxley and Thorn Hall. Leo couldn't in conscience claim to be speaking in an official capacity, but he had gained enough sense of Marston to know it wouldn't make a difference. He would speak or he wouldn't.

'Still a distinct possibility,' Leo said. 'In the circumstances, though, not the only one.'

Marston took another drag of his cigarette. 'Believe it or not, Bruno was good company when I knew him. Quite a temper, of course, and he held grudges like a Hungarian. But in the evening, when the wine flowed, he could become quite genial. He liked things outside his subject, too. You know how it can be at conferences.'

Leo nodded.

'He didn't act like a Scotsman. Or an Englishman, for that matter. There was a Continental look to him, and he knew how to drink in moderation, which the English never do. People were always thinking he was from somewhere else. A Polish count thought he must be French. A Venetian monsignor thought he was Jewish, and tried to warn him against going to a conference in Vienna, just when things all blew up there.'

'Interesting circles for a scientist to move in.'

'As I said, Bruno was good company. At ease, a touch exotic. The war changed him.'

'The war changed many men.'

'The war ought to have changed us all,' said Marston, with the first edge of real emotion Leo had heard from him. 'In Bruno's case, not for the better. He kept the act up, but I don't think his heart was in it. There was a bitter edge to him. The last time I saw him was in May, at

Foxley. Quite changed, no urbanity at all. Only wanted to talk about work, picked my brains about isotope chemistry for three hours solid. He still had an eye for a piece of skirt, though.'

'Did he quarrel over women, or simply pursue them?'

Marston gave him a sly look. 'Where did you think his scar came from?'

'He spent six months at Heidelberg. It's been taken as self-evident.'

'Oh, yes, the famous Heidelberg scar. So dashing, so distinguished in an Englishman. A Wytham Woods scar doesn't have quite the same ring, now does it? I can see you've no idea what I'm talking about, which means all those hard men in macs don't either.'

'Enlighten me.'

'I thought you priestly types had no time for the Enlightenment. Don't tell me you're hankering for the days of Torquemada after all. I shall be quite disappointed.'

Leo twitched an eyebrow. They were coming around towards the river, under the tall bare trees, towards a deserted Parson's Pleasure.

'It was just before Heidelberg, that's how he can get away with it. There was a woman.'

'Married?'

'Not this one. Divine, but heartless. A touch of the Carmen to her, and a good deal of gypsy blood. Anastasia, her name was. In any case, the usual story. Two admirers, and she egged them on. Liked the idea of them making fools of themselves for her sake. It went further than it usually did, and they ended up with a pair of old display swords or something in Wytham Woods. The swords were Rothesay's idea. He probably reckoned his chances of winning were better than if they went at it with fists. Besides, he always liked that kind of gesture. Made him different, a cut above the common throng. Quite why they chose Wytham Woods, I don't know. The place is always full of hapless zoology students trying not to crash around in the undergrowth. Long story short, they had to make a run for it, but not until the other man had laid Bruno's cheek open. He kept out of sight for a while and then took himself off. Talk of the town that there had been a duel in the woods, but not many knew who it had been.'

'I take it that things ended no better than the principals deserved.'

Marston gave a short bark of laughter. 'Indeed.'

'They were reconciled?'

'As I said, Bruno bore grudges until they died of old age, and then had them embalmed. The other man calmed down enough to make an offer of reconciliation, only to have it thrown back in his face.'

'Who was he? Another academic?'

'God, no. Not even that Jezebel could have stoked two academics into having at one another with swords. He was town, not gown. Younger than Bruno, bit of a chip on his shoulder. Worked at the Ashmolean, knew a great deal about art, but it was all self-taught. Can't remember his name. On the tip of my tongue. I keep thinking of Sunday school for some reason.'

They paused by the river's edge, looking across the grass of Parson's Pleasure to the swollen Cherwell, and out to the water meadows beyond.

Leo, a cradle Catholic like the Fitzwarins, had never been to Sunday school, but he had a good idea what it might entail. 'The name wasn't Saul, by any chance?' Leo had read that morning's papers, in which Saul's arrest featured prominently, but it seemed Marston had not.

'Yes,' said Marston, with a click of his fingers, 'Saul – Saul Ingham.'

Scene 3

'Meeting your clerical uncle, sir?' said Mr Godney, standing beside Hugo as the three-fifteen express pulled into Selchester station. Clouds of steam, the hiss of brakes, doors banging open, cries of joy or mild welcome. The wind was up still, rattling a loose door to the office and setting the station cat all at sixes and sevens.

'I shan't ask how you know that, Mr Godney,' said Hugo.

'We railwaymen have our sources, just the same as you do,' said Mr Godney with dignity. 'Always good to be one step ahead.'

Leo came striding along the platform, a tall elegant figure in a black suit and dog collar. The Selchester station staff were used to him by now.

'Good to be seeing you again, Father Hawksworth,' said Mr Godney. 'Smooth journey, I hope?'

'She's had a service, hasn't she?' Leo looked appreciatively at the engine, one of the old Southern Railway's finest. He had an instinctive liking for railways and an easy manner with the men who worked on them. Hugo had a childhood memory of his uncle on the footplate of *Mallard* at King's Cross, looking for all the world like one of her regular crew.

'Good as new. Well, aside from the paint. They don't like to maintain the engines properly these days, think it'll make everyone happier when those new diesels come in. Crying shame, if you ask me.'

'They've fixed that cylinder problem she was having, surely . . .'

They plunged deep into railway conversation, passengers flowing around them. Bill the porter was loading some luggage for Exeter into the guard's van, the crew on the footplate busy about their work.

Hugo caught sight of Miranda Pearson coming out of the ticket office, heading for the up platform. She was wearing a dirndl, such an odd thing to see at an English country station, but they seemed to be all the rage at the moment.

'Mr Hawksworth, isn't it? Shall I be seeing you at my talk on Friday?'

'I shall be going,' said Hugo, who'd heard about it from Gus. He was as intrigued as anyone else to know what the Pearsons were up to.

'I'm glad. The more the merrier.'

'Off to London?' Hugo asked, more for conversational politeness than anything else.

'Yes, my desk at the British Library awaits. We can't do everything in the field, although I like to get at local stories and customs unfiltered where possible. So much of the literature on folklore is written by people hankering for some imaginary golden age, or country parsons whiling away the hours. One has to cut through all the nostalgia and sentimentality.'

There was a whistle from down the line.

'That'll be my train. You must excuse me, Mr Hawksworth. I look forward to seeing you on Friday.'

She strode off, a swift, purposeful figure.

'Who was that?' Leo asked. Mr Godney had gone to chivvy Bill on.

'Half of the couple at Nightingale Cottage. The folklorist.'

Leo blinked. 'Ah. I had a different image of her. Shall we?'

'Meaning,' said Hugo, 'you'd like to drive.'

Hugo settled into the passenger seat, glad to be handing control to someone other than Jarrett for once.

'To the Castle?' said Leo.

'Yes, I've excused myself for the rest of the day. Leads to follow up. That is, if you've found anything.'

Leo swung the car out into Station Road with nary a jolt to be felt.

'I have indeed, although it may be rather old hat by now. Your colleagues made an arrest, I hear. Saul Ingham, the gentleman I met at Christmas.' There had been a copy of *The Times* tucked into the side of Leo's bag. Of course it was all over the papers. Even if Saul were proved innocent, his name would be dragged through the mud again.

'I'll fill you in. What did you find out?'

As they made their way down Sheep Street and over the bridge towards the Castle, slowed by a tractor, Leo recounted the story he'd heard from Thomas Marston.

'So he lied to us,' said Hugo.

'You were hoping for something less damning,' Leo observed.

'I don't find it damning,' said Hugo. 'It's the wrong way around. Bruno was the one who hung on to his grudges, Saul the one with a bad temper.'

He outlined, in turn, the story he'd heard from Oldcastle and the contents of Saul's file.

'A man shaped by violent passions, like Saul Ingham, can find it hard to control them,' Leo said. 'We form our characters by habit. Bruno never let go of a quarrel. He liked to gloat, and he wasn't shy about doing so. If he had been so unwise as to gloat in person, Saul would have found it a struggle to contain his temper.'

'It's one thing to struggle with your temper, quite another to shoot a man in the back of the neck.'

They turned through the Castle gates, Leo stepping on the pedal as the car crossed on to private land.

'You sound like a man who isn't ready to be convinced.'

'It's the convenient explanation,' said Hugo. 'We need a suspect with a particular background, and *voilà*! We have one. Sir Bernard likes it already.'

'And this Jarrett? He sounds like a man less easily fooled.'

Hugo had spoken to Jarrett by phone earlier in the afternoon. 'He wanted a list. Did Saul have any prior connections in Selchester, any known friends or enemies? I'd say that he'll be convinced if he can explain the tip-off.'

'But you won't be.'

'I think an explanation will present itself,' said Hugo. 'A perfectly plausible, perfectly coherent explanation that allows them to pin the whole thing on Saul. It works for everyone. The Soviet agent turns out to be an unpopular outsider, who has helpfully been killed in a quarrel by another unpopular outsider. Case closed. We can rest easy where scientific secrets are concerned, because it turns out all the spies are dubious types with foreign connections, just like Klaus Fuchs.'

'The Service I knew,' said Leo slowly, 'wouldn't have stopped there. Nor would the Americans, although in the current climate they'd swing to the opposite extreme. I gather you're not convinced Rothesay was passing material to the Soviets.'

'There's nothing in his record to suggest it.'

'What sparked the hunt in the first place? You couldn't tell me over the phone, of course, but I should like to hear it.'

'Ah, well, there you're in luck, because you'll be meeting the source very shortly. He's a Hungarian physicist, defected a few months back, down here for debriefing before we let him go to America, where he'd really like to be. Sir Bernard manoeuvred Gus into putting him up for a few days.'

The gatehouse was ahead. Leo, unlike Jarrett, slowed down to negotiate the passage.

'What's his name?'

'Dr Árpád Bárándy.'

'I've heard of him,' said Leo, 'but I don't believe I've met him. We're not in the same field. Is he a congenial guest?'

'Very. Gets on very well with the girls. I think even Mrs Partridge doesn't mind him, although she'd never admit it. I should mention that, as far as the world knows, and that includes the girls, he's a classicist, a colleague of Gus's rather than yours. He's very well read.'

'A man of many parts,' said Leo, bringing the car to a halt. 'I look forward to making his acquaintance.'

'He might even be here already,' said Hugo.

Scene 4

As it happened, Árpád had been and gone, no sooner back at the Castle than swept off to Veryan House by Lady Priscilla's chauffeur. Freya and Gus had left with him, the latter with a certain hesitation. Lady Priscilla might be his neighbour, and indeed his aunt, but she was a force of nature of a peculiarly English kind, and he had yet to learn the knack of dealing with her. Polly, alone of the family, had managed that, and in very short order too, by dint of simply digging her heels in.

Freya had arranged the visit that morning, which was to say that she'd rung her aunt to see about a horse for Árpád.

'Yes, I'd heard about him. You must bring him over. No, I won't hear a word to the contrary. Father in the Horthy regime, you say, I know the type. He'll be one of us, of course, not that it concerns you. Three o'clock? You don't know when the Hall will be done with him? Nonsense. I'll ring Bernard. He'll agree to anything just to get rid of me. I'll send Gerald over to the Hall, then up for the two of you. Must dash. Dogs making the most terrific rumpus out there. Don't know what's got into them. Bye!'

The phone clicked, and Freya heard Irene's voice from the exchange. 'Well, Miss Freya, you've got your work cut out with her. My granny was a bit like that. Guess that's why all my aunts and uncles went off to New Zealand, the further away the better. Pa drew the short straw, must say I think I'd have liked it out there. Bags of space, they say. Cheerio!'

Sir Archibald's smoke-grey Rolls-Royce purred into the Castle at ten to three, Dr Bárándy already ensconced in the back seat. Freya had to divert Gus towards the back seat as he tried to ride shotgun. 'No, that's the way we do it here. Just imagine you're a senator being handled into a limousine.'

Gerald gave her a grin as he closed the door for her. She sank into the seat, relishing the soft leather and immaculate trim.

Árpád looked at his surroundings with appreciation. 'I was told, Sir Archibald Veryan is sending a car for you, he is the local MP and known to your Sir Bernard, and I thought, what have I said? Then I talk to Gerald here, who is an Irishman, and it seems this is how you do social calls in the English countryside.'

'This is how Lady Priscilla does social calls,' Freya corrected him. 'Be glad we had a reason to go to her, otherwise she'd have turned up here on her hunter, and you'd have had no warning at all.'

'This Sir Archibald, I am not to see him, then?'

'He's in London, I believe. Is that right, Gerald?'

'Indeed, Miss Freya. House in session, papers to be read and suchlike. Wouldn't be the life for me, I can tell you that.'

Freya rather thought it wouldn't be the life for her either. How tedious to be confronted with piles of documents every day, all presumably to be read, marked, learned and inwardly digested, and all as dull as ditchwater. The German messages she'd handled during her war service at Bletchley, often tedious in themselves, had nevertheless been vital information. She rather doubted that could be said about most of Sir Archibald's reading matter.

On the other hand, presumably ministers and their civil servants never had to stare at blank sheets of paper for hour after hour. She was meant to be writing now, although her aunt would hardly have accepted that as an excuse.

Veryan House was mellow, reasonably sized, and immaculately kept, a Queen Anne doll's house surrounded by the gardens which were Lady Priscilla's pride and joy – indeed, her personal domain ever since she'd taken over their management during the war. Quite a contrast to the Castle, although Freya wouldn't have exchanged the two for the world. She liked the Castle's awkward corners and great thick walls.

Lady Priscilla met them by the coach house, wearing wellies and faded tweeds.

'Lady Priscilla, this is Dr Árpád Bárándy. My aunt, Lady Priscilla Veryan,' said Freya.

'We'll go to the stables first, the light will be fading soon.' Her aunt gave Árpád a sweeping glance. 'He's not dressed the part, Freya.'

'You didn't give him a chance,' Freya said testily.

'It is fine,' said Árpád, looking around curiously. 'I have not the clothes for every occasion, as you would say.'

'Some of my late brother's things might fit you. Unless you've thrown them out, Freya?'

'Nothing of the sort. The moths might have eaten them, but Sonia wanted them in one piece, probably so she could burn the lot.'

'Your cousin had good reason for feeling as she did,' said Lady Priscilla. 'Come on, then.'

Perhaps, Freya thought as they filed through an arched gate to the stables, but not for the unreasoning hatred which would have seen the Castle turned into a luxury hotel, the estate broken up, and the tenants left to the tender mercy of commercial developers. All simply to spite her father's memory. Whatever his other faults, and they were many, Selchester had been punctilious with respect to his obligations as lord of a great estate.

Lady Priscilla whisked Árpád off ahead, interrogating him at once about his life in Hungary and his level of riding ability. Her voice floated back across the stable yard. '. . . I suppose you've met that dreadful horse of Freya's; no question of you riding him. There's such a thing as too much spirit in a horse.'

'But Last Hurrah is an interesting horse. A thief would have a hard time with him. I think perhaps I might persuade him, given time, but I am not used to your English saddle, and this would be an invitation to him to play tricks.'

'We have a Continental saddle ready for you; I had Francis dig one out. My husband is the huntmaster, you see, and we've had a fair number of visitors over the years. I already have a horse in mind for you.'

'Do you think he'll be all right?' Gus asked, watching them disappear into the stables.

'He's dealt with far worse,' said Freya. 'I think she recognises a kindred spirit. They're as blunt as one another.'

They followed as far as the stable door. It was a comforting and familiar place to Freya, from childhood rides and more recent Christmases. Selchester had kept horses because he was expected to, and the Castle stables had been brisk and well run. Lady Priscilla kept horses because she loved them, and so her stables felt different. Warmer, that was it, even with the chill January wind blowing through the door.

Lady Priscilla's big hunter Jupiter was in the nearest stall. He was an uneven-tempered horse, one to be wary around, if not to the same degree as Last Hurrah. Árpád regarded him gravely for a moment. To Freya's surprise Jupiter ambled over, leaned down to whicker gently in Árpád's ear, and rested there for a moment while the Hungarian stroked his neck.

For a moment, unseen by anyone but Freya, Árpád's face lost its wary curiosity and became quite still, tranquil almost. He closed his eyes, took a long, slow breath, and then another.

A man without a country, Freya thought, but here for an instant he can be home.

The moment passed. Árpád gave Jupiter a pat and stepped away, the big hunter eyeing him reproachfully.

'A fine horse,' he said, letting his eyes wander up and down its flanks. 'There is some Arab in him, I think?'

'You know your horses, Dr Bárándy,' said Lady Priscilla, in a rather less brusque tone than before. 'I'll have to keep my stable door locked.'

Árpád's eyes twinkled. 'Hungarians,' he said, 'are first-class horse thieves.'

Lady Priscilla had picked out a roan gelding, Pompey, for Árpád to ride. Equipped with some disreputable cast-offs from a former groom, brushing off the proffered riding hat, he trotted off to take a turn around the paddock. The setting sun had dipped below the layer of grey clouds, casting everything in a rather dramatic light. Fit for a painting, Freya thought, or perhaps a chase. Yes, a horseman in the winter dusk. A horseman without a country. But who, and why? And when?

Lady Priscilla, practical as ever, broke through her musings as she came over to Gus, one eye still on the horse and rider. 'So how long will he be here?'

'I don't know,' Gus said. 'Sir Bernard thought a week or two.'

'You just have to stand up to Sir Bernard,' she said. 'He's become far too comfortable, being chief trustee of the Castle these last seven years.'

'I rather imagined he was counting on my naïveté as an American,' said Gus candidly. 'He knows I don't have the foggiest idea how things really work here. Besides, I'm glad to have Árpád here. It's good to be able to talk classics again.'

Lady Priscilla's expression suggested she knew perfectly well what Árpád's real line of work was, but she was careful not to feed crumbs to the Selchester gossip machine.

'That's as may be,' she said, 'but we can't go letting officials push us around. They do plenty of that as it is. I imagine he promised you a favour in return. Make sure you collect on it, and soon. He'll think twice before he imposes on you again. And Freya, tell Hugo to watch his step. There are people in London not best pleased with his involvement in my late brother's affairs.'

'I'll pass it on,' said Freya neutrally, not entirely sure whether it was advice or warning.

'Now, Pompey. I'll have Francis bring him over in the morning, you don't want Dr Bárándy to feel he's imposing on my hospitality every time he wants to ride. Have Ben put him at the far end of the stable-block, and that piebald brute of yours will have to like it or lump it.'

Scene 5

Supper was a cheerful affair, even in the grand dining room. Everyone except Mrs Partridge rather missed taking it in the kitchen, but she was adamant. With an earl in residence, meals should be taken properly.

They'd managed to chisel out a few exceptions, such as when only two or three of them were there.

Georgia preferred the kitchen, or failing that, something rather more gothic. 'Can't we sit at opposite ends of the table like they do in movies? Send one another messages by a cadaverous butler?'

'We don't have a cadaverous butler,' said Freya firmly. 'And before you ask, no, Gus isn't going to hire one.'

Gus had arranged with Mrs Partridge that her niece Pam would join the staff full-time, but that was as far as things had gone. Freya sensed Gus was uneasy with the very idea of servants, but sooner or later he'd need to come to terms with the sheer size of Selchester Castle, never mind the seven-year backlog of maintenance which had built up following his father's disappearance.

Árpád and Father Leo, as guests, were on either side of Gus at the end of the table. There were almost enough of them to have a more traditional placement, men and women alternating, which would have been Mrs Partridge's preference. Polly, however, helping to lay the table, had objected.

'Father will just end up talking about Latin poetry with Árpád bácsi, and Freya or Georgia or I will be stuck in the middle not following a word.'

'Your father is a very thoughtful host,' said Mrs Partridge. 'Be careful with those plates now.'

'Yes, he is, and he'll be all attentive to his guest, which means talking about things which interest him, and that means Roman stuff. Probably quoting Latin until it comes out of his ears, too, just like he always did at home,' Polly added with a scowl.

Freya, coming into the dining room just at that moment, gave Mrs Partridge a tiny nod. It was true, Gus was a courteous host, and had done his best with some difficult dinners over Christmas. It was also true that he'd spent most of his life in universities, sitting down to dinner with fellow classics professors.

There had been a faintly awkward moment when they returned. It had been clear Árpád had recognised Leo, which was hardly consonant with his cover as a classicist. Both men had the wit to cover it quickly, but Freya was fairly sure Georgia had noticed something was up. Thankfully Mrs Partridge had been out of the room at the time. Who knew how far her discretion would stretch?

There wasn't as much Latin as Polly had feared. Árpád wanted to know how things were in America, whether the country he had known in the thirties had survived the war, what had happened to this or that prominent person. They talked about the Fourth of July, and compared notes on their respective visits to Boston museums.

'Why did you go back to Hungary?' Georgia asked.

'I doubt Dr Bárándy wants to talk about that,' said Hugo.

'No, no,' said Árpád, 'it is a fair question. I went back because I had not seen my home or my family for seven years, and because I hoped that things would be better. There was an election in Hungary after the war, you see, a proper election, and the Communists did not win. You have a proverb in England, one swallow does not make a summer – is that how it goes?'

Hugo nodded.

'I thought perhaps it might, so I went home. America is a great country, full of energy, but it is not home, not my own soil. I wanted to see the house where I was born, to ride across the plains in the summer, to swim in Lake Balaton. To hear my own language all around me, to smoke Hungarian tobacco, to taste proper paprika again. When you are in exile, it is the little things which remind you, the tastes and smells which are not the same.'

'Mown grass,' said Hugo.

'Ah yes, I had a colleague at Princeton who told me this. You have a green and verdant country, not baked dry by the sun. For me, the smell of summer is more dusty, more heavy.'

'So what happened?' Georgia asked, wanting to hear the end of the story.

Árpád shrugged. 'What always happens. The Russians did not like what they had, so they changed it, bit by bit, first this restriction, then that. They made life difficult for the elected politicians, pushed them out, replaced them with their own. They are always a step ahead, with tanks and guns. I hoped until I could hope no more, this is not the Hungarian way. We are used to tragedies, to uprisings suppressed, to lands taken away. I fear I had become too American.'

Hugo said, 'Do you think this new man will change anything?' There had been a change of regime in Budapest recently, in the wake of Stalin's death. The Service was watching closely, had probably asked him this question a dozen times.

'Nagy Imre is Moscow's man too, whether he wants to be or not. If they do not like him, they will squash him, thus.' He slapped the flat of his hand on the table, making everyone jump. 'I shall not see Hungary again. I must be an American now, just as you, Lord Selchester, and your daughters, you must be British. But it is a pleasure to be here, and to spend time in a country so ashamed of its spies that it puts them in quiet country towns where they wear tweeds and pretend they are mathematicians. This is a good thing, take it from me.'

The shrill sound of the telephone sounded from Grace Hall.

'Bet it's Jarrett,' said Georgia, 'wondering why you're not in your office with your nose to the grindstone.'

It wasn't.

Pam popped her head around the door. 'Phone for you, Mr Hawksworth, the younger one that is. Someone called Valerie.'

'Tell her we're at supper. I'll ring her back.'

'She said she wouldn't take no for an answer, she's just going out.'

'If you'll forgive me,' said Hugo, putting his napkin on the table, 'I shan't be long.'

In Grace Hall, he paused a moment before picking up the telephone.

'I knew you'd be there,' said Valerie. 'You haven't called me since last week.'

'I've had a lot on my plate,' said Hugo testily. 'You may have seen something about it in the papers.'

'Oh, you're mixed up in that, are you? Thought you might be. Running around at the beck and call of that dreadful Jarrett fellow, I dare say, no life for a grown man. Interviewing scientists, too, what a bore. I was stuck next to some cousin of Reggie's at dinner last night, Cambridge professor of this or that. Honestly, you've never met a more tedious man. He spoke in a monotone, spent half the meal adjusting his knife and fork. I told Reggie if he ever did that to me again, I'd tell that ghastly puritanical aunt of his how much he'd like a visit from her. And he had the nerve to tell me it was my turn to put up with the man.'

Why was it, Hugo wondered, that Valerie's personality became so much less attractive on the phone? He made some polite noises, but Valerie cut him off.

'Can't linger. Reggie's got me a ticket to *Tosca* as a peace offering. Lady Escley has loaned him her box while she's off taking the waters. Listen. On Saturday I shall be down in your neck of the woods. Serena Hampton-Bishop had her first over Christmas, and it's the christening. They live just outside some place called Yarnley. I've added you to the guest list, no, but me no buts – there's someone you're going to meet. I haven't seen you in two months, and you spent Christmas down in the sticks when you could have been up here having a much more interesting time. I shall be on the ten-thirty at Yarnley, make sure you're there. Wear something respectable, and don't even think of bringing that sister of yours. Taxi's here, darling, see you on Saturday.'

She hung up. Hugo grimaced at the phone and followed suit.

Pam, who had been lingering in the passageway for a good eavesdrop, slipped along to the kitchen. 'Who's Valerie?' she asked Mrs Partridge.

'Mr Hawksworth's girlfriend.'

Pam's eyes lit up. 'I didn't know he had one. What's she like?'

'I can't tell you that, she's never dignified us with her presence. Lives in London. Very glamorous, so I hear, always going to nightclubs.'

'I can't say as Mr Hawksworth looked pleased to hear from her. Looked as if he'd lost a pound and found sixpence. Didn't get a word in edgeways, neither. I wonder whether she's a high-society girl?'

'I wonder nothing of the sort,' said Mrs Partridge. 'London ways may not be our ways, but there's no call to let your imagination run away with you. I imagine she's very much the same sort of person as Lady Sonia.'

'I don't like Lady Sonia,' said Pam, 'and nor do you, it's no use pretending. I heard you talking to Pa back when we all thought she'd get the Castle.'

'There you go eavesdropping again. Those as listens in will hear no good of themselves,' said Mrs Partridge. 'Now, help me with this sponge cake.'

In the dining room, Hugo took his place again.

'You look glum. What did she want?' Georgia asked.

'Since you ask, she's going to a christening nearby on Saturday, and wants me to go along.'

'Do we get to meet her?' Polly asked.

'I doubt it,' said Hugo.

'She doesn't like me,' said Georgia. 'And she's only coming to the christening to keep an eye on Hugo. You have to pry her out of London with a crowbar normally. Catch her coming down here without an ulterior motive.'

'Georgia!' said Hugo, needled too far. 'Enough of this! Be quiet or go to your room.'

Georgia's face took on a mulish expression, one both Leo and Freya knew all too well. 'Since I'm not welcome here, I shall. You know perfectly well I'm right, but you don't want to admit it.' She stalked from the room, still making sure to push her chair in before she did. They heard her voice in Grace Hall. 'Come on, Magnus, you can keep me company.'

'I'm sorry about that,' said Hugo, after a moment's silence. 'Dr Bárándy, how did you get on with Lady Priscilla?'

Scene 6

'I didn't handle that well,' Hugo said to Gus and Leo later, when Polly had gone off to bed. Freya and Árpád had taken torches and ventured out to the stables with Ben, making things ready for Pompey's arrival in the morning. Freya had mentioned moving Last Hurrah to a different stall, where he wouldn't even be able to see the other horse.

Gus gave him a sympathetic look. 'It's a hard thing, bringing up a girl on your own. When Anne died, I was quite out of my depth. You expect to have someone with you the whole way, and then suddenly you don't. You have to learn to do everything the other person did without even thinking, and you know you'll never be as good. It must be even harder for you, coming fresh to it, and with a sister instead of a daughter.'

'Does that make such a difference?' Hugo asked, wondering what he should have done instead.

'You don't have quite the same authority,' Leo said. 'Until last year, you were a distant presence to her. Now you're her guardian. She's not used to thinking of you in that way. And, rightly or wrongly, she sees Valerie as a threat to her.'

There was no mistaking his uncle's message in those last few words, but it wasn't a conversation to have now.

Gus, sensing as much, pushed his chair back. 'The fire is burning down, and there seems little point in stoking it. Shall we decamp to the Drawing Room?'

'You gentlemen go ahead,' said Leo. 'I shall venture up to see Georgia first.'

Gus said, 'I think Freya was going there after she'd seen to the stables.'

'Then I shall wait for her to return. Three would be a crowd in a situation like this.'

Scene 7

Freya had indeed gone to see Georgia, knocking softly on her door.

'Who is it?' a suspicious voice demanded.

'Just me,' said Freya.

'Oh, it's you,' she said. 'You can come in.'

Georgia was curled up in the chair in her room with Magnus on her lap, rather disconsolately flicking through a book of science-fiction stories.

'I was afraid it would be Hugo, come to lecture me on how I shouldn't be nasty about Valerie, as if he weren't avoiding her himself. He knows if he actually sees her, she'll just turn on the charm and he'll remember why he likes her.'

Freya sat down on the end of the bed, there being only the one chair.

Georgia gave her a sideways look. 'Are you going to lecture me too?'

'It's not my place,' said Freya.

'Good. Why does she have to pop up again? Everything's all right now. Horrible Sonia can't sell the Castle to the developers, and Gus isn't going to turn us out because he and Polly would rather live in Lady Matilda's wing, and it's all settled for once. I like it here. She's up to something, I know she is. She wants Hugo, and she'll vamp him until he agrees to leave the Service and move to London and become something dull, and then she'll send me off to some ghastly school where the windows always have to be open three inches and the games mistresses look at you in the showers, and it'll all be vile again, just like Yorkshire Ladies'.'

Freya had endured a full course at Yorkshire Ladies' College in the thirties, and was inclined to agree. She'd been bitterly envious of Perdita Richardson when her grandfather pulled her out to go to a London music school. How blissful to be able to leave it all behind at the end of the day.

'You know exactly what I mean,' Georgia added. She was working herself up into a right old state. 'She was pleased when he was shot, it meant he wouldn't want to stay in the Service.'

'I very much doubt she was pleased.'

'She was,' said Georgia, scowling. 'People in the Service have to pretend to be minor diplomats and shipping agents and suchlike . . .'

'Statisticians.'

Georgia's scowl softened ever so slightly. She ran a finger along Magnus's head, and he opened a yellow eye as if to say, *Why are you disturbing me?*

'And statisticians. They get sent off to odd places to do odd things, they're not really respectable. Valerie can never say he works at such-and-such a place, get everyone nodding approvingly. She'd have to pretend he's nobody very important, and she doesn't like that sort of pretending. Which is odd, because she's so good at pretending to have his best interests at heart. Don't try to say nice things about her. You haven't met her, so I shall know they're all lies.'

'I don't have anything to say.'

Georgia stared broodingly out of the window. She hadn't troubled to close the curtains before she sat down, perhaps preferring to gaze out into black night. Freya got up and pulled them to. No point letting all the heat out.

'I wish he'd marry you,' Georgia said. 'There, I've said it.'

Freya was glad she'd been closing the curtains at the precise moment Georgia said that. She moved on to pull the other set closed. 'Things aren't so neat.'

'Well, they ought to be!'

'Would you have Hugo order the whole of the rest of his life to make the next few years easier for you? In five years, you'll be off to make your fortune, university or a job or some such. The world will be your oyster.'

'The world won't be Hugo's oyster if he's married to Valerie. Or mine while I'm immured in some hideous boarding school. I like it here. I like the Castle, and Selchester, and you, and Daisy, and Mrs Partridge, and Polly. Even if she's full of peculiar Popish notions.'

'You didn't like Polly when she came.'

'Perhaps I didn't,' said Georgia grudgingly, 'but that was when she was here to throw us out of house and home. Don't tell me you wanted to leave the Castle.'

'I didn't,' Freya admitted. 'But I've had seven years here, more than I ever expected.'

'Exactly. Seven years. You like it here. You don't even want to go off to London where it's exciting, let alone be pushed from pillar to post all the time. If Valerie tries to make me go anywhere, I shall claim sanctuary in the Cathedral. Cling to the altar.'

'I don't believe you can still do that,' said Freya.

'Pity. Maybe I shall be like Luther, nail my petition to the Cathedral door. *Here I stand, I can do no other.* Miss Ormskirk told us all about him.'

Georgia was beginning to relax, although her face was still full of wary tension. Too much imagination, that was the trouble, spinning a few casual words into a catastrophe. That, and a childhood torn apart by German bombs. She wanted permanence and security, and what was wrong with that?

Freya squinted at Georgia's book with its lurid cover. She could hardly talk, look at all those buxom wenches on the covers of her Rosina Wyndham novels. Isaac Asimov, *Foundation and Empire*. 'I haven't seen that one before. Where did it come from?'

'Árpád bácsi lent it to me. He likes science fiction. Hugo's people bought some for him while he was in his safe house. I bet that annoys the bean counters back in London. A semi-detached house in Metroland, check. Agents around the clock, check. A dozen listening devices, check. Two works of speculative fiction – oh dear, we can't have that. Did you know he's met Asimov? It must be strange to meet a famous author.' A distinctly sidelong glance. What was Georgia implying?

'Really, Georgia, you do have the oddest notions.'

Georgia looked down at her book again. 'Mmmm,' she said.

Scene 8

It was much later. Hugo and Freya took Leo up to the sitting room which had been the late Lord Selchester's, well away from listening ears of any kind. Árpád showed them in, rather lost in the vastness of the room. Thick crimson drapes covered the tall windows, and a fire kept the cold at bay.

Freya carefully closed the door behind them.

'I thought, as Father Leo is a colleague of sorts, you might like some time when you could be a physicist again,' said Hugo, who knew too well the sort of strain which built up from day after day of pretending to be something or someone you weren't.

'Ah, this is thoughtful of you. But would your charming Miss Godwin not think amiss of this? She is quite a character, no – a breath of fresh air in your musty Hall? She thinks highly of you.'

'Both Freya and Leo have signed the Official Secrets Act,' said Hugo, 'which is to say that, should you let anything slip, neither of them will breathe a word about it to anyone else.'

'Quite the family business, I see,' said Árpád to Leo. 'You will not remember me, but I once went to a talk you gave. There are not so many priests in our profession that I could forget you.'

'I thought I'd seen you before,' said Leo. 'Where would it have been? I've only been to the United States once, for a colloquium at Yale in 1938, and then to see some colleagues at Princeton.'

'Yes, it would have been there,' said Árpád. 'I was visiting von Neumann . . .'

'We'll leave you to it,' said Hugo, sensing a torrent of physics on the tip of Árpád's tongue.

Leo raised a hand. 'A moment, Dr Bárándy, before we lose ourselves in shop talk. Hugo has a dilemma. A man has been murdered, a scientist at the Atomic, and the police have arrested a man who may be innocent.'

'And, of course, this is something you can change.'

'I should like to,' said Hugo.

'I do not need to tell you how lucky you are. Miss Godwin tells me you have been in Eastern Europe yourself recently. You have seen with your own eyes what passes for justice under Soviet rule.'

This Harriet Godwin seemed to talk about Hugo a great deal.

'Did you know Dr Rothesay?' Hugo asked. 'He was the victim.'

'I did not know Dr Rothesay,' said Árpád. 'Yes, I knew what happened. I have heard his name on the radio.'

'Dr Wood, Dr Vane or Dr Oldcastle?' Hugo asked.

'Ah, now perhaps I can help you. I do not know a Dr Wood. Dr Vane I have met perhaps twice, he is a very colourless man. Dr Oldcastle I know, but surely he is, how would you say it, a grand pooh-bah by now, with a knighthood and an important post in Government?'

'You knew him?' said Hugo.

'Yes, in America, and also here. I knew his type at once. In every country they are the same. They are the men who like to run things, who become provosts and presidents and heads of institutes, who always

127

know the proper way of doing things. Perhaps they are not the best scientists, but they are the best at talking to ministers, at playing the games of committees, at getting funds. They help those of their colleagues who are, perhaps, not so good at all these things.' He looked at Leo. 'Such as Paul Dirac. You perhaps have met him?'

Leo gave a faint smile. 'I have indeed. So, Oldcastle is the sort of man who becomes master of his college and leaves the lab behind.'

'A courtier,' said Freya. 'An accumulator of offices and patronage.'

Freya had put her finger on it. Oldcastle was a courtier, smooth and assured, quite out of place in the spartan surroundings of Foxley. One might have said the same thing about Philip Sidney or Walter Raleigh, though, meeting them on a Flemish redoubt or a remote South American shore.

'He is here in Selchester?' Árpád asked.

'He oversees part of the operations at the Foxley facility,' said Hugo.

'Foxley is near Selchester?' Árpád said, surprised. 'Ah, perhaps this is why they have brought me here. I told them, even in Siberia we had heard of Foxley: this is where the British nearly came to grief. We must be careful not to repeat their mistake.'

'I shan't ask,' said Leo. 'If you think of anything more about any of these men, let Hugo know.'

'To help an innocent man, I shall do nothing less.'

Hugo and Freya took their leave, closing the door behind them. The passageway beyond was dark, only a dim light shining through from the passage to Grace Hall.

'Was Leo chivvying us out just then?' Freya asked.

'Yes. Árpád mustn't realise that no one here knows about the incident. He's a clever man, used to surviving in a brutal regime: he'll put two and two together.'

Freya thought for a moment. 'That's how you know there's a leak. Something happened at Foxley. The Soviets knew, and because of Árpád we know they knew.'

She was disconcertingly quick, and he was on dangerous ground even having let her know about it. At least Árpád was confused, thought the accident had happened at Foxley rather than Ulfsgill. Hugo had to keep Freya thinking that, a necessary deception but not a pleasant one.

Freya noticed his discomfort though not its cause, drew him to a stop inside the archway. 'As you said yourself, I shan't breathe a word. But I don't like the thought of Saul being blamed for something he hasn't done.'

She had herself been accused of complicity in a murder, although for her there would have been no consequences except to her reputation. The man she was supposed to have abetted was dead, there was minimal evidence and no prospect of a trial. For Saul, accused of a cold-blooded murder in the full glare of publicity, a conviction would mean the gallows. She didn't know him that well, but a life was a life.

'I don't intend to let him,' said Hugo. 'But it may be that I shall need your help and Leo's. Talking to people from outside the Service is a murky business in a case like this.'

'Not as murky as you might think,' she said. 'Saul has nothing to do with the Atomic, aside from this past connection with Bruno. Leo and I can't go delving around in classified material, but there's nothing classified about Saul. Is there?'

Hugo shook his head. 'Nothing we haven't learned through acquaintance. Certainly no Communist connections, if that's what you're wondering.'

'The oddest people can have Communist connections,' said Freya, thinking of someone they'd both known, the last person she'd have expected to be involved in such things.

'A good point.'

'So there's no reason Leo and I can't see what we can unearth about Saul while you carry on with whatever you're doing.'

'I should also like to know,' Hugo added, 'a little more about the private lives of these various Foxley types I've been interviewing. It's hard to build a rounded picture of someone's character while Jarrett is giving them the once-over. I must say, I had a certain admiration for the way Alice Rothesay stood up to him, but I'm no closer to fathoming her character than I was before.'

'Leave it to us,' Freya said. 'And if I were you, I'd take another look at that accident of yours. If it eluded the Selchester gossip machine, it must be quite something.'

Thursday

Scene 1

It was an angry, defiant Saul Ingham who sat across the table in the police station. Hugo had brought Leo in to hand over Thomas Marston's evidence – damning, true, but evidence was evidence. Jarrett, thankfully, was out at Foxley, so Hugo was joined only by MacLeod. The room was as bare and depressing as such places always were, the busy chatter of the station a distant hum on the other side of the door.

Leo's notes on his conversation with Thomas Marston lay open on the table.

'"Didn't have much to do with him", Mr Ingham,' said MacLeod. 'Those were your exact words.'

'He was a pest,' said Saul. 'No, I didn't have much to do with him.'

'What about the duel you fought with him in Wytham Woods, Mr Ingham? Does that count as "not much to do with him" too?'

Saul began to speak, then bit the words off.

'If you wanted us to believe you, Mr Ingham, you should have told us this on Tuesday.'

'What was I supposed to say? You'd have damned me the moment the words left my mouth.'

'May I take it this account is true?'

'If you mean, did I fight with him, yes I did. He thought his degrees made him better than the likes of me. Supercilious, that's what he was.'

'Did you mean to kill him?'

'Good God, no. Just thrash him in a fair fight. Teach him he was flesh and blood, same as the rest of us. If you think I'd kill a man over something like that, you need your heads examining, both of you.'

'What would you kill a man over?'

'I killed men in the war, Superintendent, and in the Foreign Legion. I've had a bellyful of it, take it from me.'

'You didn't seem to have had a bellyful where the late Lord Selchester was concerned.'

Another mark against Saul's character.

'That man ruined my life' was all he would say.

'Did you see Bruno Rothesay in Selchester over Christmas?'

A pause.

'Yes, I did.'

'Tell us what happened. In full, if you please. You'll find things a lot easier if you tell us the whole truth.'

'Will I, Superintendent? Or have you already made your minds up? Here I am, trying to put my life back together after the last time I was stitched up by the Establishment – wrongly convicted, let me remind you – when you haul me in over a gun I've never seen before, squirrelled away in a place I didn't even live in when all of this must have happened. A place which, I'm told, has been empty since its owner died last year. Your evidence is derisory, yet still I'm here, cooling my heels in a cell while everyone in Selchester calls me a murderer behind my back. Forgive me, Superintendent, if I don't value your assurances very highly.'

'Tell us what happened the last time you met Dr Rothesay.'

'All right. Let's see how you can twist this. Yes, I met him. December the twenty-eighth, it must have been, the last day I was staying in that peculiar Nightingale Cottage. The day I found out about the Gallery. Just after all that fuss up at the Castle – don't forget I had nothing to do with that either. He knocked on my door. I thought it might be Emerson coming back. He's a friend who was staying then. Opened the door, and there Rothesay was. Didn't seem to be expecting me.'

Scene 2

It had been one of those dull wet days of the thaw, slush piled in the streets, everything damp as could be.

'You're early,' Saul had said, the other words dying on his lips. He knew this man, that aquiline face and arrogant mouth, those dark expressive eyes so beloved, it seemed, of every woman in sight. He knew that scar, too. That was his own doing. Rothesay was older now, but of course he was ageing well, merely a touch of silver at the temples. An elegant coat, Italian cut. Naturally.

'Rothesay,' he said, puzzled. 'What on earth are you doing here? I thought you didn't want another word with me.'

Rothesay frowned. 'You? I didn't come to speak to you. Where are the Pearsons?'

There was something about Rothesay's manner which got under Saul's skin every time. He sometimes wondered whether Anastasia had chosen him for that very reason. It wasn't as if she didn't have her pick of men.

'If you mean that peculiar couple who let this place to me, they're back tomorrow. I took it for a week. Clearly they didn't tell you.'

Rothesay looked him up and down. Saul was all too aware he wasn't exactly spick and span. It had been three days since his binge. Emerson was doing his utmost to keep the whisky out of reach, but Saul couldn't pretend he looked his best.

'If they're peculiar,' said Rothesay, 'it's only in their choice of lodgers. Or are you their charitable deed for the season? I see the years have hardly been kind to you.'

'Quite unlike you to come calling when the husband might be at home,' said Saul, regretting the sally at once. He didn't want anything more to do with this man. It had been twenty years since they had last set eyes on one another, and with any luck their paths would never cross again.

'I didn't come here to talk to you. When do you take yourself off?'

Saul made an effort to be polite. He'd got himself in enough trouble already. 'If you're asking when I leave here, I believe the Pearsons return tomorrow. As I said.'

'Thank you. Good day.' Rothesay turned his back and walked off. Saul slammed the door behind him and went to see where Emerson had hidden the whisky.

Scene 3

'That was all the conversation you had with him?' MacLeod asked.

'Yes,' said Saul. 'I left for London the next day.'

'But you came back' – some shuffling of papers – 'on Wednesday of last week, staying at number 3, Fisher Walk, before taking over the lease of the Selchester Gallery on Saturday.'

'I've told you all of this,' said Saul.

'Fisher Walk,' Hugo said. 'Where exactly is that?'

MacLeod answered for him. 'In Long Combe. It's a hamlet, a little way east of town, if you're wondering, Hawksworth. A dozen houses and a church, tucked down in the trees by the river, where the bogs begin. Lovely in summer, I don't doubt, but a touch damp and cold in the winter. Isolated, too.'

Hugo knew where Long Combe was, although he hadn't been there himself. A perfect place to slip a body into the river. 'Why are you staying there, Mr Ingham?'

'There was a place free for a few days, someone's cottage being cleared out.'

'Plenty of inns in town, nice and warm.'

There was a rap on the door. 'Begging your pardon, sir, but there's a call you might want to take, if you catch my drift.'

MacLeod sighed. 'I'll be as quick as I can. If you don't mind, Hawksworth?'

Hugo didn't mind. Quite the opposite, in fact. The door clicked shut, MacLeod and his constables on the other side.

'You're not saying much,' said Saul. 'I'd have expected to see you on my side of the table, all that trouble you were in with the Service when last we met.'

'It was cleared up,' said Hugo.

'Lucky for you.'

'Who knew you were in Selchester?' Hugo asked.

'Plenty of people. I came into town a few times, bought some things, chatted to some people I'd met over Christmas. Everybody seems to know your business before you do, they all knew I wasn't at Nightingale Cottage this time. Good riddance, too. I don't like it. Can't tell you why, maybe it's just that it's too crowded with stuff. You can't move for horseshoes and corn dollies and what have you. Real mishmash. Fisher Walk was half-empty, there was room to breathe.'

'And who knew you were at Fisher Walk?'

'Jim Benbow in the Fitzwarin Arms, I took a pint with him on Thursday. Vivian Witt, never expected to be hobnobbing with her. Mrs Pearson from Nightingale Cottage, bumped into her in the street. There was a walker along the riverbank, I waved to him. That tall girl in the Post Office.'

Hugo knew who he meant. 'Agnes. The biggest gossip in Selchester, so I hear, aside from the girls at the telephone exchange.'

Little joy from that line of inquiry, then. Hugo wondered what MacLeod's call would be about, and how long he might be. Best go for a straightforward approach. Sir Bernard would hit the roof if he ever found out, and so would Jarrett.

'Listen, I'll make this quick. I don't believe you did it, and I don't like the way everything is pointing at you all of a sudden.'

'Can I quote you on that?'

Hugo leaned back, crossed his legs. 'Are there any witnesses to our conversation?'

'Your word against mine. Little doubt which of us would be believed, in the circumstances. But I'm curious. What makes you so sure I didn't?'

'For one thing, I don't believe you're stupid enough to have dealt with the gun in that way.'

Saul scratched his chin. He was growing a stubble, the sort of thing which made a man look like a desperado.

'I'll get you a razor,' Hugo added. 'Safety, I'm afraid.'

'Thank you. And the other thing?'

'Providential help.'

'A tip-off?'

Hugo inclined his head just a fraction.

'The other two are policemen, and tip-offs are normal in police work. You're a spook, and don't trust information unless you know where it comes from and who's giving it to you.'

'Any enemies who might have it in for you?'

'Some. You make them easily in the art world. None I've seen in Selchester. It's hardly their turf.'

'What brought you back?'

'I heard the Gallery might be coming up for rental. Selchester seemed as good a place to settle as any. I suppose I was mistaken. Better to go somewhere no one knows you from Adam.'

There was that bitterness again, deep and ingrained. This was a man who could kill, given the right circumstances. Hugo knew that. MacLeod and Jarrett knew that. Saul himself knew that. All it needed was for Rothesay to have pushed his luck just a little too far, and Saul's fragile self-control would have snapped. As it had almost snapped once before.

Saul caught his silence. 'You're not entirely sure I didn't kill him, are you?'

A clever and perceptive man. You had to be, in that line of work. Used to being overlooked, dismissed. He'd have been an asset to the Service, if not always the easiest to handle. Without close ties or deep roots, capable and adaptable, ruthless when needed.

'I judge you quite capable of killing a man, given sufficient provocation, and Bruno Rothesay equally capable of supplying that provocation.'

'You have the measure of his character, at least. If you want to know who killed Bruno, follow the grudges. Believe me, it wasn't pleasant being on the receiving end of those.'

Heavy steps in the corridor.

'Let's go back to Fisher Walk,' said Hugo, returning to a safe subject. 'How did you find it?'

Scene 4

It had still been cold and damp the day Saul checked out.

'There's the deposit,' said Mrs Pearson, passing him a handful of change. A couple of coins slipped through her fingers. 'How clumsy of me, I'm sorry.'

'Not to worry,' said Saul, bending to retrieve the missing shillings. 'You've left it in good shape. Were you an Army man?'

'Indeed I was.'

'Jeremy said you had that military look. Was it comfortable? I suppose if you're used to barracks anything must be comfortable, but I fear it's rather cluttered.'

It was indeed cluttered with everything imaginable, there had been times he'd longed for bare barracks walls. 'I was grateful for a place to stay for a while, Mrs Pearson. Truth to tell, places in Selchester are hard to come by.'

'I know, there's been a housing shortage after the war, but somehow it's never quite urgent enough to do something about.'

Did he detect a trace of a foreign accent there?

'Do you travel much?' Four shillings and sixpence, there should be another threepence somewhere around there. He rummaged around the base of what seemed like a miniature totem – such an extraordinary collection of things this cottage had.

'Oh, all over, when I can. You can't find folklore by sitting in libraries, that's what I always say. You have to get out into the countryside, find somewhere with memories of the land still. I was sent to school in Austria when I was a little girl, for my health, you see. Years and years I was there, up in the Alps, and mountain people have very good memories. Things don't change up there.'

There it was, wedged in a crack between the flagstones.

'Oh, I'm so glad you found it,' she said.

'Tell me, is there anywhere else for rent nearby? I'm thinking I might come back, but I'd need a place to stay for a few weeks, and I can't really afford a pub for week after week.'

'Let me see now, well, there are some boarding houses up by the railway, but I can't recommend them for peace and quiet, trains rattling by all the time, and all sorts staying there. Oh, wait. You're an Army man, you won't mind roughing it a bit. There's a cottage empty down by the river. Something to do with a disappearance or a disputed will, I think.'

'There seem to be a lot of those here,' said Saul, thinking of the Gallery. Emerson had found it, nosing around after art like a bear after honey. Coming up for rent, he'd said. You want to go back into the business, why not make an offer?

'Isn't that always the way here? No, you should try it. I believe there's a local solicitor looking after it at the moment, a Mr Fortescue. You should ask around. It's a good place to be. We've found such interesting things here, with the Downs and the barrows not far. Quite remarkable what stories people come up with.'

Saul shouldered his bag, almost knocking an African mask off the wall. Clammy air seeped into the hallway.

'Don't worry. They didn't build these cottages for a crowd.'

Saul paused on the doorstep, the sight of the damp Selchester street jogging his memory. 'Oh, I forgot to say, someone called for you yesterday. Bruno Rothesay.'

'He must have been here for Jeremy, forgot we were away, and Jeremy won't even be back until next week. Most kind of you to let me know.'

'Thank you, Mrs Pearson, and thank you for the use of your cottage.'

'It was a pleasure, Mr Ingham. Have a good trip!'

Saul splashed off in the direction of the station.

Scene 5

'Did you search the cottage, back in September?' Hugo asked MacLeod, once Saul had been returned to his cell.

The cottage's previous owner had found himself in very deep water at the time of his death, in more ways than one. Hugo had been involved in the affair itself, but he'd had other things to worry about in the aftermath.

'Your people did. Sent a unit from London, turned it inside out. Nothing there at the time, so the gun can't have been a leftover, if that's what you're wondering. As to the particulars, we can confirm Ingham's story with Mrs Pearson.'

'She's in London at the moment,' said Hugo, remembering his encounter on the station platform.

'She'll be back soon enough, no particular hurry there. We've got some of our men going door to door in Long Combe to see whether there are any witnesses, but I'm satisfied with the way things are going at the moment.'

'Even with an anonymous tip-off?'

'In police work we take what we can get. Not like your world, where everything could be some game run by Moscow spymasters. In my experience of the sort of criminals we get here in Selchester, most of them would last about five minutes in the London underworld, let alone the sort of things you deal with. You can see their lies coming half a mile away. There hasn't been a single thing we've found out about Mr Ingham which doesn't fit, and if that's pure coincidence, I'll hand in my police badge right away.'

Scene 6

'Going out again, Miss Wryton?' said Mrs Partridge, as Freya came into the kitchen, booted and coated against the elements. 'It's cleared up out there, it has. There'll be a frost tonight, I hear.'

'Some things to do in town,' Freya said.

'More books to be buying? Or this business that's taken Messrs Hawksworth off? Quite the to-do, all that, and the Gallery just taken again. I'd have liked to see some pictures there myself, you never know what'll be in the window from one week to the next.'

Freya decided to be direct, since Mrs Partridge had settled for dark allusions all week. 'What's going on up at Foxley?'

'How should I know? That's Mr Hawksworth's job, debriefing all those boffins.'

'They aren't monks, you said.'

'Oh, that.' Mrs Partridge bustled along the side, collecting chopping board and knife. 'Well, that fellow who wound up with a bullet in his head, God have mercy on his soul, he had quite the eye for the ladies.'

'Even here in Selchester? Half the town would know.'

'Half the town did know,' said Mrs Partridge sternly. 'Even if you didn't, sitting up there with your typewriter and your books.'

'Do tell. It might help Hugo, he's having a time of it with this Jarrett fellow.'

Mrs Partridge looked as if she'd been boiling up toads to put a hex on Jarrett. Freya rather wished she would.

'Well,' she said. 'I don't like to say, rightly, as some of them are married women, and it wouldn't do to have dirty linen washed in public.'

'He won't be after dirty linen. They'll want it kept as quiet as possible, no inconvenient publicity.'

'I dare say they shall. Shameful. And under a Conservative government. I expect nothing better from those Socialists, but if you can't trust a gentleman like Mr Churchill, who can you trust?'

'Let me help you with those carrots,' Freya said, seeing Mrs Partridge start on a vast pile of vegetables.

'Let you go and do the things you're supposed to do,' Mrs Partridge said, batting her away. 'Like writing that book of yours, for one, instead of getting yourself caught up in all these murky dealings. You won't have any joy from it, I can tell you that for sure.'

'You didn't give me any names.'

'Well now, let me think back. There was Emma Hardcastle, her husband's a waste of space if ever there was one. Then there was some young scientist he found in London, brought down here once or twice when the missus was away. Quite something, she was, great dark eyes and hair like Sophia Loren. Then there was that woman from Nightingale Cottage.'

'Miranda Pearson? The folklorist?'

Mrs Partridge shook her head, as if lamenting the depravity of the world. 'On and off for months, they were. 'Tisn't right and natural for a woman to go tramping about the countryside like some vagrant, if you ask me, and that husband of hers is a right glum one. Don't say as I'm excusing it, mind you. Marriage vows is marriage vows, whatever some folk say these days. My Roy wasn't much to look at, and to tell the truth he wasn't much in other ways neither, but did you catch me putting myself about? No, you certainly did not. If some Jerry hadn't come along at the wrong moment, you'd not catch us having separate bedrooms like that Nightingale couple, never mind that my Roy snored like a thunderstorm.'

This was more than Mrs Partridge had ever said at once about her Roy, who'd joined the RAF when war broke out and been shot down over Germany.

'Don't tell me he used to go round when her husband was there,' Freya said.

'Oh, no, there's no true man alive would stand for such wickedness, glum or not. They had their little ways, not hard with that wife of Dr Rothesay's up in London so much. Not that they fooled anyone around here.'

'Was there anyone else, anyone he tried to hide?'

'Hide? His like don't hide, what's the need? They're not the ones who pay the price, now are they?' She gave a carrot a particularly violent blow, sending the end flying off on to the flagstones. Freya returned it to the pile of peelings. 'I hear as that Mrs Pearson thinks marriage vows are for other people. He wasn't the only man she's been seen with, nor even the only boffin. Can't think what she sees in them, myself. And that Emma Hardcastle, never had any sense, moped around for weeks when he'd tired of her. Empty-headed as they come, she is. Thought all she needed was a nice rich husband with a nice big house, never mind he's dull as ditchwater, and now she wonders why she's miserable. It won't end well, I tell you.'

Hooves clattered in the courtyard, and Ben's voice called out a greeting.

'Oh, that'll be Francis with Pompey,' said Freya. 'I'd better attend in case Last Hurrah decides to make a scene. Can't have him taking chunks out of Lady Priscilla's finest.'

The door closed behind her.

'Can't have you putting in the hours at the typewriter, either,' Mrs Partridge said to no one in particular. 'If it's not detective novels, it's playing detective.'

'What was that?' said Pam, coming through with an armful of laundry for ironing.

'Just me talking to myself,' said Mrs Partridge. 'Now, mind you pay proper attention to those shirts of his lordship's. He may prefer things the American way, but he's got standards to maintain now, whether he likes it or not.'

Scene 7

Back at the Hall, Hugo returned to Bruno's file, where he'd started. Follow the grudges, Saul had said. Bruno had plenty of those. *A vigorous participant in scientific debate*, his personnel assessment said. *Intolerant of sloppy thinking and half-baked ideas, often jeopardises relationships with colleagues by vehement dismissal of their proposals.* Well, he'd seen what that looked like in the interviews at the Atomic.

Scientific mind widely respected, yes. It seemed a great deal could be forgiven for someone who came up with solutions to so many problems. Rothesay didn't like to dwell on them, though. *Impatient to move on to the next stage once theoretical problems solved to his satisfaction*, another colleague had said. *Short-tempered with those who can't keep up.*

All of a piece. Noticeable how much more vivid it seemed now he'd been turning Rothesay's life inside out for a week. He could see the academic Dr Rothesay much more clearly. The file was full of suppressed resentments, gripes, and the reluctant acknowledgement of a first-class mind. Some vicious academic disputes, but nothing to shoot a man in the back of the head for. Numerous affairs, not unusual. No trace of homosexuality, gambling habits, academic plagiarism, anything the Soviets could have used to gain a hold on him.

Hugo turned to the last page, the material most recently added. He hadn't done the background check on Rothesay, since everyone transferred to Foxley from one of the other establishments had already been cleared.

The only serious black mark on Rothesay's file was his involvement in that accident up at Ulfsgill. The accident Árpád had heard about, far away in Siberia.

It is considered that, while a first-rate theoretician, Dr Rothesay is perhaps not suited for direct contact with radioactive material . . . His natural impatience is an impediment to working in such an environment from day to day . . . Recommend transfer to a theoretical facility along with his immediate colleagues.

He went in search of Harriet Godwin, found her at her filing cabinet with a stack of files in hand.

'You again?' she said. 'People will talk. And I'm meant to be in with Árpád. He's reading some peculiar avant-garde quarterly of Woolhope's, makes about as much sense as the Rosetta Stone.'

'He can wait. That accident at Ulfsgill,' he said, without preamble. 'There must be an official report.'

'Indeed there is. Heavily classified, I might add.'

'I need to see it.'

'No way, José. That's shoot-yourself-after-reading stuff.'

He leaned against the table, wincing slightly. 'I'd have thought it was a little late for that.'

'Nothing like locking the stable door after the horse has bolted, now is there?'

'Have you read it?'

'Yes. In London, in a secure reading room. I think Woolhope has seen it, too.'

'So give me the gist. I'm supposed to be finding the mole who leaked it.'

'Special Branch are doing that.'

'Yes, they are. Haring off after someone who has nothing to do with it.'

She put the papers down on top of the cabinet. 'What do you need do know?'

'What the report said. What Rothesay did, to be simultaneously blamed, exonerated, and transferred somewhere else to do exactly the same job.'

'The report,' said Harriet, 'is a masterpiece.'

'Of what?'

'Whitehall politics. Oh, the first half lays out the details of the accident very clearly, what happened, who was involved, what the consequences are for our reactor programmes.'

'Can you tell me?'

She sighed, thought for a moment. 'There was some sloppy work. A lot of cutting corners. Experimental improvisation, one might say. The reactors at Ulfsgill are producing contaminated plutonium, no, that doesn't mean it'll make us all glow in the dark, only that it might fizzle rather than go off with a bang.'

Hugo said, 'You mean there's too much plutonium-240.'

She grinned. 'You did your homework, I see. Most of the Service doesn't know an isotope from an isobar. In any case, Rothesay came up with a possible solution, rather ingenious, and they were conducting a small-scale test of his ideas. Reading between the lines, it was rather *sub rosa*, or as *sub rosa* as you can get in an atomic research lab. Jerry-built or borrowed equipment, and no real official sanction. They were trying to gauge the purity of plutonium ingots with the scientific equivalent of an abacus and some bits of string. Two ingots came into contact when they weren't meant to, irradiating a lab and an operator, who subsequently died.'

'I need the name of the dead man, and his next of kin.'

'You can get that for yourself. His name was Adam Sørensen, and his security file is in the archives here. Officially, he died of a pre-existing condition, the radiation merely amplified it.'

'So what did the other half of the report say?'

'It laid out, in great detail, how the organisational structure at Ulfsgill was getting in the way of progress, how the theoreticians shouldn't be stuck out in Westmorland where they could get themselves into mischief, and how the people working on fuel problems and reactor design needed to be pulled together into one high-powered department, somewhere closer to London and the universities.'

'Rothesay?'

'Should have gone through official channels on this project, distinctly slapdash where safety procedures were concerned, has the engineering expertise of a cabbage – that's not what it actually says – but is far too valuable a theoretician to be affected by this. Deserves a senior research post in this new organisation, where his talents can be put to good use.'

'And his idea?'

'Hedged around with so many *should*'s and *may*'s and *deserves further careful scrutiny*'s that no one will touch it ever again. Sørensen, I should add, gets the chief blame, for carelessness.'

Hugo drummed his fingers on Harriet's desk.

'I'll have a cigarette, since you're keeping me waiting,' said Harriet. 'You?'

He nodded absently. Harriet rattled around in the desk for her lighter.

'So the official story,' he said eventually, 'is that someone died, and it's no one's fault.'

'Accidents happen,' she said, 'particularly when you play with radiation.'

'And who wrote this masterpiece of bureaucratic doublespeak, or can I guess?'

'You can guess.'

'Laurence Oldcastle.'

'Spot on.'

Hugo had read Oldcastle's file nearly as many times as Rothesay's. 'Who went from running this wing-and-a-prayer department at Ulfsgill to Head of Division at Foxley. On the basis of his own report.'

'I believe,' said Harriet, 'that once the relevant committee had established that Oldcastle's course of action ought to be followed, it was unanimous in recommending that he be appointed to head this new division.'

'And he brought the team with him.'

'You have to admire the man. There's a certain kind of genius to it.'

Hugo held up a hand. 'So in this report, Oldcastle just about acknowledges that Rothesay's impatience caused the accident, but then does his level best to absolve him of any actual blame.'

'And succeeds. I'd say Rothesay was Oldcastle's man if ever there was one.'

'I wouldn't have said they were that friendly.'

'They needn't have been. Oldcastle may be as political as they come, but he knows his own scientific limitations. Trust me, I spent enough time with him.' She took a drag of the cigarette. 'They go right back to Los Alamos together. It was a partnership, of sorts. Rothesay was Oldcastle's ticket to chairmanships and honours.'

'While Oldcastle was Rothesay's protector, the one who smoothed over all his little peccadilloes and got him out of trouble. Ensured he could keep producing results.'

'Full-time job, if you ask me.'

'So who, aside from the immediate team, knew what had happened at Ulfsgill?'

'Special Branch looked into that. There were rumours among the researchers and in the academic community, but someone took care to circulate the "existing condition" story. It was well handled, no scandal to ruffle anyone's feathers.'

'Oldcastle again?'

'Not entirely, but I imagine his superiors in London consulted him extensively.'

'So it was all tied up terribly neatly, until Árpád turns up, fresh from whatever research gulag Joe Stalin sent him to, and innocently discloses that the Russians know all about Rothesay's blind alley. At which point the report is classified to kingdom come, lest the stable cat follow the horse out of the door, and the powers that be launch a sleeper hunt. May I have a word with Árpád?'

'Since he's staying in your country pile, you hardly need to ask.'

'Fewer curious ears here.'

'The servants get uppity and listen in, do they? Can't have that sort of thing. Come on, then, he's in Interview Room 3. You can tell me what you need to ask, and I'll think of a way to present it so he doesn't catch on.'

Scene 8

Árpád was still poring over the first page of the quarterly when Harriet returned, this time with Hugo. 'Ah, it is you,' he said. 'I wondered whether perhaps I was only allowed to speak to you in the Castle, some arcane rule of your Service.'

'No, Hawksworth is far too grand to spend much time with the likes of us,' said Harriet.

'Thank you,' said Hugo testily.

'My pleasure.'

'This magazine of Mr Woolhope's,' said Árpád, 'it is perhaps a code?'

'It's certainly a mystery,' said Hugo, 'but the mystery is whether Woolhope actually reads this stuff or just wants to make the rest of us think he does.'

'Makes Roger Bailey very suspicious,' said Harriet. 'He thinks anyone who's into this kind of literature must be a pinko.'

'Pinko? Ah, yes, a Communist. I tell you, anyone who wrote like this in Hungary, they would be in great trouble with the Party.'

'They'll be in great trouble with their bank managers,' said Harriet, ever practical. 'I can't imagine this sort of thing pays for itself.'

'Woolhope will be crushed,' said Hugo.

'He'll find another way to wind us all up. Now, Árpád, Hugo would like to ask you some questions about the personnel at Camp 39.'

Árpád put the magazine aside and sat up straight. 'I am all ears, is that how you say?'

'It is indeed,' said Hugo, pulling out a notebook and sitting down. 'Now, who was your immediate superior?'

He spent the better part of half an hour interrogating Árpád about things he had absolutely no interest in – although perhaps someone in the Service might find it valuable, further down the line. At last Árpád gave him the opening he needed, courtesy of Harriet's flash briefing on the way over.

'You said Domentzov had found favour, even though he was supposedly another political prisoner,' Hugo said. 'How did you know?'

'Well, there were little indications at first,' said Árpád. 'We noticed he was getting letters from home, this is a privilege. Of course they were read, but they were the words of his family, this made him happy.

Naturally, the MGB would not allow this unless he were doing something for them.'

'Keeping an eye on the rest of you.'

'Domentzov is not a bad man, you understand,' said Árpád. 'He is a patriot, in that Russian way where one can be a patriot even for a country which destroys one's life. But also, he went out of his way to look after the rest of us, and when he spoke up for a man in trouble, the trouble stopped.'

Hugo nodded.

'But then Moisevich had an idea, something he wanted to try. You see, we were not an important institute, because we were all recruited from the gulag. They gave us the dirty work, the things with no glamour and not much importance. Problems with reactors, for instance, particularly the isotopic composition of our plutonium, which is very dirty. You see . . .'

'Hugo is a layman,' said Harriet, well aware that Hugo wasn't interested in the physics.

'Of course. It was a matter of purifying the fuel, shall we say. Not my line of work, but I was in the meetings where it was discussed. Every week, as I said. Now, one week Moisevich has had his idea. He lays it out. Domentzov is interested, very interested. He knows Moisevich is a clever man, a meticulous man, also a cautious one. He would not propose this unless he were sure.'

'Go on.'

'So, we were all excited. We talk it through with Moisevich, we make some changes. The next week, at the same meeting, we present these to Domentzov again. But now Domentzov pours cold water on it, which is an essential thing when you're dealing with reactors.'

Harriet grinned. Hugo looked nonplussed.

'Reactors need cold water, and lots of it,' said Harriet. 'To keep the temperature down. That's why all our hands-on stuff happens up where it's wet and miserable.'

'Also for the Soviets,' said Árpád.

'What did Domentzov say?' Hugo asked. 'As clearly as you remember it.'

Árpád remembered it very well, because those meetings were always warm. They were held in Domentzov's office, which had recently had a better radiator installed – another sign of favour – and which was also too small for the purpose. With ten or eleven men packed around the desk, it was soon toasty.

'He said that a very good British scientist at Foxley had come to grief over this, a man had died,' Árpád said, 'and that the theory was not sound. It was an interesting idea, but we should concentrate on concrete plans which would produce reliable results in accordance with the targets.'

Árpád held a finger up. 'This was what he said to us. At the end of the meeting, though, he called Moisevich back. This, you understand, this was the important bit – how we knew Domentzov had friends. And this was good for us, too, because to know someone who has friends is a little bit safer.'

'Do you remember the date?'

'Yes, it was February of last year. The twenty-first or so, I'd say.'

Two weeks before Stalin died, then. A truly grim time behind the Iron Curtain.

'Do you know what Domentzov said to Moisevich?'

'Not then. Moisevich, of course, was Jewish. This was a bad time to be a Jew in the Soviet Union, there was talk of a purge. Perhaps a huge one. We had TASS and *Pravda*; we knew something was coming. A few weeks later, with Stalin gone, things were different, and that was when Moisevich told me. Domentzov said the idea was very good. He had looked through it carefully. But when the British did it, they were in a hurry, and there was an accident. The man who had the idea was blamed, this is how also it would be in the Soviet Union. Domentzov said that it would not be good for Moisevich, in the current climate, if he were to propose something risky. He would be seen as a wrecker, quite possibly shot. And so would the men who worked for him, because, you see, to make such a thing happen, Moisevich would need a group of his own, to work for him only.'

'So Domentzov's handlers were trusting him with quite detailed intelligence,' Hugo said.

Árpád shrugged. 'Who was he to tell, in the middle of Siberia?'

'Was Domentzov still in the camp when you were released?'

'He was the first to be let go. He told us that we had been rehabilitated, that the new leadership felt there were better uses for our talents. We would be given jobs elsewhere. He was transferred to an institute not far from Moscow. He said he would try to get jobs for us also.'

Just like Oldcastle, Hugo thought, taking his team with him, pulling strings for their benefit. Just as a Roman senator gave positions to his clients, in fact. Some things never changed, no matter how you dressed them up.

He followed Domentzov's story to its end, asked a few questions about the more obvious MGB minder at the camp, and then excused himself again.

'Of course,' said Árpád. 'I will return to this strange code of Mr Woolhope's.'

Hugo and Harriet walked back to her room in silence.

'Is that what the official record says?' Hugo asked.

'More or less.'

'On which basis, London launched a hunt for a traitor who'd been both at Ulfsgill and at Foxley. In other words, one of Oldcastle's team.'

'Exactly.'

'They thought, just as Árpád thinks, that Domentzov was simply protecting Moisevich.'

'He was. There's no room for manoeuvre there. Somewhere else in the files, it turns out Domentzov didn't even mention Moisevich's name when he aired the plan with his MGB minders.'

'Oh, he was doing the decent thing all right,' said Hugo, mind racing. 'But he was telling us something else, too.'

'You're enjoying this too much,' said Harriet. 'Out with it.'

'As far as Domentzov's source was concerned, the accident wasn't Rothesay's fault.'

Scene 9

'Hmmm,' said Sir Bernard. 'This is rather an inventive interpretation, isn't it?'

He'd called the people working on Foxley material in for a brief and, as far as Hugo was concerned, quite unnecessary meeting. It seemed he had hopes of getting Jarrett out of his hair by the end of the week.

Hugo, for his part, could have done with more time to prepare. There was an art to finessing Sir Bernard, and it involved dropping careful hints in the right ears before you took your case to him. Unless it was likely to upset London, he would always go with whatever seemed to be the consensus.

There were four of them and Sir Bernard, chairs arranged in a semicircle around his big desk.

'I don't think so,' said Peter Woolhope, leaning back in his chair and stretching his legs out. 'I was the one you sent up to read the report, if you remember, and it's a rum thing.'

'Dr Oldcastle is an extremely capable administrator,' said Sir Bernard, who'd clearly been won over.

Woolhope had his own views on capable administrators. 'Absolutely. It takes a first-class mind to come up with such contortions of logic. Some chap Oldcastle valued made a balls-up, so he found a way to blame it on Rothesay, who just happened to be too important to fire. Mind you, if that were me, I'd be narked as all hell.'

Roger Bailey frowned. 'If Rothesay was aggrieved, and believed himself innocent, doesn't that suggest he was the mole? The details fit, and so does the motivation.'

Sir Bernard brightened. This was exactly what he wanted to hear.

'The true story might be common knowledge among Oldcastle's people,' Harriet pointed out. 'We don't know because no one asked them.'

'So what are you after, Hawksworth?' said Sir Bernard.

'I'd like to go back to Foxley and do a few more interviews. It's a logical extension of the background work I've been doing.'

'You were looking for someone with military training. I'd say you did a splendid job pointing us to Saul Ingham.'

'Which may well solve the murder. But London won't be happy until someone pins down the source of the leak. If it was Rothesay, that's two birds with one stone. If it isn't, we need to find them.'

Sir Bernard looked around the table for guidance. Harriet and Peter were in agreement. Roger looked dubious.

'Very well, then,' said Sir Bernard. He waved a finger in Hugo's direction. 'Be quick about it. Remember what I told you on Saturday.'

Which translated to, *Don't give Jarrett a reason to stay any longer than absolutely necessary.*

Scene 10

The receptionist at Foxley was surprised to see Hugo. 'Didn't expect to see you here again, Mr Hawksworth. We thought it was all the Special Branch lot.'

'Just come to do some spadework,' Hugo said. 'Who's in with Inspector Jarrett at the moment?'

'He's taking a break with His Nibs. The Brigadier won't have interviews going on too long, says it wears his people out.'

So Caundle was still sitting on his scientists like a hen on her eggs. 'I shan't interrupt them. Who's up next, then? I shall take someone else first, so as not to get in their way.'

'They're talking to the two technicians this afternoon. They were in with Dr Wood this morning.'

'He's back?'

'Yesterday. Dr Oldcastle got him another military flight, he's been to all sorts of places on the way. Very tanned he looks, too. I'd have liked a few weeks in the sun myself, although it's hard for him to have lost his pa.'

'I'll start with him, if he doesn't mind. Where will I find him?'

'Same room as the others you were talking to, through that corridor and third on the right. I suppose you'll want somewhere private. Try the meeting room, that's two further on. Just pull the blinds down, you'll have all the quiet you need.'

James Wood was a cheerful, open man about Hugo's age with a deep tan and a ready smile. Hugo liked him at once. He might still be the mole – he'd come from Ulfsgill too – but there was no question of involvement in Rothesay's death. He'd been stuck in Singapore while his RAF transport underwent some minor repairs, everything vouched for.

'I'm sorry about your father,' Hugo said, by way of courtesy, as they settled themselves on deeply uncomfortable chairs in the meeting room. He flicked the blinds closed. Better not to have anyone looking through those.

'He had a good innings,' said Wood. 'Said so himself. Liked his cricket. Glad I got there to say goodbye.'

Hugo hadn't been granted that grace. He'd heard about his father's death in the Western Desert, the CO calling him into his tent one night to break the news that the ageing destroyer HMS *Alcyone* had been sunk by a U-boat in the North Atlantic. All hands lost, including her skipper, Commander Charles Hawksworth RNR, veteran of Jutland and the convoy battles of 1917.

'Lucky you,' said Hugo.

Wood gave him a sympathetic look. 'The war?'

'He was in the Navy.'

'Only right and proper. You too?'

Hugo had never felt the call of the sea, to his father's great bafflement. 'No. A life on the ocean wave wasn't for me. Army, Intelligence Corps.' True, after a fashion, except he'd only ever been on secondment from the Service.

'And now you're Special Branch?'

'Thorn Hall.'

'Ah, the hush-hush place. I was only ever for the Navy myself. Grew up right on the coast. Mountains for climbing on one side, sea for sailing on the other. Best place on earth.' Years in England hadn't taken the edge off his New Zealand twang.

'You're a long way from home.'

'There's no physics to be done at home. Not enough of us. I grew up reading about Rutherford splitting the atom, finding things no one ever dreamed of. Knew that was the life for me, even if it meant coming to grey old England.'

'And the greyest corner of it, so I see.'

'That was quite a shock. It gets wet and cold down in the South Island, but nothing like Manchester.'

'Why did you pick Manchester?'

'Rutherford had been there and it was still a strong department. It was that or Cambridge, and there's nothing to climb around Cambridge. Flat as a pancake, Pa told me. So it was Manchester for me. Peak District one way and the Lakes the other. Couldn't have been happier. I didn't even mind Ulfsgill the way some of the others did. Fells right on the doorstep, you see.'

'It's Ulfsgill I wanted to talk about, actually.'

'Fire away.'

If this man were a Soviet spy, he was the unlikeliest spy Hugo had ever met.

'Tell me about the accident.'

Wood shook his head. 'If you mean the one that killed Sørensen, it was a bad business all round. He was a good guy. Didn't say much, I guess they're not great talkers up in Scandinavia, but we went out walking together a few times. Get a couple of beers in him and he'd thaw out a bit.'

'What happened?'

'How up are you on the science?'

'Strictly a layman. I've read enough to have an idea what you were up to, dealing with contaminated plutonium.'

Wood folded his arms. 'It's a real bore for the weapons guys. Me, I'm more interested in nuclear energy. Strictly the reactor side. Don't care much for the Bombs, to tell you the truth, terrible things they are. But my supervisor said if I wanted to work on nuclear energy, there was nowhere better. So I went. Before you can build a Bomb, you need the fuel. For the fuel, you need a reactor, so you need reactor specialists. If we're going to get the world running on nuclear power instead of coal one day – and let me tell you, after living in Manchester, that'll make a big difference to a great many people – the training ground will be these weapons programmes.'

Hugo said, 'Which the Government pretends are all about nuclear energy.'

'Fair enough, I suppose. You see, reactors are easier than Bombs. You can get away with using much dirtier plutonium in the reactor fuel – that's the contaminated sort, by the way.'

'What's the difference?'

'Contaminated plutonium is less likely to go bang when you want it to. Not good in weapons, not good at all. Does that make sense of it?'

'So you were trying to refine the plutonium.'

'We were looking at ways to sort the gold from the dross, as it were. The Americans solved all of this already, but they won't share, so we're working it out for ourselves. Rothesay came up with an idea. I won't go into the details, but it would have speeded up the whole refining cycle. We'd have better plutonium, and faster. Bear in mind this has all been done on a shoestring, and in quite a hurry.'

Hugo was quite familiar with that way of operating. 'Was it a good idea?' he asked. 'Scientifically, I mean. Were there flaws in it?'

'Well . . . no. There weren't. It was sound.'

'So what went wrong?'

'Plutonium-240, that's the contaminant, it's tricksy stuff. Sprays out neutrons all the time, not just when you want them. Plutonium-239 is much more disciplined, you can make it do what you want. Too much 240 in a Bomb, and it could go off just fine, or it could be a squib. Makes the whole thing less dependable.'

'Not ideal.'

'Absolutely. Anyway, Rothesay came up with a very simple set of procedures to separate the types of plutonium. Relied on the different density of the allotropes – no, don't ask, we'd be here for an hour. He came up with a way to use the fizzling to our advantage, and we could do it with a very primitive experimental setup. Trouble was, there were too many things to go wrong. If something happened, you needed a safety mechanism to separate the plutonium ingots. In this case, the scram – that's the safety shutdown mechanism – was just a few wires and a pulley, to lift one ingot off the other. The day Sørensen tried to use it, it failed. He had to pull two ingots apart with his bare hands before they went critical, but that was the end of him. Nasty way to go, a radiation overdose. Takes a couple of weeks.'

'The safety mechanism, that was Rothesay's idea?'

For the first time, Wood looked distinctly uncomfortable. 'If you want the short answer,' he said, 'no, it wasn't. It was all done too quickly. Rothesay thought it could speed the whole process up. It would have been a real coup for all of us reactor types. But Rothesay was a theoretician. You wouldn't put him in charge of supply if he were the last man on Earth. We didn't even let him near the plutonium without supervision, although in fact he was in the room the day the accident happened.'

'Who was in charge of supply?'

'Look, I don't like to get a friend into trouble . . .'

'This isn't about reopening the inquiry into the accident. You have my word on that. I'm looking into Dr Rothesay's history. In the official record, he's to blame for Dr Sørensen's death. If there's a discrepancy there, it may be critical to finding out why he was killed. I also think he deserves better than to be saddled with responsibility for a death he didn't cause.'

'Very well,' said Wood reluctantly. 'Back then, supply was Dr Vane's province. He was Head of Section, the boss's right-hand man.'

Hugo might have known. He'd have to come at Vane from an unexpected direction. 'Before I talk to him, take me through the incident in a little more detail. Were you there at the time?'

'Yes, I was,' said Wood.

Scene 11

Gus had driven Vivian up to the Castle to take a look at the ballroom. Dust-shrouded, chill from years of neglect, it was like a place frozen in time. A relic of the age before the war, when such places were full of grace and elegance.

'There's enough room, I hope,' he said. 'I should like to see it used again, though I can't imagine I shall be holding many balls.'

'It's perfect,' said Vivian at once, pacing out the width. It was, aside from her ugly memories of the main part of the Castle.

'I've asked Ben to test the heating, he's working on that today. Freya says she'll organise the girls into a work party, take the dust sheets off and clear away some of the cobwebs.'

Fourteen, fifteen, sixteen, seventeen paces wide. It wasn't too far off the space they'd have in the Cathedral.

'I'll get some chairs brought up,' said Vivian. 'You don't want all and sundry sitting on these. Louis Quinze, lovely. I didn't know there was any of the Castle like this.'

'Only the ballroom,' said Gus. 'There was an orangery, too, but one of my Victorian ancestors knocked it down to build the Paxton hothouse.'

She walked over to the harpsichord, pulled the cover back. 'Gosh, I've never seen one like this. London music schools would give their eye teeth to get their hands on it. Does anyone play?'

'I'm told Hugo did when he was younger, but he won't touch it now. Doesn't like to talk about it.'

'Too many secrets, that man has. I suppose it's a good quality if you're going to be in the Service.' She walked over to the end of the room, where there was a small door set into the panelling. 'Where does this go?'

'Servants' passages.' Gus opened it, a dark musty smell came out. 'They're shut off, too much for Mrs Partridge to look after.'

'I should say so. Lots of dust, not good for anyone's lungs. I shan't try to press it into service as the Compton Chapel, then. One of the chantries in the Cathedral, we'll be using it for entrances and exits.'

Gus shut the door.

'However do you look after all this?' Vivian asked.

'I've been gently encouraged to hire more people. Ben does his best, but he's been looking after it single-handed for seven years. There's quite a backlog, and I haven't even been taken round some of the attics. It's a warren up there.'

'Sooner you than me. But then,' she said shrewdly, 'you're in even further over your head than I would be.'

Scene 12

Dr Edward Vane was, if possible, even more disagreeably suspicious than the last time Hugo had spoken to him. 'I've been interviewed twice,' he said. 'I don't have anything further to add about Dr Rothesay's disappearance or his conduct in the last few days.'

'I'm here in connection with a loose thread,' Hugo said. 'The security breach we were investigating.'

'Yes?'

'I've been apprised of your various responsibilities here, but at Ulfsgill your group was working directly on reactor construction. I need to know who was responsible for what.'

Vane began turning a pen round in his fingers. 'If you're flogging that dead horse of who knew what and when, you can forget it. We work as a team here, as you and the Inspector have been told more than once.'

'You may indeed work as a team,' said Hugo, 'but you each have your areas of responsibility, and material to which you had the most regular access. For example, Dr Rothesay was a theoretician. You presumably didn't look at his research notes on a daily basis.'

'We would occasionally ask him to take us through his reasoning.'

'But that would be his material.'

'If someone had wanted to riffle through Rothesay's notes when he wasn't looking, they would have found an opportunity, but there would have been no point. When he had something ready to show us, he would show us. Until then, anyone looking at his work would have found no more than scrawled notes on the paper. He was not a systematic thinker.'

'What else was he responsible for?'

'Very little. I considered him too unreliable to entrust with further responsibility, and Dr Oldcastle agreed. We gave him some minor administrative tasks, of the sort entrusted to every member of the team. They were done, although not with notable efficiency or alacrity.'

Hugo ran him through the other members of the team, touching on the accident once or twice, but never delving too deeply. Sørensen's speciality had been almost as theoretical as Rothesay's, but it seemed that on that particular project he'd been employed as a jack-of-all-trades, filling in wherever needed.

'Was he a good experimentalist?'

'I should say he was competent. Considerably more so than Rothesay.'

'If he was merely competent, why was he in direct charge of radio-active materials?'

Vane frowned. 'As a consequence of pursuing Rothesay's hare-brained scheme, we were attempting to do more work than we had people for. Some technicians were borrowed from another department, but they were spread thin. Other personnel were pressed into any service for which they had the necessary basic training.'

Again, that touch of Soviet planning-speak. It didn't make Vane a traitor, of course, merely a bore to work with.

'Did you make those assignments?'

'I did. I was given day-to-day oversight of the project, despite my opposition. My responsibility was to match our resources to the demands being made on them.'

'It doesn't sound as if you wanted the project to go ahead.'

Vane pursed his lips. 'I didn't speak in favour of it. I considered it quite beyond our capacity, and planned on an excessively optimistic timescale.'

'What should have happened to Rothesay's idea?'

'It should have been rigorously critiqued by other theoreticians, and then entrusted to a properly equipped engineering division supplied with adequate materials and a more generous timetable.'

'It was flawed from the start, then.'

'Indeed, as I believe the report made clear.'

'So who,' Hugo said quietly, 'signed off on it?'

'It was authorised by the people in charge of the whole Bomb project.'

'Who took the idea to them? Was it Rothesay? You? You were in charge.'

'It most certainly was not me. I would never have countenanced such a thing. Nor . . .' Vane tailed off, briefly lost for words. Too late. Hugo was one step ahead of him.

'It was Dr Oldcastle, wasn't it?'

Scene 13

Árpád was lost.

It was one thing to ride. That he could do, even though he wasn't used to the muddy English ground. To find his way was quite another.

Ben had given him directions. Across the lower meadow to find a track, that he had done. Follow the path, he'd had no problem with that. There was a fork, take the right, go down across the main road. Pompey, it seemed, regarded all cars as the enemy. Árpád had nearly been thrown when one hove into sight on the road.

The trouble had arisen on the far side of the road, where he came to something called a spinney. A clump of trees, Ben had said, but there were three clumps of trees. Paths went through, around, and to judge by the number of rabbit holes, beneath them.

The track had been sunk so deeply he couldn't see out of it, over-hung with gaunt bare trees half-drowning in ivy. Now he was out of the track, in a shallow valley between bare hills, but he could see neither the Castle nor the town.

Pompey whickered impatiently, his breath steaming in the chill air. There was something called a gallop to be found, Ben had said, on Castle land, where he could give Pompey a good run. Look for the white fences. But there were no white fences. This was a small land-scape, compared to the plains of his childhood, which stretched away in the summer haze. Its hills and valleys were mere dimples compared to the great soaring peaks of the Carpathians, where he had wandered with his sister in the meadows. Even the woods were pocket-sized. Yet somehow it contrived to be a place of infinite variety and confusion. So many little paths!

He heard footsteps, crunching on the frozen mud, a man coming down one of the paths. A farmer, perhaps, but no, it was a man with the look of town or city about him, in stout boots with a rucksack on his back. About fifty, grizzled, with eyes that had seen too much.

'Excuse me,' said Árpád, 'I am trying to find the gallops. Could you tell me where I should go?'

'You want the path I've just come down,' said the walker. 'Keep straight on, all the way up. You'll cross the gallops where the trees end. Fifteen minutes for me, less for you.'

'Thank you very much,' said Árpád. 'I was told to look for a spin-ney, this is a clump of trees, only it seemed there were three, and I could not tell which was meant.'

'All of them, actually. Hayward's Spinney, it's called. Used to be one big copse, but most of the trees were cut down in the war.'

'Ah. This I understand. So then I should have gone around to the right, at the edge of the field where there was no path, not ahead where there was a path.'

'The bridleway runs around the edge of the field, by the fence. The path through the spinney is just a deer track.'

'I see,' said Árpád politely, although he didn't see at all. It was quite mystifying.

'You must be the Castle's guest, the Hungarian,' said the man, who seemed disposed to talk.

'This is right.'

'Is it strange, to be in the West?' His tone was curious, as if he were interrogating a man from another world in one of Georgia's books.

Árpád thought a moment. 'Very strange. I lived in America before the war, for my work, but then I still had a home to go back to. Now I have no home.'

'Do you miss it?'

'Very much. Now I hardly remember it, though. I was in the gulag, in Siberia, where in winter there is snow, in summer there are mosquitoes, and always there are guards who like to use their rifle butts. There also I think of my home, of the plains in the spring, of my father's horses.' He shrugged. 'I cannot go back. I have served my time in the Soviet prison. I shall go to America, where there are also plains and horses, but where friends do not disappear in the night.'

'You never thought it would be a better world? People over here did. Still do. No more class system, no more men with money and titles owning everything, the way the Castle does here. You're lucky, you're seeing the way the other half live here.'

'This is true,' Árpád said. 'We have no class system, no aristocrats or bourgeois any more. They are all dead or in camps, and so are their wives and children. Instead, we have the Party bosses. They live in the best houses, with the best cars, but they are always in fear, perhaps they will be purged. In my country now, as in Russia, a man cannot be sure of anything, whether he is a janitor or the head of the Politburo. One moment Beria is the new tsar, the next he is dead. So each tries hard to be the most zealous, the most loyal, the most brutal, because he is afraid.'

'Doesn't sound like paradise to me.'

'You were in the war, perhaps?' Árpád said.

The stranger shook his head. 'Only on the home front. Fireman, I was. Didn't believe in killing ordinary working Germans, even if they were fighting for the Nazis. Plenty of lives to be saved here.'

'It was a bad time,' Árpád said.

'That it was. Well, I shan't be keeping you. Straight on up there, quite simple, you can't miss it.'

'This is good. I am not used to all your paths, to these hedges and bridleways and so on, there is nothing like this in Hungary or America.'

'Best network of public paths in the world, we've got,' said the stranger with pride. 'If you're on a right of way, there's nothing farmer or gamekeeper can do, doesn't matter how cross they get. Don't let anyone tell you otherwise.'

'Thank you,' said Árpád. 'A good day to you.'

'And to you.'

Árpád turned Pompey and headed for the gallops. There was a good view, Ben had said, you could see for miles and miles. 'A bit like your plains, maybe, if not nearly so flat.'

Árpád very much wanted to see this view.

Scene 14

As luck would have it, Hugo emerged from Vane's office just in time for Jarrett to bear down and haul him off outside, into the privacy of a cold wind.

'What are you doing here, Hawksworth?'

'Background interviews,' said Hugo equably.

'We've settled that question, thanks to you. Ingham's the man, quite clearly. Just heard from MacLeod. One of his sergeants has a possible match for the anonymous tip-off. Local petty criminal and black marketeer. The sergeant has looked the other way on one or two occasions when things were a little blurred, and in return this fence of his has given him a tip or two about more serious goings-on. Strictly anonymous, of course.' Jarrett still didn't quite look pleased. Anonymous tips clearly offended his sense of order.

'Do we have anything to put him in the right place at the right time?'

'There's a lay-by where Long Combe Road joins the London Road. Screened by bushes, woods on the other side. Favourite place for illegal activity, so I hear. One of MacLeod's men thought there was something going on there the last day Rothesay was seen, but by the time he got out to investigate, all he found was tyre tracks.'

'I see. You're happy with this.'

'Can't say I'm happy, but in my line of work, you take what you can get. It all fits. I dare say Rothesay riled Ingham too far. Lured out into the woods by a man with no intention of fighting fair. Bullet in the back of the neck, body weighted down in the river. Ingham's a resourceful and desperate man, he knew what he was doing. Would have worked, too, if those floods hadn't come along. We'd all have thought Rothesay had taken himself off to Moscow.'

Hugo found it difficult to imagine the dapper Rothesay, now a respectable scientist in his fifties, even taking up such an invitation from Ingham.

Jarrett brushed the point aside. 'Dr Rothesay lived a highly irregular life, just like Ingham. There are too many connections for this to be coincidence.'

'And the sleeper agent?'

'Rothesay fits the profile.'

'Rather a coincidence that he dies in a purely private quarrel just as we close in on him.'

'I shouldn't say so. Treason puts a great deal of pressure on a man, profoundly unnatural thing to do. I shouldn't say Rothesay was so very stable to begin with. Wouldn't take much to push him over the edge. There's always the chance that Ingham was doing it deliberately, orders from Moscow.'

This was news to Hugo. 'Moscow usually treats its foreign sources well, and Ingham's security checks turned up no Communist connections.'

'I'm having that looked into. Found an old associate in London who says Ingham had a thing about working men's rights in the thirties, got himself involved in more than one labour dispute which wasn't his business. Even talked about going to join the International Brigades in Spain. Scotland Yard is checking his Foreign Legion story with the *Sûreté*, just to be on the safe side. More for neatness than anything else. If it turns out his story isn't true, we've got a lever on the Soviets. What are these background interviews all about, then?'

'Following up a loose thread.' Not that it seemed to matter much. The evidence against Saul was stacking up. Hugo didn't want to believe the man guilty, his instincts said otherwise, but there was a point when you had to accept the evidence.

Jarrett gave him a hard look. 'I wasn't informed.'

'I only chanced upon it this morning.'

'Out with it, then. You're to keep me up to date with all developments.'

'If I kept you up to date with every idea one of us has up at the Hall, Inspector, you'd tell us to shut up until we had something concrete to bring you. Sir Bernard gave me his approval to look into this further, and so far there's nothing to change the story.'

Jarrett turned and began walking back to the building, too fast for Hugo to catch up. 'What's taking you so long?' he demanded. 'Oh, that leg of yours. Bad luck, that was. Or good luck, I suppose, only to be lamed. Don't look so surprised. I requested your file. I like to know about the men I work with. What they've done, what they're capable of. You must be used to it, in your line of work.'

Hugo was, but had rarely heard the knowledge used in so blunt a way.

'You have me at a disadvantage, Inspector, as the Service neglected to supply me with its file on you.'

Jarrett gave a short bark, almost a laugh, and stopped on the path. A technician scurrying between two buildings glanced curiously at them. 'I'd have thought you'd know all about me from Miss Wryton by now.'

'She hasn't talked about you much,' Hugo said. 'And then only when pressed.'

'Surprised. I saw a fair bit of her when she was engaged to Roddy Halstrop. Then again, she was something of a wallflower. No spirit, if you ask me.'

Jarrett no doubt considered virtually all women wallflowers, since he didn't let any of them get a word in edgeways.

'I should say leaving your bridegroom at the altar takes a certain spirit.'

'Funk. Pure funk. Halstrop was furious, of course, fit to burst. Took him off to a pub and poured a yard or two of porter into him. He saw it my way in the end. He's got his eye on a political career, you see, and a politician needs the right sort of wife. Someone not afraid to work behind the scenes for him, play hostess to the right sort of people. Like your Valerie Grisewood. Asset to any man's career, a woman like that. She's got high hopes for you, I hear. Might find yourself alongside Halstrop on the green benches one day.'

Hugo could hardly imagine anything he wanted less than to enter Parliament, except to have anything further to do with Jarrett or any of his friends. Certainly, Valerie had never broached the subject. Perhaps she was waiting for some more propitious moment. After all, one wouldn't do that straight from the Service.

Alternatively, Jarrett was just planning his life for him, the way he'd already planned his superior's retirement. Hugo had to believe that this was simply what passed for normal conversation with Jarrett. There was no way the man could be this rude on purpose and still hold his current position.

'Well,' Hugo said briskly. Efficiency, after all, was Jarrett's watchword. 'I shan't delay you any longer, we both have interviews to conduct.'

Scene 15

Oldcastle was his usual polished, expansive self. He leaned back in his chair, comfortable and confident, every inch the Head of Division. There were only three fountain pens lined up in the rack this time, the fourth nowhere to be seen.

Oldcastle followed Hugo's gaze. 'I've lost the other one somewhere. Probably under a chair at home, although it's a real nuisance. A good left-handed nib takes quite some finding.'

'I shall ask if anything's been handed in at the police station,' said Hugo. He would indeed, on the off-chance that it had turned up somewhere odd.

'That's very decent. What can I do for you, Hawksworth? I'd offer you a brandy, but we're on your time.'

Hugo inclined his head. He wondered, for an instant, whether he should have brought Harriet along. Scientific interrogation was her speciality. Then again, better not to tar more than one reputation if this went badly wrong.

'I'd like to talk to you about the accident which killed Adam Sørensen.'

It took experience to spot the flicker of tension in Oldcastle's body, the tightening around the eyes and the fingers, the very slight shift in posture. If Hugo hadn't been looking for it, he might not have seen it.

'I wrote a detailed report on that. I refer you to it, unless your classification level isn't high enough.'

A subtle warning: *Are you in my league, Hawksworth?*

'I've been apprised of its contents. I shall go to London to read it, if need be. Of course, I'm not a scientist, but my interest today isn't chiefly scientific.' It would be interesting to see whether Oldcastle tried to pull the wool over Hugo's eyes, to misdirect him on the scientific front.

'Of course.'

'In your report, responsibility for the accident is placed on Dr Sørensen, for carelessness, and on Dr Rothesay, for proposing a dangerous and untried technique. In spite of which, Dr Rothesay suffered no adverse consequences.'

'He was far too valuable a theoretician to lose.'

Hugo began scribbling things in his notebook, words to remind him. There might come a moment when he needed to quote something verbatim, and he didn't want to draw Oldcastle's attention to any particular answers. 'Did your staff share your opinion of the accident?'

'Several of them were interviewed in the course of preparing the report. I do recommend going to read it if you can. If you're anything like me, you'll find it much easier to take in than having me explain it to you now in dribs and drabs.'

'In general, did they share your opinion?'

'I should say so.'

'Did any of them think otherwise? Dr Rothesay, for example?'

'Rothesay was glad to be moved into a purely theoretical position. He grumbled, of course, that was his nature. We took it in our stride rather.'

'Who did he grumble to?'

'Colleagues, mostly.'

'Could he have grumbled to anyone outside Foxley?'

'I imagine he told his wife, if that's what you mean. There's always a certain tendency to confide in one's nearest and dearest, security or no security. We do try to discourage it where we can. Inspector Jarrett, I feel, would like the Los Alamos setup, all of us stuck out in the middle of nowhere with no access to anything.'

Hugo commented, 'Klaus Fuchs had no trouble getting word to his Soviet controllers from Los Alamos, so I don't imagine it would be any better here. Worse perhaps, with a city nearby.'

'Indeed. Bad for morale, too. Good for a man to feel he's part of the wider world. Tensions can build up rather in a place like this, if you know what I mean.' Oldcastle was beginning to relax, little by little. He had clearly decided this was about Rothesay, nothing to do with him.

'When he grumbled, did he have his own explanation? Another culprit, perhaps, a story of how he was hard done by?'

Oldcastle smiled. 'Don't we all have such stories?'

'So he did.'

Oldcastle's thumbs twiddled around one another. 'I think so. I suppose you could reconstruct it, if you talked to everyone in the department. You'd find the usual cocktail of scientific resentments, I suspect. Not enough resources, not enough time, the project directors weren't sympathetic.'

'They must have been, to give him the go-ahead. I suppose he could be persuasive when he chose.'

'He had a good theoretical reputation.'

'How did he convince them?'

'You understand, making a British Bomb has been a key priority of both this Government and the last. With the Americans freezing us out of their nuclear programme, we've had to make up a great deal of ground on our own, with limited resources.'

Hugo had fenced at school, and a little at Oxford. Foil, mostly, the lightest and most delicate of weapons. This was pure foil fencing, the slow back and forth, the twitch of blades, lunge and parry, riposte and counter-riposte, all in little flicks of the wrist.

'So Rothesay sold this to the top brass as a way to make up lost ground.'

'It was.'

'And it was Rothesay who persuaded them of this, was it – who got them to devote the necessary resources?'

Oldcastle picked up one of the fountain pens and twisted it around in his fingers. A rather more active fidget than any so far, visible to Miss Fitzgibbon through the glazed door.

'Who was in charge of making it happen?'

'That was Dr Vane, I imagine you've already talked to him.'

'I have,' said Hugo. He was almost certain the devoted Miss Fitzgibbon would be in shortly with an urgent matter requiring Oldcastle's attention. It was time to change tactics. 'I was attempting to establish whether Dr Rothesay might have felt unjustly blamed. Which he was, wasn't he, Dr Oldcastle? He wasn't the one who whispered in Whitehall ears, persuaded the powers that be to divert funds to your department. He wasn't the one who cut corners, used unsuitable equipment and half-trained staff. Yes, he wanted the scientific fame which had eluded him so far, and you were quite willing to give him that. It was a sound proposal.

'What it needed was to be handed over to the nuclear engineers and the reactor construction specialists, the people who make the speculative ideas happen, who know how to do it all safely. Rothesay should have been transferred to another department, given a staff of his own, perhaps even a promotion. All you'd get would be a pat on the back for bringing this to some civil servant's attention.'

Oldcastle stared at Hugo, his confident urbanity deserting him. The phone rang. Miss Fitzgibbon's voice, then steps. Oldcastle's eyes flickered uneasily towards the door.

'The Ministry for you, Dr Oldcastle, it's urgent.'

'Dr Oldcastle is busy,' said Hugo.

'Excuse me, Hawksworth . . .'

Hugo turned to Miss Fitzgibbon. 'Dr Oldcastle is being questioned by a member of the Service regarding a matter of national security, on which he has vital information. If you'll put me on the line, I shall explain.'

She looked to Oldcastle, uncertain. There was no phone call, Hugo had called their bluff.

'I'll let you know when we're done,' said Hugo.

She retreated, the door clicking shut behind her. Hugo turned back to Oldcastle.

'Sørensen died because you wanted to make the breakthrough, Dr Oldcastle, and Rothesay was blamed. He knew perfectly well the accident wasn't his fault, but you were promoted, and he wasn't. Which leaves us with two questions. Who else knew, and why is Dr Rothesay now dead?'

Oldcastle was pale. As well he might be. 'I had nothing to do with that. Nothing, d'you understand? I'm no murderer, all my movements are accounted for. The Inspector's been over this.'

'I'm sure he has. I have some different questions to ask you, Dr Oldcastle. Let's go back to the aftermath of this accident. Who knew what had really happened?'

Friday

Scene 1

Friday was market day, Sheep Street and the market square full of stalls and hubbub. Scaffolding was going up over the handsome façade of the Feoffees' Hall, Brodrick and his men working flat out to protect the roof from any further storms. The weather had been kind, there had been no more rain.

Freya had taken Árpád to see the market. Harriet Godwin was busy, so he'd been given the day off.

'There are no animals,' he said, looking around. 'In Hungary, there would be sheep and cattle for sale, also chickens, and the Roma with their horses.'

'The livestock market is up by the station,' Freya said. 'Some Victorian Feoffee got tired of all the noise and muck in the square outside his offices, so he kindly donated the money for a new market. Hideous thing it is, too, looks like a workhouse.'

'I know about workhouses, they are in Dickens.'

'The cheese stalls are around here,' said Freya, ducking under an awning. 'We're not meant to go through here, but everyone does.'

'We are told in Hungary, you English are a stodgy and law-abiding people, not like we Hungarians. I learn now, this is not true. When you break the rules, you do it quietly, you make no fuss, and often you do it all together.'

His voice was muffled as Freya let a flap of canvas go too quickly. 'Sorry!'

Dinah was casting her eyes over a selection of Cheddars. 'Who's that you're assaulting?' she asked Freya.

'This is our guest, Dr Árpád Bárándy. Árpád, this is Dinah Linthrop.'

'Ah, of the bookshop! Yes, Freya has promised to show me this when we finish with the market. Gus talks of you often, you have made quite the conquest.'

Dinah looked distinctly disconcerted.

'We don't talk about it,' said Freya.

'Why not?'

'Dinah values her privacy.'

He shook his head, bewildered. 'Privacy is for mistresses. You are not the Earl's mistress, no? I should not think ill of you if you were, but this is not the English way, I think.'

Dinah went quite red.

'Have I said something wrong?'

'We don't talk about that either.'

'What do you talk about? Ah, this I know. The weather. And things which are wrong, you love to grumble. Let me try this. It is sad that your Town Hall is falling down, because of all the rain. There were not many casualties, I hope?'

He said it with a quite straight face, but Freya caught a distinct look of mischief in his eye.

'He's making fun of us,' she said.

'Of course I am,' said Árpád. 'But perhaps I need practice. Now, you said there would be proper cheeses, cheeses with taste and moisture, not like this Cheddar of Mrs Partridge's.'

The rotund, rather amiable cheesemonger found himself on the receiving end of a full-fledged inquisition into the origin and pungency of his wares.

'He has strong views about cheese,' Freya explained to Dinah, standing back.

'He seems to have strong views about everything. I must say, the town is dying to meet him. Everyone's been agog all week. Mysterious stranger turns up at the Castle, shuttled back and forth to the hush-hush place.'

'What are the stories? Do tell.'

'Well, there was one theory that he was a member of the Hungarian Politburo who'd defected. Another that he was a Jewish doctor, possibly responsible for Stalin's death.'

'Now you're having me on.'

'I'm quite serious. Then he was seen out on horseback yesterday afternoon in his late lordship's riding gear, so it's been decided that he's a dispossessed Hungarian count, some distant relative of the Fitzwarins.'

'At least that has a germ of truth.'

'I've been doing my best. But everyone's so used to mysterious goings-on at the Castle by now, they'll believe anything. Don't forget, Selchester used to have quite the assortment of guests up there before the war. There've been lots of dark whispers about him since he turned up under a flagstone, but you can't say he was a closed-minded man.'

Freya knew rather too well why her uncle had cast his net so widely. It had nothing to do with an open mind, and everything to do with power. Lord Selchester had liked to know everything he could about people, the better to use them. Once used, they could be discarded, as Saul Ingham had been.

There was a thought. Had Selchester passed any of that material on? He'd known all about Saul's somewhat shady past, probably more than Saul ever realised. If that information had fallen into someone else's hands after his death, they'd have everything they needed to frame him for something like this.

Who would know? Her cousin Sonia, that was who.

'Freya?' Dinah said.

She shook her head. 'Just a thought. Do I spy Alice Rothesay talking to Vivian over there? I didn't know they knew one another.'

'Jamie says they were at school together.'

Freya wasn't surprised. People in Selchester always turned out to have unexpected connections.

'She doesn't look happy.'

'I'd hope not, she's just lost her husband. Although, by all accounts, she's well rid of him.'

Scene 2

Alice looked paler than ever, Vivian thought, catching sight of her on the next stall.

She gave Vivian a perfunctory smile and came over, cigarette in hand.

'I thought you'd be taking yourself off to London,' Vivian said.

'I did. Thought it might take my mind off things not to be in the same house for a bit. I had to get permission from that dreadful policeman.'

'Didn't work?'

Alice shook her head. 'You think you've taken so much grief from someone that you couldn't possibly care if they dropped dead one day. What a relief, you think, I could live my own life again. Then it happens, and suddenly you realise there's a great gaping hole in your life. Someone you shared a life and a bed with is lying on a slab in the morgue with someone's bullet through his head. I hated him, but in an odd way I miss him.'

Vivian looked at her with sympathy. 'I know that feeling, the week after a last night. Doesn't matter if you hated the show by the end, you still feel empty. I shan't pretend it's of the same order, of course.'

'That's what our marriage was, an act. Only Bruno tired of even pretending to be faithful. Don't ever marry, Vivian, that's my advice. For what it's worth.'

Vivian had neither prospect nor intention of marrying. Even in this day and age it would help her career not a bit.

'What will you do now?' she asked.

Alice fished in her handbag without even looking, drew out another cigarette and lit it straight from the first. 'Once Commissar Jarrett has finished his inquiries, you mean?'

'I suppose you'll be done with Selchester.'

'I'm done with the countryside. I shall take myself to London, find a nice little flat somewhere civilised, and never set foot outside the metro from one year's end to the next. I shall get myself a job, if anyone will have me. I say, who is that man gesticulating at Simpkins? Behind you.'

Vivian turned to look. 'That must be his lordship's Hungarian guest.'

'Hungarian guest?'

'I forget, you're not plugged into the Selchester gossip mill.'

'Thank God, no. I should pass on my thanks to that lodger of Freya's, though. He did his best to be decent while the Commissar was bearing down on me. One is grateful for small kindnesses at a time like this. Let's go over, but do give me the low-down on this Hungarian. Quite an exotic for staid old Selchester, isn't he?'

'There are all sorts of ridiculous rumours circulating. I believe he's just a professor of classics or something, couldn't stand it any more behind the Iron Curtain, and came over.'

'Is he now? To judge by the look on Simpkins's face, he might as well be a Martian.'

Freya and Vivian greeted one another, cordially if without particular warmth.

'That Hawksworth lives at the Castle with you, doesn't he?' said Alice. 'Give him my thanks for his courtesy in the interview.'

'I think he was rather pleased,' said Freya. 'I don't believe he likes Jarrett any more than the rest of us do.'

'Ghastly man. I'm due for another grilling this afternoon, no doubt he wants to know everything my husband said about this Ingham character. Well, he shall be disappointed, for there's nothing to tell, and I've engaged the sharpest, most ruthless solicitor I could lay my hands on.' She smiled with chilly satisfaction. 'As I said, at a time like this one takes pleasure in small things.'

Scene 3

Back at the Castle, Freya tackled her cousin Sonia. Thankfully June was on duty at the exchange, not in the least interested in what they had to say to one another.

'Oh, it's you.' There was a strange hissing screech in the background.

'Sonia, what's that ghastly noise?'

'Just the kettle. Breakfast coffee.'

Freya glanced across at the grandfather clock by the stairs. It was two o'clock in the afternoon.

'I can hear you disapproving, don't waste your thoughts. You lead your life and I lead mine. Victor, be a darling and finish the coffee, will you?'

The noise subsided.

'Who's Victor?' Freya asked.

'An admirer. He comes to visit after lunch. His lunch, that is, I don't believe in eating lunch before five if I can help it. Now, enough of your questions. What's this I hear about the interloping earl and that bookseller friend of yours?'

Given that Sonia had never troubled to make herself agreeable to anyone in Selchester, it was a mystery to Freya how she knew so much about its goings-on.

'Her name's Dinah Linthrop, and you know that very well.'

'So, there is something. Don't deny it – you never could tell a bare-faced lie. Are they sleeping together?'

'You know perfectly well they're doing no such thing. Gus is a devout Catholic, far more devout than you, I might add, and he's behaving perfectly honourably.'

'Oh, it's just too bad.'

'It won't inconvenience you in the slightest. The title would never have come to you, and the money's already his.'

'It *will* inconvenience me. If they marry, she might have a son, and then my father's precious earldom won't die with Gus.'

'Since they're just at the stage of spending a lot of time together, you may have nothing at all to worry about.'

'Thank you,' said Sonia's voice, away from the phone. 'Coffee, simply divine.'

'Listen, I wanted to ask you a question,' Freya said. 'We both know your father was in the habit of collecting information on people.'

'He was a blackmailer, darling, don't beat about the bush.'

'He was a blackmailer, yes. But did he write everything down? Could all that information have fallen into someone else's hands?'

Silence. A muffled sound on the phone.

In London, Sonia covered the receiver with her hand. 'Victor, could you be a darling and run down to the front door? I'm expecting a letter.'

Victor gave her a sharp look. He knew exactly what she was up to. 'Trying to get rid of me, are you?'

'Just take the hint.'

Being of an equable temperament, Victor went. The door closed behind him. Freya's voice was squawking behind her hand.

'Yes, I'm here. Not the kind of conversation one should have with strangers around, however intriguing. He knew my father distantly. I'm not taking any chances. Now, what's this about information?'

Sonia's voice was sharp, not a trace of her morning languor in it.

'I've got your attention now, haven't I?' said Freya.

'What information?'

'Your father had dealings with Saul Ingham, who was here at Christmas. He framed Saul for something he didn't do.'

'Oh, the man who joined the Foreign Legion.'

'He's been arrested for the murder of this scientist. Hugo believes he's been framed, but whoever framed him must have known quite a bit about his past.'

'I see Hawksworth is making a pest of himself again.'

'Shall I tell Father Leo you said that? He's staying here.' Sonia was rather wary of Leo.

'Good God, is he? The whole clan together. Isn't Hugo reading too much into all this?'

Freya knew an evasion when she heard one.

'So he did write things down.'

'He may have done. He was a secretive man, you know that.'

Secretive, yes, that was one word for it. The late Lord Selchester had been a man of many parts, each sealed off from the rest. Even Freya, who'd spent half her school holidays at the Castle, had seen only a fraction of him.

'Could anyone have got hold of that material? Anyone close to him.'

'There was no one close to him. He kept us all at a distance, except when he wanted to pull our strings. He never had a secretary at the Castle, you know, handled everything himself. A secretary would have seen what he really was sooner or later, and he couldn't have that.'

It sounded a bleak, cold existence. Had her uncle ever been happy, in the way a normal man or woman knew happiness? Not the cold, dark satisfaction of having another creature in your power, but bright, ordinary joy. Perhaps as a young student, when he had fallen madly in love with Gus's mother.

'So there was something, but you don't know what, and you probably wouldn't tell me, even to save a man's life.'

Sonia heard the outer door close. Victor back after his search for her non-existent letter. She knew very well what Freya wanted, because she'd searched high and low for it. Without success.

'Darling, I don't know Saul from Adam, and if he was convicted of a crime once, there'll be all sorts of records. My father wasn't the only one who liked collecting information. If Hugo's trying to get Saul out of trouble, he's got the Service's records at his disposal. What could I possibly have which is any better?'

The door opened. Victor advanced on her, his amiable face suddenly intent.

'Victor, I gave you a heavy hint,' said Sonia, clapping her hand over the receiver again. 'Do be a dear and let me finish my call in peace.'

'Saul. Saul Ingham?'

'Yes, that's his name, what is it to you? I'm talking to my cousin Freya.'

'Give me the phone, Sonia,' said Victor, very firmly. 'Otherwise I shall go outside and ring her from a call box.'

Sonia passed him the receiver.

Freya heard a new voice on the line, male and deep. 'Freya, this is Victor Emerson.'

So that was Sonia's Victor – a big, bearish former Service agent who now specialised in tracking looted art. He'd helped Hugo over Christmas, had turned out to be an old friend of Saul's. An admirer of Sonia? He'd called her a looker, but Freya could hardly believe she was his type.

'Emerson, yes, I had no idea it was you.'

'Your cousin likes to keep her life in separate compartments. I believe she gets the habit from her father. What's this about Saul?'

Freya told him.

'Why on earth didn't he ring me? He had one phone call, at least. The Saul I know would never shoot a man in cold blood like that. I don't doubt he killed men in the war, even crept up on them in the dark, but in a private quarrel? No. Hawksworth is right, it stinks. Saul needs all the friends he can get. I shall set out this evening, find myself a room at the George & Dragon, and get the full story from Hawksworth tomorrow.'

'You'll have to be early. He's going off to a christening with Valerie.'

'That's still going on, is it? I shall be at the Castle bright and early.'

He handed the receiver back to Sonia. 'I need to be going. I'll give you a bell when I'm back. Keep on trying to pull the wool over your cousin's eyes, I don't imagine you'll get anywhere. I shall see myself out.'

Sonia, rather at a loss for words, waited for the click of the lock. 'I don't know that I like him after all,' she said.

'Nonsense,' said Freya, rather pleased to have discovered a chink in her cousin's armour. 'You get your own way far too much.'

'That's the point of life.'

'Thus speaks your father.'

Silence again, then Sonia's voice, languid once again. 'This is turning into a distinctly disagreeable day.'

'You'll get over it.'

'I hear Valerie is coming down,' said Sonia, not at all liking to be at a disadvantage. 'She bears an offer for Hugo Hawksworth, one he'll be a fool to refuse. Cheerio!'

Scene 4

'I think half of Selchester must be here,' said Georgia, looking around at the packed Masonic Hall. 'We should have been earlier.'

'Mr Dillon promised he'd save us some seats,' said Gus, scanning the room. 'I must say, I can't imagine you'd fill a hall in rural New England for a lecture like this.'

'Pure nosiness,' said Freya, who had been summarily bundled into Gus's car by Polly and Georgia. They were planning a hike up to Pagan Hill over the weekend, and wanted to know what stories there were about it. 'Everyone wants to know what this pair have been up to.'

'We do indeed,' said Richard, the other Daff. 'Jamie says they had another terrible fight this afternoon.'

'Look, there's Mr Dillon,' said Polly. 'Right at the front. With a whole lot of seats reserved. There's Daisy.'

'I don't want to be right at the front,' said Georgia. 'People can see you. They notice when you whisper.'

'Guilty conscience,' said Polly. 'I'm on the end.'

'No, you're not.'

They dived off into the throng.

'Was it a good idea to bring them?' Gus said.

'Oh, they'll love it,' said Richard. 'They're just curious. We all are. Not on your level, of course. I imagine you could floor them with learned questions about Greek poets if you wanted, but we're all dying to see whether they believed a word of those ridiculous stories.'

'Are they scholars?' Hugo asked, catching the end of the conversation as he came in with Leo and Árpád.

'I hear he taught at one of the newer universities in the thirties – anthropology, I believe. Didn't like the rigidity of conventional academic study, he says. I dare say he's a Swedenborgian or some such, full of strange notions about the deep psychic wisdom of mankind. He's over there, by the stage.'

Interested, Árpád craned over the sea of heads. 'But he is the man I saw yesterday, when I was riding.'

'Tramping about the countryside?'

'He was walking, I was lost. I asked directions. He was curious about Hungary and the East, I think perhaps he was a fellow traveller once. There were many such in America when I was there, in the universities.'

'Fewer now,' said Gus. 'They've seen too much and lost their illusions, or else they're afraid of Senator McCarthy and his mob.'

'Such a terrible man,' said Richard. 'It quite makes me shudder to hear what he's up to, like something out of the Inquisition. Although by all accounts this Special Branch man is no better. It must be so hard for you, Mr Hawksworth.'

Hugo said nothing, which Richard quite rightly took for assent.

'I shan't pry,' he said. 'I only hope he takes his disagreeable self back to London post-haste.'

Mr Fortescue called them to their seats, the loud hubbub dying to a subdued mutter. He was a beanpole of a man in a pin-striped suit, a Mason and pillar of the local history society.

'I'm pleased to see such a turnout for tonight's Historical Society meeting,' he began.

'Do you think he knows we're all just here for the gossip?' Georgia whispered to Polly.

Mr Fortescue shot her a quelling look. Georgia folded her arms defiantly.

'Good evening to you all. I'm very pleased to be able to welcome recent Selcastrian Mr Jeremy Pearson, who's been doing some research on local folklore and stories with the help of his wife. Mr Pearson was formerly a lecturer at the University of Reading, where he taught in the anthropology department.'

'"With the help of his wife",' Daisy whispered to Georgia. 'Bet Mr Fortescue thinks she's just part of the furniture.'

'Mr Pearson has travelled extensively in Britain and on the Continent, gathering stories from a number of different traditions. Tonight, he will talk to us about his researches in the Selchester area, and compare his findings with those from other places. At the end, both he and his wife will answer any questions you may have about the content of his talk. Ladies and gentlemen, Mr Jeremy Pearson.'

'Stuffy old stick,' said Georgia, under cover of the applause. 'Never uses one word where five will do.'

'Ssh,' said Freya.

Scene 5

Those who had come for the entertainment, she thought, would be sadly disappointed. If Mr Fortescue was wordy, Jeremy Pearson was verbose, meandering, and barely to the point. He did at least give his wife more credit than Mr Fortescue had allowed: everything was 'we'. As far as Freya could judge, the Pearsons weren't actually interested in the stories as stories, only as exemplars of types or evidence in support of their pet theory. As to exactly what that theory might be, she was still in the dark at the end, but it seemed to have something to do with the Stone Age.

She hoped for more from the questions, perhaps Miranda would be more forthcoming. Gus was one of the first to put his hand up.

'As a newcomer to Selchester myself, I'd like to hear more about the stories you've collected from around here. Are there any you haven't encountered elsewhere on your travels? What were your favourites?'

This question was met with a murmur of approval.

It was Miranda who answered. 'We were struck by the number of stories relating to Pagan Hill, it seems to have quite a reputation. Of course, we've encountered a great many places with barrows or chamber tombs, and frequently they're the sort of places you're advised not to go at night. But there aren't usually so many stories about them.'

Then they were straight off into types again, until – rather unwisely – Mr Fortescue allowed Georgia's question. Perhaps he was keen to engage the younger audience.

'Why is it all about types?' she asked. 'You've got all these stories about witches and the Hunt and fallen kings who walk at the dark of the moon. Why do you have to fit them into boxes? It makes them much less interesting.'

'Ahem,' Mr Fortescue said. Jeremy Pearson looked resigned.

'You may be right,' said Miranda. 'Universities like us to think this way, it's how scholarship is. Perhaps we don't enjoy the stories enough.'

'I shan't go to university, if that's what they teach,' Georgia announced. There was a ripple of laughter. 'I shall listen to the stories instead.'

'Good for you,' said Miranda. 'Come and find me sometime, I'll tell you some.'

Scene 6

It was a somewhat crestfallen audience who made their way down the stairs and out into the cold winter night.

'Still feel the local farmers oughtn't to be telling them tall tales?' Freya asked Gus.

'I had hoped they'd be paying more attention to the actual stories,' he said. 'It's fascinating how epics like the *Iliad* and the *Odyssey* come to be passed down through the generations, but they didn't touch on that. I suppose it's not their focus.'

Árpád was amused. 'You have these people in England also. I thought they were only to be found in Communist universities, where the facts must fit the Party line, but no, also it seems anyone with a strange notion can take interesting things and make them wrong.'

'It was bunk' was Georgia's take. 'He was, anyway. Not sure about her.'

'Universities aren't at all like that really,' said Gus, perhaps worried that a future classicist might be lost to her calling. 'When I was a student, I had to read Homer, Suetonius, Tacitus, all sorts of interesting things.'

'In Latin and Greek?'

'Of course.'

Georgia looked doubtful.

'There's always Ovid and Catullus,' Freya said.

'I like Ovid. They won't let us do Catullus, they say he's immoral.'

'I took a course on Latin lyric, too,' said Gus. 'Ovid, Catullus, Propertius.'

'I won't go to Mr Pearson's university,' Georgia decided. 'Maybe to yours. Where did you go?'

'I went to Boston College, it's a Jesuit university.'

'Hmm,' Georgia said.

'What did you think?' Gus asked Leo. 'I know it's not your field, but you've been to plenty of lectures yourself.'

'I think Georgia made the point as well as anyone could,' said Leo. 'They've lost touch with the real things. Rather sad, I think.'

'Where's Hugo?' Freya said.

Scene 7

Hugo had taken the opportunity to catch Miranda Pearson alone. Her husband had been cornered by a retired RAF wing commander, who seemed to have a pet theory of his own and had sensed a golden opportunity to hold forth on it.

'Mrs Pearson, could I have a moment?'

'Of course, Mr Hawksworth.'

'I hope your time in London was fruitful.'

'Indeed, thank you for asking. What can I do for the Statistics Office? Do you have a mathematical query? I'm very much afraid I was never good with numbers.' A glint in her eye told him she knew as well as anyone else what his real job was.

'I wanted to ask you about Dr Rothesay.'

'A nasty business, that. To think we let a murderer into our house over Christmas, it makes the blood run cold.'

'That's why I need to talk to you.' Hugo drew her away from the throng a little. 'According to Mr Ingham, Dr Rothesay came to Nightingale Cottage on December the twenty-eighth. He expected to find you.'

'Are you asking in your official capacity as a statistician, or should I take this as a purely private conversation?'

'You may take it in whatever light you wish, but you may have evidence crucial to the investigation, in which case I shall ask you to make a statement to the police.'

'I've never had crucial evidence before. What would you like to know?'

'Well, to begin with, what was the nature of your relationship with Dr Rothesay?'

'I think you know the answer to that already, Mr Hawksworth. We were having an affair.'

'Thank you for your candour, Mrs Pearson.'

'It doesn't shock you?'

'Statisticians aren't easily shocked.'

'No. You must see data on the most dreadful things every day. So many murders, so many accidents, so many cases of this disease or that. Well, I tell you because you ask, and because I don't hold with the stuffy English way of keeping up appearances. Perhaps that was good for the past, but we're in a new age now. An age in which women should be equal to men, not required to conduct their affairs in shabby secrecy while their husbands are allowed to boast. My marriage to Jeremy broke down a long time ago, our relationship now is purely professional.'

'Why do you stay together, if you don't mind me asking?'

'Because the work we do is more important than how either of us feel. We couldn't do it alone. And' – the bold manner dropping for a moment – 'because Jeremy was raised a Catholic. Even now he's given all that up, he can't free himself from the notion that divorce is wrong.'

The public reason, and the private.

'Does Jeremy have affairs, too?'

'Now and then. They don't last long, the self-loathing gets to him after a while. A pity: it would do him some good. Sex is a natural instinct, after all, like drinking a glass of water.'

That was a quote, although Hugo couldn't remember who had said it, or even where he'd heard it before. Some freethinker of the twenties, he rather thought, whose disciple was amusing herself by baiting a representative of the Establishment.

He continued his questioning, well aware she was still trying to shock him. 'How long had you and Dr Rothesay been having this affair?'

'About a year. I met him soon after Jeremy and I moved here. He was rather a breath of fresh air at first, Selchester can be such a stodgy place. Then I discovered how much he grumbled, and it rather palled. I still liked to see him from time to time, when it suited me.'

How much of this, Hugo wondered, was actually true, and how much of it was she simply making up to needle him? Perhaps he should have Jarrett question her, he'd have an apoplectic fit. Good riddance.

'When did you last see him?'

'Soon after the New Year. His wife was away, so I went to his house.'

'Did he mention Mr Ingham at all?'

Miranda raised her eyes to the ceiling. 'I should say. He was full of indignation. Why had I let a man like that into my house, what was I thinking of? I told him that was my business and Jeremy's. He said, did I know what kind of man Mr Ingham was?'

'A scoundrel, I imagine.'

'He used far ruder words than that. I know some Italian, but let me say, even I don't know that sort of Italian.'

'Would you say he was gloating or grumbling?'

'Grumbling, definitely. It seems Ingham had been downright rude when he called, more or less slammed the door in his face.'

'Might he have tried to teach Mr Ingham a lesson?'

'I don't think he'd have set out to, but if offered the chance, very much. By his own account, he'd been a champion brawler growing up in Edinburgh. It seems his Scottish relations looked down on him for being half-Italian, and his Italian family didn't think much of him because his mother hadn't married a good Italian boy. He learned to argue with his fists, so he said. He liked to be different from his colleagues.'

'So I gather.'

'Do I make the grade for a police interview, Mr Hawksworth? I hear this Inspector Jarrett is quite the prude, thinks a woman's place is in the home.'

She was baiting him again. Hugo had another question of his own.

'Was that the last time you saw Dr Rothesay?'

'Indeed. A little of him went a long way by then. The next I heard of him was the radio report on his disappearance.'

'Did you believe he might have defected to Russia?'

'That's quite a question to ask. But since you have, yes, I thought he might have done, in a fit of pique.'

'So he talked about his work to you.'

'He grumbled about his work. If you're asking, could I have learned all sorts of dangerous nuclear secrets and slipped them to a man in St James's Park carrying a rolled-up copy of *The Times*, no. He griped about his boss, his lack of promotion, how dull his colleagues were, and so on. He wanted to be appreciated, you see, for the first-class mind he thought he had. Personally, I couldn't testify to the quality of his mind, only of his personality, and that was distinctly second-class.'

'So he might have believed the Soviets would appreciate him properly if he passed them secrets.'

'Absolutely. I think he'd have loved it, at least for a while. Feeling he was doing something none of his colleagues knew about, making a difference.'

'What about Communist sympathies? Did he have any political views?'

'Only as regarded the incompetence of the Government. He thought the Soviets were much more efficient, wouldn't do everything in a muddle. And he liked to say how timid Britain had become, unwilling to commit properly to grand projects like the Bomb.'

'He actually mentioned the Bomb to you?' Out of the corner of his eye, Hugo saw Jeremy glance in Miranda's direction as he tried to edge away from the wing commander. The room was mostly empty now, aside from a knot of Masonic types around Fortescue, and a few stragglers by the door.

'Oh, you surely can't believe there's a man, woman or child in Selchester who doesn't know what goes on at Foxley? It's quite as transparent as that statistics department of yours. The Soviets could send their rawest conscript here, it would be a gold mine for him. All he'd need to do would be to take a table in the Daffodils and keep his ears open. I look at the way your outfit handles things, and I think perhaps Bruno was right. Not that it bothers me, I think the Bomb a wicked thing.'

'Thank you,' said Hugo, who was distinctly unhappy with the way the Service handled things himself. 'I expect I shall need a statement, are you here for the next few days?'

'I shall be up in your abode tomorrow. I'm transporting chairs for the rehearsal.'

'Keen to have a look inside the Castle?' Hugo asked, unable to resist a barb of his own.

'I can't say castles hold the slightest allure for me.'

'Each to her own, I suppose. Thank you for your answers, Mrs Pearson.'

'Call me Miranda, please. I'm not an extension of Jeremy.'

Hugo turned to go, took a limping step away.

'Should I ask what you did to your leg?' she said.

'A bicycle accident.'

'Of course,' she said. 'How could I think otherwise? Good evening, Mr Hawksworth.'

Scene 8

'There you are,' said Georgia, bouncing into him in the doorway. 'Where did you slip off to?'

'Work,' said Hugo.

She gave him a dirty look. 'You wanted to talk to someone about that scientist, I know. Shall I guess who it was? It can't be anyone who's gone past us already, or you wouldn't be hours behind them. It's not any of the gossips, they went past us, so either it was that dull Mason – can't think what you'd want to ask him – or it's one of the speakers. Hah! See. I knew it was.'

'Enough, Georgia,' he said wearily. 'It's a professional matter, none of your business.' He'd had enough of Miranda Pearson's wit, he didn't need Georgia's pertness.

Her face shuttered at once. 'I shan't come to find you again,' she said, running off ahead.

By the time he caught the others up, she and Polly had gone on, waiting by Gus's car. Freya had seen Georgia's face as she came back, knew something was wrong, but this wasn't the time to talk about it.

'I hope it was a worthwhile evening,' said Hugo to Árpád, as they drove back in the darkness. He was glad Leo was driving. His leg always hurt more when someone reminded him of it. The dull ache was mostly fading, but it hadn't faded quite enough.

'But of course,' said Árpád. 'I see a slice of your English country life, as you would say, although perhaps not so typical to find a scholar full of strange ideas and an Austrian Jew.'

Hugo was baffled. 'What?'

'You do not know? She is a Mitteleuropean. Definitely she is Jewish, most likely from Austria or Bavaria, although perhaps she is from Transylvania, where there were many people who spoke German. It is in her voice, you see. When I was a boy, we lived in Vienna for a while. It was very cosmopolitan, I met people from all over the empire, and learned to recognise the way they spoke. I could tell, this man is a Croat, this one perhaps from Upper Austria, this woman is a Czech. And, of course, also you could tell, this one lives in the countryside and does not come to Vienna often, that one is a Jewish intellectual, this one is loud and swaggering, he is perhaps in the cavalry.'

'Miranda keeps very quiet about it. Her English is perfect.'

Leo said, 'It wasn't easy being a refugee in the thirties. A great many people over here didn't realise how bad the Nazis were, couldn't see why all these foreigners wanted to be in England. So many of them changed their names, tried to fit in as best they could. She has a good ear, she married an Englishman and made a life here, she may prefer to forget her past.'

'In Eastern Europe,' said Árpád, a touch mournfully, 'it is very hard to forget the past. There were things the Nazis did, then the Soviets, and then under that many old hatreds, Serbs and Croats, Romanians and Hungarians. This is why I shall go to America. They ask you to be American, it is a new start. If I were to meet a nice American girl, as they say, I should like my children to be American, to grow up away from such things. It will be hard for me, but easier for them.'

They came through the gatehouse to find a low sports car parking by the main door.

'I wonder who that is?' Leo asked.

A moment later, they had their answer when Mrs Partridge opened the door, casting light on the scene.

'Oho,' said Hugo, rolling the window down. 'Another uninvited guest to rain on Gus's parade. It's Lady Sonia. She must have decided to come down with Emerson.'

When Gus unexpectedly displaced his half-sister, Lady Sonia, as heir to the Selchester fortune, he had politely told her that she should still consider the Castle her home. Lady Sonia, with her customary ruthlessness, had taken him at his word and descended for Christmas. Now she was doing the same again.

'There you are,' said Sonia, as Gus and Freya came towards her. 'I'd have let you know I was on my way, only Emerson was in too much of a hurry, sped me right out of town.'

Hugo, who knew Emerson to be a courteous man, doubted he'd done any such thing.

'You're always welcome here,' said Gus, who surely couldn't mean it. Wondering whether he could steal away to New England again? 'Mrs Partridge, would you make up a bedroom for Lady Sonia, and another for Mr Emerson?'

'Don't worry about me,' said Emerson, who was taking Sonia's cases out of the boot. 'I wouldn't dream of imposing on you. I've booked a room at the George & Dragon, they're keeping some food warm for me. Excellent landlord, Mr Plinth. You should try luring him back to the Castle.'

Mr Plinth had been the Castle's butler before the war.

'It'll be chill tonight,' said Mrs Partridge, who had very little time for Lady Sonia. 'I don't believe in heating rooms when they aren't being used, not with fuel so scarce, and with so little notice, there's no fire burning.'

Sonia managed to look annoyed, even though she had no one to blame but herself. 'I'll have a hot-water bottle,' she said, with ill grace.

'Be polite,' said Emerson, climbing back into his car. 'Else Mrs Partridge will put hellebore in your scrambled eggs, and I shouldn't blame her if she did. I'll be around early tomorrow, Hugo – catch you before you go off.'

He revved the engine into life and roared away.

'Well, don't be hanging around out here,' said Mrs Partridge. 'You're letting all the warmth out.'

'You two go in,' said Leo, as Mrs Partridge ushered everyone inside. 'I shall put the car away.'

'I'll come with you,' said Hugo, who wanted a moment with his uncle.

'You have secret business,' said Árpád cheerfully. 'I shall leave you.'

He scrambled out, slamming the door. The car crunched away across the gravel, around to its home in the old coach house.

'Do you think a man would betray his country out of professional pique?' Hugo asked, as they locked up. 'It's been suggested to me as a motive, more than once.'

Leo was silent for a moment. 'In my experience, people are drawn to the Communist cause to give meaning and purpose to their lives, because they see a dearth of those things in the world around them. You might as aptly ask, would a man turn to God out of professional pique? To betray one's country, give one's allegiance to its enemies, is no small step.'

'Taken in haste, repented at leisure?' Hugo suggested, as they turned towards the Castle.

'Slipping classified material to the Soviets is hardly something to be done in the heat of the moment.'

Leo, then, was no more convinced than Hugo as to Rothesay's guilt.

'I should say,' Leo went on, 'that such a suggestion tells you more about the person making it than the person they're talking about. You might find they have little insight into the minds of others. Or that they wear their own loyalties lightly.'

'Marriage vows, for instance?'

'Indeed.'

'Thank you. I rather think I've slotted one minor piece into place.'

They walked under the great dark bulk of Freya's tower, back towards the door.

Saturday

Scene 1

Emerson pulled up promptly at half past eight, while Lady Sonia was still asleep. She groaned, turned over, and gave the clock an annoyed look. Why did he have to be so early? Why, for that matter, was he so keen to get Ingham off? Sonia was a firm believer in letting sleeping dogs lie, except where they had something of value to her. If Hugo and Freya hadn't meddled, the Castle would have been in the hands of the developers by now, her father's precious home being altered out of all recognition. Too bad he couldn't have stayed buried there, to see it all in progress.

She turned over to go back to sleep.

Georgia and Polly had gone off on their bikes, bound for school and then their expedition to Pagan Hill. Gus had told them in no uncertain terms to be back before sunset, and no quibbles. Mrs Partridge had slipped a solid slice of fruit cake into each of their lunchboxes, to keep them going.

Hugo was up and about, his sleep short and disturbed. His dreams had been full of dark corners of Berlin, shadowy figures stalking him, gunshots from behind. He'd found himself in the Lago, unable to move, being driven towards a cliff by a faceless MGB man while Valerie waved inanely from the pavement. All in all, not a good night.

Emerson had breakfasted at the George & Dragon, and breakfasted well, but he still found space for two slices of toast and some scrambled eggs he'd charmed out of Mrs Partridge. He was intrigued by Árpád, and promised to come back after Hugo was done with him.

Hugo took Emerson up to the sitting room he and Georgia shared, far from listening ears, and unfolded as much of the story as he could. There were certain details he couldn't reveal to anyone outside the Service, Official Secrets Act or no, which made the whole process rather more frustrating.

'The Saul I know,' said Emerson, who quite filled the large wing-back chair Hugo normally sat in, 'wouldn't have done that.'

'I don't believe he did,' said Hugo, glancing out over the Castle gardens. It was a lovely morning, misty with the promise of sun to come, a frost glinting on grass and trees. Lucky Georgia, to have a day like this for her expedition.

'He mentioned this Rothesay quarrel to me once, years ago. During the war. One of those conversations around a fire where everyone brings out their stories on a particular theme. In this case, it was fights they shouldn't have picked. He told us he'd fought a duel with a scientist, but they'd chosen the wrong place, been discovered by a coterie of witless undergraduates and had to run for it.'

'That matches the story my uncle heard.'

'The important thing about Saul,' Emerson went on, 'is that enormous chip on his shoulder. I twit him about it. He knows it's there, and he tries his best, but sometimes it's stronger than he is.'

'Strong enough to kill a man for gloating over his misfortune?'

'Aha,' said Emerson, 'that's my point. Saul needs to prove he's better. It's not about winning, it's about showing his mettle.'

Hugo understood. 'He wants them to know he won.'

'Exactly. I dare say he might have killed an unwary German sentry, but the point of killing a sentry is to stop him raising the alarm.'

'Whereas the point of fighting Dr Rothesay would have been to show him which of them was the better man.'

'I won't say he might not have killed someone accidentally, punched them too hard . . .'

'Or run them through with a fencing sword.'

'Indeed. I think he might well have killed the late Lord Selchester, if they'd ever met again. God knows, he had reason enough. But he'd have done it face-to-face, so Selchester had time to realise what had happened, and he'd have done it to show Selchester he could bleed and die like any other man.'

As indeed Selchester had, at the hands of someone he'd believed to be in his power.

'The trouble is,' Hugo said, 'that none of this will count for much with the police.'

'They are rather literal-minded.'

'Anxious to get rid of this Inspector Jarrett.'

'My God, is he here? The man's a menace.'

'You've come across him before?'

'Put a lot of pressure on one of my clients who was trying to recover a looted painting. Goering gave it to a Luftwaffe ace for his hundredth victory or some such. Being a fighter pilot rather than a Nazi, he's become a big cheese in the new West Germany, and the Government didn't want to alienate him. Jarrett dropped a lot of heavy hints about how unpatriotic it was to pursue private justice at the cost of public interest.'

'He seems to me to be after justice at any price.'

'Order is more like it – an order with him on top. Saul won't get any mercy if he's involved in the case. They'll find a hanging judge to try it. I did some ringing around yesterday, seems the Service is quite keen to have this all closed up.'

'They don't like Jarrett poking around any more than we do. I've had a fair number of veiled invitations to take myself off to a new line of work.'

Emerson laughed. 'They did that to me. Take the offer and run, is my advice. If they want you out, they'll just keep making life difficult.'

'They're not pushing me out while an innocent man is in peril of the gallows,' said Hugo. 'I'm running out of ideas, though. I know you're here to help Saul, but I don't know how much you can do.'

'I shall take myself off to visit him. I must say, I'm intrigued by the gun which was found at his cottage. Planting something like that without being detected takes a degree of skill.'

'It was searched from top to bottom not long ago, been empty ever since. The owner of the cottage died last year in very murky circumstances. Possibly a Soviet spy, certainly a sympathiser. That's why there was so much attention from the press, and other quarters, when Dr Rothesay first went missing. Georgia was hassled after school by an unpleasant fellow called Jenkins. We've seen him around Selchester before.'

Emerson sat bolt upright. 'Jenkins? Tall, cold-looking, pale blue eyes?'

'Yes.'

'He's no journalist.'

'Known to the police, apparently, some sort of private investigator. He told Freya he'd worked for the late Lord Selchester. She thought he might have been an official, although he didn't have the feel of one.'

'That he may have done, but she was right, he was never an official. There isn't really a description for what he does. You might call him your unofficial counterpart. He's worked for several powerful men in a hemi-demi-semi-official capacity. Situations where the Government absolutely can't be seen to have a hand in things, but the people he's negotiating with need to be sure their message will reach the right ears.'

'An odd sort of man to be turning up in Selchester. Is he on the level?'

'No,' said Emerson, 'he was involved in some very murky dealings. I came across him in Madrid during the Civil War, meeting several high-level people in the Republican government. Then he turned up in the Nationalist HQ too, bold as brass, straight into a meeting with one of Franco's aides. I couldn't enquire too closely, he had some dangerous friends and it wasn't a safe place to be.'

This Jenkins was a piece that didn't fit. Crossing the Atlantic with Gus, poking his nose around the town, asking intrusive questions on trains. Working for Lord Selchester, too.

'Lord Selchester was in the Government during the Civil War,' said Hugo. 'And well into the war too. Could he have been meddling?'

'Everyone was meddling in Spain and pretending not to. From Selchester's record, I'd have expected him to be a Franco sympathiser, but the Republicans were the official government. Perhaps there was something to be gained in talking to them.'

'I'll see if Jenkins has a file.'

'You'll be lucky to find one. I queried him to London when I was in Madrid. Slapped down at once, mind your own business. Met him again in Lisbon in even murkier circumstances. Same request, same response. You might have an easier time of it now, with Selchester and others of his generation safely in their graves.'

'Any history of violence?'

'He's a hard and capable man. Whether he ever gets his own hands dirty, I can't say.'

Hugo rather thought he did, from the number of suspicious accidents which had befallen Gus. Why try to kill Selchester's son, though? What was there to be gained? He'd apparently given up, too. Left Selchester at Christmas, hadn't been seen until he popped up outside Georgia's school.

'I should say,' Emerson added, 'that he'd be more than capable of planting evidence in a country cottage. Particularly if the owner had odd connections. You never know who might have a key.'

'Are they letting you in to see Saul?'

'They are indeed, although I suppose they'll watch me like a hawk.'

'Ask him about this Jenkins, see whether their paths ever crossed. See whether he ever dealt directly with any of Selchester's other people. We already know Selchester involved Saul in one sort of dubious business in post-war Berlin. We might be able to trace the other people who did his dirty work. Find out what they're up to now. I should be off, Valerie awaits.'

Emerson heaved his bulk out of the chair. 'Thank you for not giving up on Saul, by the way. Decent of you.'

'He isn't out of the woods yet.'

Emerson felt in one jacket pocket, then the other, then the inside. He frowned. 'I had a note for you from Henry Surcoat. Sends his regards, scrawled a few lines and sealed it in blood, as it were. Seem to have left it in my room, though. No wonder the Service didn't want me.'

'Bring it when you're finished with Saul. I shan't be back for a few hours. Better still, give it to Leo, it'll be safe with him. I'd rather not have it lying around where anyone can pick it up, we'll have all sorts in for the rehearsal this afternoon.'

Scene 2

Yarnley should have been a pleasant place to wait in the morning sunshine: a small market town with a merry river, assorted old pubs and a slightly sleepy air. The stationmaster gave Hugo a civil greeting and they exchanged a few words about the weather. The station tabby was so similar to the one in Selchester that Hugo wondered whether it was the same cat, prone to hop on and off the trains to ensure itself extra meals.

The cat seemed at ease, stalking among neatly bordered flowerbeds; Hugo was not. He hadn't worn his formal suit in more than a year, and it didn't seem to fit any more. Mrs Partridge had been a touch enthusiastic with the starch on his collar, too.

'There you go, Mr Hawksworth,' she'd said. 'Can't have Londoners saying we don't know how to dress in Selchester.'

Scene 3

Mrs Partridge clearly hadn't met Peter Woolhope. He and Harriet had wangled five minutes in private with Hugo on Friday afternoon, an illicit conference in Peter's chaotic office. They'd all been pulled off their regular work for a special job of Sir Bernard's, a task of extreme tedium and no apparent urgency. This happened about once a month, as Sir Bernard tried to impress his superiors in London, but on this occasion the timing was suspicious.

'Did you get anywhere at Foxley?' Harriet asked.

'I did indeed,' Hugo said. 'The rat I smelled turned out to be Laurence Oldcastle. Tried to get his group to pull off some tricky plutonium processing on a wing and a prayer. No proper equipment, no competent experimentalists, and a great deal of pressure from above.'

'What did he stand to gain?' Peter asked.

'The credit. It was time for Rothesay to get his own department, but Oldcastle knew he'd lose his ace in the hole.'

'Who knows?' Harriet said.

'They all do. Rothesay wasn't shy about telling anyone. He was the source of Árpád's leak, we can be quite sure of that. I think I know how that got back to the Russians. One of his numerous amours was

Miranda Pearson, who I'm told has fairly radical views. I think if we delved, we'd find they'd been fellow travellers in the thirties.'

'Shall we look her up?'

'I'm going to.' He had already resolved to tackle her at the talk that evening.

'In which case,' Peter said, 'you don't think Rothesay is the source of the more recent material.'

Hugo shook his head.

'Who else could it be?' Harriet asked. 'I know you're not keen on Rothesay the Communist, nor am I. But Rothesay full of sour grapes, that's much more plausible.'

It was Peter who supplied the answer. 'Oldcastle's the man Hugo has in mind. He's wide open to blackmail, given Rothesay's habit of grumbling to anyone who'd listen. We'll need to do a full inquiry, temporary suspension and everything.'

'I don't know whether you gentlemen have noticed,' Harriet said, 'but Sir Bernard thinks Oldcastle is a Good Egg. We'll have the devil of a time getting approval for this.'

'The evidence is there,' Hugo said. 'That was my task for today.'

'A task you now don't have time for,' Harriet said, 'thanks to this ridiculous wild goose chase of Sir Bernard's. Orders from London, my foot. He wants you out of the way.'

Peter's eyes narrowed. 'Oho! Mischief afoot. A quiet phone call from Oldcastle, pouring his woes into our exalted chief's shell-like?'

'Sticky territory for Sir B if so,' Harriet said, 'but I wouldn't put it past him. They seem to be getting on very well indeed.'

Hugo had entertained the same suspicion. 'Reconvene on Monday,' he said. 'First thing, let's give ourselves a head start.'

'If it's enough,' Harriet said. 'The cat's out of the bag now. If Oldcastle is desperate enough to pull Sir Bernard's strings, who else has he talked to?'

Who else indeed, Hugo wondered. Oldcastle was a better Soviet source than Rothesay in every respect – more senior, more influential, and most importantly more discreet. Hugo had handled sources like Rothesay himself, men with private grudges. Loose cannons, unreliable in the extreme. Dangerous to someone in Oldcastle's position, dangerous to their controller.

But who was that controller? Someone in London, where everything was anonymous? Or in Selchester, close by? Instinct said the latter. Whoever had dumped Rothesay's body and stitched Saul up knew the area well.

Scene 4

The train pulled into the station in a hiss of steam. Hugo wished for a moment it had gone straight through, then caught himself. What on earth was he thinking?

Valerie stepped down from one of the first-class carriages, chic and immaculate as ever. He winced as he caught sight of her shoes: high-heeled kid leather, utterly unsuitable for the country. Lady Sonia might wrap herself in mink, but she'd never be caught out like that.

'There you are, darling.' Valerie glanced around. 'Pretty enough, but I shouldn't like to be stuck here. I wonder if they talk about anything but dogs and horses.' He rather thought one or two of the other passengers were off to the same thing, but Valerie didn't seem to know them.

Hugo handed Valerie into the car. 'Where are we heading?' he asked.

'Wulfsy Manor. Straight up the high street, Serena said, and it's on the right, a mile out of town.'

It was indeed, a rambling and rather charming assortment of gables, Elizabethan windows, and Jacobean timbering. Yarnley's church stood by the gate, well out of the town, one of those peculiar mediaeval survivals.

'Rustic' was Valerie's verdict. 'I suppose Serena married him for his house. She always wanted to live somewhere rural and have hordes of children. There's no accounting for taste.'

'Who's her husband?'

'His name's Arthur. Good-natured, but a bit dim if you ask me.'

Hugo couldn't remember which of Valerie's many acquaintances Serena was until she met them at the porch. Fair, round, with laughter lines around her eyes. She looked happy, he thought, not at all like a woman who'd married for the sake of the house. Her husband was equally fair, blond and cheerful. Hugo recognised him at once, they'd been at Oxford at the same time.

'Hawksworth,' said Arthur, giving him a firm handshake. 'History at St John's, am I correct?'

'Indeed. You were at Christ Church.'

'Forestry.' He grinned. 'Can't say I paid much attention, but I haven't had to sell the place yet, so I must be doing something right. Where are you now?'

'Selchester.'

'I had no idea. Shows you how much I get out and about. D'you know Archie Veryan? He's coming today.'

'I lodge at the Castle, his niece lives there.'

'Freya Wryton. Rides a big ugly piebald with a foul temper.'

Hugo would have to tell Freya how far Last Hurrah's reputation had spread, although he suspected Arthur was the sort of man who knew horses better than people.

Valerie shot Hugo a sidelong look at the mention of Freya's name.

'So you'll know this new American earl. I must say I'd rather like to meet him. Fancy being plucked from New England and planted down here. Serena tells me he's much too clever for the likes of me, though. Come in, come in, we're assembling here before we go over. One or two

207

still to arrive. Didn't want all this mummery myself, but my mother insisted, likes to do things properly.'

Wulfsy Manor was as oddly laid out as the Castle, although on a rather more friendly scale. They were led through into a beamed hall, barely the size of one of the Castle's Drawing Rooms, with a minstrels' gallery. A chorus of barks sounded from the other side of a door. Arthur was exactly the sort of man to have half a dozen dogs.

Valerie extricated Hugo from Arthur's company. 'There's someone you should meet. Over there, talking to the Veryans.'

Lady Priscilla's husband was large and florid, quite a presence in the House. Hugo had only met him once or twice, as he was away a great deal. He didn't know the other man, although he had the look of a senior civil servant about him.

'Hawksworth,' said Sir Archibald. 'Good to see you here, heard you'd be coming. This is Hammond Stainer, of the Board of Trade.'

They shook hands, Hugo concealing his wariness. He had a good idea what was afoot. One didn't work for the Service without learning the ways of British officialdom.

'So this is Valerie,' said Lady Priscilla, sizing her up. 'Come, let's leave them to the Official Secrets Act, best to get business out of the way first. I believe you know my niece, Lady Sonia . . .'

Valerie had not the slightest objection to leaving Hugo the moment they came into the room. It was all very effectively managed. The Service could hardly have done better, although they might have maintained the pretence of a social occasion for a few moments longer.

'We knew one another when I was on the Trade Committee,' said Sir Archibald. 'He was in your department for a while, although before your time. You joined the Service from the Army?'

'Service first. I was seconded to the Army during the war.'

'And now you're on the bench, with this leg of yours. Heard about that, nasty business. How's it healing?'

'It's on its way,' Hugo said. There was a script to be followed, the only question was what they wanted to offer him. 'The doctors tell me I'll always limp, but nothing worse.'

'How are you finding life at Sir Bernard's outfit? Worked with him for a while. Good man, if perhaps a touch pedestrian. Not in the Chief's league.'

There wasn't much Hugo could, or indeed should, say to that.

'You know to keep your mouth shut,' said Sir Archibald approvingly.

Stainer took over. 'I wanted to meet you, informally you under-stand,' he said. 'We've an opening at the Board, quite a step up from your present position. Needs a man with some experience in your line of work, untangling truth from falsehood, bit of a nose for what's been hidden.'

'I'm no economist,' said Hugo.

'We've plenty of economists, you'll pick the numbers up quickly enough, or what's an Oxford education for? What I need is someone who's used to thinking the way the Soviets do. Who's up, who's down, who's in, who's out. Keeping track of the politics of it all, so we know who we're dealing with on the trade front, and who we might be dealing with in a year's time. I've all sorts of bright young men who know their numbers, but none who knows the Soviets. London-based, of course, you'll have access to all the information you need, and a hefty increase on your Service salary. Can't have a man like you mouldering in the sticks, now can we?'

'Don't let Sir Bernard hear you say that,' said Sir Archibald.

'I'd have thought,' said Hugo carefully, 'there were men on the Russia desk who'd be better suited than I am.'

He heard Valerie's laugh across the room. She'd already gathered an admiring circle about her.

'None I can get hold of,' said Stainer. 'Come, don't beat about the bush. I'm told you're a man who wants to serve your country, not jump ship to work in a bank. I admire that. But the Service can't use a field officer with a gammy leg. The Board can. I dare say that girlfriend of yours would take it kindly, too. You'd be in line for one of our official flats, just off the edge of Mayfair, and school fees for your sister. I understand you're her guardian.'

'Thank you,' said Hugo. 'How soon would you want me to start?'

'Soon as possible. We'd treat it as an internal transfer, you'd be on your way in a few weeks.'

'It's quite an offer. May I give you my answer next week?'

Stainer frowned. 'I was rather hoping you'd jump at it. Won't be able to hold it open for long.'

'Mr Stainer, I've been with the Service for fourteen years. I owe it my loyalty, and I won't simply leave it because I've had another offer, no matter how generous that offer may be.'

'Good answer,' said Sir Archibald unexpectedly. 'Give him a day or two, Stainer, it's only courteous. Man wants to serve his country, you should expect him to have a sense of duty to the branch he serves in.'

'Of course.' Stainer fished a card out of his pocket and scribbled a number on the back. 'This is my private line. Give me a ring, Tuesday at the latest.'

Hugo tucked the card into his pocket, and the talk turned to mutual acquaintances in the Service.

Scene 5

Valerie caught up with him as they made their way over to the church, square and archetypally English in the winter sunshine.

'Well?'

'Well, what?'

She cast her eyes upwards.

'What do you think?'

'I take it you know what he was offering.'

'It's a job at the Board of Trade, who'll appreciate you considerably more than the Service, give you a good position with a decent salary, and not exile you to a decaying Victorian pile in the middle of the countryside to do the job of a glorified librarian. As to exactly what it is, no I don't know, although I suppose it's something in your general line. Do I have it right?'

'More or less.'

'Then, for heaven's sake, what did you say?'

'I'll give him an answer in the week.'

'You leapt at the chance to come down here.'

'I virtually handed in my resignation my first day on the job.'

'Why on earth didn't you?'

'I owe the Service. And, as it turned out, I like the work.'

He didn't expect her to understand, and she didn't. She was, however, wise enough not to say anything more. She gave his arm a squeeze, and they walked through the porch into the musty quiet of the little church. St Osmund's, said the noticeboard.

It was a still, hallowed place, full of box pews and pale sunlight. The walls were scattered with memorial stones to generations of Arthur's family sleeping in the churchyard, the hassocks threadbare with use, the stone floor worn and uneven. There was a rood screen, old as the church, with a gaunt mediaeval crucifix above.

The guests stood around the font, hushed by habit. The christening party came in, Serena radiant and Arthur solemn. That must be Arthur's mother, she had his look. Not nearly so much a dragon as Lady Priscilla, though. There was the rector, tall and bony like a heron, with a voice which seemed much too resonant for him. There was the baby, Hugo hadn't caught its name. He felt like an imposter. What was he doing here, at the christening of a child of two people he hardly knew? There couldn't be twenty people in the church.

Stainer was one of the godfathers, Sir Archibald another. The Hampton-Bishops clearly believed in an abundance of godparents, there were seven around the font.

Hugo's eyes wandered over the church, the words of the service washing over him. Dust danced in the sunbeams, bell ropes hung looped beneath the west tower. He wondered whether Freya had rung here. Change-ringers were a convivial lot, always popping around to one another's churches to try out the bells.

He looked at Valerie, poised and attentive. Very much a hatch, match and dispatch Anglican, although with the number of weddings she went to, that was no inconsiderable level of churchgoing. He'd hardly made it to the christenings of friends' children, always abroad. He did remember Georgia's, in a blacked-out London church at the beginning of the Blitz, his father granted a single night at home by a sympathetic admiral. A next-door neighbour and Aunt Charlotte for godmothers, his father's first officer as godfather, smart in his naval uniform. His parents, worn by war and worry, had for one night looked as radiant as the Hampton-Bishops now. Georgia had been a gift to them, quite unexpected and greatly treasured.

In a grim symmetry, the neighbour had died in the doodlebug strike which killed Hugo's mother, while Lieutenant-Commander Melmerby, a reservist like Hugo's father, had gone down with the *Alcyone*.

A memorial stone just beyond the font caught Hugo's eye, pale grey stone with RAF wings at the top. Flight-Lieutenant Charles Hampton-Bishop, only son and heir to another Arthur. Killed on the Marne aged twenty-three, 1st November 1918. Arthur had never even known his father.

'I demand, therefore,' said the rector, his voice louder of a sudden, 'dost thou, in the name of this child, renounce the devil and all his works, the vain pomp and glory of the world, with all covetous desires of the same, and the carnal desires of the flesh, so that thou wilt not follow, nor be led by them?'

A confused mumble from the phalanx of godparents, no individual words discernible.

Stainer had just offered Hugo the vain pomp and glory of the world, and not a few covetous desires of the same, so he clearly wasn't forswearing them. But then, he wasn't required to do so for himself. He was forswearing them for the Hampton-Bishops' child, a tiny Arthur or Serena to grow to adulthood in this quiet corner of England, to skip down the stone path to the church and fidget in the pews, no doubt to complain loudly about having to go at all.

The child was held out over the font, the water poured. It broke out in an indignant wail.

'Charles Augustus Osmund, I baptise thee in the name of the Father, and of the Son, and of the Holy Ghost.'

A boy, then. Another Charles, like Arthur's father and Hugo's. New life, to keep the Hampton-Bishop name alive. To make a life of his own, perhaps into a ripe old age, if there was hope for any of them in a world full of A-bombs and H-bombs.

Hugo was in the oddest frame of mind today. It was a social event, full of strangers and distant acquaintances, in a place he'd never been before and would probably never visit again. Why were his thoughts wandering like this?

Valerie had noticed. 'Wool-gathering again?' she said as they came back out into the sunshine, back between the graves towards the house and a spread for lunch. 'The countryside must be getting to you. Bright as a button, you were, in London.'

They walked on. A gust of wind rustled the yews, wafting snatches of conversation towards them. Valerie fell silent, alert for gossip.

'. . . second reading of the Housing Bill . . .'

'. . . due back on leave next weekend . . .'

'. . . always said he was wrong for her, but it's hard on the children . . .'

'I suppose they've put him down for Eton?' Stainer said, close behind.

Sir Archibald's voice, in reply. 'No, they haven't. Some odd ideas about education, both of them. Tried to reason with them, but they're not having any of it. Say they'll send him somewhere close. Bryanston perhaps, or Millfield.'

'Peculiar places, the both of them. Felicity and Walter are sending my grandchildren to a day school. Don't know where these notions get into their heads. Won't do any good.'

Stainer and Sir Archibald strolled past them with courteous nods. Hugo's limp was slowing them down, only the grandmothers were left to pass them.

'. . . Yes, after his grandfathers. The Osmund is a family tradition . . .'

'This will all be done by two or three,' said Valerie. 'You can show me Selchester afterwards. I've a ticket on the evening express.'

'I thought it was fearfully dull.'

'I'm sure it's perfectly charming, as provincial towns go. Wouldn't want to live there myself, but you'll have been six months or so here. I should like to see it.'

Scene 6

The Castle had come to life.

Freya was glad of it. There hadn't been this many people there since the war, and then it had all been camouflage trucks and the like. The courtyard was a cheerful bedlam of cars and vans, far too many for the usual spaces. Ben had to direct some to park on the grass in the inner court, the great circuit within the ruined walls.

The ballroom, cleaned and lit for the first time in almost fifteen years, was alive with voices. Gone were the dust sheets, the dim gloom, even the chill. Ben had fixed the radiators, with some uncomplimentary words about the Army plumbers. Gus, always ready for some electrical tinkering, had tested the chandeliers before handing them over to Mrs Partridge for a good polish. Naturally, they gleamed.

The professionals were clustered in one knot, perhaps more curious than usual, but acting as if they'd seen it all before. The local cast members were wandering around excitedly, peering out of windows and into corners. Vivian was briskly impersonal, laying out the limits of the stage.

The Pearsons were setting up folding chairs under the direction of Mrs Partridge, who wasn't having anyone else take charge in her house. Sonia had drifted in earlier, cigarette in hand, casting a jaundiced eye over the proceedings.

'Amateur dramatics, how worthy.'

Emerson was having none of it. 'Weaned on a pickle, you were. It's not amateur, for a start, not with Vivian Witt directing and Sir Desmond Winthrop playing Becket. I shall be coming down to see it, and I shan't be the only one.'

Sonia didn't have much time for Vivian either. 'Hardy Amies, ugh. I wonder if they're keeping her on retainer.'

'She wishes it were builders, in to strip the place bare and turn it into a hotel,' said Freya.

'I do,' said Sonia, 'and I shan't pretend otherwise. I hope you've locked the doors. Look at all those hangers-on. Some of them will have light fingers, believe me.'

'I could put one of those pikes across the passage,' Freya said. The staircase hall was thick with displays of mediaeval weapons, relics of various arsenals the Fitzwarins had built up whenever the Crown wasn't looking.

'Just put that bear in the way,' said Emerson. 'The one lurking at the foot of the stairs. It has an accusing look, if you ask me.'

'I should have an accusing look if I'd been shot by an English earl on a tourist jaunt,' said Freya. The bear in question had been unlucky enough to come within the sights of her grandfather's gun during his tenure in Canada. Since her grandfather had been notoriously short-sighted and too vain to wear spectacles, family tradition suggested it had simply died of old age at a convenient moment.

'Hideous thing,' said Sonia. 'Like something out of the Dark Ages.'

'So it'll deter burglars,' said Emerson. 'Let them wonder what else they have to contend with. Are there oubliettes in the Castle?'

'There's a room at the bottom of the Old Tower,' said Freya, 'but I don't believe it was anything so gothic. Just a storeroom.'

'I shall keep myself out of the way until they're all gone,' said Sonia. 'At least Aunt P isn't about, off at that christening with Hugo and Valerie, or she'd feel the need to haul me over for tea.'

Freya knew very well this was a dig at her, and was determined not to let her cousin get under her skin. Sonia was being more than usually waspish at the unwonted interruptions in her life.

Despite which, she showed no sign of actually getting rid of Emerson. He lingered after she'd left, quite content to watch the bustle.

'Did Saul know anything about Jenkins?' Freya asked. Hugo had brought her up to date on Jenkins before he left.

'I did. He gave me one or two names to follow up, men he knows were associated with the late Lord Selchester. He doesn't know Jenkins, but recognised him from my description. Turns out Saul saw him down on the river path last weekend. Took him for a reporter, that was the day they were all nosing around.'

'Did he now?' Not enough to convince Jarrett or MacLeod, but perhaps a glimmer of hope, a thread to follow.

Vivian clapped her hands. The room fell silent.

'Thank you. We're late starting, so let's not have any further delay. We'll start with the entrance of the Second Tempter. Father Leo Hawksworth has kindly agreed to read in for Becket today. I'm reliably informed he was a pillar of OUDS during his time at Oxford.'

'He'd make a good Becket,' Emerson whispered, seeing Leo tall and commanding in clerical black.

They settled down to watch.

Scene 7

Bicycles safely chained to a fence post at the base of Pagan Hill, Georgia, Polly and Daisy were making their way up its slope.

'The path goes this side of the fence,' Polly insisted. 'Look, you can see the line on the map.'

The map belonged to the Castle, tracked down by Mrs Partridge with dire warnings as to the consequences if it was muddied, drenched or torn.

'Maybe it does,' said Georgia, 'but there's a path on this side of the fence, too, and the view's much better. Look, you can see all the way to the Atomic.'

'The best view is at the top,' Daisy pointed out. 'And if you two won't stop squabbling, we won't have time to get there.'

'It doesn't look far,' said Polly.

Half an hour later, she was thoroughly disabused of that notion. 'How many summits does this hill have?' she said, planting herself on a tree stump. 'Every time it looks as if we're there, it just goes on.'

'Hah! No stamina, you Americans.'

'I've been to Yosemite,' said Polly. 'Half Dome could squash Pagan Hill and not even notice.'

'Does Half Dome have a pagan barrow on top?' Georgia said. 'Revenant kings who ride with the Wild Hunt? I think not.'

'You didn't say anything about the Wild Hunt,' said Daisy, who was rather envious of their night-time excursion with Árpád. She'd quite like to stay at the Castle more – home was nice, but not nearly so interesting. 'Only lights.'

'Of course it was the Wild Hunt,' said Georgia. 'What else would it be?'

'Martians,' said Polly, who after initial resistance had succumbed to the lure of Georgia's science fiction, and was now catching up with Árpád.

Polly was chivvied off her perch, and they all pressed on.

'Look, we're nearly there,' Daisy said as they reached a fence and a belt of woodland. 'This is on the map, just before the top. It can't be more than a couple of hundred yards now.'

'How do we get over the fence?' said Polly, practically.

'There's supposed to be a stile. Look, there it is.'

Georgia and Daisy gathered that stiles were an unknown quantity to Polly. She found it distinctly wobbly, but persevered. Georgia leapt off the top of the fence, landing in a shower of dry leaves.

'Where does that go?' she said, pointing to a path leading off into thick undergrowth.

Daisy consulted the map. 'It's a right of way, but it doesn't go anywhere.'

'What's the point of a path which doesn't go anywhere?' Polly said. 'Only in England would there be anything so ridiculous.'

'Maybe it goes into the hill,' Georgia said. 'Maybe there's another entrance to the barrow, and we'll find a network of tunnels under the hill. With skeletons.'

'I think if there were skeletons, someone would have found them already,' said Daisy, but Georgia was already charging off.

Much to Georgia's disappointment, the path petered out in a briar patch after a mere fifty yards.

'I think foxes and things must use it,' said Daisy. 'Look, it goes on into the undergrowth, but it's much too small for us.'

Georgia was looking for a way around. 'Hullo, what's this?'

She picked up something tortoiseshell, with gold bands.

'Fountain pen,' said Daisy. 'Give it to me. Pa likes fountain pens.'

Georgia handed it over.

Daisy surveyed it with a knowledgeable eye. 'No name on it. But it's an Osmiroid. Expensive. Must have fallen out of someone's pocket while they were looking for a way through. They'll be cross.'

'We can hand it in at the police station,' said Polly. 'Come on, let's go back, the sun's low and we don't want to be late. Think how long it took us to get up here.'

A few moments later they were standing on top of the barrow, a stiff wind blowing their hair back.

'You can see half the county from here,' said Georgia.

'Chilly place to be buried, though,' said Daisy.

'Pagan kings didn't care about that. They're probably off in Valhalla, feasting with the Valkyries. Maybe they were burned in a funeral pyre, here where everyone could see.'

'There were midsummer fires up here until the sixteenth century,' said Polly. 'They used to light them on every hilltop roundabouts, but this was the chief one. It wasn't called Pagan Hill until after the Reformation, when the Protestants decided they didn't like bonfires any more and put a stop to it.'

'That's because bonfires ought to be in November, when it's dark. They were just more sensible.'

'Will you two stop that?' Daisy said, glaring at them both. 'It's bad enough you arguing about it over homework. You only do it to wind the adults up anyway. Now, let's have a look in the barrow while there's still light.'

Scene 8

The three of them came freewheeling down the path through the Castle gardens just as Hugo's car pulled up outside the front door. The inner bailey was still packed with cars, the rehearsal just coming to a close. The sun had set, but the western sky was still a clear pale blue with a faint dusting of bright stars.

'Who's that with him?' Daisy asked, quite innocently.

Georgia scowled. 'That's Valerie.'

'Uh-oh,' said Polly. 'Too late, they've seen us now.'

Hugo had indeed seen them, although Valerie was still look-ing around her. 'So this is Selchester Castle,' she said. 'I must say, I hadn't imagined anything quite so grimly impressive. More something Victorian with turrets.'

'There are turrets aplenty around the back,' said Hugo. 'The Earl lives in a Victorian wing.'

'So you're here, in this louring pile. I must say, it's not where I'd imagine you living.'

'It's not nearly so grim inside. Come on, let me show you.' He took her arm. It had been a good lunch, his odd mood of the christening temporarily forgotten. Valerie had been in fine form, sparkling with anecdotes, charming all and sundry. Hugo had renewed his acquain-tance with Arthur, in considerably more depth than it had existed before. He was pleasant company, a man quite at peace with himself and his limitations, consequently very easy to be around. Indeed, for a while Hugo had managed to put Stainer and his offer quite out of mind.

She smiled. 'I should like that.'

The girls raced along the edge of the inner bailey, coming to a halt in as near a screech of brakes as bicycles would allow, although Georgia was now lagging distinctly behind.

'How was your expedition?' Hugo asked. 'No, don't tell me now, put your bikes away before there are cars everywhere. The rehearsal's just finishing.'

It was indeed. The first few cast members, with places to be or no disposition to linger, were making their way across the terrace to their cars. A big black car came through the gatehouse, on its way to pick someone up.

'I'd have liked to see Father Leo as Becket,' said Polly.

'He'll be doing it again tomorrow,' said Hugo.

He ushered Valerie into the kitchen, the door closing behind them.

'Where's Georgia?' Daisy asked, as she put her foot on the pedal.

Polly looked round. 'She was just behind us. Probably gone the long way around, so she doesn't have to see Valerie.'

'What's wrong with Valerie?'

'Everything, to hear Georgia say it. I'm sure she can't be that bad.'

'You haven't met Lucy Cheriton's stepmother,' said Daisy. 'I thought Lucy was laying it on too thick, until I met her.'

'Valerie wouldn't be Georgia's stepmother.'

'Step-guardian. Bad enough. Come on, let's put these away before we end up stuck in a traffic jam.'

Scene 9

Gus, sensible of his duties as host, gathered them all in for tea in the library. Freya was glad of the extra bodies. Emerson's warmth and Árpád's impolite questions were more than enough to smooth over the awkwardness of Valerie's presence and Georgia's pointed absence. Hugo hadn't talked about the offer he'd received, and Valerie hadn't mentioned it.

The rehearsal was over, the chandeliers dark, the ballroom closed up. Father Leo had been a splendid Becket, Freya rather thought. Perhaps they could revive the old tradition of theatricals at the Castle. They'd still been going on well into the 1880s, just as in Jane Austen's day. Somewhere up in the attics, boxes and boxes of costumes and props still gathered dust. Perhaps the moths had got them, perhaps not.

Hugo was trying not to think too hard about Georgia, but no one could conceal that every other current resident of the Castle was there, and his sister wasn't. He took advantage of the arrival of a fresh pot of tea to ask Mrs Partridge to call her down. A few moments later, the door opened, but it was Mrs Partridge again.

'She isn't in her room, Mr Hugo, nor in your sitting room, nor anywhere else I've poked my head in.'

Hugo caught Freya's eye and drew them both out into the hallway.

'Did you or Sonia have hiding places, if you didn't want to be found?' he asked.

'I imagine Sonia did,' said Freya. 'There'd be plenty. I never needed them. My uncle liked his peace and quiet, and he was always very meticulous about ensuring his guests were extended the same courtesy if they wanted it. Unless he had business with them, of course.'

They both knew what sort of business that would be.

'It's too bad of her,' said Hugo testily. 'All she had to do was make polite conversation for half an hour. You'd think I was threatening to pack her off to a nunnery.'

'Polly and Daisy say she took herself off as soon as she saw you at the door. Have you seen her bike, Mrs Partridge? Perhaps she put it inside and came up the back stairs.'

'If she'd left it in a corridor, I'd have given her a good talking-to, but there's no sign of it, and Ben hasn't seen it neither.'

'Could Ben make a tour with a torch, see whether he can find her? Or at least the bike – we'll be able to tell where she came in. He'll know all the nooks and crannies.'

'That he can,' said Mrs Partridge. 'He's fond of Miss Georgia. We all are.'

She took herself off towards Ben's domain.

'I'll have a look around inside,' Freya said. 'She might come out for me.'

'She'd better,' Hugo said. 'It's one thing not to like Valerie, quite another to behave like this. She was brought up to have good manners. Aunt Charlotte was very careful about that, after Mother died.'

'She's also thirteen years old,' Freya said, 'and longing for some stability in her life – a stability conspicuously lacking in the last year or so. When did your aunt announce her engagement?' Aunt Charlotte's decision to marry an American and move across the Atlantic had prompted a great deal of turmoil in Georgia's life, and the transfer of her guardianship to her brother.'

'Last December,' Hugo said.

'She's had thirteen months of uncertainty, and just when everything looked settled, it may all be about to turn upside down. It's a wonder she's borne everything as well as she has. You've led a very rootless life yourself, by choice. Georgia may be made of the same stuff, but she shouldn't have to find out until she's older.'

Hugo nodded, feeling distinctly out of his depth once again. He'd meant to ask his uncle for advice, but the opportunity had yet to present itself, with the question of Saul's guilt hanging over everything. He'd make time tomorrow, Leo wasn't due back in Oxford until Monday.

'Thank you,' he said. 'At least let me know when you find her, if you can't coax her down here.'

Hugo returned to the library, no doubt to watch Árpád interrogating Sonia and Valerie. Freya was a little sad to miss that – it wasn't often Sonia came across someone as tactless as she was, and Valerie's face was a picture – but she was worried about Georgia.

She took a torch from the cupboard by the door and set off into the upper reaches of the Castle, one room at a time. Ben and Mrs Partridge did their best to keep everything in order, but not all the rooms had working bulbs, and there were plenty of dark corners.

It was quiet, dark, chill. The corridors were familiar but empty, some still with bare stone, the rooms musty and long deserted. She walked quietly on slippered feet, calling out Georgia's name every so often, listening in each empty room for the sound of breathing. She rather thought Georgia wouldn't have gone in search of darkness, but of warmth and familiarity.

She checked in her own tower just in case, but it was as she had left it, shrouded in gloom aside from the desk light, pages of scribbled notes all over the table. She was almost ready to go: she could feel a new version of the story looming in her mind, much stronger and more dramatic. Monday morning, she would start on Monday morning. An imprisoned Puritan major-general, a Royalist peer compromised by Thurloe's little book of secrets, a web of intrigue with its roots in the grim years of the Commonwealth, it was all there.

She crossed back along the gallery of Grace Hall.

'Miss Freya?' It was Ben's voice.

She leaned over the balustrade. He'd come in through the door at the back, holding his own big torch, looking rather puzzled. 'Yes? Any sign of the bicycle?'

'None that I can see,' he said. 'I've looked in the shed, and the Old Guardroom, where she sometimes stows it when she's come back for something, but there's no sign of it.'

'The gardens?' Freya said. 'They were on their way from Pagan Hill. They must have come down through the upper gate and the Italian garden.'

'I wouldn't want to be searching in the dark,' Ben said. 'You could pass two feet from it and not see it, if it's behind a hedge. Besides, Miss Polly said Georgia was right behind them when they came down on to the circle. Doesn't stand to reason she'd take herself back up again, it's a steep way. Shouldn't like to come down it myself, like to break my neck, but girls will be girls. You don't think she might have taken herself off elsewhere, do you?'

Freya was alarmed. Georgia hiding in the Castle was one thing, Georgia cycling off into the dark was quite another. It was something very close to running away, and on a bitterly cold winter's night. Even hardy Ben was bundled up in a heavy coat.

'Could you try the attics?' she said. 'I don't see why she'd have gone up there, but it's a real rabbit warren. Maybe she thought she'd go exploring where we can't find her. There might be footprints.'

'Might be, but I don't know how she'd have got the key. Very careful with those, I am, and Mrs Partridge, too. Accidents waiting to happen, those attics are, and dry as tinder besides. One silly fool poking around with a candle or gas lamp, and the whole Castle's on fire before you know it.'

'Don't say such things, you'll frighten us all witless.'

Ben shook his head. 'I doubt very much she's up there, but I shall take a look nonetheless. Best to be sure.'

They parted company, Ben to the attics and Freya to the guest rooms above her father's suite, in the Jacobean part of the Castle. She passed through the Long Gallery, generations of ancestors watching her from the shadows. Two or three of the girls' skittles had fallen over and rolled into corners, had that been Georgia's doing? She called, but no answer came. Now thoroughly worried, she pressed on.

Scene 10

Freya came back in alone. Seeing her face, Hugo fell quiet, and the whole room with him.

'Something's the matter,' said Father Leo at once, putting his cup down. 'What can we do?'

'Nothing that Ben and I haven't already done,' said Freya. 'There's no sign of Georgia anywhere, nor of her bike.'

'Then we must search,' said Árpád. 'For one to wander through the corridors calling her name, this she can ignore. But to hear all of us, worried, in search of her, then if she is hiding she will come out.'

'But she was just behind us,' said Polly, looking around for reassurance.

'Árpád is right,' said Gus at once. 'I'm sure we shall find her soon, but we should split up. There are plenty of us.'

'What if she tripped and hit her head?' said Polly. 'She could be lying out in the gardens somewhere.'

'It is too cold to be outside for long,' said Árpád. 'She will be in danger.'

'Ben couldn't search the gardens on his own,' Freya said.

'Then we must help him, it is our duty,' said Árpád. 'Perhaps the gentlemen can search outside, and the ladies inside?'

'Should we tell the police?' Gus asked. 'We'll need them if we have to search the grounds.'

'Let's try the house and gardens first,' said Hugo, who had no mind to call out the county police force only to discover Georgia sulking in a cupboard somewhere. If he were to clear Saul's name, it was essential Jarrett and MacLeod took him seriously.

'Must we?' said Sonia. 'She's just after attention. Leave her alone and she'll come creeping out of whatever hole she's hidden herself in.'

Valerie was of like mind. 'You should have left her at Yorkshire Ladies', they'd have put a stop to such nonsense. I shall call a taxi to take me to the station, you'll need all hands on deck here.'

Árpád, standing behind Valerie, scowled at her, but it was Lady Sonia he spoke to. 'I do not believe that Miss Georgia would act as you say. Shall we proceed?'

Scene 11

It was a cold and dispirited group who trudged back towards the house an hour or so later. There was a chill north wind across the valley, a frost on the ground, and no sign of Georgia.

Polly had ventured out, bundled in coat and hat, to show them where she'd last seen Georgia, between the box hedges on the sweeping path down from the Italian garden. They tried to follow the imprint of her tyres, but the path emptied on to gravel trodden by too many feet at the end of the rehearsal.

Nowhere in the gardens was there a trace of Georgia, bicycle, or even of intruder. Undertended these past seven years, the gardens were untidy and overgrown, but nowhere could they see so much as a hint of someone pushing their way through a hedge or lying comatose behind a wall. They looked in summerhouses, sheds, the Gothick folly at the gardens' far edge. They shouted out across the parkland, beneath bare winter trees bright with ice.

The searchers of the house were back in the kitchen, hastily drinking mugs of hot tea. Sonia looked distinctly put out, this wasn't what she'd signed up for.

Freya didn't need to ask to know they'd been unsuccessful. She'd heard no joyful shouts or cheerful murmur of voices.

'I shall phone the police,' said Gus.

'We thought,' said Polly, 'that some of the people coming out of the rehearsal might have seen something. We could try them.'

'That's my girl,' said Gus. 'Let's get the Superintendent in, then we'll see.'

He disappeared through into Grace Hall.

'She must have run away,' said Hugo. 'But where? I can't imagine who she'd go to.'

'She'd not run away,' said Mrs Partridge. 'Poor thing's so desperate at the thought of being uprooted again, leaving's the last thing she'd do. She feels safe here.'

Then where had she gone?

Gus came back in. 'The phone's down. I can't get a dial tone.'

'Can't be,' said Sonia. 'I rang a friend this afternoon, while you were all hanging around at that rehearsal.'

Probably chatted for hours on Gus's phone bill, too.

'What time was that?' Freya said.

Sonia shrugged. 'Three o'clock, perhaps? It was still daylight when I hung up.'

'I shall go to the police station in person,' Hugo said.

'I'll come with you,' said Leo at once. 'Hot tea can wait.'

They headed back outside. Hugo had left the Lago by the front door, expecting to drive Valerie to the station. He opened the door, it wasn't locked. There was a folded sheet of paper on the driver's seat, where none had been before. He went very still.

Leo saw his expression. 'What is it?'

Hugo came back around to the light, unfolded the paper. Ordinary typing paper, a few lines.

> Mr Hawksworth,
>
> If you wish your sister to be returned, you will put in writing your considered opinion that Dr Bruno Rothesay, Soviet spy, was killed by Mr Saul Ingham in the course of a personal quarrel, and ensure that this report is received by the police. If you do so, she will be released unharmed.
>
> You will then return this note by any means you wish to Major Lukács at the embassy of the People's Republic of Hungary.
>
> Should you subsequently attempt to retract this opinion, suggest that your sister has done anything more than attempt to run away from home, or mention the existence of this note to the police at any point, you will never see her again.

Hugo took a deep, furious breath, and handed the note to Leo. He took in the contents in a second.

'The oldest and ugliest way to make a man do what you want,' he said. 'I doubt it will be any consolation that this has quite convinced me on the matter of Mr Ingham's innocence.'

Hugo struck the edge of his fist against the doorpost, all those years of training counting for nothing in the face of such a letter.

'Could they carry through on such a threat?' Leo asked. 'To make her disappear again?'

Hugo nodded. 'There was a case in Berlin in '47, I think, when the Soviets were just getting a grip. The parents went to the police the moment the child was returned. A month later, she disappeared again. They never found her.'

'Harder to pull off in England, I think.'

'I can't risk it,' Hugo said.

'The alternative,' said Leo, 'and I say this with as much concern for my niece as you have, is to allow Saul's trial to go ahead, a trial which will almost certainly end with a death sentence.'

'I know,' said Hugo. 'I should like to send whoever wrote this note to the gallows, believe me.'

'That's your anger speaking. The immediate priority is to ensure no one else finds out about this,' said Leo. 'Here, tuck it in your pocket. We can tell Freya – she must know what's really going on – and Gus, but that's as far as it must go for now.'

Hugo took the note and slipped it inside his jacket, wanting rather to throw it in the fire and scour his hands clean. His sister had been kidnapped, was in the hands of people capable of any barbarity if it served their ends. He'd seen plenty of it in Berlin.

'Emerson?' Someone else who knew Service procedure would be invaluable.

Leo shook his head. 'In any normal situation, I would trust Mr Emerson, but cold logic tells me that he's a man who knows Saul very well indeed, more than well enough to frame him. He's also been to Selchester before, and has all the necessary connections to arrange something like this.'

Leo was right. Where were Hugo's wits?

'Then to the police station it is,' he said, turning to the Lago. 'They can put an appeal out, one of the people leaving the rehearsal may have noticed something.'

'Not in the Lago,' said Leo. 'I'll get the keys to Gus's car. Someone capable of kidnapping is equally capable of cutting a car's brake lines. From their point of view, silenced is good, but dead is better.'

Scene 12

The duty inspector was brisk, sympathetic. 'Terrible thing to happen, Mr Hawksworth,' he said, 'but they can be right awkward at that age, and it sounds as if she's had a hard time of it. Likely as not she's gone to someone she knows, but we'll do our part. Not much to be done now, mind you, it'll have to wait till morning before we go around asking questions. You say there were a deal of possible witnesses, do you have a list?'

'Vivian Witt will. She's directing the play.'

'I know about Miss Witt and her play, I shall give her a ring this very moment. Bad time for your telephone to go down, but we'll send a constable up if there's any news.'

'Thank you, Inspector.'

'Don't worry, Mr Hawksworth, this is a good area, and people are friendly. If she's wandering around lost, someone will look out for her. We'll have her back with you in no time.'

Hugo gave a tight smile. 'I hope you do.'

Scene 13

Georgia drifted up out of a strange groggy sleep. Her head was thick and fuzzy, and when she opened her eyes she couldn't see a thing. She waggled her fingers slowly in front of her face, still nothing.

The air was cold, and she was wrapped in rough blankets. The floor was made of boards, dry and dusty. She reached her other hand up and banged into something, a beam, only just above her head. Her skull was throbbing. She had cut her head, and it hurt.

'I must be brave,' she said, feeling nothing of the kind. She hated dark enclosed spaces, cupboards and holes and suchlike. Until she was eight she had always slept with a nightlight. Otherwise she remembered the long ghastly hours trapped in the ruins of her parents' house after the doodlebug hit. The dark, and the cold, and the rafters pressing down on top of her, throat choked with dust so she couldn't even scream.

She wrapped one of the blankets more tightly around her, movements slow. Her head was really very foggy indeed, all she wanted was to go back to sleep. Her throat was dry again. Where was she? What time was it? What had happened? She remembered seeing the little doorway in the turret ajar, going into the dark servants' stairs, then something soft held over her face, a cloying smell like hospitals.

She groped her way around the room until there weren't beams over her head any more. Not a chink of light. It was quite dark, and her head was swimming. The walls were wood, or bare brick, it felt like a shed. She worked her way around, not finding a door, until she came to something earthenware. It was a jug of water. She tried a little, gingerly, but it tasted just like water out of the taps.

So tired, why was she so tired? She would sit down against the wall for a bit, wrap the blankets around her. Just for a few minutes.

Scene 14

'Kidnapped?' said Freya.

Hugo pulled the note out of his pocket. It was much later, the Castle quiet at last. Mrs Partridge had served a plain supper, and everyone had gone in search of a fitful sleep, alarms set for first thing. A constable had cycled up to inform them that the police had a list of the cast, and would be attending the rehearsal on Sunday afternoon to appeal for witnesses.

He and Leo had come to find Freya in her tower, where they wouldn't be overheard. She had hastily cleared her notes into a pile, plonked some worthy tomes down on top of them, propped some dull eighteenth-century prospect of the gardens and Castle open on the desk.

She felt a little ashamed for bothering. What was the point of keeping secrets when something like this was going on? Force of habit, no doubt.

'I suppose Bruno wasn't the spy, then,' she said, 'and Saul didn't kill him. But surely no one from Foxley could have done this? A scientist?'

'Science is a rational, analytical endeavour,' said Leo, 'no more moral than any other profession. It can attract those rather detached from ordinary human sympathy. I've met men of genius who were almost completely dissociated from the world around them. But in this case, I'd have said the skill and tradecraft were beyond any of them.'

'Then who could have done this? They must be desperate, which means Hugo was close to the truth.'

'As to the spy,' said Hugo, 'I'm almost certain it's Dr Oldcastle. Not willingly – he's being blackmailed. I should say Dr Rothesay's compulsive grumbling came to the ears of someone who could put two and two together. They, whoever they are, realised Oldcastle had covered up his own part in a serious accident, and contrived to gain promotion on the back of it.'

'And you believe this person killed Dr Rothesay,' Leo said. 'Do we have a motive?'

'To silence him, surely?' said Freya, staring at the ghastly note. 'That's what this is all about, to keep things quiet. They'll threaten a thirteen-year-old girl to halt Hugo's investigation. Why would they cavil at shooting a troublesome scientist in the back of the neck?'

'Making it look as if he'd taken himself off to Russia,' Leo added. 'Thus neatly wrapping up the investigation into the source of the leak.'

'Why do they want you to return the note?' Freya asked. 'And why to the Hungarian embassy, not the Russian?'

'To keep the evidence in their hands,' Leo said. 'And to implicate Hugo to a degree. His fingerprints will be on the note, don't forget, and he'll have to get it there somehow. As to the Hungarian connection, might it be the AVH running this, rather than the MGB?'

The AVH were the Hungarian secret police, an unpleasant bunch.

'It could be all sorts of things,' said Hugo. 'To undermine our trust in Árpád? They're well aware we've got him here. To throw us off the scent? After all, the Service isn't quite as concerned about Hungarians as about Russians. The AVH is efficient enough when it comes to boots stamping on faces, to use Mr Orwell's term, but they're not in the MGB's league when it comes to foreign espionage. They don't have the experience – they've only been going a few years.'

'Whoever did this is an expert,' said Leo. 'To abduct Georgia from the Castle, to cut the phone line and leave the note, all without any of us noticing, takes quite a deal of skill. Not to mention making such a convincing case against Saul. I was inclined to believe it myself.'

'Jenkins may well have the skill,' said Hugo, 'but we know far too little about him, and we don't know whether he's been in Selchester since Monday.'

Freya said, 'Surely it must have been someone in the cast?' It wasn't something she cared to think about. They were mostly locals of some kind, while Vivian would surely know who the professional actors were.

'What makes you think that?'

'It would be the perfect cover. In and out of the Castle all afternoon with no one really keeping an eye on them.'

'There were cars arriving to pick people up at the end, though,' said Hugo. 'One was just behind the Lago, coming up the drive. A big black Vauxhall, if I'm not mistaken.' He was trained to observe inconsequential details, car makes and number plates. It could be a bore sometimes, he found himself paying attention to a car on the road if he caught sight of it more than once.

'The trouble is,' he went on, 'I can't ask the police to look out for it. Whoever's behind this seems to know everything the police do. Doubtless the Selchester gossip mill at work again.'

'That would rule Jenkins out,' said Freya. 'He's hardly here enough to be plugged in to the gossip mill, and everyone's quite tight-lipped about blabbing to outsiders.'

'You seem intent on the idea that it's a member of the cast.'

'Yes, although it's a very disagreeable thing to think. Call it instinct, the way you didn't believe Saul was guilty. I think whoever it was had the whole afternoon to prepare. It's too much of a stretch to imagine they could hope to turn up at the right moment, like your black Vauxhall.'

'Then they could as easily be someone who'd just come to nose around, watch the rehearsal,' said Leo. 'I saw several people with no particular reason to be there, aside from the fame of Miss Witt and the chance to see inside the Castle. I shall enquire who they were this afternoon. After all, they could quite legitimately have seen Georgia making her way off.'

'I can record the cars as they come in,' said Freya. 'I have a good view from that window. I shall see all the comings and goings.'

'Which reminds me,' said Leo, reaching inside his clerical jacket. 'Emerson gave this to me. I believe it's from one of your colleagues in London.'

Hugo read it, read it again, with a look almost of bafflement. He reached down and rubbed his bad leg, the one he always said was the result of a bicycle accident. Freya had her suspicions, but she rather suspected Leo knew the whole story.

'I think we should turn in,' she said, to give them an opportunity to talk without her. 'At least try to sleep.'

The men took their leave, down the spiral stair past her bedroom, back towards their own wing of the Castle.

'What did it say?' Leo asked, as they paused at the door to his room. 'Was it indeed from Henry?'

Leo also knew Henry Surcoat, although they hadn't been in the Service at the same time.

'It was. Once the police discovered that Luger, they asked the Service to take a look at it, and the ammunition. It seems, although nobody has thought to inform me through official channels, that the bullets match one the doctors took out of my leg last year.'

Scene 15

Pacing the Castle, unable even to contemplate sleep, Hugo's steps brought him to the ballroom. The drapes were still drawn back, light from the new-risen moon spilling silver across the parquet floor. The chairs were still there, arranged in two distinctly disordered rows along the edge of the room, the stage clear, the harpsichord pushed to the corner.

He stared at it for a very long moment, his mind full of terrors and torments, of what had been and what might be, of his sister terrified in the dark somewhere. Such things belonged to the world he'd reluctantly left behind, not to the peace of Selchester. Where could Georgia be safe, if not here?

He pulled the stool out and lifted the lid. For a moment, his fingers hung above the keys, uncertain, and then he began to play.

The sound carried through the tall windows and the heavy drapes of Árpád's room, bringing to an uneasy mind memories of a happier time, Vienna before the first war, when all seemed stable and everlasting, when music floated from balconies on summer evenings.

He woke, and hearing it still, took himself in search of it, to hear it more clearly.

Scene 16

Freya's room was too far away for the sound to reach her across the roofs. Restlessness had driven her to walk the corridors, until she caught the plangent tones of a harpsichord drifting up through Grace Hall. She saw a figure vanish into the darkness below, and caught up with him again at the half-open door to the ballroom.

Árpád gave her a grave smile, said nothing. Hugo played on, quite lost in the music. It was a ghostly sound, well fit for moonlit tranquillity even amid a sea of troubles.

Hugo reached the end of a movement, went straight into the next with barely a pause. She'd had no idea he was so good, nor that he had so much music in his head. There were wrong notes and fractional hesitations here and there, but he played as a man listening to the angels, determined above all not to stop.

They stood there in the darkness for a long time, until finally Árpád nodded again and slipped away, back up the stairs to her uncle's bedroom. A moment later she realised why. He'd known the sonata was coming to its end, and hadn't wanted to intrude. Freya, lingering to hear the last of it, was caught unawares. She turned to go, but her slipper scuffed on the floor, and Hugo looked around. For once, though, no defences went up. Tonight, he wasn't the spy, the keeper of secrets, only a man in anguish, worried for the safety of kith and kin.

'Scarlatti?' she said, walking out to join him.

He nodded. 'I can't have woken you.'

She stood by the side of the harpsichord, running her fingers over the wood. 'I couldn't sleep. Much too worried. It's harder at night.'

Hugo said, 'Now entertain conjecture of a time/ When creeping murmur and the poring dark/ Fills the wide vessel of the universe.'

'*Henry V*,' said Freya. 'He must have seen the world in a most extraordinary way, to come up with so many such lines in the middle of all that tumult, players and Puritans and conspiracies all about him.

I didn't know you were a Shakespearean, was it all that lighting you did for OUDS?'

Hugo pulled a small, scarred volume out of his inside pocket. Freya turned it over in her hands, to see in the moonlight. *Complete Works of Shakespeare*. The type was tiny, she'd have had to squint to read it even in daylight.

'My perpetual companion on the road. I've had it since before the war. A few more years and I shan't be able to make the words out, but it's done its duty. I must have read most of them through at least half a dozen times. After my father's ship went down, I read *Hamlet* over and over again. After my mother died, it was *Antony and Cleopatra*, don't ask me why.'

'But not tonight.'

'Tonight . . .' He rested his fingers on the keys. 'I couldn't have changed what happened to my parents, and they wouldn't have wanted me to. They did their bit, they were happy to be doing their bit. Georgia didn't ask to get mixed up in all of this.'

'No more and no less than your mother,' said Freya. 'Georgia was born into this time, and you're doing what you can to ensure she grows up in a free country, not a hell like Árpád's Hungary. The difference is that you're responsible for her. You weren't for your parents.'

'Cold comfort.'

'I shan't try to varnish it. You're worried sick about her, and so am I.'

'She means a great deal to you.'

'Yes, she does. I didn't expect it. I didn't want either of you here, as it happens.'

'I remember. Never mind cold comfort, your welcome the first time we met was distinctly chilly.'

'She's quite won me over. I never had a younger sister, and I doubt she'd have been as quirky and original as Georgia.'

'You do yourself too little credit.'

'Georgias aren't ten a penny.'

'No,' said Hugo, 'they're not.'

Neither spoke for a moment. Then Hugo gently closed the lid of the harpsichord and rose from the stool. They turned back towards the door.

'I forgot,' said Freya, fishing in her dressing-gown pocket. 'The girls found this on Pagan Hill. It was at the end of a dead-end path. Rather an odd thing to lose in such a place, don't you think? If I owned such a thing, I wouldn't tramp around the countryside with it.'

Back in the light, Hugo examined the pen, and unscrewed the cap to look at the nib. Left-handed.

'Very curious indeed,' he said. 'Now what would an eminent scientist be doing in a place like that?'

'You know whose it is?'

'I do indeed. It belongs to Laurence Oldcastle.'

Sunday

Scene 1

Hugo woke abruptly from a shallow, restless sleep, full of threatening dreams and Georgia's voice calling from a bottomless abyss. He'd fallen asleep in the library chair, a half-finished whisky close by his head.

Freya had come in, already dressed, with a cup of tea.

He sprang to his feet. 'What time is it?' A faint promise of daylight glimmered around the edges of the curtains. How long had he been asleep?

Freya said, 'Don't fret. It's half past seven, time to have a quick bath and put some fresh clothes on. MacLeod sent a constable up, he's sending more to comb the grounds. They may not find Georgia, but they'll be able to tell if anyone's been in or out. There's quite a heavy frost.'

'I hate to have everyone out combing the countryside when she won't be there,' said Hugo.

'The more people know, the more hope of something being picked up.'

Hugo said, 'If only the rehearsal were sooner.'

Mrs Partridge was up and about, ladling scrambled eggs on to toast. The kitchen was full of people – Emerson already up from town, Árpád in a coat borrowed from her uncle. As Hugo wolfed down a few bites, there was a great roar from outside, and dogs barking.

'Who's that?' Polly asked.

That, it turned out, was Arthur Hampton-Bishop, driving a mud-spattered Jeep with a bloodhound in the back. In a Land Rover behind him were Lady Priscilla and Sir Archibald, with two of the Selchester Hunt's finest, tails wagging furiously. Magnus took one look and bolted.

'Heard what was up,' Arthur said. 'Roped the godparents in. Do you have something of your sister's, a shirt she's worn recently? Or shoes. Shoes are good.'

'You shouldn't,' said Hugo.

'Course I should. Can't imagine how you feel. My mother says I've the imagination of a cabbage in any case, but I'll lend a hand, and Morpheus here can lend a nose. He's not the brightest tool in the box, I'm afraid. I'm having rather a time training him up, but he'll do his best.'

Freya had to concede that Morpheus was a distinctly dim-looking bloodhound, but even a dim bloodhound was better than none. Mrs Partridge left Pam to stir the eggs, with strict instructions to hand out flasks of tea to all and sundry, and went in search of Georgia's clothes.

'Right-ho,' said Arthur, as she came back. 'Who saw her last?'

'I did,' said Polly.

'Lead on, Macduff.'

They spilled out of the kitchen into the morning sunshine. Thank heaven it was another clear day. The circle was full of people and noise, and there was someone else coming through the gatehouse on a bike. For a moment, Hugo's heart leapt, thinking it might be Georgia, but it was Dinah Linthrop, come to join the search.

Polly led them in a gaggle to the last place she'd seen Georgia. Morpheus set off, combing the ground this way and that, then loped along towards the ballroom.

'She did go this way,' Polly said, excited.

They came to a corner at the back of the ballroom, through an arch into a disused service courtyard with two or three doors, one into a little turret.

'What's this for?' Hugo asked Freya.

'It leads into the servants' corridors, it's the quickest way from the kitchen to the ballroom terrace.' She remembered uniformed footmen coming in and out with drinks during a summer party long ago, following them back.

They had to find Mrs Partridge for the keys, but no sooner was the door opened than Morpheus lost the scent entirely. Arthur frowned.

'What was she doing in here?' Leo asked. 'We'd better have a look upstairs and downstairs, just in case.'

'I don't think you'll be finding her in here,' said Mrs Partridge. 'I keep this locked. You never know what sort of people are on the loose these days. I'd say I haven't turned that key these five years.'

'What about the other side?' Gus asked. 'If I judge rightly, that corridor leads through to the door Vivian and I opened the other day, in the ballroom. We didn't go in. Too dusty.'

'Where is this bicycle, though?' Árpád asked. 'We know she was on it.'

'Something a bit fishy about this, if you ask me,' said Sir Archibald. 'Are you quite sure she's run away, Hawksworth? Don't like to be the one to suggest something worse, but a man's got to face the possibility.'

'I have, Sir Archibald, believe me.'

'Well, no use all of us clumping about in a huddle like this, we'll put Morpheus right off his game. I say we split up, comb the grounds again in daylight. You did your best last night, by all accounts, but a winter evening before moonrise is no time to be out searching.'

Scene 2

When Georgia woke again, it was to the greyest, the dimmest of lights. Her head was fuzzy still, her muscles aching. She was cold, very cold, hunched along the wall in the inadequate cover of the blankets. How had that happened? She'd only meant to rest for a little while.

She blinked a few times, to clear her eyes. Her stomach was groaning, and she had a crick in her neck. Weren't they going to come back, whoever they had been? She realised she could see a little of the room. Wood and brick, just as she'd thought. There was a line of light high up, a rectangle, like daylight around the edge of a curtain or shutter. Better than the dark, anything was better than the dark, but the room was so small. She must have been around it twice last night, it was barely big enough to lie down in.

Groggy, she heaved herself up and reached for the line of light. It was above her head, too high to see out, but there was a latch of some kind. Her stiff fingers fumbled to open it, and at last it moved, with a creak. She looked up, out, to a distant slice of blue sky, an expanse of brick and lead. She was in an attic somewhere, the roof of the school looked just like this. She could just about see a line of shadow on the brick, the sun was quite high. She must have been asleep for hours and hours and hours.

She shouted, but her voice barely echoed in the passage. She looked around the room again. There was no door, not even a hatch in the floor. Her heart began to pound. How could she be in a room with no door? Her mind raced to oubliettes, like the ones they used in the Middle Ages, where you couldn't even climb out. She pushed and prodded and poked and shouted until she was hoarse, but there was no reply, not even a sound. She didn't drink the water, a little suspicious of it. What if it had sent her back to sleep?

In the corner, she found a panel which opened when she pressed a corner, but only into a tiny dusty cupboard, almost bare and empty.

Two old books sat on a shelf. She picked them up. They looked ancient, when had they last been used? They were full of Latin in blotchy type, a great big papal emblem on the front page of each, the last few pages blank. Underneath them was a little black notebook, much more recent, full of indecipherable squiggles. Wedged in a crevice at the end of the shelf was an old pencil, almost too blunt to use.

She looked at the tiny little room, then very deliberately she tore out the last page of one of the old books, wrote HELP, and then after consideration a proper message: MY NAME IS GEORGIA HAWKSWORTH I HAVE BEEN KIDNAPPED LOCKED IN A CUPBOARD UNDER ROOF OF BIG OLD BUILDING PLEASE HELP, like a telegram. Then she folded it into a paper plane. She hated to spoil the old books, heaven knew when they were from, but the paper was so thick, surely it would fly well? She didn't know whether anyone would find it, whether it would just flutter a few feet and lie on the roof, but it was all she had.

She stood on tiptoe, threw the dart with all her might, and returned to tear out the next-to-last page.

HELP MY NAME IS GEORGIA HAWKSWORTH . . .

Scene 3

By half past eleven, Hugo's leg could take no more. He'd stayed with the search parties right through the garden, out into Upper Wood, and back down to confer with MacLeod by the Lodge. It was more exercise than he'd taken in a year, and it showed.

It was Leo who insisted he take a rest, bundling him into a police car for a lift back up to the Castle, where he hobbled through into the kitchen. Mrs Partridge bundled some ice cubes up in a cloth for his leg.

'Don't you go doing yourself a mischief,' she said sternly. 'Miss Georgia needs you in the best of shape. Look at your shoulders, crooked as can be.'

They were indeed. He'd found in the last hour or so that he could keep going if he held himself at an angle, the better to put less weight on the leg.

'Just a few minutes,' said Hugo. 'I want to look at that doorway again, without a great crowd of people hovering around.'

'You stay right here,' said Leo. 'I shall take a look. I've much the same training as you, and I shan't be limping around like Richard III on a bad day.'

'Don't you speak ill of him,' said Mrs Partridge sharply. 'The Castle won't like it, d'you hear.'

Although she'd spent most of her life out of the Fitzwarins' service, only returning after the late Lord Selchester's disappearance, Mrs Partridge had nevertheless firmly adopted most of the family's ancient prejudices. Save those where Papists were concerned.

'An excellent and much-maligned king,' said Leo diplomatically, and took his leave. He knew why Hugo wanted to have a look. It made no sense for Georgia to have headed towards the Castle before reversing her course and running away. It made rather more sense if, say, she had seen something amiss, gone to investigate, and run instead into a kidnapper lying in wait. A kidnapper with keys to the Castle, though, that was the oddest thing.

He paced along the corridor. There were footprints on the stairs, but they were those of the searchers, trampling over the evidence in their search for Georgia's bicycle – nowhere to be found, of course. Perhaps there was a trace of it outside, though. There was a path along the back of the Castle at cellar level, through the old pantries and workshops. Someone could well have taken a bike along there, brought it around the far side of the gatehouse and loaded it into a car.

He let himself out, followed the path down the steps, past dusty and shuttered rooms – carpenters' and joiners' workshops, unused boiler rooms, sculleries, and the cavernous nineteenth-century kitchen, designed for a staff of dozens. He came out on to a lawn by the hot-house, just where the mediaeval and Elizabethan wings met. There was Magnus rushing about on the grass, chasing something which flitted in the breeze.

One of several somethings, actually. What were they? Paper planes, how odd. He picked one up, prompting a furious attempt by Magnus to retrieve possession, and a claw in his finger.

'Ouch. Off, cat!'

He unfolded it, read it.

With quick precision, he gathered up every one of the planes he could find, and went back to the staircase, an indignant Magnus trailing at his heels.

Scene 4

Freya saw Leo as she came freewheeling down the garden path, laden with thermos flasks – her turn to ride back to the Castle and replenish them. The searchers were out at the edge of the park now, a constant trickle of people joining in from the town. Some of the cast had arrived early with packed lunches and spare sandwiches, ready to lend a hand.

Leo waved, abruptly. *Come here.* She veered off, stopped by him. He pulled a piece of oddly folded parchment out of his pocket and showed her the message on it.

'The priest hole,' she said. 'I told you about it, it's called The Room That Has No Ears.'

Leo knew all about priest holes. 'Does anyone know where it is?'

'I never did,' she said. 'I can ask Sonia, although it'll be tricky to hide why I'm asking.'

'Can we trust Mrs Partridge to keep a secret? She may know.'

'Show her the note,' said Freya. 'For something really important, she won't breathe a word.'

Mrs Partridge was incandescent. 'It's a wicked, wicked thing. Not a shred of decency these people have, and to think here in Selchester. I shan't breathe a word indeed, not to anyone. To threaten Miss Georgia's life like that. Savages, that's what they are.'

'Do you know where the priest hole is?'

She shook her head. 'I've looked for it, shan't pretend otherwise, but never found it. Plinth's your man for this. He was in service here forty years and more. It was his business to know everything.'

'The Selchester priest hole was Nicholas Owen's work,' Leo said.

'Who?' Hugo asked.

'He was a carpenter, a recusant, and a genius at hidden rooms, false panels, double walls and such. The searchers could be very thorough and sophisticated. They'd take a week to comb a house, measure everything to see where there were unexplained spaces, but some of Owen's priest holes were never found. The Throckmortons had one, up in Warwickshire, went undiscovered until the late nineteenth century.'

'I've been there,' said Freya. 'They're distant cousins, all these Catholic families marry one another. It's not nearly as complicated a building as the Castle. You could probably hide a whole secret apartment up in the roofs here. They searched the Castle for a week after the Babington Plot, I know that. There was a Jesuit in the attic, the seventh Earl's brother, but they never found him.'

'See what you can find in your books,' said Leo. 'Get Polly to help you. She's been trailing about the fields long enough, she must be exhausted. She'll keep a secret. I shall take myself to the George & Dragon to find Plinth.'

'I'd best come with you,' said Mrs Partridge. 'He knows me, he won't ask too many questions.'

'Such a nuisance, having to do all of this *sub rosa*,' Hugo said. 'At least we know it must be on the east side of the Castle, that's where you found all the darts. I shall take myself off to the upper floors and sing lays like Blondel seeking the Lionheart. Perhaps Georgia will join in the chorus.'

Leo said, 'Be sure to sit upon the ground every so often, tell some sad stories of the deaths of kings, and give that leg of yours a rest.'

'I shall be all three Richards at once,' said Hugo, with the ghost of a smile. 'Come on, Magnus, let's see if you're more use than that bloodhound.'

Scene 5

Coming back past the Lodge with Plinth beside him, Leo was flagged down by Superintendent MacLeod.

'Could I impose upon you for a lift up to the Castle, Father Hawksworth?' he said. 'I've sent both my cars off, and the cast are trickling in. I'd like to get a head start on interviews.'

'Of course, Superintendent, jump in.'

MacLeod sat himself in the back, and Leo roared off up the drive. 'Excellent car, this,' he said approvingly. 'Good day, Mr Plinth, Mrs Partridge. Gathering reinforcements?'

Leo made a swift decision. 'We think it's possible she got herself locked in a priest hole, Superintendent. There's one hidden up in the roofs of the Castle. She knows it exists, and if she'd found it while look-ing for somewhere out of the way, she might well have been unable to get out. They were designed to muffle sounds.'

MacLeod gave him a keen look in the mirror. 'I should say it's worth a try, but I'm not so comfortable with this running away as I was. It's too cold for a girl to have spent the night outside, and if she'd gone to friends I'd have expected to hear by now. Sir Archibald is a little concerned she might have been kidnapped. It's that missing bicycle, you see. There hasn't been sight nor sound of her on any of the roads around Selchester. I didn't like to broach the subject with Mr Hawksworth yet, but I wondered what you thought.'

'I should say that was worth following up,' said Leo, 'although relations between her and Hugo have been a little strained this week. Do you have any particular reason to believe she might have been abducted?'

'Mr Hawksworth is currently involved in some rather sensitive Government business,' said MacLeod. 'It's not beyond the bounds of possibility that someone might be attempting to put pressure on him. Nor, for that matter, that he's had some form of ransom demand he daren't share with us, for Miss Georgia's safety. It's a familiar enough *modus operandi* in kidnapping cases.'

Leo met his gaze. 'If this were the case, it would be better for you to come to your conclusions quite independently of Hugo.'

MacLeod nodded. 'Thank you, Father Hawksworth. You've been most helpful.'

He let himself out at the door and headed off towards the ballroom. The circle was packed with cars again, searchers and cast members all together, sometimes double-parked for lack of room. It would be a job to disentangle. There was Vivian Witt, dressed more for the search than for the rehearsal, talking to the Pearsons, Stanley Dillon, Daisy, and a pale woman Leo didn't know. Daisy was pointing over towards the gardens, tracing out their route of the night before.

'I see a number of his late lordship's connections are involved,' said Plinth as he got out of the car. 'I had wondered if this had something to do with him.'

'With the murder?' Leo asked. Both Vivian and Stanley had fallen foul of the late Lord Selchester's nastier ways.

'You don't work for a man such as his lordship without getting to know him better than he suspects,' said Plinth, closing the Lago's door with care. 'He mixed with unusual people, and I can't help noticing there are plenty of them around at the moment. Miss Witt and Mr Dillon there, and I've seen her before – she visited his lordship a few times. That gentleman who makes out he's a journalist, he's been in town too.'

'Today?' Leo asked.

'He stayed at the George on Friday night, said he was on his way down to see friends in Cornwall,' said Plinth. 'Chattier than usual, if you ask me. Took himself off yesterday afternoon.'

'What time, Plinth?'

'About one, I should say. Took lunch in the parlour, then off in that big black car of his.'

'A Vauxhall?'

'I didn't note the make, sir, but I couldn't say otherwise.'

'Well, well,' said Leo. 'And you say you know him.'

'He's stayed at the George a few times, not a talkative gentleman, but I saw him once before the war. He belonged to the part of his lordship's life which was lived in London, if you'll take my meaning. His lordship kept a town house, but not a big one, nor a big staff, and the estate steward didn't have anything to do with it. He dealt with all the accounts himself.'

They turned to go in when something else struck Leo. 'Who else did you say visited his lordship? Was it her?' He nodded towards the pale woman.

'Not her, no, that's Mrs Rothesay. It was that one, talking to Miss Witt. Miriam her name was, or something like it. Came over as a refugee, from Austria I believe, just before the war. Some diplomatic connection of his lordship's. He offered her hospitality while she found her feet here, so to speak.'

'Was his lordship often generous like that?' Leo asked.

'I shouldn't say so,' said Plinth. 'To his own sort, yes, you couldn't fault him on that. But one came to see, in time, that the other sort, the likes of Miss Witt and Mr Dillon, it was more a question of what they might do for him. They didn't often like it, if you catch my meaning.'

'Did she?'

Miranda caught their gaze, and gave Leo a nod.

'I should have said they got on well, he was much taken with her. But she was a stranger in a foreign land, and quite dependent on him. People can be very good at keeping up appearances, when they've nothing else.'

Scene 6

In the faint hope of a miracle, Freya had knocked on the door of her cousin's room. Polly was still up in the New Tower, flicking through Freya's books on the Castle. Not somewhere she wanted prying eyes, but it was out of the way, couldn't be helped. The job of tracking and recording all the cars had been entrusted to a joint team of Emerson and Árpád in one of the guest rooms. They didn't know why they were doing it, and doubtless would ask some awkward questions later, but they could at least be relied on to work meticulously.

'Priest hole?' Sonia said. 'What on earth does that have to do with Georgia?'

'We think she might have been looking for somewhere to hide,' Freya said. 'Found it, went inside, couldn't open the door again.'

Sonia didn't look at all convinced. 'I don't think you're telling me the truth,' she said.

'Then we understand one another perfectly,' said Freya, who wasn't in the mood for her cousin's games. 'Do you know where it was?'

'Father knew,' Sonia said.

'You're quite sure?'

'Yes. But he didn't tell, if that's what you're about to ask.'

'Might he have told Tom?'

Tom had been Sonia's brother, killed in Palestine shortly after his father's death.

'He liked his secrets, you know that very well. He might have told Tom, some sort of family tradition, but I doubt it. Not that you'd get much joy out of Tom unless you're desperate enough to resort to a Ouija board.'

Scene 7

Superintendent MacLeod joined Vivian outside the ballroom. 'Thank you for your list, Miss Witt,' he said. 'Much appreciated. Are you planning to continue the rehearsal?'

'I shall for the sake of the professionals, but I was thinking of releasing the chorus to help with the search.'

'If you'd be kind enough to gather everyone first, I shall go through them all together, and then they can go. I doubt I shall be very long. We're just looking for anything which might help.'

'Of course,' said Vivian. 'I saw some of them going over to the kitchen with offerings of sandwiches, we'd better gather them up. Stanley can go and get them – where's he gone?'

'I'll go,' said Miranda, who was just behind them. 'Through the passageway?'

'And across Grace Hall. You'll need to go around that dreadful bear someone put to block the Hall off. Thank you!'

'Is there anyone on the list who isn't coming today?' MacLeod asked.

Vivian bent over the list. 'Let's see . . .'

Scene 8

'Listen,' said Polly, brandishing a book from the library, as Freya came back up the stairs. Freya recognised it. She'd brought it up here mostly to look as if she were studying the family history, although there'd been some useful tidbits about Restoration England in it. '*Keeping the Faith: The Fitzwarins and the Papacy*. It's not half bad, full of letters and messengers and secret Jesuits. Anyway, in 1586 the Earl's youngest brother was a priest, Father Eudo Fitzwarin, and he was hidden in the Castle for four days while the priest-hunters turned it inside out. When he was an old man, in 1626, he told one of his fellow priests about it. Here, read this.'

Freya read.

> I passed above four Days in a Hiding-Place so cunningly Wrought by the late Master Owen that were all the Legions of Satan to make Search and Inquisition until the last Days, yet would it through the Grace of God elude their wicked Purpose. It lieth in the uppermost Part of that House, which being an antient Abode greatly Altered by the Fashion and Whim of following Ages, is wrought and Joined with great Confusion even unto those Masons and Carpenters to whose diligent Care the Fabrick is Entrusted. The Entry being by means of a false Masonry, the Genius of the Design is such that a first secret Room concealeth a second, made with no Less an Artifice, so that not a Sound may reach the questing ears of impious Hereticks, further that the first being Found and Discovered to be Empty, the search may be Confounded.

'False masonry,' she said. 'That narrows it down. One of the chimney breasts, perhaps. Shall we take a look?'

Polly swept the book up and ran ahead, to find Hugo sitting on a chair at the bottom of the stairs to the Long Gallery.

'Are you the sentry?' she said.

'More a weary traveller who walked the length and the breadth of the top floor singing his throat raw, but all in vain.'

'Won't work,' she said. 'It's soundproof. There are two secret rooms, one behind the other.'

'I wish I'd known that first.'

'I liked your singing,' said Freya, who had heard snatches of it on her way to and fro. '*HMS Pinafore*?'

'Indeed. Not perhaps in the same class as Blondel's lays, but considerably easier to remember. How have you found that out, Polly?'

She brandished the book. 'Georgia will have to be thankful to all those Papists now. The entry is behind a false masonry.'

'That narrows it down, most of the rooms up here are panelled. We can start in the Long Gallery, there's some masonry in the fireplaces.'

'There are always the attics,' Freya said. 'She mentioned roofs.'

'There are indeed the attics,' said Hugo, standing with painful resolution. 'Still, it must be done. Once more unto the breach, dear friends, once more.'

'I would we had one ten thousand of those in England,' said Freya, 'who do no work today.'

'The fewer men,' said Hugo with a grim smile, 'the greater share of honour.'

'Father Leo was quoting Shakespeare,' said Polly. 'It must be contagious.'

They clattered up the stairs and into the Long Gallery, fanning out in search of masonry to poke, prod and push.

'It's got to be here, in the attics above, or in one of the guest rooms off the Gallery,' said Freya. 'If you go towards the front, it's all altered.'

253

'Smells smoky in here,' Polly said, attacking the middle chimney breast with a heavy old-fashioned poker. 'I didn't know these chimneys were used any more. Hullo, Magnus, come to help?'

'He was helping me,' said Hugo, 'but I can't say he contributed very much.'

Magnus gave a let-me-in yowl, poking his nose into a corner of the fireplace.

'I've looked there,' said Polly.

'Maybe you dislodged something,' said Freya, worming her way in and patting her hands over the stonework. 'Yes, you have, there's a draught. I can feel it.'

'I can't imagine it's that easily found,' said Hugo, frowning.

'Not originally,' said Freya. 'But it's four hundred years old, and whoever closed it last didn't need to hold off Walsingham's priest-hunters for a week. Give me a hand, Polly. Push here.'

There was a creak, an indignant squeal. Two of the stone panels swung back, revealing a brick-lined staircase which twisted and turned. Hugo and Freya exchanged a glance over Polly's head, both wondering how anyone could get an unconscious girl up such steps.

'I'll go first,' said Freya firmly. 'We don't know the floor is safe.'

Polly sniffed. 'I can definitely smell smoke,' she said. 'The chimney must be in use.'

'The chimney shouldn't leak,' said Hugo, but his voice was muffled as Freya climbed the stairs. She shouted. 'Georgia!'

A croaky reply from behind one of the panels. 'Freya!'

'Hullo, Georgia!' said Polly, scampering up behind Freya.

'I can't find an entrance,' said Georgia, still muted. 'I've pushed and poked and everything. Where am I?'

'In the Castle,' said Freya. 'Up in the attics.'

'That's odd,' said Georgia. 'But you found one of my gliders.'

Freya could smell it now, too. She hammered on the panel, increasingly desperate. She wasn't strong enough. 'Hugo,' she called, 'we could do with a blunt instrument up here.'

There was no reply.

'Maybe we're going about this the wrong way,' Polly said. 'Priest-hunters were violent types, always hammering and smashing. What if it's just pressing gently on the corners or something?'

'You try. I'll go back down for that poker of yours.'

Hugo had emerged back out into the fireplace. He heard footsteps walking along the Long Gallery, and froze.

They weren't the footsteps of someone in a hurry, Leo or Árpád or Emerson come in search of them. No, they were the footsteps of someone with deadly purpose and fell intent. Slow and deliberate, tap-tap-tap along the floor of the Long Gallery.

Scene 12

A memory flashed into his mind of a dark rainswept alley in Berlin, rubble all around, a lone dull streetlight. Footsteps behind him. He'd taken them for an ordinary pedestrian at first – he'd seen one or two go past when he'd scouted the street in daylight. He was waiting in the side entrance to a small apartment block. There was an East German upstairs, a man who wanted to defect. A man with every reason to defect.

It was the rhythm of the footsteps which alerted him. A woman's footsteps, with low heels. A woman who, in a dangerous city, saw a man waiting in a dark and poorly lit alley, but who didn't turn around, didn't so much as falter.

It was a trap. A voice sounded on the intercom. He ignored it, walked away from the door and down the street, his back itching. A voice behind him, a man's. The door opening, a swear word.

His car was waiting just around the corner, Roland Chamberlain at the wheel. A good man in a tight corner, possessed of a sixth sense. He'd been wary about the whole thing, even with the weeks of research they'd done.

Hugo ran. Shouts, a volley of shots. The screech of tires in front of him. Roland, suicidally bold, had reversed out of the space, driving backwards into the traffic. Horns sounded, irate and impatient. A sudden hideous pain in Hugo's leg, almost sending him headlong. Somehow, he managed to drag himself those last two paces. The shots stopped, running feet. He pulled himself into the car, Roland stepping on the accelerator before the door was even shut, weaving away into the traffic.

There had been blood on the floor when they came to the checkpoint, it was sheer luck that the Russian on duty was a bored, jaded Red Army sergeant coming to the end of his shift, not some keen-eyed MGB man eager for promotion. Hugo had passed out before they reached the hospital.

He remembered the footsteps, though.

Scene 13

Freya appeared at the foot of the stairs. Hugo motioned her to silence.

She, too, had heard footsteps behind her in the mist, on the Embankment in London, when she'd been delving too deeply into Lord Selchester's past.

Hugo closed his fist around Polly's poker. The footsteps came closer and closer, brisker now. There was some commotion elsewhere in the house.

Hugo struck out with the poker, hit someone, hard. A snap like breaking bone. Something metallic clattered away across the floor. A gun, another Luger. Before Hugo could strike a second blow the owner darted to pick it up, one-handed, breathing heavily.

Miranda Pearson turned, the gun levelled in her left hand. He'd broken her right arm.

'Back,' she said, nudging the gun at them. 'Into the priest hole.'

'I don't think so,' said Hugo. 'If they find bullets in us, your plan won't work. Too many questions.'

Polly's voice from above, excited. 'I'm through! Georgia!'

There was smoke swirling in the Gallery. Miranda's face, mocking at their last meeting, was set and savage, devoid of all remorse.

'I don't care how you die,' she said, her accent suddenly a great deal stronger than it had been. Austrian. Árpád had been spot on. 'I missed you last time, I shall finish the job.'

She cocked the gun. 'Into the priest hole.'

Footsteps at the other end of the Gallery. 'No, Miriam,' said Jeremy's voice. 'I don't think so. Not any more.'

'Keep out of this!' she snapped. Her finger tightened on the trigger.

Two shots rang out, shockingly loud in the panelled space of the Long Gallery. Miranda jerked backwards. The Luger hit the floor with a thud. Dark blood spread across her chest, Jeremy's aim had been perfect. She slumped back, her expression in the final seconds almost outraged. A shower of stone fragments clattered down on to the floor. Her bullet had struck a carving on the chimney breast.

'What's going on down there?' Polly shouted.

'Stay where you are!' Freya called.

Hugo stepped out into the Gallery, just in time to see Leo and Plinth run up the stairs, Plinth brandishing a halberd. Jeremy Pearson stood in front of them, lowering his gun to the floor. He caught Hugo's eye.

'Enough is enough,' he said. 'I shall turn myself over to the police, but for now, let me help.'

Scene 14

'Her name was Miriam Rubinstein,' said Jeremy.

He, Hugo, Leo and MacLeod were in Gus's study, tucked away on the far side of Lady Matilda's wing, two constables guarding the door. Jarrett had been summoned, but thankfully had yet to arrive.

The Castle fire was under control, thanks to Gus's bucket chain and some ingenious use of the attic water tanks by Ben and John Brodrick. Miranda – Miriam – had started it in one of the old servants' bedrooms at the top of the Elizabethan wing, just below the priest hole. It seemed she'd been aiming to create smoke more than fire, since she'd wedged the chimney full of heavy wool blankets from a cupboard.

Two of the servants' bedrooms and an attic had been gutted, along with the roof above them. So had the priest hole, keeping its secrets to the end. The civilians had all been evacuated to the ballroom, and the firemen were in charge now, hunting for stray smoke.

Hugo knew that once Jeremy started talking it could be a torrent, unguarded and incoherent. A confession, in fact: an anguished conscience unburdening itself in the heat of the moment.

'The Service knew about her,' Hugo said, keen to keep him talking. He'd seen her file, what there was of it, but there'd been no picture. 'She was a Viennese Communist. An English fellow traveller married her in 1937, to spirit her out of the country. As far as we know, the marriage was never dissolved. Once she came to England she slipped between the cracks. We had nothing more on her, not even a photo, which in retrospect is very odd.'

'That was the late Lord Selchester's doing,' said Jeremy. 'He thought she could be useful to him, used his considerable influence in your outfit and elsewhere to erase her old identity. Men like him think they're above the law. As for her first husband, they never bothered to divorce. Marriage was bourgeois nonsense, she always claimed. She only married me because she wanted an official record. All that time, she was married to him, too. I didn't find out until he died.'

'Is your real name Jeremy Pearson, sir?' MacLeod asked. He wasn't in formal mode. No point starting that before Jarrett arrived.

'Yes, it is,' he said. He looked ten years older and twenty years younger, all at once, as if a terrible weight had been lifted from his shoulders. 'She was Austrian. I'm as English as Mr Hawksworth here.'

'Did she recruit you?' Hugo asked.

'After a fashion. I was a lecturer, at the University of Reading. I suppose you might have called me a Fabian socialist back then. The Nazis were doing terrible things in Germany, I wanted to do something to oppose them. She took some of my courses. I thought she was a student, but she wasn't. She was young and angry and full of passion. I fell for her. Her, and her cause.'

'Did you become a member of the Communist Party?' MacLeod asked.

'For a while. Then she said it was better we left, that was when Molotov and Ribbentrop signed their pact. I thought we were done, but no, she just wanted to be less visible. The war was a good time. I was on the same side as her, and as England. Then the peace came, and we started getting instructions from Moscow. Little things at first, then bigger and bigger. Mostly she was the one who did them. I provided the cover. They thought our being folklorists was inspired. Believe it or not, I actually thought that was important, work worth doing.'

Hugo nodded.

'It didn't matter to her. All she ever cared about was the cause. She went off to East Germany several times. Training, I think, though there may have been more. I only went with her the once. She didn't talk about it much. Then we came here. She had work to do with someone at Foxley, and she knew the area from her connection with Lord Selchester.'

'His lordship,' said Hugo, 'wasn't all he seemed.'

Jeremy's face was bitter. 'I'd gathered that. He was everything I'd thought the aristocracy were: double-dealing and deceitful, saying one thing and feathering their own nest. But by then I couldn't care less, it was all just words. I saw what was happening in Eastern Europe, Uncle Joe acting just the way Hitler had done.'

'She didn't waver?'

'Never. Not once. She'd have done anything for the cause.'

'Kill children?' MacLeod asked.

Jeremy nodded. 'That was the last straw. She killed Dr Rothesay when he twigged to what was going on. I knew she'd blackmailed Dr Oldcastle into feeding information to her, they used to meet on Pagan Hill. She wanted to protect him as a source. I didn't know she was going to kidnap Miss Hawksworth until she came home last night, told me what she'd done. I was in it with her, she said.'

'When did you realise what she planned?' Hugo asked.

'Only at the last minute,' Jeremy said, 'when I saw the smoke. You'd realised where Miss Hawksworth was, I think she'd cottoned on. She assumed you'd found the priest hole. Then I saw she hadn't come back, the smoke . . . I came as quickly as I could. I knew I couldn't let her do it.'

'Had you killed anyone before?' MacLeod said.

'Never. Never once! I'm a pacifist, Superintendent, or I was until today, when I realised that my conscience wasn't worth four lives. When the East Germans trained us, they taught us how to shoot. That's how I could hit her. They said we might need it.'

A rap on the door, one of the constables put his head round.

'Inspector Jarrett's car outside, sir, I thought you'd like to know.'

MacLeod got to his feet. 'I'd better fill him in, save us going over the same ground.' He reached for the door handle, and paused. 'I didn't say this, Mr Pearson, but don't let Inspector Jarrett bully you.'

'Thank you,' said Jeremy.

MacLeod went out, closing the study door behind him.

'What will happen?' Jeremy asked.

'You'll be hauled over the coals by Special Branch,' said Hugo. 'I imagine one of us will be involved, too. It'll probably be me. Don't give Jarrett anything you don't have to.'

'I don't want to hide any more. Perhaps that sounds strange. I shall probably regret it in a few days, but I'd like to make amends.'

'That's commendable, but you'll find him a vengeful man. He'll demand the harshest possible sentence. However, if you agree to cooperate in return for a shorter term, the Service will greatly appreciate it. We'd like to know what she got up to. She was clearly involved with Soviet activities directed at our agents, which puts her in our purview, not that of Special Branch. We'd particularly like to hear anything you know about Jenkins, too, and we'll be in a position to make sure you get something in return.'

Jeremy nodded. 'I see. I must say, I didn't expect sympathy.'

'You saved my niece's life,' said Leo. 'Twice, in a manner of speaking. I saw you going upstairs, thought you were going to help your wife.'

'You knew who she was?'

'Oh yes,' said Leo. 'I only realised at the last moment. Plinth had seen her at the Castle before the war, which made me very suspicious. You fitted the final piece of the puzzle into place for us, and then you acted with courage and resolution. If the measure of a man is how he handles himself in a supreme crisis, you did all the right things.'

'She was always telling me I was in too deep to change my mind,' Jeremy said, staring out of the window at the bare trees. 'That I'd committed myself, I'd made my choice and there was no turning back.'

'She was wrong,' said Leo. 'There's always a choice. We might not like it, but it's there.'

Heavy footsteps in the corridor, then there was Jarrett coming down like a wolf on the fold. Leo rose. 'I imagine the Inspector will consider me surplus to requirements, so I shall take myself off. If you need to reach me, Mr Pearson, I shall be here for another couple of days after all of this, as I believe my niece will need me. I normally live at St Giles College, Oxford.'

Scene 15

It was MacLeod who finally put an end to the interrogation, quietly but firmly. 'It's a Sunday afternoon, Inspector. Mr Pearson and Mr Hawksworth have been through a great deal today. Mr Hawksworth's sister will need him a great deal more than you need to ask questions now rather than tomorrow. Constable!'

Jarrett gave MacLeod a glance which was almost admiration. 'A word with you before you go, Hawksworth.'

'I shall see Mr Pearson to the police station,' said MacLeod, pulling his coat on.

'Has Mr Ingham been released?' Hugo asked.

'That's been done, he'll be back at his cottage now. I've advised the solicitors to get all of the locks changed. Rather too many people seem to have had the keys to that place.'

He ushered Jeremy Pearson out.

'I wasn't at all happy about the way you handled Oldcastle,' said Jarrett. 'Quite clearly tipped his hand. If you'd come to me first, we might have avoided all this business. Kidnapping, murder, two Soviet spies turning on one another – the press will have a field day.'

Hugo was in no mood for this. 'If I'd come to you with my suspicions at that stage, you'd have dismissed them out of hand. The case against Mr Ingham was well crafted. Even my uncle believed him guilty until we received the note.'

'This note which you didn't trouble to inform the police about.'

'With good reason, Inspector. We've seen very clearly what Miranda Pearson was really capable of. You wouldn't have been willing to provide my sister with the permanent protection she'd have needed, and I wouldn't have been willing for her to live in constant fear.'

'You'd sooner have betrayed your country? You're in very murky waters, Hawksworth. This will be in my report. I doubt the Service will see this in a good light, and I can't say I'm happy with official secrets resting in the hands of a man who made the decision you did.'

'You may write what you please, Mr Jarrett, and I shall do the same. You might care to ask yourself one question, though.'

'And what would that be?'

'How you came to draw exactly the conclusions a Soviet spy wanted. Good day, Inspector.'

Scene 16

Georgia had been put to bed in Polly's room, so as not to be alone. She was running a chill – from the cold night and the shock, the doctor had said.

'Nothing to worry about. A couple of days off school, rest and friendly faces, and she'll be right as rain. Dare say she won't mind missing school. They never do, however much we should like them to.'

Hugo came in after supper to find her propped up on a pile of pillows, deep in an Asimov. Magnus was stretched out beside her, deep in slumber and taking up a good half of the bed. Hugo pulled up a chair.

'Mrs Partridge said you finished your supper. That's a good sign.'

'Of course I finished it, she made apple crumble.'

'How are you?'

She considered for a moment, letting her book flop down. 'I wish I didn't have a cold. No one ever gets colds in films, not even when they've been rescued from sinking ships or chased over moors in the middle of the night.'

'That's because the people who write the films have never done anything of the kind.'

She gave him a sly look. 'And you have, of course. All those dangerous statistics.'

'I don't suppose it's really any use pretending, but one must keep up appearances.'

Her smile faded. 'I heard people saying you'd been offered a job in London, something really with statistics this time. Are you going to take it?'

'That depends.'

'On what?'

'On what you'd like to do.'

'You're asking me? Really?'

Hugo nodded. 'You said you didn't feel safe in London, but now with this, and that man on Monday . . .' Both the police and the Service would be looking more closely at Jenkins after this. At the very least, he'd have to tread extremely carefully from now on.

She shook her head violently. 'I still feel safe here. When I go missing, half the town turns out to look for me, even though they'll all mention it and I shall never live it down. Then there's you on my trail, and Leo, and Freya, and Polly, and even stuffy old MacLeod. When that man came up, Mr Dillon was there straight away. In London, you'll have a flat somewhere, and you'll never meet your neighbours, and I should have to go off to boarding school.'

'You wouldn't,' said Hugo. 'I know you don't like that idea.'

'Some frightfully posh day school, then. Polly said Valerie was telling her about some of them, I think she was trying to make it sound better.' She paused. 'Do you want to go to London? It sounded frightfully important. I suppose I could get to like it, although I'd miss Freya and Mrs Partridge and Magnus. Even Polly, though you mustn't tell her so.'

'My lips are sealed. I'm good at secrets, remember?'

She gave him a keen look, tipping her head to one side. 'Not as good as all that. I think you've already made your mind up, you're going to stay here.'

'What makes you say that?'

She grinned. 'Instinct.'

'As a matter of fact, I had come to a decision, but it was all down to you. I thought you'd be happier here. If you'd changed your mind about Selchester, though, I should have taken the job.'

'Valerie won't like it one bit.'

'I think the time has come for the two of us to go our separate ways,' said Hugo. 'She may well come to the same conclusion herself, when I tell her what I'm doing. She'll say I'm throwing away a golden opportunity.'

'Are you?'

'I don't think so. But if I am, it's for the right reasons. Mr Pearson did something this afternoon, something he knew would result in him going to prison, but he did it anyway, because it was the right thing.'

'If it was the right thing, why will he go to prison?'

'Because it's brought all the other things he did to light.'

Her hand strayed to his. 'Is Mrs Pearson really dead? I thought I saw . . .'

They'd done their level best to hide Miranda's body from Georgia and Polly, but the first priority had been to get the girls out of harm's way. Perhaps they hadn't done enough.

'Yes, she is,' said Hugo. 'She was the one who kidnapped you.'

'MacLeod told me. He said she was a spy.'

'She was.'

'We have rather a lot of spies here, don't we? I'm glad you're here to keep an eye on them all. Even if I do have to pretend my brother spends his days poring over a lot of dull Government statistics.' She paused. 'Is Leo cross I didn't save those old books, by the way? They must have belonged to that Jesuit who hid up there.'

'Good heavens, no,' said Hugo. How like Georgia to worry about something so inconsequential. 'None of us would exchange them for a single singed hair on your head.'

She considered that for a moment. 'Maybe a few singed hairs would be good when I go back to school. I could get special consideration from the teachers. Pulled from the flames and all that.'

'I can see your teachers are in for a very long term,' Hugo said.

Georgia grinned. 'There was something odd there, under the other books. I meant to bring it with me, but then there was all that smoke, and I forgot. It was in code, I think.'

Hugo was intrigued. 'An Elizabethan code?'

'No, it wasn't old. Just a black notebook with lots of strange writing in it. I'd have used it for gliders instead of those old books, but there was nowhere to write a message, I was worried people wouldn't see.'

'Perhaps someone hid it there as a game,' said Hugo.

'Perhaps,' said Georgia with a sidelong glance. 'This is a statistician thing, isn't it?'

'In a way,' said Hugo. 'If it's what I think it is, believe me, it's much better burned.'

Scene 17

Hugo came out into the corridor to find Leo lurking.

'I thought I'd have a word, but I didn't like to interrupt,' he said.

'I told Georgia I wasn't taking the job,' said Hugo.

'What made up your mind, if I may ask?'

'Her well-being, for the most part. Everyone's been telling me how much stability means to her, and I'm afraid I've been rather deaf to it of late.'

'We all have moments of wilful deafness.'

'Even you?'

'Even me. Miranda's real identity was staring me in the face once Plinth recognised her, and I was still dwelling on Jenkins. You said Georgia was the most part. What was the rest?'

'If you're going to offer a man a bribe,' said Hugo, 'don't do it at a christening.'

'Ah,' said Leo. 'I see. Your father would be proud of you.'

Scene 18

Árpád had been in Freya's tower.

He had come bounding up the stairs to tell her Saul and Emerson had arrived. She hadn't been quite in time to rearrange her desk.

'No, no, you should not hide this,' he said. 'I know that you are not writing a long dull history of the family.'

'Who told you?' she demanded, quite shocked to hear him say it so openly.

'No one tells me, I keep my eyes open. You know I have met Isaac Asimov?'

'Georgia told me so.'

'I have met him more than once. We have friends in common, I went to dinner with him several times. We get on very well. I even sleep on his couch one night, just before I go back to Hungary. I see a writer at work, a writer of fiction. I see his frustrations, his evasions, his pro-crastinations. I see the ideas slowly forming in his head. Now I have met people who labour long and hard over monographs. They are worthy enough, but they do not behave like you. No, you are someone who writes plenty, and well, but you have been stuck.'

Freya regarded him coolly, rather taken aback by all of this.

'No, do not look at me thus. I am not the only one. I do not think anyone here in the Castle believes you, except perhaps Gus, who is a straightforward person. It is one thing to hide what you do from the world, this is reasonable. In my country, now, it would be the only way you could survive, to live in a lie. But you are not in my country, and you should not hide from those who are close to you. You should tell them, this is who I am, and what I do. It is not a dishonourable thing.'

Freya said, 'It's not something I choose to make much of.'

'And you would not be. But to live with people and to keep such a thing from them, it is not right. I think also you know this, but you have a habit not to tell. It is very English. You say to yourself, *Oh, it would be awkward, what would they think of me?* I tell you, they are good people, they would be glad for you. They would keep your secret, even Mrs Partridge, because they are fond of you.'

Árpád's eyes twinkled. 'I have said too much, it is my way. I forget, you English, you like to come at things slowly, little by little, to leave much unsaid. I shall go now, you have had enough for one day. I was sent to tell you, we are gathering for drinks in the library. Gus would like to celebrate Georgia's rescue, and perhaps also that his ancestral home has not burned to the ground.'

He turned to go back down the stairs. Freya stared at her desk, at the same piles of books she'd been staring at for year after year, threads for the endless Penelopean tapestry of a book she wasn't writing and had no intention of writing. Although it might, for all that, be interesting, when there were priest holes in the attic.

'Thank you,' she said, turning to her desk. 'I'll be down in a little while.'

She listened to him go, then picked up a pile of wordy eighteenth-century tomes and carried them over to her bookshelf.

Scene 19

Making slow time with his stick, Hugo met Árpád on the landing in Grace Hall. 'Have you seen Freya?' he asked.

'I have just come from her, in her tower. She has something she wishes to tell you. Also, we are beginning our celebration of Georgia's rescue. There are several people with Gus in the library, also some excellent whisky. There is Lady Priscilla and her husband, Mr Dillon and his daughter, also Emerson and this Saul, who I think would like to thank you.'

Hugo digested this for a moment. 'I shall be down shortly.'

'I do not think Leo knows this yet. Where will I find him?'

'He's upstairs with Georgia.'

'I was on my way to see her. She must come also. I shall deliver my message, and talk to her later. Have you decided what you are doing?'

Hugo told him.

'This is very good,' said Árpád. 'I did not like to say, this Valerie, she is not right for you. When Georgia was in trouble, she took herself back to London.'

'She didn't want to be in the way,' said Hugo, a touch defensively.

'There is no "in the way" at such a time. There is present, or there is absent. Freya was present. Lady Priscilla, she was present, and her husband who is so busy and important. This Hampton-Bishop, who you hardly know, he is present. Half of Selchester, they are also present. Valerie was absent. Do you see?'

'I do,' said Hugo.

'I think perhaps I shall not be here as long as I thought, now you have found your traitor. Sir Bernard, he tells me the Americans have agreed to give me this green card of theirs, and my friend Leo Szilard thinks he has found me a job.'

'We shall be sad to see you go. When are you off?'

Árpád waved the question away. 'Maybe in three or four days. The important thing is, you and I must talk about music before I go. You can make beautiful music. I heard it last night, but I am told you never play. You must change this.'

'I'm no professional.'

'Perhaps, perhaps not. I am only an amateur, a lover of music, and I know that there is music in your soul, which you do not let out. There is in the world now a great deal of ugliness, of desecration. This is what the Soviets have brought, and the Nazis before them. Sometimes to stand against this takes courage, like Mr Pearson. But from day to day, it is important that we do not hide the beauty we have, that we commemorate those who made it, and share it with others. Some things must be kept secret, but not music.'

He jabbed Hugo in the chest, a friendly jab.

'I have said my piece. But we shall talk, you and I. You shall not slip out of it like a wily Odysseus.'

Scene 20

Freya heard Hugo's knock at the bottom of the stairs. 'Come up,' she said.

It was a slow and painful progress. No wonder, given everything he'd put his leg through recently.

'There seem to be twice as many stairs in the Castle today,' he said, sinking gratefully on to her sofa. She saw him eyeing her desk, rather changed from the last time he'd visited. It was full of notes and manuscript, the books she used to keep up the pretence of research cleared away to a shelf of their own. 'I hear you've had a visit from Árpád.'

'Yes,' she said. 'He had Words with me. I was distinctly disconcerted, but I think he's right.'

'Was this about your book?' Hugo asked. 'Or books, I should say.'

She narrowed her eyes. 'How much do you know?'

'As much as any self-respecting spy ought, were he going out of his way not to trespass upon your secret. I imagine I could have found out exactly what it is you write, but I felt it more courteous not to enquire. Georgia has no such scruples, of course. She's speculated more than once, and not only to me.'

'It's too bad of her.'

'She finds it exciting. She'd be thrilled to know the truth.'

'And you?'

'I should simply be honoured,' said Hugo, 'were you to confide in me.'

She was still a touch put out by Árpád's bluntness. 'I haven't been left much choice.'

'You could keep on exactly as you were. He won't breathe a word to anyone else. If it's any comfort, he had Words for me on the subject of the harpsichord.'

'Quite right, too. You play beautifully.'

'Thank you.'

She reached into the bottom drawer of her desk, under a pile of books, and pulled out a Rosina Wyndham to show him. He gave a pleased smile.

'Oh, now this is first-class.'

'They're bodice-rippers,' she said, not entirely sure he wasn't making fun of her.

'I meant it. They're well written, full of mischief and fun. Like Dumas. Leo enjoys them immensely. I should be pleased to have written them myself, had I the slightest inclination in that direction. You should be proud of this.'

She plopped herself down in the ancient Queen Anne chair she kept for reading in, suddenly self-conscious and eager to change the subject. 'How's Georgia?'

'Full of apple crumble.'

'Mrs Partridge will be pleased.'

'I asked her whether she wanted to leave, after what's happened. She said no, of course not. She's touched that everyone turned out to look for her, says she doesn't want to be anywhere else.'

'So you won't be taking a job in London.'

He shook his head.

'I'm glad,' she said. 'For Georgia's sake, too. It's a kind thing to do.'

'She needs a home,' said Hugo. 'It wouldn't be right to drag her back to London.'

'Are you pleased?' she asked. 'To be staying at the Hall.'

'Yes, I am. I don't know what that job in London really entailed, but I don't think they needed me. Someone wanted me out of the way, to stop me asking awkward questions. Which is exactly why I was sent here.'

'Saul has every reason to be glad of your awkward questions.'

'I hope he'll stay,' said Hugo. 'He's had a bad time of it these last few weeks, but I think he'll fit right in. On which note, shall we take ourselves to the library? They'll be waiting for us.'

'Absolutely,' said Freya.

They walked companionably down the stairs and along the corridor. On the landing in Grace Hall, they met Leo with Georgia, who was wrapped up in an enormous burgundy dressing gown in archaic velvet.

'Goodness, where did you find that?' Freya asked.

'Polly found it in a closet in Lady Matilda's wing. She said it belonged to Lady Matilda herself.'

'It's rather too big,' said Hugo, a touch doubtfully.

'I shall grow into it,' said Georgia, quite unrepentant, though the effect was rather spoiled by another sneeze.

'I think you shall,' said Freya. Lady Matilda had been a woman of some character, by all accounts. As Georgia would doubtless become, although not perhaps if she had to reach for a handkerchief every two minutes.

Leo said, 'Georgia was telling me about the notebook. She has a very good idea of what might have been in it.'

'Which notebook?' Freya asked.

'Lord Selchester's black book,' said Hugo. 'The one he kept all his secrets in. It was hidden in the priest hole.'

Like Thurloe's little black book. 'Gone?' she asked.

'Burned to cinders. I shall go up in the morning to make quite sure. With luck, there'll be a few fragments to show Superintendent

MacLeod. Best to get the word out that it's been destroyed, and there's nothing left to hunt for.'

'It must have been full of terrifically important things,' said Georgia. 'Everyone wanted it.'

'Indeed. I think you'll find a great many of the odd things which have happened here in Selchester had their roots in that little book.'

'As if he were still alive,' Freya said, with a shudder. She didn't like to think of her uncle wandering the Castle's halls still, full of secrets. Watching, observing, twisting everyone out of shape for his own ends.

'He was a man who allowed his worst instincts gain the upper hand,' said Leo.

'Like the way he threw over Gus's mother,' Freya said. 'Cut her off without a word, kept their marriage secret, sent her back to France believing she'd committed mortal sin, all so as to protect his inheritance.'

'Indeed. Such a man taints the lives he touches. By writing every-thing down, he handed that taint on. He made it possible for others to gain that same power, to destroy lives and reputations. Had it been found by Lady Sonia, it might in time have transformed her into an image of the father she hates so much.'

'Worse still,' said Hugo, 'it might have been found by Miranda, and through her fallen into the hands of the Soviets.'

'She must have been within a few inches of it,' said Georgia. 'Only she never knew it was there.'

'For which we can all be thankful. As to its contents, we shall never know, and I think that's the best end it could have come to. For Lady Sonia's sake, if nothing else.'

'She wanted it, too,' said Georgia. 'Won't she be cross.'

'I can live with that,' said Freya.

'So will she,' said Leo. 'But enough of this dwelling on secrets – we've all had more than is good for anyone. They'll be wondering where we are.'

'You can conduct me down the stairs,' said Georgia, hastily muffling a sneeze. 'Red and black go well together.'

'Very well,' Hugo said. 'But you're to be back in bed in half an hour. You're only allowed out because it wouldn't be fair to celebrate your rescue without you.'

She gave him a sidelong glance. 'Can I have some wine?'

'You're far too young for wine,' Hugo said.

'If I were a Papist, I'd have wine at Communion.'

'If you were a Papist, you'd have to agree with Polly,' said Hugo. 'But the two of you may have a libation, as it's a very special occasion.'

Leo gave Georgia his arm, and they set off down the stairs, Georgia as regal as any queen. Hugo and Freya fell into step behind them, as side by side they made their way down through Grace Hall to the waiting company.

Afterword

It goes without saying that I never wanted to write this book.

I was to be its editor, as I had been for its two predecessors. As I had been, often in a more informal capacity, with almost everything my mother ever wrote. I learned my trade both as writer and as editor from watching her at work, from seeing first-hand how a gleam in the eye became a novel. I grew up inside storytelling, and for that I shall always count myself blessed.

My mother's death, like much of her life, took us all by surprise. Until two weeks before the end, we had no inkling that anything was seriously wrong. Until six days before the end, we had no idea it was beyond curing. On the last afternoon of her life, I left the hospital with the injunction to track down certain of her notes, so that in the morning I could help her nail down the last few chapters of this book. She had been given perhaps four or five weeks to live, and had every intention of finishing a first draft in that time. Her editor at Thomas & Mercer, Emilie Marneur, had with incredible kindness arranged an amanuensis to take dictation for her once she was moved to the hospice.

Half an hour later, the duty nurse rang me and told me to come back; she had fallen into a sleep from which she wouldn't wake. I was able to gather a priest to give her the Last Rites, and to summon my sister and two old friends to the hospital in time to say goodbye. My mother was never one to linger, and her desire to rejoin my father proved stronger than her desire to finish the book.

Nevertheless, a book there had been, and a book there might still be. When I spoke to Emilie at the funeral, I didn't quite realise how little had already been written – a few scenes, a nearly complete outline, a copious quantity of notes. I knew something of it from phone conversations, and one or two fellow authors had been her sounding boards.

From this, *A Matter Of Loyalty* came into being. I knew her style inside out, I knew her plans for the book, and something of her intentions for the rest of the series. I made some editorial decisions at the outset. There were one or two plot developments I thought had come in the wrong place, and had intended to raise with her; I cut some surplus relationships; and I introduced one character who hadn't been in the outline. Other than that, the book you've just read is, as far as human power permits, the book she intended to write in those last few weeks.

This will be the last Selchester book, and the last book of her career. It was written to honour her valiant effort, and to ensure that one, at least, of all the stories she still wanted to tell would see the light of day. A few years before her death, she told the *Oxford Times* that she had far more books in her than time to write them; this proved all too true. I knew enough of this one to write almost the book she intended, but I can't do justice to the remaining books in the series. They should exist as her creations, or not at all.

Before I take my leave with words from two of my mother's favourite authors, I owe thanks to more than the usual array of people, and for more than the usual run of reasons.

Those who lent their aid during those awful weeks and days in early 2016, and who gave comfort to my mother as she faced the last and most terrible of life's mysteries. In particular: Bridget, Jonathan, and

Theresa Rowland; the Fathers of the Oxford Oratory; Tessa Caldecott; Amy Mason; Andrew and Anne Wilkinson; William Maddock; Daniel Dolley; Lyn Whiting; the nurses of the John Radcliffe Short Stay Medical Ward, in particular Alice, Jade, and Mauro, and a fellow patient named Sandy whose last name I never learned; St Hilda's College, Oxford, which laid on its alumna's final farewell.

Those who helped bring the book first into being, and then to completion: Nancy Warren and Elizabeth Jennings, fellow authors and good friends; Emilie Marneur and Jane Snelgrove, who encouraged me to finish it and brought it to publication; Susan Opie, who did a first-rate job with the editing; William Edmondson and Tony Harker for advice on physics and many related things beside; Jean Buchanan for her expertise on the fifties; Stephen Edmondson for being an excellent godfather.

To those whose love, strength and support were, and are, a light in darkness and a comfort in adversity, in particular Von Whiteman, Naomi Harries, my sister Eloise, and Katherine Richardson.

Last of all, to the co-author of this book, who can no longer hear my words: *Thank you.*

'It is only a novel . . . or, in short, only some work in which the greatest powers of the mind are displayed, in which the most thorough knowledge of human nature, the happiest delineation of its varieties, the liveliest effusions of wit and humour, are conveyed to the world in the best-chosen language.'

—*Jane Austen, Northanger Abbey*

'. . . But your nightingales live on; Death who takes all things cannot lay his hand on them.'

—*Callimachus, Elegy for Heraclitus*

About the Authors

© David Morgan

Elizabeth Edmondson (1948–2016) was born in Chile, educated in Calcutta, London and Oxford, and worked in EFL publishing before turning her hand to writing novels. She had more than thirty books published in a variety of genres, but her lifelong preoccupation was on the one hand with English manners and eccentricities, and on the other with the conflicts of the thirties, the Cold War, and espionage, in all of which her family had been involved. The Very English Mysteries, her last series, brought all of these preoccupations together in stories of the fictional cathedral city of Selchester, full of spies, gossip, and goings-on.

A lifelong nomad, she lived in five countries and six English counties, founded a youth orchestra, rode horses, rang bells, enjoyed Baroque music, and was never without an enormous collection of books, a wardrobe of sleek clothes, and the latest gadgets.

A Matter Of Loyalty, left unfinished at her death in January 2016, was finished by her son Anselm Audley, also a published novelist.

Anselm Audley is a fourth-generation writer whose antecedents include authors, linguists, spies, and even a dictator. He grew up chiefly in cathedrals, has lived in an assortment of historic English towns and landscapes, and was educated at Oxford and the British School at Rome. His passions are stories, landscapes and the past, with honourable mentions for making music, ringing bells, and sailing the ocean blue. He now lives in yet another cathedral city.

He is the author of four fantasy novels with a historical twist. More recently he has written three non-fiction Kindle Singles, combining storytelling with historical understanding to bring the real predicaments of historical figures to life. He also worked as editor and informal story consultant on the two previous Selchester books.